# Wedd

*For richer, for poorer…*

**Three passionate novels!**

In January 2007 Mills & Boon bring
back two of their classic collections,
each featuring three favourite
romances by our bestselling authors…

## WEDDING VOWS

*In the Best Man's Bed*
by Catherine Spencer
*The Wedding Dare* by Barbara Hannay
*The Wedding Challenge* by Jessica Hart

## BEDDED BY HER BOSS

*Back in the Boss's Bed*
by Sharon Kendrick
*Her Boss's Marriage Agenda*
by Jessica Steele
*His After-Hours Mistress*
by Amanda Browning

# Wedding Vows

## IN THE BEST MAN'S BED
*by*
*Catherine Spencer*

## THE WEDDING DARE
*by*
*Barbara Hannay*

## THE WEDDING CHALLENGE
*by*
*Jessica Hart*

MILLS & BOON®

MILLS & BOON and MILLS & BOON with the Rose Device
are registered trademarks of the publisher.
Harlequin Mills & Boon Limited,
Eton House, 18-24 Paradise Road, Richmond, Surrey, TW9 1SR

WEDDING VOWS © by Harlequin Enterprises II B.V. 2007

In the Best Man's Bed, The Wedding Dare and The Wedding
Challenge were first published in Great Britain by Harlequin
Mills & Boon Limited in separate, single volumes.

In the Best Man's Bed © Kathy Garner 2003
The Wedding Dare © Barbara Hannay 2001
The Wedding Challenge © Jessica Hart 2002

ISBN 10: 0 263 85134 6
ISBN 13: 978 0 263 85134 2

05-0107

Printed and bound in Spain
by Litografia Rosés S.A., Barcelona

# IN THE BEST MAN'S BED

*by*

## Catherine Spencer

**Catherine Spencer**, once an English teacher, fell into writing through eavesdropping on a conversation about Harlequin Romances. Within two months she changed careers and sold her first book to Mills & Boon in 1984. She moved to Canada from England thirty years ago and lives in Vancouver. She is married to a Canadian and has four grown children – two daughters and two sons – plus three dogs and a cat. In her spare time she plays the piano, collects antiques, and grows tropical shrubs.

# CHAPTER ONE

*ETHAN BEAUMONT...Ethan Andrew Beaumont...Monsieur Beaumont.* Ever since the wedding date had been set, his was the name on everyone's lips; his was the name uttered with the kind of reverence normally accorded only to royalty, popes or dictators.

*So given that it's Philippe Beaumont who's marrying my best friend, what's wrong with this picture?* Anne-Marie Barclay wondered, sipping thoughtfully at her champagne. *Why is it that, where other people's weddings are concerned, the bride and groom take center stage, but in this instance, it's all about Ethan Beaumont? And why is Solange allowing it?*

"If you look just beyond the tip of the starboard wing, *Mademoiselle,* you'll catch your first glimpse of Bellefleur." Moving with surprising stealth and grace for such a big man, the flight attendant materialized from the galley at the rear of the private jet, and pointed over Anne-Marie's shoulder. "It's the island shaped like a crescent moon."

She craned her neck and scanned the specks of land floating like emerald gems on the sapphire-blue water, thousands of feet below. "Yes, I see it," she said, and wondered why the sight of the island, tranquil and beautiful even from this distance, should fill her with such odd apprehension. "How long before we land?"

"We'll begin our descent shortly. Please remain seated and keep your seat belt fastened." His smile flashed brilliant white in his ebony face. "Not that you need to be reminded. You haven't moved since we left the mainland. Are you by chance a nervous flyer, *Mademoiselle?*"

"Not as a rule." She glanced again out of the window and found nothing but blue sky beyond, as the jet banked in a steep turn. "But nor do I usually travel in so small an aircraft." *Especially not over miles of open water.*

He smiled again, kindly. "You're in excellent hands. Captain Morgan is a most capable pilot. *Monsieur* Beaumont hires only the best."

There it was again, the Beaumont name rolling off the steward's tongue with lilting Caribbean reverence, as if her host ranked head and shoulders above other mortals. And again Anne-Marie felt that disturbing little surge of misgiving. She was not looking forward to meeting the almighty *Monsieur* Beaumont.

"He's nothing like Philippe, although there's quite a strong family resemblance, even though they're only half brothers," Solange had told her, when she phoned with news of the forthcoming wedding. "He's larger in every respect. Larger than life, almost, and certainly lord of all he surveys. They practically curtsy to him when he passes through the town. I can see why Philippe was a little anxious about breaking news of our engagement to him. Ethan can be…how shall I put it? *Un peu formidable.*"

"In other words, he's a tyrant." Anne-Marie had rolled her eyes in disbelief. "Imagine a grown man being afraid to tell his family that he's getting married. It's positively medieval! If you ask me, all that wealth and power has gone to the formidable Ethan Beaumont's head."

A thoughtful pause followed before Solange replied, "*Oui,* he is powerful, but underneath it all, he's a very good man. Not cuddly like *mon cher* teddy bear, of course—he's much too distant for that. I can't imagine him ever allowing grand passion to rule the day."

"He did, at least once," Anne-Marie pointed out. "He's got a son to prove it."

"But alas, no wife. Maybe he inherited too much English reserve from his mother, and that's why his marriage lasted so short a time." Solange sighed, and Anne-Marie had imagined her shrugging in that uniquely French way of hers. "Such a pity! Such a waste!"

"Such a blessing, you mean! No woman needs the kind of man in her life who'd deprive her of her child. I feel sorry for the little boy, being at the mercy of such a father."

"But that was not Ethan's fault, Anne-Marie! The mother chose to leave both her husband and her son."

"Which just goes to show how bad things must have been for her, that she'd give up her baby rather than put up with the husband!"

Solange's initial burst of laughter, rippling over the phone like music, had dwindled into hushed alarm, as if she were afraid she'd be sent to her room without dinner for disturbing the peace. "It's all right to say such audacious things to me in private, but you must take care not to speak so in front of other people when you join me on Bellefleur. They would not take kindly to a stranger criticizing their *Seigneur.*"

*Seigneur,* indeed! Anne-Marie leaned back in her seat and closed her eyes as the blue Caribbean Sea rushed up to meet the jet on its final approach to the island. How feudal—and how utterly absurd!

Feudal, perhaps, but her notions of absurdity wavered alarmingly during the journey from the airport to the Beaumont estate. Seated in solitary splendor in the back of a black Mercedes limousine, she experienced instead the unsettling sense that *she* was the only anomaly on Bellefleur.

As the chauffeur-driven car rolled sedately through the winding streets of the small town, residents stopped to acknowledge its passing with a respectful nod which came close to a bow. Dark-eyed children waved chubby hands.

*Should she wave back?* she wondered, hating the sudden uncertainty usurping her normal self-confidence, *or wouldn't the Seigneur approve?*

Probably not!

"He'll be very charming, very attentive to your comfort and needs, but don't expect him to treat you the way a North American host would," Solange had warned. "He's much too reserved for that. He'll probably call you *Mademoiselle* Barclay, the entire time you're here. It took him ages to unbend enough to call me by my first name."

When she'd descended the steps from the jet and set foot on the tarmac, the sun's shimmering heat had hit Anne-Marie like a wall, and she'd been glad to take refuge in the dim, air-conditioned comfort of the Mercedes. But as the vehicle left the town behind and climbed the hill leading to the Beaumont estate, her friend's warning settled unpleasantly in the pit of her stomach like a too-large meal of badly prepared food.

More than a month of having to bow and scrape to some domineering individual given to feudal delusions of grandeur was enough to kill anyone's appetite! Worse, it promised to leach all the pleasure out of her coming to Bellefleur to be her best friend's maid of honor, and instead threatened to turn the visit into a penance for sins not yet committed.

That an autocratic stranger should wield such power that he cast a pall over Solange's wedding was indefensible. But more troubling by far, in Anne-Marie's opinion, was the fear that his domination would spill over and influence the marriage, as well.

She had met Philippe Beaumont, and liked him. He and Solange were well-matched. But he'd never struck Anne-Marie as a particularly strong or forceful man. Given a choice, he'd choose the easy route over the difficult, and whether he'd be any match for his assertive half brother seemed questionable, given what she knew about the latter.

Her concerns intensified as the Mercedes swept through the gates guarding the entrance to the family estate and, a short time later, drew up in the forecourt of the main house.

She was no stranger to luxury. She'd attended the best schools, seen something of the world, never known what it was to lack money or material comforts. Yet, quite apart from its architectural beauty, the sheer size and opulence of the Beaumont mansion overwhelmed her.

She'd heard that royalty had slept under its roofs and she could well believe it. This was no mere villa, no rich man's private island hideaway. This was a palace which, surrounded though it might be with smothering tropical heat, nevertheless exuded an intimidating aura of cool, dignified formality. If it was representational of its owner, then small wonder Solange held him in such awe.

*"Mademoiselle?"*

With a start, Anne-Marie realized the passenger door stood open, and a manservant, immaculate in starched white Bermuda shorts and tailored, short-sleeved white shirt, waited to hand her out of the car. Bracing herself to cope with whatever situation might await her, she slid across the leather seat and stepped into the courtyard.

Somehow, that made all the difference to her perceptions. Everywhere she looked, she saw flowers. But rather than viewing them from behind the tinted windows of the

Mercedes, her eyes were assaulted by the splendor of color spilling over cream stucco walls, and tumbling from huge stone jardinieres in a riot of purple and scarlet and bright orange.

She became instantly aware of the cooling splash of fountains, and the raucous shriek of brilliantly feathered birds; of the exotic scent of gardenias; of ginger blossom and plumeria.

Shading her from the sun with an exquisitely painted parasol, the manservant escorted her up a shallow flight of steps and into the building—not by way of a front door because, for all its luxury, the villa didn't appear to possess one. Instead, a pair of curved iron gates, so delicately wrought that they resembled black lace, led directly to a covered inner courtyard, circular in shape and large enough to serve as a ballroom.

Solange waited there, her dark eyes liquid with emotion, her smile tremulous. "Oh, how I've missed you!" she exclaimed softly, gliding forward over the marble-tiled floor, and kissing Anne-Marie on both cheeks. "Welcome to Bellefleur, *ma chère, chère amie!* I'm so glad to have you here at last!"

"Glad?" A little teary-eyed herself, Anne-Marie held her friend at arm's length and inspected her searchingly. "If you're so glad, why are you crying?"

"Because I'm happy."

"You don't look happy, Solange."

Solange gave her little Gallic shrug, cast a furtive glance over her shoulder, and said, "Come, let me show you where you'll be sleeping. We can talk more freely there. Ethan instructed the staff to put you in the guest pavilion next to mine."

"You mean to say you're not staying here in the house?"

"Not until I'm a married woman. Ethan wouldn't approve. Philippe might be tempted to sneak into my bed at night."

"The way he did when you were still living in Paris, you mean?"

"Hush!" Solange pressed a nervous finger to her lips. "No one must know that, Anne-Marie. Standards are different here."

"So I gathered," she muttered, following Solange through another curved gateway on the opposite side of the foyer, to a paved terrace overlooking an enormous, infinity-edged pool. The view beyond was breathtaking; a sweeping panorama of sky and sea framed with swaying coconut palms and poinciana trees. "Tell me, do the guest pavilions have doors and windows, or must we whisper all the time we're there, as well, in case anyone overhears?"

"We'll be quite private, except for when our maids are present. Then we must be discreet." She led the way down a shady path which wound among a series of ponds connected to each other by miniature waterfalls and pebbled, man-made streams. "We're a good distance from the main house, as you'll see, but the suites are very luxurious and spacious."

"That's good. I'll need plenty of room to finish working on the dresses."

Solange flung a glance over her shoulder and, just for a moment, her usual vivacity showed in her face. "I can hardly wait to see mine. The drawings you sent were gorgeous."

"We can have a fitting later on, if you like, to give you an idea of how you're going to look in the finished product."

"It'll have to wait until tomorrow. Because you've been

traveling all day, we're having an early dinner, and I expect you'll want to shower and change first.''

"Presumably, I'll be meeting the formidable Ethan Beaumont.'' Anne-Marie grimaced. ''I've got indigestion already!''

"Not tonight, you won't,'' Solange said with a laugh. "I ordered a private meal to be delivered to my suite. Ethan's aunt and uncle are visiting friends until tomorrow afternoon, and he's away on business.''

"I understood running this island and the lives of everyone on it was his business.''

"*Mon Dieu, non!* He has investment and real estate portfolios all over the world, though he's recently begun delegating Philippe to take charge of them, and concentrating all his energy on his oil interests. That's what's taken him away this time.''

"To the Middle East? Good! The farther away he is, the better! I already dislike the man and I'm in no hurry to meet him.''

"Oh, he's much closer than the Middle East, I'm afraid. Just off the coast of Venezuela, in fact, which is no great distance from here at all. He'll be back in a few days, I'm sure, but until then you'll have to make do with his aunt and uncle, who also live on the estate, and with Adrian.''

"Who's Adrian?''

"Ethan's son.'' Her voice softened. ''He's an adorable little boy. I don't think you'll find being around him a very great hardship, regardless of how you feel about his father.''

The path opened onto a wide expanse of lawn just then, and she stopped to point out a pair of villas perched high above the sea. ''Well, here we are, *chérie*. This where we'll be living for the next little while.''

Given her first impressions of the Beaumont estate,

Anne-Marie ought not to have been surprised by the sight confronting her now. Surrounded by showy flower beds, and separated from each other by a covered walkway, the villas were miniature replicas of the main house, with the same deep verandahs, lacy iron French doors, and a smaller version of the infinity-edged swimming pool.

"I have to say that, whatever else his shortcomings, your future brother-in-law knows how to treat guests," she exclaimed, captivated by the serene elegance of the setting. "This is paradise, Solange. Perfection! We're going to have a lot of fun here over the next few weeks."

Solange smiled wistfully. "I hope you're right."

"There shouldn't be any question but that I am! The days leading up to the wedding are supposed to be a happy time for the bride, and I don't understand why you're not glowing with your usual radiance. What is it, Solange? Are you having doubts about marrying Philippe? Because if you are, it's not too late to call the whole thing off."

"Oh, it's not Philippe! I adore him, more than ever, and I'm always happy when he's with me. But the rest of the time…" Her mouth drooped sadly. "…it seems so foreign here."

"How can it be foreign? It might be a long way from Paris, but it's still French. Imagine how much worse it would be if everyone spoke Spanish or Portuguese, and you couldn't understand a word they were saying."

"Perhaps what I should have said is that, even though the language is familiar, I feel like a foreigner." She gestured at the lush spread of land stretching to either side, and the jungle-clad hill rising behind the estate. "There are two kinds of people on this island, Anne-Marie: those who belong because they were born here, and the rest of us, who weren't."

"If that's true, how are you going to cope with living here?"

"Philippe tells me that once we're married and start a family, I'll feel differently. I'll be accepted. Maybe he's right. Maybe it's just that I've been alone too much lately."

"Why hasn't Philippe been with you?"

"He's been taking care of business in Europe, and Asia. Right now, he's in Vienna and has been for the last week. Ethan says that since he'll soon be a married man, he has to take a more active role in the family business."

*Ethan says, Ethan thinks, Ethan decrees…!*

"Tell me Solange, has anyone ever dared to say, to hell with what Ethan wants?"

Solange rolled her eyes like a frightened foal caught in quicksand. "*Mon Dieu,* don't ever say something like that in front of anyone else! It would be considered…." She fluttered her hands, groping for the right word.

"Treason?" Anne-Marie supplied witheringly. "Good grief, girlfriend, who is this browbeaten little creature reciting the party line with every breath? What's happened to the woman I used to know?"

"I'm still the same inside." Solange squared her shoulders and made a determined effort to look more cheerful. "I've just had a little difficulty adjusting to my new situation. But now that you're here, I'll soon be my old self again."

They'd reached the guest houses by then, and looking through the open entrance to the one she'd been assigned to, Anne-Marie saw that her luggage had been delivered and that a maid was busily unpacking her suitcases.

"I don't want her messing around with the wedding outfits, so I'd better get in there and take charge before the hired help starts on the travel trunk," she said. "But this conversation is far from over, Solange. You might fool everyone else with your polite, subdued little smile, and your docile acceptance of the all-important *rules,* but you aren't fooling me. Something's not quite right in paradise, and I intend to find out what it is.''

''It's nothing—just pre-wedding nerves and difficulty settling into a new situation,'' Solange insisted, edging nervously toward her own suite. ''I've always been shy, you know that, and it's all taking a bit of getting used to, especially with Philippe away so much. I suppose, if truth be told, I'm just plain lonely.''

*Small wonder!* Anne-Marie thought. *And that's something else we can thank the almighty Ethan Andrew Beaumont Lewis for!*

She thought she'd sleep late the next morning, but even though she'd fallen into bed exhausted the night before, Anne-Marie awoke at sunrise. It would be hours before breakfast was served, but after last night's dinner, she needed exercise more than food, especially if she wanted to fit into the dress she'd be wearing at the wedding.

''Always assuming,'' she murmured, slipping between the folds of filmy mosquito netting draped around the bed, and hunting through the dresser drawers for a bikini, ''that the wedding takes place which, from everything I've surmised, might not happen if the lord and master has his way.''

The pool glimmered invitingly when she looked outside, but there was no sign of life from Solange's villa, which was probably a good thing. She'd looked very pale and hollow-eyed by the time dinner was over, as if she hadn't been getting enough sleep, and could probably use a few more hours of rest.

Better not to disturb her, Anne-Marie decided, pulling a

cover-up over her bikini and slinging her camera around her neck. Hiking down the hill to wade in the milk-warm Caribbean would serve just as well as a dip in the pool.

Finding a way down to the beach turned out to be a more frustrating experience than she'd expected, though. Even in the bright light of midday, many of the paths winding through the estate gardens lay in the protective shade of trees. At that hour of the morning, with the sun still not high enough to penetrate the dense green canopy overhead, she found it almost impossible to keep track of the direction she took.

Twice, she ended up back where she'd begun. Another time, she found herself on the edge of the cliff, with a sheer drop down to the shore. Finally, when she was so confused that she wasn't certain she'd even find her way back to her villa, she came across a man tending one of the ponds.

He knelt with his back to her, and her first thought was that he must have spent most of his life toiling in the hot sun for Ethan Beaumont. How else would he have developed such a physique, or his skin acquired such a deep and glowing tan? And who else but a manual laborer would be allowed to wander about the estate wearing nothing but faded denim cutoffs?

*"Bonjour,"* she began, unsure of the protocol involved in approaching a gardener—because whatever else she might have missed at dinner the previous evening, she'd quickly learned that, with regard to the house staff, protocol was paramount. The wine steward did not refill the water goblets; the butler who served the food did not remove the empty plates.

That being the case, it was entirely possible that this lowly employee with his face practically submersed in the pond, might not be allowed to speak to guests. Certainly, the way he ignored her greeting suggested as much—unless he was deaf or didn't understand her French.

*"Excusez moi,"* she said, stepping closer and speaking a little louder. *"S'il vous plait, monsieur—"*

Irritably, he flapped his hand at her and, in case she hadn't understood the message *that* was supposed to convey, said curtly, "Lower your voice. I heard you the first time."

His English might be flawless, albeit slightly accented, but his manner left a great deal to be desired. Offended, she snapped, "Really? And how do you suppose your employer would react, if he knew how rude you were to one of his guests?"

"Disturbed," he replied, still bent double over the pond. "But not nearly as disturbed as he'd be with the guest for interfering with the delicate business of keeping his prize koi alive and well."

"You're the fish man?"

The way his broad shoulders sort of rippled and shook at the question made her wonder if he was having some sort of fit. "You could call me that, I suppose."

"What does your employer call you?"

"Nothing," he said carelessly. "He's never conferred a title on me. In his eyes, I'm not important enough to warrant one."

"Yet you continue to work here. You must love what you do, to put up with that sort of abuse."

"Oh yes, lady," he replied, his deep baritone suddenly adopting a musical Caribbean lilt. "Master lets me feed and tend his fish. Gives me hut to live in, and rum to drink. Fish man very lucky guy."

"There's no need to be so offensive. It's not my fault if the work you do isn't properly appreciated." She tipped her head to one side, intrigued by his preoccupation with the task at hand. "Exactly what *is* it that you're doing?"

"An egret's had a go at the koi. I'm repairing the damage."

"I didn't know that was possible. How do you do it?"

"I get the fish to come to the surface so that I can treat their injuries."

"Of course you do," she said mockingly. "And because they're obedience trained, they stay put while you bandage them."

"Not quite. But they stick around long enough for me to disinfect the puncture wounds inflicted by the bird."

She stepped closer and saw that he wasn't exaggerating. One fish, over a foot long, was happily nibbling food pellets from one of his hands and, with the other, allowing him to dab some substance on the nasty-looking hole piercing its back.

"You really care about them, don't you?" she said, impressed despite herself.

"I respect them," he said. "Some are over fifty years old. They deserve to be well cared for. Is there a reason you're wandering around the gardens at this hour?"

"I'm looking for a way to get down to the beach. I'd like to go for a swim."

"What's wrong with the guest pool?"

"My friend's still sleeping and I don't want to disturb her. She hasn't had a very easy time of things lately."

"How so? Isn't she about to marry the man of her dreams?"

"It's the other man that's part of the package who's causing her grief."

He ran a caressing finger over the back of the fish he'd been tending. "There's another man in the picture? That hardly bodes well for the marriage."

"Not *that* kind of other man. But never mind. I shouldn't even be discussing the matter with you. *Monsieur* Beaumont wouldn't approve."

"No, *Monsieur* Beaumont certainly wouldn't," he said. "There isn't a path to the beach on this side of the property. If you want an early swim, I suggest you go up to the main house and use the pool there."

"Oh, I don't think so. It's probably against the rules for a guest to dip her toe in the family pool without invitation."

"You don't seem fond of the Beaumonts. Do you know them well?"

"Except for the bridegroom, hardly at all. I haven't even met the big cheese yet, but what I've heard hasn't exactly swept me off my feet."

He wiped his hands on the seat of his cutoffs, and jumped lithely to his feet. He was very tall. Very. "The big cheese will be crushed to hear that."

"Who's going to tell him—you?"

He laughed, and turned toward her just as the sun lifted over the side of the hill and afforded her first good look at him, and she almost cringed.

This was no common laborer! He had the face of an aristocrat, with high, elegantly carved cheekbones, and a mouth set in the lines of one unaccustomed to suffering fools gladly. His jaw, faintly shadowed, was lean, and his eyes, vivid beneath dark sweeping brows, the bluest she'd ever seen. And she didn't need an introduction to know his name.

"You don't work here!" she said, weakly.

"Certainly I do. Very hard, in fact."

"No, you don't, and you're not the fish man. You're Ethan Beaumont!"

He inclined his head. "And where is it written that I can't be both?"

*Oh, rats! Talk about putting her foot in it!* "Why didn't you say something sooner?"

"Because it was more informative listening to you running off at the mouth. Is there anything else you'd like to tell me about myself?"

"No," she mumbled, so embarrassed she wanted to die. "I don't have anything else to say right now."

"In that case, allow me to escort you up to the house where, at my invitation, you may swim in the pool to your heart's content."

"I don't think I feel like swimming anymore. I think I'll just go back to the guest house."

"And disturb the delicate bride-to-be? I won't hear of it." He towered over her and took her elbow in a not-to-be-thwarted grip. "Come along, *Mademoiselle*. Let's not waste any more time debating the issue. It's already been settled. By the big cheese."

# CHAPTER TWO

"You're supposed to be digging for oil in Venezuela," she panted, struggling to keep up with his long-legged stride.

"We don't dig, we drill."

"You know what I mean!"

"Oh yes," he assured her, the seductive baritone of his voice laced with irony. "You have a way with words which leaves a man in little doubt about their meaning."

Although she'd sooner have poked hot needles in her eyes than offer an apology, she knew one was called for. "I'm afraid I was out of line, talking to you the way I did when I first saw you, and I'm sorry."

"You should be. Is it customary in your part of the world to criticize one's host to his employees?"

The distaste with which he said "your part of the world" made it sound as if she'd emerged from under a very unsavory rock. "No," she said. "But where I come from, hosts aren't usually so inhospitable. Nor do they go around impersonating other people."

"Inhospitable?" His sleekly elegant brows rose in mock surprise. "Your accommodation falls short of your expectations? The food is not to your liking? My staff have treated you discourteously?"

"Dinner was exquisite, your staff couldn't be kinder or more helpful, and my accommodation," she replied, thinking of the delicately fashioned iron four-poster bed with its Sea Island cotton sheets, and elegant draperies which more closely resembled silk wedding-veil tulle than mosquito netting, "is everything I could wish for. It's the atmosphere around here that leaves something to be desired."

"A sentiment which my future sister-in-law appears to share. Dare I ask why?"

"Let's just say she's hardly the poster child for bridal bliss, and leave it at that."

He held back the fronds of a giant fern and waited for her to pass by. Just there, the path was narrow, an iridescent green lane awash with the scent of the jungle, a thousand hidden flowers—and him.

He smelled of morning and cool water faintly kissed by the tropics. He oozed raw strength, the kind which defied the elements. He would neither wilt under the sun's heat, nor bend before the storms which swept over the island during hurricane season, and as long as she didn't look at him, she could prolong the illusion that he was exactly what she'd first assumed him to be: a subordinate born to the grinding, endless toil of working the cotton plantation or tending the gardens.

But one glance at the elegant conformation of bone and muscle underlying the gleaming skin, at the well-shaped hands, the patrician features, and most of all, at the intelligence in those cool, spectacular eyes, and she felt herself dwindle into insignificance. This was a giant of a man, not so much because of his size and physical beauty, which were considerable, but because of the innate bearing in his manner. The mantle of authority, of culture and refinement, sat easily on his shoulders.

"Please proceed," he said, waving her ahead with an imperious gesture. "And explain your last remark."

She scuttled past and muttered, "I've forgotten what it was."

"Then allow me to refresh your memory. You said you don't find Solange the picture of bridal bliss."

"Well, do *you?*"

"I hardly know her well enough to say."

"Oh, please! Even a complete stranger, if he bothered to take a good look at her, would see at once that she's anything but brimming over with happiness."

"She *has* struck me as moody and difficult to please." He gave a careless shrug. "Unfortunate traits in a woman about to become a wife, wouldn't you say?"

Irked by the casual way he'd pigeon-holed Solange without bothering to learn what was really causing her so much distress, Anne-Marie said tartly, "Almost as unfortunate as finding yourself related by marriage to a man so ready to assume the worst of you!"

"If I've misjudged her—"

"There's no 'if' about it! I've known Solange for over ten years and I can assure you she's normally the most equable woman in the world. But finding herself sequestered as far away from the main house as possible, as if she's carrying some horrible, contagious disease, doesn't do a whole lot for her self-esteem."

"I'm preserving her good reputation."

"You're isolating her and making her feel unwanted!"

"That's ridiculous," he said bluntly. "During the day, she's welcome to spend as much time as she likes with the rest of the family."

They'd reached the upper terrace by then. "She's too intimidated," Anne-Marie said, stopping to admire a bed of tall pink lilies with burgundy leaves. "She'd feel she was imposing, especially on those days when Philippe isn't there to run interference for her."

"If she thinks he'll constantly be at her side once they're married, she's in for a rude awakening. By his own choosing, Philippe has led a very carefree bachelor life up until now, and is no more equipped to be a husband than I am to tame a tiger. In order to fulfill his marital obligations, he'll be kept very busy learning to pull his own weight in the family business. And that, I'm afraid, will involve his spending a certain amount of time off the island.''

''Will it?'' she said heatedly. ''Or is this simply your way of sabotaging a marriage you don't approve of?''

His mouth curved in displeasure. ''I've never found it necessary to stoop to such underhand measures. If I don't like something, I make no secret of my intent to change it.''

Who did he think he was—God? ''And what if you can't?''

''There's always a way,'' he said impassively. ''It's simply a matter of finding it. But you may rest easy on one score at least. I take no pleasure in reducing innocent women to tears or despair. Whatever else might be upsetting Solange, she has nothing to fear from me. I have only her best interests at heart.''

''I'd like to believe that's the case.''

''I'm not in the habit of lying, *Mademoiselle*.''

He uttered the words with such a wealth of dignity that she was ashamed. No, he would not stoop to lying. Whatever his faults, he would never compromise his integrity.

He indicated the pool, stretching before them like an eighty-foot length of satin undulating in a whisper of breeze. ''Enjoy your swim. You look as if you need it. You're more than a little flushed.''

Hidden by the shadowed fretwork of the door opening onto his bedroom verandah, he watched her approach the shallow end of the pool, and cautiously lower herself over the side. In every other respect, she appeared to be exactly as he'd anticipated: brash, abrasive, and disagreeably self-confident, like most North American women.

It surprised him that she was so tentative in the water, and it annoyed him, too. He didn't want to be made aware of any vulnerability she might possess. Dealing with Solange's fragility was more than enough.

"Papa!". The door burst open and Adrian catapulted into the room. "When did you come home?"

"Last night," he said, scooping his son into his arms.

"You didn't kiss me good night!"

"Of course I did. But you were sleeping so soundly, you didn't know."

"I'm scared when you go away, Papa." The sweetly-rounded arms crept around his neck and held on tight. "What if you forgot to come home again?"

"Don't be scared, *mon petit*," he said. "Parents never forget to come back to their children."

"They do, sometimes. I heard *Tante* Josephine say that's why I don't have a mama."

*Damn you, Lisa!* Inwardly cursing his ex-wife, he said, "You'll always have me, son," and made a mental note to remind his aunt to watch her words around the boy.

Adrian wriggled to the floor and tugged at his hand. "Teach me to swim some more, Papa."

His glance slewed back to the pool. She'd ventured in a little farther and was floating on her back, with her hair fanned out around her head like the tentacles of a pale sea anemone. Just as well she wasn't expending much energy. Any sudden movement, and she'd lose the flimsy excuse for a bathing suit clinging precariously to her frame.

*To her very slender, distractingly feminine frame.*

He turned away, annoyed again. "Not right now, son. Later, perhaps."

"But you said you would as soon as you came home again. You *promised!* And you've been home for *hours!*"

"You're right." He sighed, accepting defeat.

"And you told me it's bad to break a promise."

"Right again." He buried a smile. "Okay, you win. Give me ten minutes to clean up and change, and we'll have a quick lesson before breakfast."

Perhaps she'd be gone by then, and they'd have the pool to themselves.

The water lapped around her like warm cream. Very pleasant, very relaxing. *I could make a habit of this,* she thought, stretching luxuriously and breathing deeply of the flower-scented air. *Given enough time and exposure, I might even learn to enjoy it.*

From within the house came the faint clink of dishes and the whispery sound of soft-soled shoes hurrying over marble-tiled floors. She had no idea of the time, but it occurred to her that if the servants were readying breakfast for the family, she should vacate the premises. She had no wish for further contact with Ethan Beaumont. She'd seen enough of him, for one day.

But even as she rolled over and swam sedately toward the steps at the corner of the pool, a child in bright blue swimming trunks came roaring across the terrace, squealing with glee the whole time. And right behind him came Ethan.

"Wait!" he called out.

But the child either didn't hear or chose not to, and with another squeal, shot through the air like a bullet and landed practically on top of her. The relatively calm surface of the water churned in a turbulent froth, smacking her in the face and blinding her. Choking, she lunged for the side of the pool, misjudged the distance, and went under.

To panic when she knew all she had to do was stand up and she'd find herself only waist-deep in water was ridiculous, but that didn't stop her from flailing and thrashing around like a wild thing. The humiliation of that exhibition, though, paled beside the insult of suddenly finding herself being hauled upright by the hair.

Spluttering, she surfaced again and came eyeball to eyeball with Ethan Beaumont. He knelt on the tiled deck, his mouth quivering with suppressed laughter. "Idiot!" he said softly.

"Caveman!" she spluttered. "Do you make a habit of dragging women around by the hair?"

"Only when they're in danger of drowning or otherwise causing themselves grievous bodily harm." Releasing her, he rose smoothly to his feet, and she saw that he'd exchanged the denim shorts for black swimming trunks which showed rather more tanned skin than she felt able to cope with at that moment. "Stay put and I'll give you a lesson on water survival."

"No, thanks," she told him, but she might as well have saved her already tortured breath. He'd turned away and was striding to the other end of the pool, and any inclination she might have had, to escape while she could, faded as she watched him. Tall, broad at the shoulder and narrow at the waist, he moved with the sort of masculine grace few men possessed.

A splashing at her side drew her attention to the child treading water furiously to stay afloat. "That's my papa," he panted, his sweet little face beaming with pride. "He can teach you to swim. He can do everything."

*Perhaps not everything,* she thought, swinging her gaze back just in time to see Ethan Beaumont dive into the pool so cleanly that he barely caused a ripple, *but I can see why his son might think so. The man is frighteningly competent.*

He surfaced next to her, his hair seal-dark against his skull and water streaming down his torso in sparkling rivulets. "Lesson number one," he said. "Learn to be comfortable with your face submerged."

"It'll never happen," she said flatly. "At least, not with me."

"That's what Adrian said, in the beginning. But he soon changed his mind." He looked at her inquiringly. "Have you met my son?"

"Not formally. I'd hoped to meet him last night, but by the time we'd finished dinner, it was past his bedtime."

"Then allow me to introduce you now." He extended his arm for the child to grasp. "This is Adrian, who just turned five."

"Hello, Adrian." She smiled at him. He was a beautiful child, black haired like his father and with huge dark brown eyes fringed in long black lashes. "I'm Anne-Marie."

He smiled back, but Ethan frowned disapprovingly. "I prefer that he call you *Mademoiselle.*"

It was on the tip of her tongue to tell him she didn't care what he preferred, but decided it was something better said when they didn't have an audience. So, keeping her smile in place even though doing so made her face ache, she said, "I should be getting back to my quarters. Solange is surely awake by now, and wondering where I am."

"No hurry," he said, clamping his free hand around her wrist. "I sent a message for her to join us for breakfast on the terrace. She should be here any moment. We'll make use of the time until she arrives, and start your swimming lesson. Now, to begin—"

"I'm sure you mean well, *Ethan,*" she said, taking private delight in the way his mouth tightened at the familiarity, "but just as you have your preferences, so do I have mine. And I prefer not to take advantage of your offer, especially not if it means leaving your son to his own devices when he's clearly expecting to spend this time with you."

He released her just long enough to boost Adrian onto the pool deck and murmur something in his ear which sent the boy scooting over to a canopied stall loaded with towels and swimming paraphernalia. Then, turning his attention back to her, he said implacably, "Adrian doesn't mind waiting a few minutes. So, to begin, I'll fit you with a face mask. That way, you'll be able to see under water without discomfort to your eyes."

"I don't want a face mask. I don't want a lesson. How much more plainly do I have to put it?"

"You're afraid."

"Yes, I'm afraid. Is that all right with you?"

"No, it isn't. As long as you're cavorting in pools on my property, I'm responsible for your well-being. I could ensure it by forbidding you to use them, but in this climate they're less a luxury than a necessity. So for your own comfort and my peace of mind, I must insist you allow me to teach you the rudiments of water safety." He paused and surveyed her mockingly. "If a five-year-old can master them, surely a woman your age can at least try to do likewise?"

For a moment, she glared at him without replying, but already the heat was intense and she knew that, as the day progressed and the sun climbed higher in the cloudless sky, it would only get worse. So when it became obvious he wasn't about to accept silence as an answer, she said grudgingly, "Much though I loathe to admit it, it's possible you're right. On all counts."

He selected one of the two masks Adrian had dropped on the side of the pool, declared with irritating superiority, "Of course I am, so let's get on with it," then proceeded to clamp the wretched contraption snugly over her face, and adjust the strap holding it in place. "How does that feel?"

"Fine, I suppose," she said, vibrantly conscious of his touch and the proximity of their near-naked bodies. Although harmless enough on the surface, there was something implicitly intimate about the situation.

"Excellent!" Quickly, he slipped on the other mask, and taking her by both hands, backed away from the steps.

Instantly, the fear grabbed at her. "Don't pull me into deep water!" she begged, resisting him.

"Relax, *Mademoiselle!* All we're going to do is remain perfectly still and look at the bottom of the pool, like so...." He took a breath, lowered his face into the water, blew out a stream of bubbles, then raised his head. "Very simple, very safe, yes?"

"You make it look easy."

"Because it is. Try it and see for yourself."

Cautiously, she followed his instructions and surprised herself. It wasn't nearly as terrifying or alien an experience as she'd expected. The tiles on the bottom of the pool glimmered in the sun-shot blue light. By turning her head slightly, she could see the steps in the corner, a reassuring sight. And when she felt herself running short of air, she simply lifted her face and filled her lungs with a fresh supply.

"I can't believe I'm able to do this!" she said, absurdly pleased with her small accomplishment.

"But you are, and very well, too." Without warning, he tugged her off her feet. "So now we progress to the next level and float."

*"Ahh!"* She let out a little yelp of fright as, powerless in his hold, she found herself traveling even farther away from the steps.

But he wouldn't let fear get the better of her. "Concentrate," he ordered, his voice low and hypnotic as he towed her effortlessly alongside him. "Remember—lift and breathe, lower and blow."

She did, becoming so engrossed in following his directions that she didn't notice how far they'd traveled until a shadow fell across the water and, looking up, she found herself under the diving board at the deep end of the pool. Again, the familiar panic rose up, and again, before it got the better of her, he tightened his hold and said soothingly, "You're perfectly safe, *Mademoiselle*. I won't let anything happen to you."

"I believe you," she panted, and the amazing thing was, she did. A total stranger had lured her far out of her depth and into dangerous territory, and for some insane reason, she trusted him implicitly. Not for years, not since she was a little girl, had she known such a sense of security, and she rather liked it.

Her voice must have betrayed something of what she was feeling because he pushed up his face mask and, for the first time since they'd met, he smiled. The problem then was not that she'd forget to breathe properly with her face in the water, but that she'd forget to breathe at all. Because his smile transformed him and he became not merely handsome, but truly gorgeous. Flawless in every detail, from his dazzling white and perfect teeth to the brilliant azure of his eyes. And she, fleetingly paralyzed by the moment, could only gaze in spellbound admiration.

Slowly, he disentangled his fingers from hers, as if he were as reluctant to release her as she was to have him let go. "One more thing, and then it's Adrian's turn," he said, giving her slight push. "Swim to the ladder over there, under your own steam." Then, before she could give voice to the protest rising in her throat, he added. "It's either that or make your way back to the shallow end which is five times the distance away."

Did pride give her the courage to do as he asked, or was winning his respect what motivated her? That she hardly knew how to answer the question disturbed her. What he thought of her shouldn't matter. And yet, it did. Rather more than she cared to admit.

Heart pounding, she breast-stroked to the ladder, grasped the lowest rung and pushed off her mask. Then, aware of his gaze focused on every inch of her as she climbed out of the water, she hoisted herself onto the pool deck, resisted the impulse to check that her bikini remained in place, and said, "Thank you for the lesson."

Then, with as much nonchalance as she could muster, she strolled to where Solange waited with Adrian on the bench at the shallow end of the pool. "I thought you'd never get here," she muttered, picking up a towel.

A smile twitched at the corners of Solange's mouth. "I hardly think you missed me."

Anne-Marie waited until Adrian had jumped into his father's waiting arms and was happily splashing his way toward a huge red ball floating on the water, then she said, "Exactly what do you mean by that?"

"Just that you and my future brother-in-law appeared too wrapped up in each other to notice anyone else."

"He insisted on teaching me to use a face mask." She mopped the dripping ends of her hair, then tucked the towel around herself, sarong-style. "And all I can say is, it's a pity no one ever taught him how to take 'No' for an answer. He's very bossy."

"And you're unusually flustered."

Unwilling to debate the truth of that statement, she said, "Never mind me. How are *you,* this morning? You're looking a bit more cheerful than you were last night."

"That's because you're here. I don't feel so alone anymore." She gestured to the terrace. "Breakfast is ready. Shall we go over and sit down?"

Anne-Marie glanced covertly at Ethan who was still in the pool with his son. "Shouldn't we wait for the lord and master to give us permission to eat?"

"He's not an ogre, Anne-Marie! He won't be upset if we help ourselves to coffee. Finish drying off and let's go. I'm never properly awake until—"

"You've had your morning *café au lait.*" She laughed, then pulled on her cover-up and slipped her arm through Solange's. "I remember!"

The inflated ball hit Ethan squarely on the shoulder and bounced into the water. "Papa," Adrian called out reproachfully, "you're not paying attention!"

"I know." How could he be expected to, with her laughter floating through the air like music, and the graceful, easy way she moved her scantily-clad body distracting him every other second? But since he could hardly tell his son that, he sniffed conspicuously, boosted the boy onto the pool deck, and said, "I'm thinking about food instead. Jeanne made fruit crêpes for breakfast. I'll race you to the terrace."

The women were chatting animatedly as he approached, and Solange had color in her cheeks, for a change. "You're looking more rested this morning, *ma petite,*" he said, dropping a kiss on her head. "Having *Mademoiselle* Barclay here appears to agree with you."

"*Oui.* I am very happy."

"As happy as when you're spending time with Philippe?"

His technique must leave something to be desired because, as usual, she didn't recognize that he was teasing her. "Oh, never that, Ethan!" she said, horrified. "No one can take his place."

"I'm glad to hear it, especially since he phoned this morning to say he'll be home in time for dinner tonight."

Her face lit up—she really was a pretty little thing which, no doubt, was what had first caught Philippe's eye—but she had a fragility about her, and a desire to please at all costs which, combined with a lack of confidence in her own judgment, worried Ethan. This friend, this Anne-Marie Barclay with the long, tanned legs, minuscule bikini, and outspoken manner, didn't strike him as the best influence. The sooner Philippe reappeared and kept Solange occupied, the better.

"So, *Mademoiselle,*" he said, taking a seat opposite his guest, "tell me something about yourself."

# CHAPTER THREE

"WHAT would you like to know?" Anne-Marie asked pertly, ticked off by his patronizing attitude. Clearly, his expectations of her possible accomplishments hovered around zero.

He shrugged. "As much as you care to tell me. Let's begin with your work. You've designed Solange's wedding trousseau, I understand."

"Yes."

"As a professional, or is this a favor between friends?"

"Both," she said sharply. "I'm a graduate of *Esmode International* in Paris, one of the foremost schools of fashion design in the world."

"Very commendable, I'm sure. And you work—?"

"In Vancouver, on the west coast of Canada."

"I'm aware of where it is, *Mademoiselle.* I've visited your beautiful city a number of times and greatly enjoyed its many attractions. But it hardly struck me as the center of *haute couture.* For which fashion house do you design?"

"My own."

He almost curled his lip in disdain. "I see."

"Do you?" she inquired, matching his condescending tone. "Then you're no doubt aware that my designs have won a number of prestigious awards."

"Anne-Marie worked in the movie industry in Hollywood for a while," Solange cut in, trying to be helpful. "She was even nominated for an Oscar, once."

*"Hollywood?"* This time, he *did* curl his lip, as if he'd

discovered something disgusting crawling around in the mango-stuffed crêpe the butler placed before him. *"The movie industry?"*

"Yes," Anne-Marie purred, taking a certain vengeful delight in his ill-contained horror. "Theatrical costume has always interested me."

"But you're no longer connected to the entertainment world? You've moved on to a less...flamboyant clientele?"

"Not really. We have a thriving movie industry in Vancouver, too, which is what originally drew me back to my hometown. As a result of the contacts I've made there and in California, I number quite a few well-known stars among my private clients, as well as celebrities from other walks of life."

"And you've designed Solange's wedding dress," he said glumly, rolling his eyes. *"Mon Dieu!"*

"Why does that disturb you, Ethan?" she asked. "I assure you I'm up to the challenge of creating an appropriate wedding ensemble for the bride and her entourage."

He compressed his rather beautiful mouth. "We are a small, close-knit community on Bellefleur. Tradition plays a big part in our lives. A wedding—particularly a Beaumont wedding—is a significant cultural event. My family has certain standards to uphold, certain expectations to meet."

"What a shame," she said blandly. "Where I come from, a wedding's simply a happy event where people who care about the bride and groom come together to celebrate their commitment to one another. And although I don't expect you'll approve, it's also an occasion when the bride gets to call most of the shots. It is, primarily, *her* day."

"How unfortunate for the man who chose her as his bride."

"Why?"

"Because such an attitude shows a distinct lack of consideration for what the groom might prefer—and that does not bode well for harmony in the marriage."

"What a load of rubbish!" she scoffed, ignoring Solange's gasp of petrified horror. "Marriage is a lifelong contract whose success depends on mutual consideration and respect. A wedding, on the other hand, is a one-day affair in which, historically, the bride takes star billing. For a man who professes to set such store by tradition, I'd have thought you'd know that."

"And you're qualified to make that distinction, as well as dictate fashions trends, are you?"

"I've never been married, if that's what you're asking."

"Then you'll forgive me if I take your opinions with a grain of salt."

"Of course I will," she said sunnily. "Just as I'm sure you'll forgive me if I treat yours the same way since, as I understand it, you're divorced—which certainly indicates *you* don't have much of a grasp on how marriage is supposed to work, either."

Only eyes as intensely blue as his could assume such a hard, metallic sheen. "We appear to have strayed from the subject at hand," he said coldly. "Namely, this family's wedding."

"Which you're afraid I'll turn into a tasteless Hollywood spectacle."

He inclined his head in offensively tacit agreement. "I don't mean to insult you."

"Insult me?" Very much aware of Adrian taking in everything without really understanding the subtext of what was being said, she swallowed the temper threatening to get the better of her, and cooed sweetly, "You're downright offensive, Ethan, and on the strength of what? You know next to nothing about me.''

''I know that you're afraid of water.''

He, too, spoke lightly, as if trying to defuse the tension swirling through the air, but she was having none of it. ''I'm not afraid of *you,* though,'' she said. ''Nor do I care what you think of me or my achievements. I'm here to lend moral support to Solange, not win your approval.''

''I applaud your loyalty, but just for the record, *Mademoiselle* Barclay, you're not the only one with Solange's best interests at heart. We all want to see her happy.''

''Then we really don't have anything to disagree about, do we, Ethan? And since I'm calling you by your given name, you may call me Anne-Marie.''

He choked on his coffee at that. ''Thank you, I'm sure,'' he said, when he recovered himself. ''So tell me, *Mademoiselle*, what are your plans for the rest of the day?''

''I'll be working on Solange's wedding gown.''

''Would you care to join us for lunch and perhaps take a tour of the island this afternoon?''

''No, thank you.''

He lifted his brows in faint surprise. Clearly, he wasn't accustomed to being turned down. *Well, he might as well get used to the idea,* she thought, pushing her chair back from the table, *because I've got a feeling he's in for quite a few more upsets before this visit's over.*

Ever the perfect gentleman, he also rose to his feet. ''You're leaving so soon? I hope I'm not the reason. Just because we don't see eye to eye—''

''Don't flatter yourself, Ethan. You have nothing to do with my leaving. As I said a moment ago, I have work to do.''

"Very well. Would you like me to send our in-house seamstress to give you a hand?"

"That's not necessary. I'm perfectly capable of mastering this project on my own."

For a moment, he chewed on the concept that the world could indeed spin without his directing it, and didn't seem to find the notion very appealing. At length, he said, "You have everything you need in the way of equipment?"

"Absolutely...except for—"

"Ah!" He favored her with another smile, a Cheshire-cat kind this time, full of smug satisfaction, as though to say *I knew all this fine independence wouldn't carry you very far.*

"I will need an ironing board."

"We have staff who take care of ironing."

"Not with my projects, you don't! I'm the only one who touches them."

"As you wish." He inclined his aristocratic head again, as though conferring enormous favors on an undeserving minion. "Is there anything else I can supply?"

"Yes," she said, spurred to be difficult just for the sake of proving that he wasn't as all-powerful as he liked to believe. "I could use a worktable—something about eight feet long and at least three feet wide—with a padded muslin top to protect the delicate dress fabrics I'm working with."

"I'll see to it that one is delivered to your suite immediately," he replied, promptly dispelling any illusion she might have entertained that she could play one-upmanship with him and win. "You do realize, of course, that it's going to leave you rather short of living space?"

"That's not a problem. I'm sure Solange won't mind sharing her sitting room with me, should the occasion arise that I need one."

"If she does, feel free to relax here at the main house."

*I'd rather live in a hovel on the beach than spend a moment more than I have to under your roof!* she was tempted to reply but, aware of Solange nervously following the tenor of the conversation, said only, "Thank you. I appreciate the offer."

"You're welcome." He leaned down to ruffle his son's dark hair. "I'll arrange for the worktable to be delivered. Come along, Adrian."

The boy looked hopefully at Solange. "I want to play at Solange's house."

"You'll just be in the way now that *Mademoiselle* Barclay is here. She'll be keeping Solange very busy."

"As long as he doesn't mind my borrowing her for a fitting once in a while, he won't be in the way at all," Anne-Marie said, smiling at the child. "Let him come. It'll give us a chance to get to know one another better."

"Very well." As he passed behind her chair, Ethan laid a surprisingly affectionate hand on Solange's shoulder. "Just phone when you've had enough, *chérie*. Don't let him wear you out."

"He almost sounds as if he cares about you," Anne-Marie muttered, watching Ethan lope gracefully up the steps and disappear inside the villa.

"He does. I already told you, he's very kind and very well-intentioned." Solange covered her mouth to smother a giggle. "But you were deliberately baiting him, Anne-Marie, and succeeding rather well, I might add. I nearly had a heart attack at the way the two of you were going at each other."

"He's the kind of man who brings out the worst in me."

"Is that what you call it?" This time, Solange didn't try to hide her amusement. "From where I sat, it looked more like two people taking refuge in hostility, because they didn't want to admit to the instant attraction between them.''

''That's the most ridiculous thing I ever heard!''

Although her reply held a convincing ring of certainty, Anne-Marie couldn't prevent an annoying shudder of awareness skating over her skin. Ethan Beaumont's penetrating blue gaze *had* unnerved her—more than she was willing to acknowledge. She *was* vibrantly conscious of the physical presence of the man, no matter how much she tried to ignore it.

''I didn't say it made sense,'' Solange replied cheerfully. ''That sort of spontaneous combustion seldom does. But that's no reason to deny it.''

Oh yes, it was! Just because Ethan Beaumont was all smooth, male beauty on the outside didn't mean he wasn't full of flaws on the inside, and she wasn't about to compromise her heart by allowing a purely physical reaction to rule the day!

He heard the laughter long before he reached the guest pavilions: Adrian's high and exuberant, Solange's rippling with unusual delight—and *hers,* breathless, musical, alluring.

Emerging noiselessly from the path, he stood a moment in the filtered shade cast by a giant tibouchina at the edge of the terrace, and saw at once the cause of so much hilarity. A kitten, one of the stable cat's latest litter and not yet as surefooted as it should be, was chasing a balloon tethered to a length of ribbon tied around Adrian's wrist.

The gleeful expression on his son's face sent a stab of pain through Ethan's heart. There'd been too much grief and not nearly enough laughter in the boy's life. Too many nights filled with bad dreams and tears; too many questions left unanswered. Because how did a man explain to a three-year-old that the woman he'd once called "Mommy" had grown tired of the role? Had gone and was never coming back?

Ethan's personal sense of betrayal had long ago faded into indifference. If he thought of his ex-wife at all—and it happened rarely—the most he felt was pity and disgust. But what she'd done to their son left a permanently bitter taste on his tongue. It had been two years since she ran off, and although Adrian no longer asked about her, the damage she'd done had left its mark on the boy.

Certainly, Ethan tried to pick up the slack. Loved enough for two parents. Did everything in his power to create a secure, impregnable world. His shoulders were broad enough to carry the child all day, if need be; his arms strong.

But when the gremlins came and filled the night with terror, he lacked a woman's tender touch, her soft, reassuring voice and sweet, welcoming curves. And seeing how Adrian leaned against the North American visitor and instinctively hid his face against her breasts as the kitten lunged at him, Ethan realized with fresh awareness just how much was missing from his son's life.

"You ought to stay out of the sun, *Mademoiselle*," he said, driven forward less by concern for her welfare than the surge of jealousy which struck out of nowhere and whispered that she had no right trying to supplant him. She was a stranger, a temporary fixture in their lives. She didn't belong and never would. He didn't want her insinuating herself into his boy's affections, just to leave him high and dry when she grew bored with playing nursemaid. "Fair-skinned people like you burn very quickly in this part of the world."

"I used sunscreen," she said offhandedly, nuzzling Adrian's neck.

She'd exchanged the bikini for a yellow sundress held up by shoestring straps. Her arms and feet were bare. As for the parts in between...unwillingly, Ethan noted how the fabric clung to her tiny waist, flared over her narrow hips, and ended halfway down her thighs.

The kitten swatted again at the balloon, missed, and attacked her toes instead. Giggling helplessly, Adrian curled up in her lap and wiggled his toes, too.

"That's enough, Adrian!" Ethan called out, more sharply than he intended. "You're making a nuisance of yourself."

Fending off the kitten, she hugged the boy and stroked the hair from his forehead. "No, he's not. We're having a wonderful time playing, aren't we, Adrian?"

"Yes." He squirmed against her, and wound his arms around her neck.

Almost choking on outrage, Ethan said, "I thought you were here to work, *Mademoiselle.*"

"I am," she said, the sweetness in her voice belied by the evil glance she cast him from beneath her lowered lashes. "But since I'm my own boss, I don't need anyone else's permission to take time off for a little fun."

And if he didn't soon put a leash on her tongue, she'd create even more trouble than was already brewing! "That doesn't give you the right to countermand my instructions to my son."

"Good grief!" Rolling her eyes, she released Adrian, gave him a little pat on his behind, and said, "The master calls, sweet pea. Better not keep him waiting. But come back soon, okay?"

"I know how busy you are, Ethan," Solange cut in, eyeing him apprehensively, "and if you'd phoned, I could have brought Adrian home and saved you having to come and get him."

"I was headed down here anyway," he said, wishing she wouldn't tiptoe around him as if she were walking on eggshells all the time. "I wanted to be sure *Mademoiselle* Barclay has everything she needs for her work."

"I do," the other one said, rising languidly to her feet and tugging the skirt of her sundress snugly around her thighs.

He averted his gaze and pretended an interest in the diving board. "The table's satisfactory?"

"Perfectly. Thank you."

"Would you like to see my wedding gown?" Solange asked. "It's truly gorgeous, Ethan."

"He's not interested," her bossy friend informed her. "He's got more important things to do,"

Not sure what demon of curiosity provoked him—she herself or merely her work—he said, "Certainly I'm interested! Nothing's more important than pleasing my family, *Mademoiselle*. By all means, show me the dress."

Anne-Marie Barclay stared at him, her mouth set in a delectably stubborn pout, and for a moment, he thought she'd refuse him. After a moment's reflection though, she grudgingly led the way to her villa and waved him inside.

Brushing past her—an unsettling experience, fraught with awareness of her scent and the proximity, again, of her cool, creamy skin—he paused under the covered entrance and stared in disbelief at the sight before him.

Except for the foyer which looked more or less as usual, he barely recognized the place. Gone were the elegant arrangement of furniture, the silk-shaded reading lamps, the bowls of fresh fruit and vases of cut flowers.

The silver candelabra normally gracing the middle of the table in the dining alcove had been banished in favor of her sewing machine, with the iron and ironing board stationed close by.

The main salon was barely recognizable. All the furniture had been pushed against the walls to make room for the worktable, leaving so little floor space that two people couldn't pass one another without body contact—something he'd be wise to avoid where she was concerned, he reminded himself.

"Well, there it is." She indicated some sort of dummy figure in the corner, with the wedding gown draped over it. "Perfectly respectable, as you can see."

"I never doubted that for a moment."

"Oh, please!" she exclaimed, putting the length of the table between them in order to make some small adjustment to the dress. "You anticipated nothing of the sort. The only reason you professed an interest in seeing my work was to prove conclusively how totally ill-equipped I am to handle the task I've undertaken."

"Possibly." He inched his way down the other side of the table and circled the garment, taking note of the myriad pearl-headed pins holding the cobweb-fine fabric in place. Even he, ignorant though he was when it came to the finer points of women's fashions, could appreciate the clean, clever lines of the bodice and the artful drape of the skirt. "But if so, my reservations were clearly misplaced, although I confess I expected the dress would be more or less finished by now. As it is, you appear to have quite a bit of work still to do."

"It just needs to be put together," she said, as if such a major feat of engineering was a mere trifle to a person of her expertise. "I wanted to be sure of a perfect fit before any permanent stitching went into place. This fabric's too delicate to tolerate much in the way of alterations."

"So you did the preliminary work ahead of time on the dummy? How'd you manage to fit it into a suitcase?"

"I didn't," she answered saucily. "I pack my equipment in a small cabin trunk and although it's roomy enough for most things, try as I might, I couldn't squeeze myself inside. But if you're referring to the dress form, it comes apart and actually takes up very little space."

Unable to repress a smile, he said dryly, "We appear to have difficulty communicating, *Mademoiselle*."

"Oh, I don't think so," she replied, around a mouthful of pins. "I think we understand one another perfectly. Neither of us is the least bit impressed with the other. If it were up to you, I'd be on my way home by now."

The glance she flung at him dared him to deny it, nor was he inclined to do so. "Yes, you would," he admitted. "But since that's clearly not about to happen, the question now becomes, what can we do to reverse such an unfortunate state of affairs?"

She removed the pins from her mouth and poked them into a fat pink cushion designed for the purpose. "You mean to say, you're not even going to pretend to deny one exists?"

"Certainly not. I have good reason to mistrust you, although I fail to see why you should be so antagonistic toward me."

Her mouth fell open, whether in mock surprise or because she truly was amazed by what she obviously interpreted as unabashed arrogance on his part. But much though he'd have preferred to take advantage of her discomposure and emerge the winner in their little contest of wills, he found to his chagrin that his attention was drawn to how deliciously pink and ripe her lips were. Would they taste as sweet, he wondered.

She planted her fists on her hips. "What possible reason do you have to mistrust me?"

"It's not something I'm prepared to discuss at present," he said, glancing meaningfully to where Adrian was playing with his kitten under the covered walkway. "More to the point, why are you so hostile?"

"That's easily answered," she said bluntly. "You're not my type. I've never cared for overbearing men. Not that either issue matters one iota since I'm here for only a few weeks and, once the wedding's over, we'll never have to see each other again."

"I disagree. Even a day can seem like a very long time when two people find themselves frequently thrown into one another's company. And make no mistake about it, *Mademoiselle*. We *will* be spending a great deal of time together in the coming weeks."

"Why? We're not the couple getting married."

"Indeed not, and for that I'm deeply and enduringly grateful," he said, taking private pleasure in the flush which ran under her skin at his response. "But weddings, at least Beaumont weddings, amount to a bit more than a church ceremony and a reception. As best man, it's my duty to escort the maid of honor to the various social events taking place between now and the big day itself. That being so, surely you agree we need to arrive at some sort of truce?"

"I'm perfectly capable of looking after myself. So thank you anyway, but no thank you, Ethan. I neither want nor need you to act as my chaperon."

A third voice, young and filled with confusion, brought them swinging around to find Adrian standing just inside the foyer. "Don't you like my papa, Anne-Marie?"

"Oh, sweetheart…!" Gray eyes wide with distress, she hurried around the worktable and dropping to her knees, cupped his face in her hands. "I didn't say I didn't like him."

*Not in so many words, perhaps!* Annoyed as much with himself as with her, for forgetting how easily sound traveled through the open shutters of the building, Ethan joined her and placed his hand on his son's shoulder. "I thought I told you to stay with Solange, *mon petit?*"

"She went inside to answer her phone," he said, his gaze fixed adoringly on the face of his new friend. "She was gone a long time, and the kitten ran off, so I came to find you."

"You did the right thing," the Barclay woman murmured soothingly. "It was very rude of us to leave you alone, but your father and I are finished our conversation now, so why don't you and I play another game?"

"No," Ethan said, taking Adrian's hand firmly in his. "I already made it clear he won't be staying."

"And I made it clear he's no trouble."

*But you are,* he thought. *You're nothing but trouble, and I intend to put a stop to it before you cause irreparable damage to my boy.* "No," he said again, more forcefully this time. "He comes with me. You can't possibly attend to your work and keep an eye on him at the same time."

"I'm a woman," she retorted, as if he hadn't already noticed. "I can multitask."

"I'm a father, and I don't care to have my son left to his own devices around a swimming pool, especially not with someone who doesn't have the first clue about water rescue or life-saving techniques."

"Oh, rats!" She made a comical face and rubbed her nose against Adrian's, thereby reducing him to another fit of giggles. "Father's right again, but never mind, sweet pea. We'll have lots of other chances to play."

Not if he had anything to say in the matter, as she'd discover soon enough, Ethan thought grimly, steering Adrian outside just as Solange emerged from her quarters.

"There's someone waiting to see you in your office,"

she told him. "A Señor Gonzales from Caracas. Something to do with the oil operations, I understand."

"I wasn't expecting him until tomorrow." He pointed Adrian toward the path leading uphill. "Guess we'd better head home, *mon petit.*"

"Yes, do," Anne-Marie Barclay said, with unflattering enthusiasm. "There's certainly nothing to keep you here."

"Not at this moment, perhaps," he said, determined to have the last word, "but I'll be back. And when I return, it'll be to establish a few ground rules. Because you'll surely concur that we need to arrive at some sort of harmonious understanding of who's calling the shots around here."

"You haven't left me in much doubt about that."

"I'd like to think not. But you don't strike me as someone who concedes defeat easily."

She lifted one shoulder in a delicate but decidedly defiant shrug.

"Precisely," he said. "So for the good of everyone, but most especially my boy, you and I will arrive at a mutually acceptable agreement which will preclude any further clashing of wills. Because I will not subject him to any more such displays, nor will I allow our incompatibility to turn my brother's pre-wedding festivities into a battle zone."

# CHAPTER FOUR

ANNE-MARIE didn't see him again until that evening when, unlike the day before, dinner was a formal affair involving the whole family.

"You look lovely," Solange told her, as they made their way through the gardens to the Sunset Gazebo for the cocktail hour. "Is that outfit one of your own creations?"

"Of course. I make all my own clothes."

"Well, seeing you tonight ought to put an end to any doubts Ethan still has about your talent. He's sure to be impressed."

"I didn't dress to please him," she said sharply, but it wasn't true. She'd deliberately chosen the violet chiffon dress for its dramatic neckline which left one shoulder bare, and for the way it lent her gray eyes a smoky purple depth at the same time that it emphasized her ivory-toned skin.

*I'll knock his socks off!* she'd vowed defiantly, glaring at herself in the mirror as she secured her hair in a smooth coil on the crown of her head, and swept a trace of lavender shadow over her eyelids. *Before this evening's over, there'll be no doubt in anyone's mind about which of us knows the most about good taste!*

But when they finally came face-to-face, she was the one left speechless. If Ethan stripped to the waist in the cool shade of morning was spectacular, Ethan in white dinner jacket and black tie, with the setting sun turning his skin to glowing bronze, was breathtaking.

"I'm delighted you decided to join us," he said, as if

there was even a remote possibility that *anyone* would have the nerve to refuse a Beaumont invitation. "Allow me to introduce my aunt and uncle, Josephine and Louis Duclos. This," he said, drawing her toward the couple waiting to the rear, "is Solange's friend, *Mademoiselle* Anne-Marie Barclay."

*"Enchanté, Mademoiselle,"* Louis Duclos murmured, kissing her hand with old-world gallantry. "Welcome to Bellefleur."

"Indeed," his wife said, with a cool smile, and tapped him on the shoulder. "That's enough, Louis! Release *Mademoiselle* Barclay's hand, if you please, before you swallow it whole, and allow her to make my acquaintance. *Mademoiselle,* you may sit with me under the canopy."

Issuing orders under the guise of invitations must be a Beaumont family trait, Anne-Marie decided, accepting the proffered seat. And with the exception of her eyes, which were the same dark brown as Adrian's, Josephine's striking resemblance to Ethan marked her as a Beaumont born and bred.

"Tell me about yourself," she commanded, her gaze raking over Anne-Marie with daunting candor. "I know nothing about you except that you and Solange are old friends. How did that come about, given that she is French and you're Canadian? Were your parents also members of the diplomatic corps?"

"No. My parents died in a boating accident when I was eight."

Josephine's gaze softened marginally. "I'm sorry. That was a grievous loss for such a young child to endure. Were you left completely alone?"

"Not quite. My mother had a brother who became my guardian. But he was a bachelor in his early twenties. He hadn't the first idea how to cope with a little girl who cried every night for her mother and father. So he sent me away to boarding school where I'd at least be with other children my own age, and eventually to the Swiss finishing school where Solange and I met.''

"And became friends because you had so much in common. Not that she was orphaned, of course, but she might as well have been since her parents so seldom showed interest in her.''

"They didn't really abandon me, *Tante* Josephine,'' Solange said, leaping to their defense just as she always had, no matter how often they forgot her birthday or canceled plans to meet her during school vacations. "It was just that my father's work in the Consulate was very demanding and involved a great deal of travel. The only reason I spent so much time in boarding school was that he and my mother wanted to maintain some sort of continuity in my education. But they always made sure I attended the *very best* schools.''

"Rationalize it any way you like,'' Josephine replied, "but the bottom line is, they farmed you out to an institution and left someone else to bring you up while they partied their way through Europe. You're just too nice a child to speak as plainly as I do.''

"I met Solange's parents on several occasions, and they always struck me as very caring people,'' Anne-Marie said, knowing how devastating Solange would find such blunt criticism.

"I'm sure they were, and are,'' Josephine Duclos replied. "They care a great deal about their own pleasures.''

"They were always extremely kind to me.''

"I'm not saying they were deliberately cruel, young woman.'' Josephine spared Ethan a telling glance. "Merely self-involved to the exclusion of those around them, like someone else we once knew.''

"Let's not air our dirty linen all at once," he said mildly. "*Mademoiselle* Barclay's opinion of us is already tarnished enough."

"I don't know why you'd assume that," Anne-Marie replied, accepting a glass of champagne from Louis Duclos. "Adrian is adorable."

"But I'm not." Although his tone remained cheerfully uncaring, Ethan's smile held more than a touch of irony and caused a minor upheaval in Anne-Marie. Even when he wasn't *trying* to be charming, she found him attractive, so what sort of fool did that make her?

"No," she said, striving to match his insouciance. "You're thoroughly obnoxious!"

At that, Solange visibly cringed but, surprisingly, Josephine let out a squawk of laughter. "I think you've met your match, Ethan," she crowed. "And as for you, child...." She tapped Anne-Marie on the arm. "I do believe I might like you!"

"From which you'll no doubt gather that my aunt doesn't confer approval on too many people," Ethan said dryly. "Would you care for more champagne?"

"Stop trying to make her tipsy. I'm not yet finished quizzing her." Brown eyes snapping with lively curiosity, Josephine turned back to Anne-Marie. "What else about you is interesting, child, beside the fact that you're refreshingly outspoken?"

"Very little. My work keeps me too busy to pursue much in the way of hobbies."

"I'm not talking about what you *do!* It's who you are inside that I want to hear about—your thoughts and opinions. How, for example, do you feel about Solange marrying a Beaumont?"

Dusk was descending rapidly. Already, the shot-silk blue of the sea had deepened to rich plum. But the squat

pillar candles encircling a bouquet of scarlet hibiscus on
the table threw out enough light for Anne-Marie to be vividly aware of Ethan's gaze sliding from her face to her
bare shoulder, dipping slowly all the way to her ankles,
then returning to dwell on her face as if he were trying to
penetrate her mind and discern her most private thoughts.

He made her wish she'd worn something a little more
conservative. Something that didn't reveal quite so much
of her. She wanted to hug her arms over her breasts,
smooth away the gooseflesh suddenly pebbling her skin.
Turn away from that probing regard.

Instead, she found herself hypnotized by it…by him. His
hair, dark as night, lay smooth against his skull. Except
for his eyes which, even in the fading light, gleamed blue
as lapis lazuli, he was a study in tones of sepia, black and
white. He lifted his glass in that negligently graceful way
with which he appeared to do most things, his hand and
wrist tawny against the snowy cuff of his shirt. He blinked
slowly, and the charcoal shadow of his lashes flickered
over the polished bronze of his cheekbones.

His mouth lifted in a slow smile. "We're all waiting to
hear your answer, *Mademoiselle*," he said softly. "Do you
think Solange is insane to throw in her lot with a family
such as ours?"

"I hope she isn't," she said forthrightly. "I hope
Philippe lives up to her expectations."

"But you have doubts that he will?"

She hesitated, hating how he was putting her on the spot,
and wishing he hadn't so accurately pinpointed the reservations she'd kept from Solange. The Philippe she remembered was charming and attentive, but he didn't possess a
fraction of his brother's strength of character. Solange was
emotionally fragile, though. She needed a strong man by
her side.

"I haven't seen Philippe in almost eight years," Anne-Marie said, choosing her words with care. "I expect he's changed, so I prefer to withhold comment until we become reacquainted."

Ethan, though, wasn't about to let her off the hook so easily. "Changed from what?" he persisted.

"From the way he used to be, of course—a boy barely out of his teens, playing at being a man of the world. I expect he's grown up somewhat in the time since."

"Don't hold your breath," Josephine Duclos muttered. "Louis, hand me my wrap and escort me back to the house. My stomach tells me it's time I ate."

Even as she spoke, the telephone beside Ethan rang. Lifting it, he strolled to the edge of the gazebo and carried on a brief, low-voiced conversation before turning back to announce, "Your stomach is right on time as usual, *ma tante.* And you, Solange, will be happy to know Philippe arrived home half an hour ago, and will be joining us for dinner."

"He's here already? I wasn't expecting him until much later." She sprang to her feet, her face illuminated with joy. "Will you excuse me if I run ahead?"

"Sure," he said. "Go welcome him back."

She raced off, light-footed as a gazelle, and since Josephine and Louis also had already started back, Anne-Marie was left with no choice but to walk with Ethan.

"So," he said, cupping her elbow in a firm, warm grasp which made it clear he wasn't about to let her wriggle free from his hold or his questions, "now that we're alone at last, tell me exactly what you really think about this marriage between your best friend and my half brother."

"I have mixed feelings, Ethan. Philippe struck me in the past as being very likable but rather spoiled. If he hasn't matured, I'd worry about how ready he is for something as permanent as marriage. On the other hand, I never thought his relationship with Solange would last more than one summer. I take it as a very good sign that it's survived nearly ten years.''

''There have been other women in between, you know.''

''And Solange has dated other men. Yet, in the end, no one could come between her and Philippe. They always found their way back to one another.''

''Does she know how you feel—that you're not sure she's made the wisest choice?''

''No. Solange's confidence is easily crushed and I wouldn't dream of saying anything which might undermine her at this stage of the game. If she'd asked me six months ago, I might have been more candid.''

''It strikes me as strange that, for such good friends, you don't confide in one another more readily. I'd have thought you'd be the first person she'd tell when she became engaged.''

''I'm the person she turns to when things go wrong, Ethan. When life's treating her well, the people she shares her happiness with are her parents, because she knows they don't have either the time or the inclination to involve themselves in her troubles. The only news they're interested in hearing is the good news.''

''So my aunt's observations weren't far off the mark?''

''Sadly not.''

''It makes me wonder why some people bother having children in the first place,'' he said, the note of savagery underlying his tone echoed in his almost bruising grip on her elbow.

''Do *you* have any regrets about fathering Adrian?''

''Good God, no! What sort of question is that?''

''One prompted by the fact that you're practically pulverizing my bones!'' Wincing, she extracted herself from his hold. ''To some men, a child is a sort of status symbol, a mark of their masculinity, if you like.''

''And to some women, a child is a toy to be cast aside when they grow tired of playing with it!''

''Are we talking about your ex-wife now?''

''Yes, though I can't imagine how she merits being included in the conversation. She was, if you'll forgive my speaking plainly, a living bitch, and undeserving of a son like Adrian.''

''Abandoning a child is completely contrary to a woman's natural instincts. I think she must have been desperately unhappy to resort to such action.''

''Are you suggesting I'm the one who drove her away?''

''I'm not suggesting anything, merely expressing an opinion I believe in. Normally, it goes against the grain for a mother to abandon her young.''

''There was nothing 'normal' about Lisa! The pity of it is, I didn't recognize the fact sooner. If I had, I could saved everyone, particularly my son, a lot of heartache.''

*And what about your pain, Ethan?* she wondered, hearing the ragged edge in his voice. *Does it still eat at you when you wake up alone in the night? Is Adrian the only one who misses her?* ''If she were to ask to come back, would you let her?''

They had emerged from the path into a clearing swathed in moonlight. The drugging scent of flowers filled the still air but not a sound disturbed the silence—except for his uneven breathing. ''Yes,'' he said from between clenched teeth, and it was as if his reply had been torn from his very heart and left him mortally wounded. ''Yes, I would let her. How could I not?''

She shouldn't have cared. But his anguish flowed out and entrapped her like a living thing, filling her with an

inexplicable, illogical sense of having been robbed. Yet
how could that be, when she had nothing to lose in the
first place?

When they arrived at the house, they found Josephine and
Louis admiring an urn full of gardenias at one end of the
dining room verandah, and Philippe and Solange at the
other, locked in the kind of uninhibited public embrace
which was their habit.

Either his annoyance showed on his face, or else he
made an involuntary sound of disapproval because, as they
approached, Anne-Marie flung him a scornful glance and
said quietly, "What's the matter, Ethan? Jealous?"

"Not in the least," he muttered. "But there's a time
and place for everything."

"Not in their case. You've made sure of that by keeping
Solange and Philippe apart as much as possible, so who
can blame them for making the most of whatever opportunity presents itself?"

"Not you, apparently," he said dourly. "Should I take
that to mean you exercise no restraint in your
own…affairs?"

"You make 'affairs' sound like a dirty word, Ethan, as
if you think men line up around the block, eager to sample
whatever sexual favors I choose to bestow."

As though drawn by a powerful magnetic force, his gaze
lingered a moment on the graceful sweep of fabric draping
itself from her shoulder and across the swell of her breasts
to her tiny waist. "I could hardly blame them, if they did."

A delicate peach blush ran over her face. "I'm not sure
whether I should be flattered or insulted by that remark."

He was spared having to answer by Philippe who, having finally noticed them, crossed to where they stood
and swept Anne-Marie into a hug which struck Ethan as

being considerably more enthusiastic than the occasion called for.

"I swear, if I weren't marrying Solange, I'd propose to you, Anne-Marie!" he said. "How come no other man's got my good sense?"

Hearing him, Josephine said tartly, "Perhaps Anne-Marie's the one with sense. Put her down, you fool, and let your brother lead her into dinner before I faint from weakness! What took you so long to get here, Ethan?"

"We were talking and time got away from us."

"Talking about what?" Never one to be fobbed off with half-truths, Josephine stared at him, beady-eyed.

"Children, and how best to deal with them," he replied, trying to ignore the uneasiness which assailed him at the expression on Solange's face as she watched his brother. Did Philippe have any inkling of the depth of her adoration? Did he *deserve* it?

Ushering them all into the dining room, Ethan indicated that Anne-Marie should take her place to the right of where he sat, at the head of the table. She slid onto the chair in one easy, graceful movement, with her dress rippling down her body to swirl in waves around her ankles, thereby drawing his unwilling attention to the physical attributes of the woman wearing it.

The candelabra suspended from the ceiling awoke glimmers of palest wheat in her blond hair and painted fetching shadows on her face. Over the course of the day, she'd picked up a touch of sun—just enough to gild her creamy skin with honey.

She sat close enough that, without it appearing deliberate, he could have nudged her knee with his. Touched her sandaled foot in private intimacy. Had he wished, he could have reached over and covered her hand. Fingered the thin gold chain at her narrow wrist, or the diamond studs winking fire and ice at her ears.

And, shockingly, he did wish—for all those things. Which made him, for once, very glad of his aunt's insatiable interest in other people's lives. It spared him having to make polite conversation with a woman he found altogether more distracting than she had any right to be.

"How old are you, child?" Josephine inquired, over hot papaya-orange soup.

"Twenty-eight."

"And never married?"

"No." She smiled, seeming not at all put out by such a personal line of questions. "I haven't had the time. Or perhaps it's just that I haven't yet met the right man."

"But you have no objection to marriage as such?"

She thought about that for a moment, tipping her head to one side and lowering her lashes so that they lay like miniature fans against her cheeks. Finally, she said, "No. Eventually, I would like a husband and children, and the trappings that go with them."

"By 'trappings,' do you mean money?"

"Good grief, no! I've already got plenty of that."

"Social status, then?" his aunt persisted.

"I consider I have that, too." She cast an amused glance at Ethan. "Although not everyone around this table might agree with me."

"Oh, never mind Ethan," Josephine chortled. "He's the kind of man who, once he makes up his mind about something, there's no moving him. But that's not to say he's always right."

"If I might be allowed to say something in my own defense, I haven't reached any hard and fast conclusions about you, *Mademoiselle*," he said mildly.

"Certainly you have," she retorted. "You've pegged

me as brash, flashy and uncouth when, in fact, I'm guilty only of being brash.''

''Don't put words in my mouth. And don't presume to read my mind.''

Josephine flapped her hand imperiously. ''Ignore him, Anne-Marie. Instead, tell me more about these trappings you're so anxious to acquire.''

''They're not material, if that's what you're wondering,'' she said. ''I want things money can't buy—traditions, I suppose you'd call them, like taking my child to choose his own pumpkin for Halloween, or helping him trim the tree at Christmas, then drinking hot chocolate and singing carols with him, afterward. If I had a daughter, I'd want to sew pretty party dresses for her, and bake special cakes for her birthdays.''

''Because they're the things which were taken away from you at much too early an age. Yes, I can see why they'd be important to you now.'' Josephine nodded sympathetically. ''Would you like to have more than one child?''

''Oh, definitely! Heaven forbid they'd suffer the same loss I did, but at least if it should happen, they'd have each other. In my experience, an only child is too often a lonely child.''

''It doesn't have to be,'' Ethan said defensively.

''No, of course not.'' She shrugged. ''It all depends on the circumstances.''

''And yours were particularly tragic.'' His aunt paused long enough to sample her soup, then started in on another barrage of questions. ''You've worked very hard to make a name for yourself in the world of fashion, my dear. Do you see yourself being able to give up your career in order to raise a family?''

''Not permanently, perhaps, but certainly over the short

haul. I consider motherhood to be a very worthwhile career in itself and deserving of the best a woman can bring to it.''

"*Eh bien,* isn't it fortunate that you're going to be here for several weeks!" Josephine glanced at Ethan meaningfully. "And what a pity we didn't meet you seven years ago."

"For someone who claimed she was starving, you're doing a lot more talking than you are eating," he said, knowing full well where his aunt's remarks were leading. She'd never liked Lisa, and had made it her mission in life to fix him up with someone more suitable.

*You're my firstborn nephew and my favorite,* she'd often told him. *I need to know you're with someone who truly deserves you, before I die.*

"I'm merely being sociable," she said now. "Tell me, Anne-Marie, how do you like this room?"

"Very much. The detailed flower painting on the walls is exquisite. *Trompe l'oeil,* isn't it?"

"Quite right, child, and how delightful that you're cultured enough to recognize it," Josephine replied, too transparently pleased at discovering her newfound protégée's latest virtue to recognize her remark came across as insultingly condescending.

"I saw many fine examples of the same in the chateaux I visited when I lived in France," Anne-Marie said, further enhancing her image with his aunt. "In fact, I followed a similar technique with some of my textile designs during my studies."

"And won a gold medal for them, too," Solange said, managing to tear her attention away from Philippe long enough to contribute something to the conversation.

"Did you indeed?" Josephine smiled, as satisfied as a cat who'd just devoured a bowl of cream, and Ethan privately admitted he was rather impressed himself. Perhaps there was more depth to Anne-Marie Barclay than he'd originally thought.

Still, he was relieved when the butler, Morton, appeared to direct the serving of the second course and Josephine, recognizing her favorite heart of palm salad, turned her attention to her plate.

Leaning toward Anne-Marie, Ethan said in an undertone, "I hope you didn't find my aunt's comments offensive. She means well, but her interest sometimes takes on the tone of an inquisition, and I apologize if it made you uncomfortable."

"It didn't," she replied. "I appreciate her being so direct and I envy you her devotion."

"If you're sincerely interested in the decor of this room, I'll be glad to give you a tour of the house someday when you have an hour to spare."

"That would be very nice."

Would it, or was she merely being polite? he wondered. Was she really as serenely composed as she appeared, or was it more a case of her having perfected the act of appearing so?

As the meal progressed, he found himself observing her. Watching for a hint of what really lay behind her lovely smile. Listening to the musical lilt of her laughter, the slightly husky timbre of her voice. And when, after coffee and cognac, the other four excused themselves and left him alone with her, he heard himself offering to escort her back to her villa with an eagerness which made him wonder if she'd somehow bewitched him.

He'd probably live to regret it, but the prospect of delving below her surface and discovering the real person underneath struck him suddenly as too appealing an undertaking to ignore.

# CHAPTER FIVE

"This really isn't necessary," Anne-Marie said, as he ushered her past the pillared entrance to the room and out through a side door to the paved terrace. Just when the other four members of the party had drifted off until only the two of them remained lingering over coffee, escaped her, but she did know the prospect of being alone in the deserted gardens with Ethan filled her with peculiar trepidation. "I assure you I can make my own way back."

His laugh flowed over her, low and oddly intoxicating in the warm night. "I somehow doubt that, since you couldn't even find your way here in broad daylight. And the path is steep in places. It wouldn't do to have you fall and hurt yourself. Solange would never forgive me. In any case, I could use a breath of fresh air, and it'll give us a chance to get to know one another better."

"Better? How about 'differently'?" she said.

"I'm not sure I know what you mean."

"Then let me speak bluntly. Your opinion of me underwent a subtle change over dinner and I'm curious to know why. Was it my informed appreciation of the decor in your dining room and the fact that I didn't try to steal the family silver that persuaded you to temper your animosity toward me, or did it take your aunt's stamp of approval to soften your attitude?"

"Have I been such an ogre?" he said lightly. "If so, I apologize."

"That doesn't answer my question."

"Then perhaps this will. Not for a moment did I think

64

you'd steal the family silver, Anne-Marie, nor was your intelligence ever in question. As for my aunt...." Again, his laughter caused an inexplicable sensation of pleasure to ripple over her skin. "I'm so used to Josephine putting her two bits' worth into the conversation every other minute that I barely notice it anymore."

*Putting her two bits' worth into the conversation...* The American idiom struck an incongruous note, coming as it did from a man who appeared to have little respect for anything remotely American. "You speak with a slight accent," she said, "yet your English is very colloquial."

"French was my mother tongue, but I spent several years studying at Harvard."

"So not everything from my neck of the woods is necessarily bad?"

"Not necessarily, no." She heard the smile in his voice. "I have a number of friends and many business acquaintances in the U.S. But before you accuse me of misleading you, you should know I'm also fluent in Spanish and Portuguese, and have contacts throughout South America, too."

"Then you're one up on me. I speak only French and Italian."

"That would matter only if we were in competition with each other, but since we're not, let's try to put aside our differences and get along, for Solange's sake." He took her hand, tucked it in the crook of his arm, and led her down a gravel path on the far side of the pool, different from the one by which he'd brought her to the mansion earlier. "It's pleasant out here, don't you think?"

"Pleasant" hardly began to describe it. The night was full of stars, some winking down from the heavens, and some gazing up from the ground—exotic lilies, and other flowers she didn't recognize, which looked ghostly pale and almost insubstantial by moonlight, yet were heavy with a scent redolent of earthy passions. It was an enchanted scene, so magical she thought she heard music drifting on the quiet air, and stopped to listen. Yes, there it was: something old-fashioned and rather haunting, in three-quarter time.

"*Deep In My Heart*," Ethan said, pausing too, and she reared back, for a moment startled into thinking he was speaking to her. But then he continued, "It's the refrain from *The Student Prince,* my aunt's favorite operetta. She and my uncle dance to it almost every night. It has great sentimental value for them. He proposed to her the night he took her to see the musical revival on Broadway, over fifty years ago."

"And they still honor the tradition today?" It was such an unexpected story, and one so touchingly reminiscent of the way her own parents had behaved toward one another, that Anne-Marie turned away, embarrassed by the sudden tears stinging her eyes. "That's the way marriages ought to be."

"But seldom are." He thrust a handkerchief at her. "Here. I believe you need this."

"I don't know why I should," she said, feeling like a fool.

"You were caught by surprise. You didn't think there'd be much room for passion or tenderness in a relationship where the wife appears to wear the pants."

"Well, your uncle does seem a little henpecked," she said, smiling again at the odd blending of formality and slang in his speech.

He clasped her hand again, and didn't let go. "On the surface, perhaps, but he's the steel in the backbone of their marriage, which just goes to show how wrong first impressions can be, Anne-Marie, and is a lesson to both of us not to leap to unfounded conclusions. Louis is the light of my aunt's life, and she of his.''

*Anne-Marie,* he'd called her, and the way he'd said it rendered it so intimate that a flush ran over her.

''That's the way I remember my parents being,'' she said, projecting a calm she was far from feeling. ''I've often thought it was as well they died together because I can't imagine how one would have survived without the other. They needed each other the way other people need oxygen.''

The path opened into a clearing just then, with a lily pond in the middle spanned by a small stone bridge. Leading her toward it, he said, ''But you had needs, too, and I'm beginning to think they've been left neglected too long.''

The moon shone full and bright, splashing the surrounding jungle with silver and flinging long, deep shadows across the surface of water. A night creature let out a sleepy squawk which somehow intensified the utter stillness of the setting.

''Needs?''

''Yes,'' he said—a simple enough answer and, on the surface at least, not without merit, because the feeling of belonging, of being connected to another person in the most vital way possible, had been missing from her life from the day she'd learned about her parents' death.

She'd searched for it without success in every relationship which had come her way since, but never in her wildest imaginings had she thought she'd find it with a man she'd met little more than twenty-four hours earlier. Yet, all at once, there it was, so tangible she could almost reach out and touch it.

''Why didn't you tell me the reason you're so afraid of the water?'' he said. ''If I'd known your parents drowned when you were just a child, I'd have been more under-standing.''

''Would you?'' she stammered.

''Yes,'' he said again, standing so close that his answer this time feathered over her lips.

How had it come about, she wondered, dazed, that in the space of a second, her association with Ethan Beaumont had shifted to assume a totally different dimension? At what precise moment had they suddenly ceased being wary host and defensive guest, and become instead a man and a woman helplessly drawn to one another by forces beyond their control?

She had no answer. She knew only that it had happened, and a breathless, reckless expectation seized her. Without thought for the consequences, she lifted her face and drank in the essence of the blossom-scented night. Of him and the pure masculine magnetism he radiated. She closed her eyes and waited…waited….

Seconds ticked by, marked only by the urgent thud of her heart. And then, when she thought she'd been mistaken after all and nothing had changed between them, he said raggedly, ''Am I supposed to kiss you now, Anne-Marie?''

She'd have been humiliated beyond endurance if she hadn't detected the torment behind his remark and realized the reason for it. But the battle he was fighting—and los-ing—so closely paralleled her own emotional turmoil that she found the courage to whisper, ''How about a little truth, for a change, Ethan? How about 'I *want* to kiss you, Anne-Marie'?''

''No,'' he muttered. But his hands betrayed him and slid through her hair, working at the pins holding it up until it fell loose around her shoulders. ''No,'' he said again, al-most savagely. ''It'll never happen.''

''Why not?''

"Because," he said, "it would be a mistake."

But either he didn't really believe what he was saying, or he, too, was at the mercy of impulses beyond his control, because he dipped his head lower...lower...until it blotted out the moon peeping over his shoulder, and his breath taunted her senses with the memory of the pale gold wine he'd drunk at dinner.

And finally, when she was trembling all over with anticipation, his lips searched out hers. Unable to help herself, she rose to meet him, felt his arms lock around her, and was lost.

His kiss was so much more than a meeting of mouths. It was an introduction to paradise; a promise of something beyond earthly comprehension. Its imprint scorched her soul and left her melting against him.

He awoke every female instinct she possessed and set it free. He reduced every other kiss she'd ever known to ashes; every other man to a featureless shadow.

His mouth lingered, explored, discovered, persuaded. At his instigation, her lips parted to allow her tongue to engage in shameless, erotic intimacy with his. He tasted divine and the more she sampled, the more she craved. The more he demanded, the more she gave.

At length, inevitably, he broke all contact and stepped back to examine her from hooded, unreadable eyes. "I was right," he said hoarsely. "That was a big mistake."

"But not necessarily fatal, surely?" she said, trying not to whimper with disappointment. "Sometimes, people can learn a great deal from their mistakes."

"Yes, but that was a lesson I could do without. It taught me nothing I want to know."

*It taught me things I never want to forget,* she longed to tell him, but he was in no mood to listen. The warmth he'd briefly lavished on her was gone and he was once again the cool, unwilling host under obligation to a guest not of his choosing.

"Come," he said, gesturing for her to precede him across the bridge. "Your suite is only a few yards farther on."

A moment later, the flickering yellow flames of the tiki lamps bordering the guest pavilions' terrace appeared. The maid had left a small lamp burning in Anne-Marie's foyer, but the adjoining villa was in complete darkness. Just as well. She was in no shape to face Solange.

"You'll be all right now?" he asked.

"Perfectly, thank you."

"Then I'll say good night. I hope you sleep well."

*Fat chance, Ethan!* "I'm sure I'll sleep like a baby," she replied and, still shaken, went inside and leaned against the wall beside the filigree ironwork at the window of her bedroom, listening.

Over the still-thudding extravaganza of her heart, she heard his footsteps crunch over the gravel and fade away, and wondered how she'd ever face him again without blushing. Because she knew that if he'd asked, she'd have let him stay and would have spent the night in his arms. But worse by far was that she was afraid he knew it, too.

Over the next several days, she avoided him altogether by concentrating on putting together the wedding party's outfits and using that as an excuse to keep away from the main house. She established a routine of working during the early mornings and cool evenings, and spending the stifling midday hours either by, or in, the pool outside her door.

Although by no means ready to tackle anything too ambitious, she found that, with daily practice, she gained a new measure of confidence in the water and took real pleasure in finally being able to swim the forty foot length of the pool without panicking. The sun turned her skin a delicate honey color and lent streaks of shimmering highlights to her already blond hair.

She arranged for her meals to be sent down from the main house. Three times daily, one of the servants would arrive in a small golf cart, with a covered tray—fruit, hot sweet rolls and coffee for breakfast, a salad with more fruit for lunch, and for dinner, whatever the family was having. It was always immaculately prepared, always delicious.

Adrian came to visit most afternoons. His nanny dropped him off about half past two, and picked him up again around four. During their time together, he'd climb on Anne-Marie's lap and beg, "Tell me another story about living in Canada, Anne-Marie. Tell me about snow."

He'd never seen snow, never built a snowman, never made snow angels, poor, deprived darling.

Once, when he caught her drying her hair after a swim, he leaned against her and said sadly, "*Maman* had gold hair like yours, but she went away. Papa says you'll go away, as well, but I wish you wouldn't. I'll miss you."

"I don't have to go yet," she told him, knowing it was small comfort. "We still have lots of time to spend together. And when I do go home, I'll send you pictures of my house and garden, so you'll know where I live."

He looked at her for a long time, his dark eyes wide and solemn, then buried his face against her shoulder. "It won't be the same," he said, his voice muffled and quivering. But he didn't shed a single tear because he already knew that crying wasn't enough to make a person stay. It broke her heart that he'd learned such a hard lesson so early in life.

Later, when she thought he'd forgotten all about their conversation, he asked, "I can read a bit. Will you write letters to me, as well? I like it when I get mail. The mail-man brought me lots of cards on my birthday.''

"I'll send you lots of letters," she promised. "And just so that you get them faster, I'll e-mail them to you on your daddy's computer."

"No. Papa might be angry. He says I shouldn't keep bothering you."

"Then I'll send them to Solange instead, and it'll be our little secret."

It wasn't the only secret she kept from Ethan. The first evening of her new regime, after she'd finished work, she wanted to stretch her cramped muscles before turning in, and decided to explore the gardens. That was how she found the rough-hewn steps leading down the cliff.

At the bottom was a quiet cove, a perfect crescent of white sand with a big flat rock in the middle where she sat for the longest time, watching the moon rise over the sea. On her return, she almost bumped into Philippe as he materialized silently from the shadows on the far side of the pool, and let himself into Solange's villa.

Every night after that, Anne-Marie went down to the beach, aware that under cover of dark, Philippe sneaked down to spend the night with his fiancée. Solange was not sleeping alone, whatever Ethan might like to think, and he'd be furious if he ever found out.

Anne-Marie wasn't all that thrilled, herself. The smallest sound carried clearly on the quiet air and try as she might, she couldn't help hearing the muffled laughter from next door, or the murmured voices, or, worst of all, the smoth-ered moans.

She was, she realized with disgust, jealous. Jealous of her friend's happiness. Jealous that Solange had someone to love, when she had not.

Then, just after ten on the fifth night, with Solange's

place already in darkness, Ethan showed up at Anne-Marie's door. "I saw the light on and thought I'd stop by," he said. "Are you still working?"

He wore a shirt made of some lightweight, oatmeal-colored fabric, matching drawstring pants, and black molded Teva sandals. She, on the other hand, had just stepped out of the shower. She was barefoot, wore a thin cotton robe which barely covered her knees, and her hair was wrapped in a towel turban.

*Of course! I always dress like this to work,* she was tempted to reply, but decided she was in no position to be saucy. He might be dressed casually, but at least he looked decent which was more than could be said for her. "No," she said mildly. "I'm done for the day."

"Then may I come in? I'd like to talk to you."

Given that he already had one foot inside the door and wasn't about to pay the least mind to any objection she might raise, she moved aside in tacit consent. "About what?"

"First off, my son." The foyer was just large enough for a couple to tango if they felt so inclined, but it shrank to insignificant proportions under the aura of disapproval radiating from his imposing six-foot-plus frame. "He's spending altogether too much time with you."

"I enjoy his company."

"If it's company you're looking for, there's plenty to be had at the main house."

"Then let me rephrase it. I *prefer* his company."

"To my aunt and uncle's?"

"No," she said. "To yours."

His mouth twitched with amusement. "I'm crushed, my dear! But I'll survive—and so will you. Adrian, however, is a different matter. *He* is far too vulnerable to be left to your mercies."

"What are you afraid of?" she exclaimed incredulously. "You can't seriously believe I'd do anything to hurt him?"

"Not intentionally, perhaps, but however well-intentioned your motives, in the long run you'll end up doing him more harm than good."

"For heaven's sake, Ethan, I don't rot his teeth by feeding him sugar, or teach him foul language, or let him wander off into the jungle unsupervised! He's never in the pool unless Solange is with him because I know I'm useless in the event of a water emergency. All I do I *play* with him."

"I know," he said, loping past her to take a turn about the salon, and pausing to admire the shimmering aquamarine fabric laid out on the worktable. "But he's not a toy, Anne-Marie. And he doesn't understand the games played by women like you."

There wasn't another man on earth who could match his ability to put her back up and leave her so angry she could almost smell smoke! "What's that supposed to mean— *women like me?*"

He stopped before the dress form to inspect the beadwork on the bodice of Solange's wedding gown. "The fly-by-night kind who flits without warning or reason from one obsession to another. Right now, you're enjoying the adulation of one small, impressionable boy, but once the novelty wears off and his neediness becomes a burden, you'll drop him and move on to the next thing to catch your fancy, without any thought for the hurt you'll inflict on him."

"You must be confusing me with your ex-wife," she said acidly. "I wouldn't dream of treating a child, or any other living creature, for that matter, as shabbily as you seem to think."

"Leave my ex-wife out of it!"

"Why should I, when we both know she's smack in the middle of it?" she retorted, prepared to go toe-to-toe with him on this one. "You're saddling me with her failings and holding me accountable for them."

"Can you blame me? You're part of that glitzy, artificial world that lured her away from here in the first place."

"To assume that makes me glitzy and artificial is a bit of a stretch, don't you think?"

"We're reflections of our tastes and inclinations, *Mademoiselle*," he said, making his way to where she stood.

"Oh, good grief, are we back to the *mademoiselle* nonsense again?" She smacked him smartly on the shoulder which probably wasn't the wisest thing she could have done, but it beat rapping him on his thick skull, which was what she really felt like doing. "Well, listen up, *Monsieur!* Believe it or not as you please, but I'm not in the habit of treating people as disposable commodities. Having known firsthand how it feels to be left with virtually no one, I treasure friendship above all else and I'm sincerely fond of Adrian. I fail to see how anyone could not be. He's adorable."

"He's fond of you, too. That's my whole point. He misses his mother and is constantly looking for someone to take her place. But you're only a temporary fixture in his life and how your leaving will affect him isn't something you'll have to deal with. I'm the one responsible for his happiness and well-being, which is why I'm taking steps now to protect him from you."

"Are you forbidding me to associate with him?" she asked hotly. "Because if you are, I want your word that you'll explain it to him without making me out to be the villain of the piece. I won't have him think I've abandoned him by choice."

''There's no need to take quite such drastic steps. He understands you have work to do and that he can't disturb you whenever the mood takes him. All I'm asking is that, instead of fostering this close one-on-one relationship which, ultimately, must come to an end, you instead spend time with him at the main house and become part of our larger family group. Which brings me to my second point. You *do* recall there were two matters I wished to discuss?''

''Sweet heaven, how could I possibly forget? I've been waiting with breathless anticipation for the other shoe to drop!'' She lowered her lashes and sighed with deliberately melodramatic emphasis. ''All right. I'm braced for the worst. Let me have it, and don't spare my feelings.''

''You've been avoiding me.''

''Is it any wonder?''

Purposefully, he stepped closer, and the expression in his eyes made her quake a little inside. If ever there was a man on a mission, he was it! ''Do you think avoiding me is going to change what happened between us the other night, Anne-Marie?''

''No,'' she said, not so transfixed that she wasn't woefully conscious of how absurd he must find her, in her too-short robe and too-large towel turban which made her head look at least three times bigger than it ought to be. ''But not having to see you helps me to put the whole unfortunate incident into perspective. I didn't come here looking to have an affair.''

''I don't recall suggesting you did.''

''You might as well have! From the way you kissed me—''

He shrugged. ''I'm no saint, Anne-Marie. When a beautiful woman makes it plain she's both willing and available, I'm as susceptible as the next man to what she's offering.''

It was as bad as she'd feared! He'd interpreted the moment all too accurately, right down to her practically throwing herself at him. "You're also more imaginative than most!" she snapped, humiliated. "We kissed—*kissed,* Ethan, and by mutual consent at that, so don't make it out to be more than it was—a colossal, foolish mistake."

"Exactly—as I believe I said, both before and after the fact."

"I ought to have guessed you'd be an *I told you so* kind of man."

"But I have been known to be wrong on occasion." A slow smile crept over his mouth, and try as she might, she couldn't drag her gaze away from it, or quell the rising heat in her blood as he covered the remaining distance between them.

"You have?" she squeaked.

"Indeed yes. You look very appealing in that thing, by the way." He hooked a finger between the buttons on the front of her robe and tugged her even closer. If he'd touched her skin, she swore she'd have burst into flames. "But *this* doesn't do a thing for you."

Before she could guess his next move, he'd unwound the towel from her head and was running his hands through her hair. "There," he said, his voice about as seductive a purr as she'd ever heard. "That's much better. Hair such as yours should never be hidden from sight."

"I don't think you should be doing that," she protested faintly, as he continued massaging her scalp. "I think it could lead to our making another really colossal mistake."

"Or not," he murmured, moving in for the kill. "It depends on your point of view."

She'd wondered often enough over the last few days if memory had played her false; if it had blown the other night out of all proportion and left her vulnerable to huge disappointment, should there ever be another such encounter. As his mouth came down on hers a second time, though, she learned the folly of such thinking. If that first kiss had taken her by surprise, this one took her by storm. More deliberate, less cautious, it caught her up in a deluge of sensory pleasure so intense that the world tilted on its axis.

Nor, for once, was he entirely in command of the universe. His mouth was hot and possessive, his hands hot and urgent as they traced down her back from her neck to her hips. In truth, he was hot and hard all over, a fact made glaringly apparent by the flimsiness of the clothing separating their two bodies.

And she, clinging to him for fear that she'd melt in a puddle at his feet if she let go, wanted to submit to his implicit demands, and never mind that they barely knew each other and didn't much like what they'd so far discovered. Because Solange had been right. All that superficial animosity had been nothing more than camouflage to mask the attraction which had exploded between them with the suddenness and force of spontaneous combustion.

If, rather than meeting him formally amid the grandeur of his estate, she had instead come across him in a street market, the outcome would have been the same. She didn't need to know his name, nor he hers. He didn't have to be rich and powerful, nor she successful and independent. They could have been beggars, and still the *only* reality that would have mattered was the primal knowledge that, somehow, out of all the other men and women in the world, they had recognized each other.

*This is insane! You're both crazy!*

The admonishment fought to surface in her befuddled mind, and was swamped. What chance had reason against such elemental force?

None at all! She was ready to yield to him completely, there on the cool marble floor of the foyer, and hang the consequences. But even as a whimper of surrender rose in her throat, another, fraught with equal passion, floated faintly through the night and turned her rigid with trepidation.

"Oh!" she moaned, loud enough to drown out the other sound, and then, just to be on the safe side, "Oh, oh, oh!"

If she'd hoped to distract him, she succeeded, but hardly in the way she'd hoped. He lifted his head, stared at her as if she'd lost her mind, and said coldly, "You sound pained. Is it because of something you ate?"

"No," she said, embarrassed.

"Then it must be me. I had no idea you found my attentions so unappealing."

The next moment, she was alone, feeling so let down and frustrated that she could barely stand.

## CHAPTER SIX

AN INVITATION to afternoon tea with Josephine arrived at Anne-Marie's door the following day, and turned out to be such a mutually pleasant event that it became a daily ritual after that. Sometimes Solange joined the party, and Adrian was always there, hopping with impatience for his new best friend to put in an appearance.

The refreshments, served in the shade of a verandah overlooking the hummingbird garden, consisted of an array of delicacies wheeled out on a trolley, to where Josephine presided at a low table set with snowy linen and a magnificent sterling tea set.

"Ethan's mother started the tradition," she explained, one day when Solange had gone to visit friends with Philippe, and Adrian, bored with too much grown-up talk, had wandered off into the garden to play with his kitten. "She was born in London, you see, and although her father was a doctor on Saint Vincent, here in the Caribbean, she grew up in England and held its customs very dear to her heart."

Anne-Marie helped herself to a buttery scone heaped with imported preserves and clotted cream. "How did she happen to meet Ethan's father?"

"She came out here on holiday when she turned nineteen and met him at the races in Barbados—horse races, that is. They're very big in this part of the world. You must get Ethan to show you his stables, someday when you're not both tied up with work."

"I'd like that." Not that there was any chance she'd

ever get it! She'd seen neither hide nor hair of him since the night he'd stopped by. At first seeming as helplessly attracted to her as she was to him, he'd initiated a kiss that fairly singed the already steamy night.

But her attempt to cover up what was going on in Solange's quarters had soon put paid to that, and the worst of it was, Anne-Marie had been able to offer no reasonable explanation for her sudden, inexplicable behavior. If only he was more approachable, less inflexible, she might have tried, but that was like wishing for snow on Bellefleur—a notion too fanciful to be entertained.

Josephine handed her a wide-lipped cup balanced on its saucer as gracefully as a lotus blossom floating on water, the china so translucent, a person could almost read print through it. "Earl Grey today, my dear. I hope it's to your taste. Help yourself to lemon, if you prefer."

"Thank you." She sipped the hot, fragrant liquid, and found it delightfully refreshing despite the tropical heat visibly shimmering above the flower beds beyond the verandah. "And they fell in love?"

Josephine blinked. "Who? Oh, André and Patricia, you mean? She was a Hythe-Griffiths, you know, of Griffiths pharmaceutical fame. Very well to do, very aristocratic. And André—well, the Beaumonts are the *crème de la crème* in these parts. Ethan's great-grandfather bought this island in 1921. It had been a French territory before that and was in very sad shape. A few fields of cotton, some peas and corn, wild cattle and sheep—nothing you'd want to live with nowadays, I can assure you. But he rescued it from neglect and turned it into a viable community. Have another scone, child. They'll only go to waste if you don't eat them."

"And Patricia?" Anne-Marie prodded, her curiosity about Ethan's background itching to be satisfied.

"I'm getting to that part. My father was a profligate. When he took over, he drank away the family fortune and let the island fall back into decay, so it was a blessing all around when his horse threw him and broke his neck, because that left André, my younger brother and Ethan's father, in control."

"I see." Anne-Marie hid a smile. Clearly, her hostess was not one to waste sympathy on those she deemed to be undeserving!

"André slaved to restore Bellefleur," Josephine continued. "All those citrus groves and coconut palms you passed, the day you arrived here, are part of his legacy, as are the cotton plantations. He built the roads, an airstrip, a school. And he started a horse breeding program which is what took him to Barbados."

"Where he met Patricia."

"Exactly. It was love at first sight for both of them. She was a beauty, a true English rose, and André...." Josephine sighed, her dark eyes misty with fond memory. "Oh, he was handsome! All the eligible women on Bellefleur wept a little when he brought home a bride. Ethan looks very much like him, but he has his mother's eyes."

"You say André *was* handsome. I take it that means...?"

"Restoring this island to prosperity eventually killed him. He worked himself to death." She blinked, and stroked the wedding ring on her left hand. "And he did it on purpose, because he didn't care to go on living."

"And Patricia?"

"Died in childbirth, a year after she came to Bellefleur as a bride. A terrible tragedy. It never should have happened. But we had no hospital here at the time that she went into labor, and a wicked storm had blown in from the Atlantic, which made getting off the island impossible.'' She sighed. ''It was only after Ethan was born that André built the medical facility, and named it after her. Too little, too late, as the saying goes.''

''Poor man. He must have been heartbroken.''

''More than that, it broke his spirit. He blamed himself for his wife's death, and became frighteningly withdrawn for months afterward. But he had a baby to look out for, a son who needed a mother, and I didn't live here then because Louis's work kept us in Europe. So, two years later, André remarried. Celine was a good woman, a devoted wife. She gave him another son, Philippe.''

''How did Ethan feel about that?''

''Oh, he was thrilled! He was five at the time, and had no memory of Patricia, remember. Celine was the only mother he'd ever known, so there was none of the resentment you might have expected from an older child who'd seen another woman come in and take his birth mother's place. He was very protective of his baby brother.''

''And yet, from your tone and expression, it seems there was no happy ending for this new family.''

Josephine sighed again. ''I'm afraid not. Celine loved André deeply, and he loved her, too, after a fashion, but not the way he'd loved Patricia. Celine knew it, and she was proud. She grew tired of competing with a ghost and always being second best, so she left when Philippe was eight. André wouldn't let her take the boy, and because she was Roman Catholic, divorce was out of the question, so she joined a French convent as a lay person, and took the veil after she became a widow, seven years after that. Ethan was twenty when his father died and left him to take charge not just of the island, but of Philippe, too, who was a very unruly teenager.''

A faint sound overlaying the soft whir of the ceiling fan

in the room behind had both women looking over their shoulders to find Ethan standing in the open doorway, blatantly eavesdropping. "I can't imagine our guest cares one iota about our family saga, Josephine," he said stiffly, his glance skating over Anne-Marie with stunning disregard.

"On the contrary," she said. "I'm enjoying hearing about the Beaumonts and their doings."

"Why?" He flung the question at her baldly, resentfully.

*In the hope that it might persuade you I'm not quite as reptilian as you seem to find me,* she nearly told him, shivering in the cool blast of his indifference. "Family histories always fascinate me, I suppose because I have so little of my own."

"I didn't know you were back already." Josephine extended her hand in welcome. "Have a cup of tea with us, *mon cher,* and tell us about your trip."

So he'd been away and hadn't necessarily been avoiding her, after all! An untoward flush of pleasure rippled over Anne-Marie, but it barely had time to register before he squashed it.

"I was able to take care of the problem in a matter of hours," he said, accepting the cup his aunt offered and looking out at the sweep of jungle and ocean beyond the garden.

"You were up very early this morning. It was still dark when I heard the car leave."

"Did I disturb you? I'm sorry."

"I never sleep well when I know you're en route to the oil platform. That whole operation makes me very uneasy."

The smile he turned on his aunt, warm and full of teasing affection, filled Anne-Marie with envy. "You don't like having an oil baron in the family?"

"I don't see the necessity for it. We're Caribbean land-owners, not Arabian sheikhs."

*But he could have passed for one,* Anne-Marie thought, sneaking a look at him as he stood surveying his tiny kingdom. *A blue-eyed western sheikh, as proud and powerful as his desert counterpart.*

"Running Bellefleur costs money, *Tante* Josephine. We have an obligation to the future generations of this island."

"Your father relied on its natural resources."

"They're no longer enough. And I enjoy the change of pace."

"Do you?" she replied tartly, clearly put out at having her opinion dismissed. "Well, Anne-Marie could use a change of pace, too. She's working much too hard. I told her you'd show her the stables."

Once again, his cool gaze drifted over Anne-Marie. "I doubt she's really interested."

Anger rushed in to take the place of that wayward flash of optimism. "Why don't you try asking me, instead of behaving as if I'm a piece of furniture incapable of speaking for myself?"

He raised one arrogant eyebrow. "Do you ride?"

"Not as well as you, probably," she said. "But I'm as capable as the next person of appreciating a fine animal."

"You know what to look for in a horse, do you?"

"Besides two legs more than you possess, and a head more handsome?"

He grimaced, annoyed, but Josephine let out a squawk of laughter. "Child, you are a breath of fresh air, and just what this man needs to remind him there's more to life than work!" she crowed, tossing down her embroidered napkin. "Help me up, Ethan. It's time for my pre-dinner siesta."

"I expect you have to go, too," he said hopefully to Anne-Marie, once his aunt had left.

"I suppose I do." Bereft, she brushed a few crumbs from her skirt, and drifted toward the steps leading to the garden.

"You can find your way?"

"Certainly. I've become quite familiar with the layout of the grounds."

"And the wedding gown? Is it finished yet?"

"Not quite. I ran short of seed pearls and am waiting for more to be sent from Vancouver."

"I hope you didn't rely on them arriving by ordinary parcel post."

"No. I always use a courier."

"That's good. Because mail delivery to the island is unreliable, to say the least."

Such inconsequential conversation seemed out of character for a man who, a moment before, had been insultingly anxious to see the back of her. "What's the purpose of these delaying tactics, Ethan?" she inquired boldly. "Is there something else you'd like to say to me that has a relevant purpose beyond wasting both your time and mine?"

"Not at all," he said, staring out at the landscape.

"If you're worried that I've ignored your edict that I stay away from Adrian, don't be."

"I'm not," he said, apparently engrossed by the hummingbirds fighting each other to feed at the flower beds. "It never occurs to me that my requests will go ignored. That being the case, and since you're at a temporary standstill with the wedding project, I'll expect you at the stables at nine tomorrow."

"Then brace yourself for an upset, because this is one time your expectations aren't going to be met. I'm still busy with the bridesmaids' dresses, and can't afford to waste the morning.''

It was a lie. Apart from final finishing, the dresses were done and, for once, she had the luxury of time on her hands—a rare occurrence when she was at home, with the phone constantly ringing and new designs being commissioned daily. But his implicit censure of everything she said or did cast a long shadow and took the shine off the bright afternoon.

Why expose herself to more of the same, tomorrow? She still had several weeks left on the island and she wanted to enjoy them. Why let him strip her of the pleasure?

''That's a pity. Some other day, perhaps?''

She shrugged. ''Perhaps,'' she said, matching his non-chalance, and without bothering to spare him another word or glance, set off across the lawn.

The dazzling, sun-splashed days and scented, star-spangled nights fell into a pattern of lazy indulgences. At least three times daily, she swam in the guest pool. She took tea with Josephine. She drew pictures for Adrian, and played croquet with Louis. She and Solange lazed in recliners on the shaded walkway connecting their suites, and sipped tall, cool drinks while they reminisced about old times. Before she went to bed, she walked down to the beach and sat on her favorite rock to watch the moon rise, and soak in the tranquility and beauty of the sleeping island.

Apart from showing up each night for dinner, Ethan kept his distance, but that didn't lessen her infatuation with him. The meal tended to be long and leisurely, often lasting two or more hours but, no matter how delicious the food or entertaining the conversation, they couldn't compete with him.

Sometimes, she feared the memory of him sitting at the

head of the table in that spectacularly elegant dining room, his immaculate white dinner jacket in gleaming contrast to the burnished bronze of his skin, his rare smile bringing life and youth to his often somber face, would stay with her the rest of her life and make it impossible for any other man to take his place.

Nor was he as oblivious to her as he tried to make out. Occasionally—*very* occasionally!—they'd share a moment's amusement at something Josephine said, but most of the time he treated Anne-Marie with distant courtesy.

Yet for all that he tried to hide it, she was sublimely conscious of his gaze resting on her when he thought she wasn't looking. Once, she caught him at it, and he immediately lowered his eyes and scowled at the broiled pheasant in front of him, as if the poor thing had risen up from the dead and laid an egg on his plate!

All that being so, she was surprised to receive a phone call from him at the beginning of her fourth week on the island. "A replacement part for some machinery which I ordered from the mainland arrived this morning, and I'm headed out to the airport to pick it up," he told her. "You want to come with me? There's a package waiting there for you, as well."

"Yes," she said, the chance to be alone with him, for however short a time, more than she could resist.

"Meet me in the front courtyard in half an hour, then," he said. "And wear a hat. The heat's enough to kill you today, and I'd hate for you to get sunstroke."

No "please," or "will you," but his concern for her well-being took the sting out of his command. Hanging up the phone, she hurried to exchange the knee-length sarong she always wore around the guest quarters for a gauzy cotton dress in pale apple green sprigged with tiny pink rosebuds, and a wide-brimmed straw hat.

"You look delicious as a sherbet sundae," he surprised her by saying, when he saw her. "All cool and shady, except for your skin. You've picked up quite a tan."

She'd have told him he looked entirely fabulous himself, if his compliment hadn't left her tongue-tied. What a mass of contradictions he was; charming one minute, and chillingly aloof the next. How was a woman supposed to know where she stood with him?

He walked her out to the forecourt and handed her into a white Rolls Royce Corniche. Fairly tingling from his touch, she said, "Is Adrian coming with us?"

"No. He's in school."

"I didn't know he attended school. I suppose he has a private tutor?"

"You suppose wrong. He goes to the local school, but only in the morning. He's still in kindergarten. Have you had a chance to explore the town, at all?"

"No."

He put on a pair of sunglasses and nosed the stunningly elegant convertible down the steep driveway. The big iron gates swung smoothly open as the car approached, then glided closed once it had passed through. "I'll show you the sights, after we've collected our stuff. I assume the package waiting for you is the beading you need to finish Solange's dress?"

"I hope so. The wedding's fast approaching."

"We'll fly to Florida and shop in Miami, if necessary. One way or another, you'll have your supplies."

"I hope it won't come to that, but it's very nice of you to be so accommodating."

"Not really," he replied, dashing any hope she had that winning a few Brownie points with her was his prime objective. "It's a Beaumont wedding. It has to be perfect."

"Of course! Silly me, to have thought for one second

that it might be because you were willing to go out of your way on my behalf.''

His expression inscrutable behind the reflective lens of his glasses, he said, ''The two go hand in hand, surely? The guest list runs close to three hundred and all those people will see your work and no doubt admire it enough that some will want you to design for them. This could be a real boost for your career.''

''I don't need a boost, thank you very much,'' she said. ''I already have more than enough clients.''

''Aren't you interested in seeing your company grow?''

They were passing through the town by then and the open car afforded her an unobstructed view of the quaint conical roofs on the houses, and the pretty flowering vines climbing over fences and doorways. Down near the quay, a street market hummed with shoppers clustered around stalls loaded with fresh fish, fruit, vegetables, and other food.

The kaleidoscope of color, bright orange, red and yellow against a backdrop of azure sky and turquoise water, added to the scent of blossoms mingling with fresh baked bread and the sharp tang of the ocean, presented a feast to the senses like nothing she'd experienced before. And yet, despite the bustle of activity, the pace of life was so much less frenetic than what she was used to in Vancouver.

Here, people really did take time to smell the flowers. Here, there was always tomorrow on which to take care of the things that didn't get done today.

''Well, Anne-Marie? *Don't* you want to increase your business assets?''

''No,'' she said, surprising herself almost as much as she no doubt surprised him. ''I love my work, but it doesn't consume me, nor does it fill all the corners of my life. It never will.''

"How so?"

Again, she surprised herself. "Because, at the end of my life when I look back at what I've achieved, costume design won't be what counts."

"And what will?"

"A real home."

"You don't have one?" He sounded skeptical.

"I have a very smart town house, if that's what you mean. It's extremely comfortable, very well located, quite charming, and it suits me well enough for now. But I want to be remembered for something more meaningful than a pile of lumber and a few dramatic designs which will be forgotten even sooner than I will. I want to leave behind a legacy of love."

"And just how do you propose to do that?"

"With a family," she said, her heart swelling with a need which went back twenty years, to the day she'd learned she was an orphan. "With a husband and children."

He turned onto the road leading to the airport. "Successful career woman giving it all up for the dubious joy of changing diapers and scrubbing floors? Somehow, I don't see you fitting into such a picture—unless, of course, you plan to marry for money."

She could have slapped him. He certainly deserved it. "Did I forget to mention that I don't need to go searching for a rich husband? That I have enough in the way of assets that I can afford to marry a poor man and the only criteria is that he love me for myself, and not for what I own?"

"Is that ever enough to keep a woman happy?"

Annoyed, she threw the question back at him. "Is it enough for men?"

"Yes," he said. "Often to their lasting regret. Because

most men are very straightforward about their objectives, whereas women too often have an ulterior motive.''

An invisible cloud seemed to pass over the bright day. ''Are we talking about your ex-wife again?''

''She fits the type, certainly.''

She longed to ask him what the woman had done to disillusion him so thoroughly, but sensed he'd rebuff her. Instead, she said, ''Do you think Solange has an ulterior motive in marrying your brother?''

''Solange is different.''

''We're *all* different, Ethan, that's my whole point, and you're too smart a person to make such dangerously sweeping statements and really believe them. We have minds of our own, we choose how to live our lives, and sometimes we make mistakes. But most of us learn from them and go on to make wiser choices in the future.''

He brought the Corniche to a stop outside the small terminal. The sun scorched blinding white on the tarmac. The heat hung in the air, dense and breathless. He swung open his door and climbed out. ''And some of us don't,'' he said flatly. ''Some *mistakes* as you choose to call them, are unforgivable. Are you coming in, or do you want to wait here?''

''I'll come in,'' she said, wilting under his unflagging bitterness. How he must have loved his wife, that she'd been able to wound him so deeply!

# CHAPTER SEVEN

SHE played her part well, that much he had to give her. Hardly ever a false step and even when she stumbled, a man had to have his wits about him to notice. And therein lay the problem because, when he was around her, his wits took second place to other, more primitive instincts.

"We'll have lunch at the Plantation Club," he said, when the business at the airport was done. "It overlooks the yacht basin and if there's a breeze to be found anywhere, it'll be there."

"Sounds lovely," she said demurely, dipping her head so that her face was hidden under the brim of her hat, and if he hadn't known better, he might have been fooled into thinking she was shy.

The club was crowded, as usual, but he had a permanent reservation and they were led to his table immediately. Fully aware of the interest aroused by his appearing with a stranger who swept into the place with her pale green skirt swirling just above her ankles like the sudden onset of a cool Canadian spring, he nodded to the familiar faces already at lunch and, wanting to observe her reaction to the stir she'd created, sat her in the corner and took the chair next to her, so that they both looked out at the room.

"Iced tea," she replied, when he asked her what she'd like to drink.

"Try the planter's punch instead," he suggested. "You'll find it very refreshing." And before she could voice a protest, ordered one for each of them.

She took off her hat and dropped it carelessly next to

her straw bag on the floor. "Are you going to choose my food, as well?" she wanted to know, the impudence he found so attractive sparkling in her eyes.

"As a matter of fact, yes." She'd wound her hair up on top of her head, but a strand had fallen loose and spilled down the nape of her neck like a skein of pale silk ribbon on a honey-gold background. Suppressing the urge to tuck it back into place, he nodded at the waiter who'd served both his father and grandfather before him. "We'll have the conch salad, Hamilton."

The man took off to the bar, and returned a short time later with the drinks. After he left a second time, she ran a finger lightly down her throat and turned her head to catch the drift of breeze created by the overhead fans. "You were right," she said. "It is much cooler here."

"I'm glad you approve."

A smile tugged at her mouth. "Aren't you going to tell me you're always right?"

"I'm only right ninety-nine point nine percent of the time."

The smile gave way to a teasing laugh, a bewitching musical fall of amusement that captivated him. "You mean, you once thought you'd made a mistake, but you were wrong?" Then, touching her fingers to her mouth, said contritely, "Oh, I'm sorry! That wasn't a very nice thing to say, and I really didn't mean it!"

"Why do I have trouble believing that?"

"I think because you and I become very good at not saying what we really mean, Ethan. Very good at leaping to all the wrong conclusions about each other." She clinked the rim of her glass against his. "How about a toast to not doing that anymore?"

The memory of their last kiss surfaced in his mind, right down to the artificial moans of ecstasy she'd let out. Too bad she'd had her eyes wide open at the time, and looked more like a terrified mare about to be mated with a raging stallion, than a woman wildly overcome with passion! "Is that possible?"

"We could always try, couldn't we?"

"For what purpose?"

"Well, you said yourself that we can't avoid each other. Why make things any more awkward than they have to be?" She sipped her punch. "This is delicious, by the way. If the conch salad's half as good, I'm going to have to swallow my pride and let you do all the ordering in future."

"For the remainder of your time here, at least," he said, his attention caught by the silhouette of the man poised on the threshold leading from the outside deck. Although backlit by the early afternoon sun, there was no mistaking his identity.

So, Roberto Santos was back on Bellefleur!

Ethan fixed him in a stare, and silently dared him to acknowledge it. Santos stood a moment, scanning the tables, then, sensing he was being observed, his glance swiveled and collided with Ethan's.

His mouth twitched, the full, almost feminine lips tightening a fraction. He tilted his head, aiming for arrogance, but the attempt wilted under his enemy's unblinking regard. Aware that just about everyone else present was interested in how he was going to handle the situation, he squared his shoulders and wove a jaunty path among the tables until he reached Ethan's.

"It has been a long time," he said, the heavily-accented English some people found so irresistible more pronounced than ever. "How are you, *amigo?*"

"Like most people on the island, better off not having to share it with you. What brings you back here, Santos?"

"What always brings me back? The beautiful ladies, of course," he drawled insolently, bending an oily smirk on Anne-Marie who lowered her too-long, too-dark lashes, and smiled back prettily. "Are you going to introduce me to your lovely companion?"

"No. That's a privilege I reserve for friends and you hardly qualify. You're not looking your usual buff self, Santos. Prison didn't agree with you?"

An ugly flush darkened the man's face. "I see that trying to smooth over our differences was a mistake. You are clearly a man who prefers to hold on to a grudge." He clicked his heels and gave a stiff little bow. "Good day, *Señorita!* Perhaps we'll meet another time, under happier circumstances."

"Not if I have anything to say about it," Ethan assured him.

Looking thunderstruck, Anne-Marie fortified herself with another sip of punch before jumping into the silence left behind as Santos beat a retreat. "Did you have to be quite so cruel? The man was just trying to be sociable."

"Did you not hear me refer to his having been incarcerated?"

"Oh, yes," she said, with heavy sarcasm. "I doubt anyone in the room missed it!"

"Then what makes you think I owe him any sort of courtesy?"

"Maybe the fact that he's served his time and shouldn't have his past held against him any longer?"

"You know nothing about his past. If you did, you might not feel so charitably inclined toward him."

"Perhaps not. But all I know right now is that you were intolerably rude, and went out of your way to humiliate him in front of a roomful of people who obviously know him."

Ethan drew in a long breath, and debated the wisdom of telling her more, because she was right in one respect. The past was over. But if, by keeping his silence, he allowed Santos to come across as the victim rather than the perpetrator, could he live with that?

"He was convicted of impaired driving on a neighboring island," he said brusquely, settling for the short version of the story.

"Oh." She looked down, her expression somber. "Well, I agree, that's hardly to his credit."

"No, it isn't," he said. "Especially not when he had a child in the car at the time of his arrest."

Her gaze, wide with distress, flew back to his face. "Was the child hurt?"

"No. Neither the child nor the mother was injured."

She drew in a shocked breath. "His wife was there, and did nothing to stop him from getting behind the wheel of a car and risking their child's life?"

"It wasn't his wife, nor was it his child. They were mine."

"Oh, Ethan!" Impulsively, she covered his hand. "I'm sorry!"

"Why? You had nothing to do with it."

"But I misjudged you. And so soon after we'd made a pact not to leap to conclusions about each other."

"Actually, we never did reach agreement on that, but it doesn't matter. Santos doesn't matter, either, not any more, and he's not worth spoiling our lunch over. Here comes our salad. Would you care for another rum punch?"

"Good grief, no! I've hardly touched this one, and already it's going to my head. I'd like some water, though."

He ordered a bottle of Perrier, and turned the conversation in another direction. "The package you picked up were the beads you need to finish Solange's wedding gown?''

"Yes," she said, her attention caught by something or someone beyond his view. Well, what had he expected? That she'd hang on his every word as if she really cared about anything he had to say? She was every bit as shallow as he'd first supposed, and any inclination he might have had to change his mind on that had died the other night. "They had to be ordered specially, which is what took so long for them to arrive, but now that they're here, I'll have the dress done in no time."

"Then perhaps once it's finished, you'll change your mind and take me up on my invitation to visit the stables."

"Perhaps I will," she said vaguely, her glance again sliding past him.

"What's so intriguing, Anne-Marie? Don't tell me Santos is still hanging around, ogling you from afar?"

"No," she said. "But a woman just came in the door and from the way she keeps looking over here, I think she must recognize you. In fact, I'm certain she does because she's headed right this way."

He glanced up in time to see Desirée LaSalle approaching. Following so soon after Santos's unwelcome visit, it was something he could have done without.

"It *is* you, Ethan!" she warbled. "I was sure I must be mistaken."

"Have I changed that much since the last time you saw me?" he said lightly, standing up and kissing the proffered, perfumed cheek.

She stepped back and pursed her lips in a pretty pout. "Well, it has been weeks, *Chéri*. And I hardly expected..."

That he'd be with another woman? She might as well have come out and said what she was so clearly thinking. Her hazel-eyed glance, as it slid dismissively over Anne-Marie, spoke volumes of protest.

Knowing he couldn't very well refuse an introduction this time, he said, "I'd like you to meet Solange's maid of honor, Anne-Marie Barclay. This is Desirée LaSalle, Anne-Marie."

"Oh, she's the seamstress! I've already heard about her from Angelique. Well, aren't you a sweetie, treating her to lunch at a place like this, Ethan." Desirée slid a familiar arm through his, her pout melting in the sudden warmth of the smile she turned on Anne-Marie. "Is the sewing going well, dear?"

"Oh, yes, ever so!" Anne-Marie cooed, too sweetly for his peace of mind. "Thank you so much for asking! And I'm ever so grateful to *Monsieur* Beaumont for letting me take a few hours off and showing me the sights. It's a real honor."

"I'm glad you realize what a very lucky woman you are. Ethan doesn't usually bother to squire the hired help around the island."

"Are you here alone, Desirée?" he asked, not liking the direction the conversation had taken, or the crackling tension that went with it.

"Actually not." She bathed him in another smile. "I'm with friends."

"Well, don't let us keep you from them."

"They won't mind. They won't even miss me, if you're thinking of asking me to join you."

"Some other time, perhaps. We're about ready to leave," he said, hurriedly detaching himself from her grasp. "If you're finished toying with that salad, Anne-Marie...?"

"Quite," she said, the frost in her voice rivaling the ice cubes clinking in her water glass. "I find I don't have as much of an appetite as I first thought. In fact, I believe I have a touch of indigestion.''

"Too much sun, perhaps," Desirée suggested.

"Too much hot air, certainly," she replied, plunking her hat on her head and disappearing behind the brim.

"Feel up to a stroll to help settle your stomach?" he asked snidely, once they were outside.

"Not if you're in a hurry to get back."

"I wouldn't have offered, if I was. We'll go as far as the market, and give you a taste of local life."

"Whatever." She shrugged indifferently.

"Do you like sailing?"

"No. Why do you ask?"

"Because I own the white yacht moored at the end of the second dock over there, and I'd offer to take you for an evening cruise, but if you're not interested...."

"Perhaps you've forgotten already how my parents died," she said icily. "But if it's company you're looking for, I'm sure Ms. LaSalle would be more than happy to join you."

"I apologize," he said, truly contrite. "That was insensitive, even for me."

"Fine," she replied, and sank into stony silence.

They walked in silence for another hundred yards or so, then turned down a narrow lane enclosed on both sides by high walls beyond which ornamental palms clacked and swayed in the breeze.

Still cursing himself for being so thoughtless, he tried again to engage her in conversation. "Some of the oldest residences on the island lie along here," he said. "Fine houses set in beautiful gardens. You'll see one for yourself in a few days. The Tourneaus are throwing a pre-wedding party on the Thursday before the wedding. You've already met their daughter, Angelique. She's the other brides-maid.''

Another silence ensued. Finally, she said, "You're sleeping with her, aren't you?''

"Who, Angelique Tourneau? Good God, no! Why would you even ask such a question?''

"Not her,'' she snapped. "She's much too charming and well-bred! I'm talking about the other one. That LaSalle creature.''

"Desirée's harmless, Anne-Marie.''

"She's a viper in panty hose!''

"Well, not that it's any of your business,'' he said, hardly able to keep his face straight, "but no, I am not sleeping with her. Nor do I intend to.''

"Why not?''

"Because she's not my type, and she wants more than I'm prepared to give. Now I have a question for you. Why do you care?''

She didn't lie very well. "I don't,'' she said, turning pink.

"Is that why I had to get you out of the club before you ripped her throat out?''

"I didn't like her condescending attitude,'' she said primly.

"I didn't like the unflattering innuendo in your remarks, a moment ago, either. What do you mean, Angelique's *too charming and well-bred to sleep with me?*''

Her blush deepened to the color of the fuchsia bougain-villea hanging over the wall behind her. "I didn't mean it quite how it came out.''

"So we're back to that again, are we? Saying one thing, and meaning another?''

"It's your fault!'' she shot back, flustered. "You make me do and say things I don't mean, all the time.''

"I guess that explains your phony, melodramatic response to my kiss, the other night."

Her mouth dropped open. "I liked being kissed by you!" she exclaimed, on an indignant puff of breath.

"Oh, please, Anne-Marie! Save it for someone too inexperienced to know the difference between play-acting, and the real thing."

Her lashes swooped down to hide whatever expression her eyes might betray and, this time, the color stained her throat and neck as well as her face, leaving him wondering how far down it went before it stopped. "How did you know?"

It was the last thing he'd expected her to say. Denials, yes; injured innocence, certainly. But outright admission of guilt? Never! In his experience, few women were capable of that kind of honest introspection.

"That you weren't exactly swept away by the moment?" He shrugged. "Oh, I don't know. The unconvincing moans, perhaps. Or the way you latched onto me and tried to drag me farther inside all the time that your eyes were wide open and filled with something other than overwhelming desire. Shall I go on, or have I made my point?"

She pressed her lips together, reminding him all too vividly of how soft and silky they'd felt under his, and ventured an uncertain glance at him from beneath those absurdly long lashes.

"I'm sorry. I was distracted by…night noises."

Her embarrassment, rather than her words, were what clued him in to what she really meant. "Are you perhaps referring to the goings-on next door?"

She paled a little and nibbled the corner of her mouth. "You mean, you *know?*"

"I'm neither blind nor stupid, Anne-Marie," he said,

wearily, resuming their walk. "I'm fully aware my brother spends most nights with his bride-to-be."

"You are? And you're not doing anything to put a stop to it?"

"They're consenting adults. As long as they're discreet, I'm not going to make a fuss."

"But I thought that was the reason you insisted Solange not stay in the main house. I thought—"

"You thought I was a controlling bully whose chief pleasure in life was wielding his clout to make those around him as miserable as possible."

"Well, you *do* like to have your own way!"

"Where my son is concerned, yes, I do. I will not have him exposed to behavior which will only confuse him. He had enough of that with his mother's carryings-on."

He hadn't realized he'd set such a brisk pace that she was almost running to keep up with him until she caught his arm and said, "Slow down, Ethan, please, and let me catch my breath enough to apologize. I've misjudged you on a number of points and I'm really sorry."

"Are you?"

"Yes. I hate that other things and other people keep coming between us."

"Given that your stay here is temporary, it hardly matters."

"It matters," she said firmly. "Everything matters in life, Ethan. Every ant you step on accidentally, every petal that falls, everything and everyone—especially us."

"Us? How do you figure that?"

"Well, Solange is like a sister to me, so after the wedding, you and I will be…sort of related."

"Related?"

She blushed again, a lovely, delectable shade of rose.

"Stop looking at me like that!" she mumbled. "If *related* is too strong a word for you, how about *friends,* instead?"

She was the kind of woman who eroded a man's defenses. Warm, forgiving, generous, and a damn sight too alluring. If he'd met her seven years ago…!

But that kind of useless thinking did nothing but provoke the urge to kiss her again, and *that* annoyed him enough to say brusquely, "I'm not the kind of man who makes friends casually or easily, Anne-Marie."

"Well, at least we're on speaking terms again. Isn't that progress of a sort?"

"It's a beginning," he allowed.

"And that's enough," she said, lifting her face and bathing him in a smile which threatened to topple what was left of his reserve. "At least for now. Tell me more about the island, Ethan. How does it feel to know you hold the welfare of its residents in the palm of your hand?"

They'd left the old residential section behind by then, and reached the center of town where the market clustered around the fishing harbor. "No different from any other job where a man's responsible for his employees," he said, then stopped to greet the young mother passing by with a baby balanced on her hip. "*Bonjour,* Madeleine! That's a fine-looking boy you've got there. How's your husband?"

"Getting stronger every day, thanks to you, *Monsieur,*" she replied. "The operation saved his life, and we can never repay you for your generosity."

"You already have, Madeleine, by being there when Jean needed you," he told her. "Give him my best, and take care of each other."

"No different from any other job?" Anne-Marie said, watching as Madeleine went on her way. "I rather doubt that."

"I might own the land, but I don't own its people, nor could I run it efficiently without their cooperation."

"But they revere you as if you're a god, and I'm beginning to understand why."

"I'm as mortal as the next man, Anne-Marie. I've made my share of mistakes, and there's not a soul here who doesn't know it."

"Do you ever get claustrophobic, living on such a relatively small patch of land, with everyone knowing your business?"

"I don't," he said, the question giving rise to far more unpleasant memories than she could begin to imagine, "but there are some who do. You might find, if you stay here long enough, that you're one of those people."

"Oh, I don't think so!" She flung out her arms and spun around, sending the skirt of her dress dancing around her slim ankles. "I love the open vistas of sea and sky. There's a feeling of freedom here that I've never experienced anywhere else."

"There's also a lack of sophisticated culture. No opera or theater, or ballet. No glitzy hotels or resorts."

"That's what the rest of the world's for, Ethan, and in this day and age, it's only a short hop away. After all, aren't you the one who said, just this morning, that if my sewing supplies didn't arrive in time, we'd go shopping in Miami? But this…!" She climbed on the low stone wall separating the market from the park behind the beach and, taking off her hat, sent it skimming through the air like a saucer. "This is paradise!"

A boy of about eight, dark-skinned, dark-eyed, dark-haired, left the soccer game he was involved in, picked up her hat from its landing spot on the grass, and ran over to present it to her. *"Pour vous, Mademoiselle."*

"Thank you, angel," she said, jumping down from the

wall and bending so that she was at eye level with him. *"Merci beaucoup!"*

He held her gaze a moment, broke into a worshipful smile, then ran back to join his friends.

"Isn't he beautiful?" she murmured, straightening.

"They all are, at that age," Ethan said, giving in to the stab of regret assailing him at the way she'd addressed the child.

Had any woman ever spoken to Adrian with such a wealth of tenderness in her voice? He thought not. Though loving enough, Josephine wasn't given to extravagant demonstrations of affection, and Lisa.... Lisa had saved her endearments for men outside her marital sphere.

"You sound so sad," Ann-Marie murmured. "Why is that?"

"Because they learn too soon about betrayal, the world stops being a shining, perfect place for them, their innocence is lost, and they never get it back again."

"Not always, Ethan," she said, catching his hand and folding her fingers around his. "There are happy endings, sometimes, and I should think that on this protected, beautiful island, the chances are better than just about anywhere else. There's a sense of family, of belonging here, that you don't find in big cities. It's a wonderful place for a child— safe, free from crime and poverty."

"And still it's not enough for some people."

"It wasn't enough for your ex-wife," she said. "But that was a failing in her, not you."

"Try telling that to Adrian, the next time he wants to know why he doesn't have a mother to come to school concerts, or tuck him in at night, the same as all his friends do. Try answering some of the other questions he asks, as well, while you're at it."

"Well, I don't pretend to be an expert on children," she

said thoughtfully, "but it seems to me that all you can do is answer as honestly as possible."

"You think it's that easy, do you?" He laughed bitterly. "Then tell me, how should I have answered when my son asked me why his mommy was kissing a man behind the pool cabana and why she wasn't wearing her bikini top at the time?"

"She did *that?*" Anne-Marie exclaimed, on a shocked intake of breath. "Oh, Ethan, I'm so sorry! Was she with Señor Santos? Is that why you hate him so much?"

"No. He was just one of several, and when he wound up behind bars, she moved on to a member of my house staff—a blond Adonis responsible for maintaining the swimming pools. They left the island together, just five minutes ahead of my boot, but not before she'd flaunted the affair in front of Adrian." He paused long enough to swallow the bitter anger souring his tongue. "I made up some excuse at the time, but if you think I should now spell it out to him candidly, in all its sordid detail—"

"No, of course I don't! He's too young to understand, and even if he weren't, that's more information than he ever needs to know."

"Right now, perhaps. But in time he needs to understand, if only to protect himself against repeating my mistake when he's old enough to choose a wife."

"Why do you assume you're the one who made a mistake?"

"Because I knew the risks, but I married her anyway."

"When two people are deeply in love, risks aren't something they always consider. It's easy to be wise, after the fact. Hindsight's a wonderful thing."

"So is foresight." He swung around and started retracing their steps. "I wish I could subscribe to your dewy-eyed belief that love conquers all, Anne-Marie, but the plain fact is, it doesn't. It's fragile and, in the romantic sense at least, short-lived.''

''Are you saying you don't believe in marriage?''

''No. I'm saying it's up to a man to choose wisely. I didn't, and Adrian is still paying the price.''

She was silent for so long that he thought—*hoped*—the topic had exhausted itself. He lived with the knowledge of his own culpability every day. Rehashing it all with this woman, who stirred up emotions and desires best left sleeping, merely added another wrinkle to an already messy situation. He didn't need it. He didn't need her.

But when had she ever been satisfied to let someone else have the last word? ''So if you had everything to do over again,'' she began, the minute they were in the car and headed back to the estate, ''what would you do differently?''

''That's easy,'' he said promptly. ''Choose a woman with Bellefleur blood flowing through her veins—someone born and bred to the rhythm and tempo of this island—instead of settling for an outsider.''

# CHAPTER EIGHT

THE second the convertible cruised to a stop in the fore-court, Morton, the butler, came out to meet them, his face creased with worry. "Thank goodness you're home at last, *Monsieur!* I'm afraid there's been an accident. *Madame* Josephine took a bad fall just before lunch."

"Good God! Why wasn't I informed sooner?"

Just how significant a matriarchal role Josephine played showed in the alacrity with which Ethan leaped out of the car while the engine was still running, and in the staccato burst of alarm in his voice as he fired off his question. Equally concerned, Anne-Marie reached across to turn off the ignition, then hurried after the two men as they strode into the house.

"We tried to reach you at the club, but you'd already left, *Monsieur,*" Morton was explaining, when she caught up, "and we were unable to contact you on your cell phone."

Ethan slapped the heel of his hand to his forehead. "I forgot to take the damn thing with me when I went out, that's why. Has the doctor seen her?"

*"Oui, Monsieur."*

"And? Does my aunt require hospitalization?"

*"Madame* refused to entertain the idea and Doctor Evert agreed she could recuperate at home. She's resting comfortably now, and asked that you and *Mademoiselle* Barclay stop by her room as soon as you returned. She's quite agitated, I'm afraid, and *Monsieur Louis* is beside himself with worry."

"I can imagine," Ethan said grimly. "We'll go up right away." Already halfway across the inner courtyard to the curving staircase at the other end, he crooked a peremptory finger at Anne-Marie. "Follow me."

He'd already taken the bloom off her day with his remark about never entrusting his heart to anyone but an island woman, and that he was now flinging orders at her without so much as a *please* would ordinarily have been enough for her to remind him in no uncertain terms that she was not one of his lackeys.

In this instance, though, Josephine's condition took precedence over Ethan Beaumont's manners, or lack thereof. Still, Anne-Marie couldn't suppress a twinge of regret that the intimacy they'd shared on their stroll through town had lasted such a brief time.

A central hall lined with many closed doors ran the length of the upper floor of the house, with tall, open windows at each end and numerous ceiling fans whirling lazily to keep the air circulating. On the walls between the doors hung portraits of dark-haired, noble-looking men and finely-featured women. Beaumont ancestors, she guessed, glancing at them as she sped by; the resemblance was unmistakable.

The Duclos's suite of rooms lay in a wing at the far end of the house and, as Anne-Marie might have expected, was a spacious, elegant affair with a sitting room, small private dining room and study, all opening onto the usual deep shaded verandahs overlooking a fabulous view down the hillside to the sea.

A shaken Louis ushered them into a bedroom furnished in shades of blue and ivory. Josephine, wearing a froth of beribboned lace and satin, sat propped up on a bank of silk-covered pillows like an aging Cleopatra about to set sail in her barge.

"This is not how I planned to spend the next several days," she proclaimed, waving aside her husband's anxious hovering and patting the edge of the bed in invitation for Anne-Marie to sit. "I've twisted my ankle rather badly, and I'm afraid it's going to create a serious inconvenience, in light of all the entertaining we're facing in the coming days."

"Never mind all that. We'll manage somehow." Ethan glowered affectionately at her from the foot of the bed. "More to the point, how come you fell in the first place? I suppose you were in your usual hurry and not looking where you were going?"

"Don't blame me!" she snapped. "It was that benighted kitten's fault. Ever since Adrian took a shine to it, it's forever underfoot. It's a miracle I didn't break my neck."

His scowl melted into an unabashed grin. "You're an indestructible old woman, *ma tante,* and I don't know why we're wasting sympathy on you. If anyone needs comfort, it's probably the cat."

"The cat," she assured him irascibly, "is perfectly fine, and you have bigger problems to face than worrying about it. Or have you forgotten that the French Trade Envoy and his entourage are joining us for dinner tonight, and staying over until tomorrow?"

"Oh, hell! Yes, I had."

"I expected as much. Well, lucky for you that Anne-Marie is able to take my place as hostess, or you'd be left to cope single-handedly with *Monsieur* Pelletier and that insatiable wife of his."

"Me?" Anne-Marie said. "Oh, surely not! Surely Solange is the one who should take your place?"

"Good heavens, child!" Josephine snorted. "Solange and Philippe are too wrapped up in each other to spare a thought for anyone else. Why, the Envoy could choke on a fish bone and fall face first in his plate, and they wouldn't notice! No, you're the only possible choice.''

''I'm afraid my aunt's right,'' Ethan said. ''Solange isn't up to the task, not these days. Too caught up in wedding fever.''

''Precisely.'' Josephine smiled, gracious in victory. ''And now that we're all in agreement, Ethan, have Louis show you out. I believe the cook wants your approval on some last-minute changes in the menu. No, my dear, not you,'' she added, when Anne-Marie rose to leave also. ''You stay and keep me company a little longer.''

Before leaving, Ethan rested his hand on Anne-Marie's shoulder; a passing touch only, but as always where he was concerned, it stirred up an aftermath of sensation out of all proportion to the occasion. ''Will you come up to the house half an hour earlier than usual, Anne-Marie, so that we may greet our guests together?''

''Yes,'' she managed, more elated than she had any right to be at the idea of being his consort for the evening.

''I should warn you, it'll be a somewhat more formal occasion than usual.''

''*More* formal than usual?'' She blinked, taken aback. ''I have a hard time imagining how, since everyone here always dresses for dinner.''

''When it's just family, we make an occasion of it, yes, but not to the degree that Mimi Pelletier expects. She shows up looking as if she's about to be presented to the crowned heads of Europe. Full length evening dress, enough jewelry to set up shop, and all that sort of thing. It'll be a long and rather tedious evening, I'm afraid. Are you sure you're up to it?''

''I'll manage,'' she said, her gaze trapped helplessly in his.

"You have something suitable to wear? If not, I'm sure Solange—"

"I have something. Don't worry, Ethan, I won't embarrass you."

"Having never seen you look anything but lovely, it never occurred to me that you might. I was thinking only of how you'd feel if you found you were under-dressed for the occasion."

"I appreciate your concern," she said, drawn ever deeper into the beguiling depths of his blue, blue eyes.

He rewarded her with one of his rare and charming smiles. "Until later, then."

She watched as he dropped a kiss on his aunt's cheek, then followed Louis from the room. The door clicked shut behind them, and left behind a hanging silence marked only by the discreet tick of the exquisite ormolu clock on the bedside table.

At length, Josephine said quietly, "Your face is a picture, child. Everything you're feeling is written there and what I see at this moment is utter turmoil. Is my nephew the reason for it?"

"Yes," she said simply. "He's…different from other men I've known."

"In other words, you don't understand him."

"I don't understand myself, Madame Duclos!"

"Because you're hopelessly attracted to someone who's working so hard to keep you at arm's length?"

"Crazy, isn't it?" Anne-Marie attempted a laugh which fell sadly short of the mark.

"Not really, my dear. Sex has you by the throat, and that tends to befuddle one's faculties."

Appalled, Anne-Marie exclaimed, "Ethan and I haven't had sex!"

"But you've thought about it. Indeed, that's almost *all* you can think about where he's concerned."

"Is it so obvious?" she muttered, burning with embarrassment.

Josephine laughed, not unkindly. "There's no need to look so ashamed. It's mostly about sex at this stage of a relationship, and that's as it should be. Sex is crucial to love between a man and a woman. It's a gift beyond price, and it's meant to be enjoyed. *I* enjoy it. Louis is a magnificent lover! There, does that shock you?"

"In all truth, yes. But not in the way you might think. I just never expected you and I would ever have such a frank discussion."

"We are women, Anne-Marie. It is part of our nature to confide in one another in matters of the heart." She laughed again, a little wickedly this time. "Men are dismayed by that, of course. They don't care for the fact that we…what is that American expression which puts is so well? *Gang up* on them."

By then as curious as she was mortified, Anne-Marie said, "Is that what we're doing? Ganging up on Ethan?"

"Possibly."

"He'd be furious, if he knew."

"He won't hear about it from me." Josephine stroked the fine cotton sheet covering her and sighed. "Ethan is very good at orchestrating other people's lives, but he's in danger of making a terrible mess of his own. And that's why I'm speaking to you so bluntly—because from what I've observed, you might be the one woman to change all that. So the question now becomes, what else can you bring to the relationship, apart from the obvious sexual attraction?"

"At this point, I'm not sure we even have a relationship!"

"Well, the potential for one is certainly there. I'm neither blind nor stupid. I know what to look for. He drives you pleasantly crazy. You can't think straight when he's near. He fills your mind, your heart, your soul. You crave him, even as you fear him, because he threatens to turn your world upside-down. But Ethan will run in the opposite direction if he believes you're drawn to him only because he's beautiful."

"Oh, there's more to it than that!" Anne-Marie protested. "But he's a complicated man. Overcoming the barriers he throws up isn't easy."

"If you can bring yourself to understand what makes him the man he is today, you might find it worth the effort. His experience has been that women can't distinguish between love and infatuation—that they value things like money and prestige and appearances, over unwavering devotion, integrity and, yes, passion. Passion not just for him but for his family, and for the people of this island."

"All the things his ex-wife lacked, in other words."

"Precisely. And once you recognize that, your options become very clear-cut. He'll probably have sex with you, if that's all you want and don't mind walking away without regret afterward. But he'll never again compromise Adrian's happiness, or his own, by allowing himself to fall in love with you, unless you can convince him that you're as capable of loyal commitment as he is."

"That kind of thing takes time—more than I can afford. Once the wedding's over, I'll be gone from here."

"Then make the most of every minute you have left."

"But how, on such short acquaintance, does a person tell the difference between infatuation and love?"

"*Mon Dieu,* child, I don't have *all* the answers! I know only what I see, and bring to those observations only the wisdom of my years. Perhaps what exists between the two of you will never amount to more than a superficial attraction and that, indeed, only time will tell. However, if you sincerely wish to begin the journey of discovery, then for heaven's sake get on with it! Start showing him that you're not someone to be easily dismissed, regardless of where you'll be living a week or two from now! Dare to reveal to him all that's in your heart.''

But did she have that kind of courage? The question plagued Anne-Marie for the rest of the afternoon and throughout the time it took her to dress for dinner.

It was almost midnight, yet the air remained as heavy and close as if the sun still cast its powerful light over the gardens. Exchanging her elegant navy dinner gown for a short sarong printed with scarlet hibiscus, Anne-Marie slipped quietly out of her villa and headed for her favorite retreat.

Though shrouded on either side by deep shadows, the hillside steps lay clearly defined in the moonlight and the sand, when at last she reached the beach and took off her shoes, sifted between her toes like warm flour.

The evening had been a triumph from the moment she set foot in the main house and found Ethan waiting for her. That he'd said not a word when he stepped forward to greet her hadn't mattered. The firm, almost possessive touch of his hand in the small of her back as he guided her into the salon, and the unspoken approval in his eyes as he poured champagne and regarded her over the rim of his glass, had been enough.

It wasn't enough now, though. Everyone else might be so sated with good food, wine and conversation that all they wanted was to flop into bed and sleep off the meal, but she was filled with a restless sense of unfinished business, of anticlimax.

The night should not have ended as it had, with formal handshakes, Gallic air-kissing on both cheeks, and her slipping quietly away in a rustle of midnight silk while Ethan directed the Pelletiers to their overnight accommodation.

There should have been something more exciting to round off the occasion, just as the thimble-sized glasses of fine orange liqueur served with rich island coffee had completed the magnificent dinner.

Maybe that was why she cast aside her usual caution and ventured into the sea. Not far at first, to be sure; just enough for the gentle tide to ebb and flow idly around her calves. Stooping, she swished her hands back and forth, and sent tiny sparks of phosphorescence shooting through the water.

*Magical,* she thought. *As magical as this night was meant to be.* And made bold by the benign pleasure of the moment, she raised the hem of her sarong and waded in deeper until the waves caressed her thighs as sensually as a lover's hands.

"Oh, Ethan...!" She murmured his name on a tiny breath full of longing which only she could hear.

Or so she thought. But scarcely had the words escaped her than, with blood-chilling suddenness, a hand slid under her hair and closed around the back of her neck. Letting out a muffled shriek of terror, she spun around to find him standing behind her, with the waves lapping at the hem of his khaki shorts.

"For someone who claims to be afraid of anything deeper than a glass of water, you're taking a hell of a chance wading in the shallows at this time of night," he chided. "There are dangers out here, and not all of them lie below the tide line."

"You mean, I could be mugged and robbed?" She pressed a fist to her ribs, to try to settle her erratic heart, and managed a laugh. "I doubt it! I don't have anything on me worth stealing."

His eyes were inscrutable in the dark, his expression unreadable. But his touch, as he trailed his fingers up her throat to her mouth, betrayed a hunger in him which electrified her. "I disagree," he said, his voice deep and dark. "You possess something any man in his right mind would covet."

"I do?" She trembled on the edge of expectancy, sure he would kiss her, and hoping it wouldn't be enough, that he'd want more. That he'd want everything she longed to give.

He didn't—but why should that surprise her? He seldom did what she hoped or expected. He merely led her to the brink of anticipation, and left her dangling there, hungrier than ever.

"You surprised me tonight," he remarked, directing her back to shore. "I knew you spoke some French, but I had no idea you were so fluent in the language, or so conversant with current affairs as they pertain to these islands in general, and to Bellefleur in particular. Pelletier was quite smitten by you."

*And you, Ethan?* she yearned to ask. *Did I misinterpret the warmth in your gaze at dinner? Was there a reason you glanced at me so often, and always with a hint of a smile playing over your mouth, as if we shared a secret too deeply personal to admit to anyone else?* "His wife was charming, too, but very quiet."

Ethan's laughter echoed across the water. "His wife likes attention—her husband's and that of every other man in the room, but she found slim pickings tonight. You stole the show. Why didn't you tell me how accomplished you are?"

''Why didn't you ask, instead of presuming I'd be an embarrassment to you?''

''I didn't say that, Anne-Marie.''

''Perhaps not, but I can read what's going on in your mind.''

''Can you really?'' he murmured, his voice a smoky, sultry counterpoint to the cadence of the sea. ''In that case, this shouldn't come as too much of a surprise.''

And then, when she *wasn't* expecting it, he *did* kiss her, bringing his lips to hers in a fierce, erotic invasion of heat which sent her senses swimming. He explored her mouth, and when he knew it as thoroughly as he knew his own, went on with thrilling dedication to discover her throat, her ear, the bare slope of her shoulder.

''I have wanted to do this all night,'' he said roughly, his hands skimming the length of her spine to her hips, and pulling her so close she could feel the urgent throb of his erection through the layers of his clothing.

She clutched at his upper arms, dazed. How was it possible that, with the simple brush of his lips over her skin, he could reach a place within her unfettered by physical boundaries? By what divine intervention did he know how to touch her soul?

His fingers toyed with the top of her sarong. Dipped into her cleavage with tormenting finesse. A moment later, the fabric whispered down her body and left her breasts bare to his gaze.

''From the moment you appeared on the terrace, right through that interminable dinner and all the civilized conversation that went with it, the only thing I wanted was to get you alone and rip that incredibly sexy gown from your body,'' he said hoarsely, grazing his palms lightly over her nipples. ''Thank God you saved me the trouble. It would have been a pity to lay waste to such a lovely garment.''

A spasm of pleasure shot through her and left her skin puckered with sensation. "I didn't realize you felt that way," she whispered. "You seemed so much in command."

He ripped off his shirt. Wrenched open the buckle at his waist, and kicked off the rest of his clothing. Moonlight glimmered over him, painting his bronzed limbs with silver, and she thought that Josephine had said it best: he *was* beautiful.

He took her hand, and placed it against his chest, right over his heart. "Does this feel to you like a man in command?" he rumbled, and when she shook her head in mute denial, drew her fingers lower and boldly closed them around his penis. "Does this?"

Her breathing, shallow enough to begin with, seized up altogether at the power and vitality of him. She felt the strength seep from her legs, the warm, damp heat surge between her thighs. Her knees buckled, and she sank to the sand.

He knelt above her and traced the shape of her from head to toe, his hands warm and possessive. He murmured her name and made it sound like angels singing.

He removed her panties, and parted her legs. Touched her—a single brush of his finger only, but it was enough. Enough to make her cry out in exquisite agony and reach for him, desperate to verify that this was no dream; that he really hovered over her, all lean and hard and ready.

He let her touch him. Thrust himself, hot and smooth, against the curve of her palm, before retreating far enough for a whisper of ocean breeze to flutter over her naked body.

"No...!" she begged on a long sigh. "Come to me, Ethan...please! Come now!"

"All in good time, my lovely *Canadienne*," he murmured hoarsely, touching her again, this time with his mouth…and its talent defied mortal boundaries.

He made her shimmer from the inside out. His tongue delved and stroked, until she arched like a bow, and flew like an arrow. Until she shattered into a million shining fragments, and came together again more alive than she'd ever been before.

He left her begging and pleading and clutching at him. Reaching for him. Wanting more. Wanting *all* of him— everything he ever was or ever would be. And when he finally ended the glorious torment and drove into her, she knew that she'd never again be complete without him.

She closed around him, tight and sleek as a second skin. Contracted around the powerful length of him. And briefly reveled in the hot, sweet rush of his seed flooding into her before, once again, she splintered on another wave of ecstasy.

Of course, it had to end, unrehearsed miracle that their coming together had been, and she braced herself, expecting that, once the rush subsided, he'd pull away and again disappear behind the cool reserve that was too often his stock in trade.

When he did not, and instead lay with his weight pressing her into the soft white sand, and his breath gusting damp at her ear, and his hand idly stroking her hair, a slender hope sprang alive that perhaps he'd been taken by the same emotional storm as she had. Was it possible, she wondered dreamily, that they'd embarked on that journey of discovery Josephine had talked about?

At last—too soon—he stirred and, lifting his head, planted a kiss on the corner of her mouth. "Well?" he said. "How do you feel? Full of regret?"

"Mm-mm." She shook her head, loving the feel of his cheek rasping slightly against hers. "Blissed out! What just happened between us…it was so much more than I dared to hope for!''

Laughter rumbled deep in his chest. ''I'm not sure that's a compliment!''

''Oh, Ethan, never doubt for a moment that it was wonderful!''

*''Oui.''* He kissed her again, lightly, tenderly. ''For once, you and I are in agreement. What a pity that it has to end so soon, that we can't spend the rest of this singular night together. But my son—''

''I understand,'' she said. ''You have to be there when Adrian wakes in the morning.''

''Yes.'' He ran his finger over her mouth, unaware of the surge of desire to which his casual embrace gave rise. ''And you, too, must leave, Anne-Marie, because I meant what I said earlier. This is not a smart idea, to be wandering alone in such an isolated spot.''

''But I love it here,'' she reasoned. ''I love to watch the shooting stars streaming across the sky, and the reflection of the moon rippling over the night-calm sea. I love the tranquility of the island at rest, soothed by the quiet lullaby of the surf.''

''Very lyrical, I'm sure, but don't be fooled by it,'' he replied, unmoved. ''The sea can turn into a monster without warning, and who do you think would hear your cries for help and come to your rescue, should you find yourself in difficulties?''

''You,'' she said, leaning into him. ''If there's one thing I've learned since I came here, it's that you're always there when you're needed.''

''Not always. I'm as fallible as the next man, Anne-Marie. You can count on me for only so much.''

It was as close to a warning as she wanted to get, that she shouldn't expect one night to translate into forever.

"Then I'll be more careful," she said lightly. "I'll only ever come here again after dark if I know I won't be alone."

"Temptress!" He smiled, sprang lithely to his feet, and offered his hand. "Come. I'll take you home."

"No." She shook her head, aware that if she presumed too much, pushed too hard for a closeness he wasn't ready to accept, then the regrets he'd spoken of would arise, and they'd be all his. "I can make it back on my own. I've traveled the cliff path often enough in the dark that I'm familiar with it."

"But I have another way, safer and swifter." He gestured down the beach to a spot where the encroaching jungle met the sand in a tangle of lush undergrowth, and she saw a horse grazing there; a ghostly, graceful creature, its flanks dappled by moonlight. So that was how he'd managed to sneak up on her so easily!

"Come," he said again, climbing into his clothes and draping her sarong around her breasts. "This way, we can prolong the pleasure of the night a little longer."

Denying him was beyond her. He vaulted astride the animal, then reached down and hoisted her up behind him. "Hold on tight," he ordered—as if she needed any encouragement!—clicked his tongue, and they were off in a powdery thud of hooves, a mile or more along the shore to a place where a broad trail opened out.

She'd never ridden bareback before; never clung to a body so lean and strong and capable; never felt so secure, so cherished. And she knew that if she lived to be a hundred, the memory of this night would remain, undimmed by the passing years.

It ended too soon, of course. Cresting a final slope, Ethan drew the horse to a halt in the lee of guest pavilions, and dismounted. "*À demain, ma chère,*" he murmured, as she slid down into his waiting arms. "Sleep well."

*À demain*—until tomorrow.

Oh, yes, she'd sleep! And with such implicit promise to pave the way, in her dreams she'd hoard every touch, every kiss, every word they'd exchanged. "*Oui,*" she breathed, lifting her face for one last kiss. "*À demain.*"

## CHAPTER NINE

She did indeed see Ethan the next morning, but only from a distance. Since he appeared to be in a hurry and too preoccupied to notice her, she didn't attempt to draw his attention. Refusing to allow the keen sense of letdown to take hold—for what woman wanted to learn that she was so soon forgettable?—she instead took herself back to her workroom, and told herself to stop behaving like a teenager in the throes of puppy love. One encounter, no matter how memorable, did not amount to a lifetime commitment, except in romance novels.

Later that afternoon though, when she stopped by to visit Josephine, and learned that he and Adrian had flown to Miami and would be gone at least overnight and possibly longer, her disappointment wasn't so easy to contain.

"Did he not bother to tell you he was called away?" Josephine inquired, skewering Anne-Marie in her penetrating, all-seeing gaze, and discerning far too much.

"Why would he?" Anne-Marie looked out at the blue afternoon with pretended indifference. So much for making an indelible impression on the man! "He hardly needs my permission to go wherever he pleases."

For the next forty-eight hours, she put aside her dented pride and drove herself to the point of exhaustion, finishing the dresses. But best intentions notwithstanding, nothing could silence the questions hammering in her head. *Why hadn't Ethan told her he was leaving? Was he deliberately avoiding her? Was this his way of telling her that, in the greater scheme of things, she simply didn't count?*

It didn't help any that the heat grew intolerable. Heavy as a wet cloth pressed to one's face, it sapped both her energy and her normally sunny disposition.

"You're awfully crabby," Solange remarked, toward the end òf the second day.

"You would be, too, if you were shackled to a sewing machine for fifteen hours at a stretch in weather like this!" she snapped.

Solange flinched. "Oh, you're working too hard, and it's all my fault. I shouldn't have imposed on you like this."

Ashamed, because she knew how brittle her friend's self-esteem was, Anne-Marie took as deep a breath as the humidity would allow, and said apologetically, "It's no one's fault but my own, Solange, and I had no business taking my frustrations out on you."

Nor had she. She was twenty-eight years old, and if she didn't have a string of past lovers to draw on for comparison, she'd at least been around long enough to know that impulsive one-night stands seldom amounted to anything permanent. Never mind that Ethan had said and done all the right things after the fact. He was too much the gentleman to behave otherwise.

That evening, the clouds swept in from the east, dark and threatening. Rather than get caught in a downpour, she and Solange had an early dinner delivered to their quarters. By eight o'clock, lightning split the night sky, and thunder rolled down the hillside. A gale rattled the palm tree fronds and tore blossoms from the shrubs bordering the little terrace. Shortly after, the lights went out.

"Power failures happen regularly during stormy weather," Solange told her, lighting candles. "It's the one drawback to living here. But candlelight's so romantic, don't you think?"

"For you, perhaps," Anne-Marie said, and took herself off to her own rooms, there to lie alone in a bed large enough for two, but with only the filmy mosquito netting for company.

She awoke the next morning to tranquil skies, calm seas and the overwhelming scent of freshly washed flowers. Bellefleur was living up to its name in fine style.

Refreshed herself, for the storm had cleared her mind as well as the air, she hung the finished gowns in garment bags and supervised their shipping to the main house, for storage until the big day. After seeing them safely stowed in an empty dressing room, she came back along the upper hall to find Ethan waiting for her at the foot of the stairs.

"I hear you've been busy," he said, his glance sweeping over her as she descended to the main floor.

"I hear you've been away," she shot back, and could have slapped herself for sounding so piqued.

His lips twitched. "Did you miss us, Anne-Marie?"

"I missed Adrian," she said scornfully. "But you? I barely noticed you were gone."

The twitch became a full-blown grin. "We missed you, too."

"Sure you did," she said, hanging on to her annoyance because it was her only defense against such an onslaught of charm. "And the little pigs of Bellefleur have wings, and fly."

He pressed his lips together, but although that contained his laughter, it did nothing to quell the amusement dancing in his eyes. "There are no pigs on Bellefleur, *Chérie*. Only sheep, horses and cattle. Oh yes, and a little boy who's learning to sail, and panting to have you come and applaud his progress." He caught her hand and drew her down the last two stairs. "And now that you're finally done with the wedding gowns, you have no reason to refuse him."

Resolve growing weaker by the second, she muttered, "I suppose not."

"Excellent! Perhaps you'd like to try handling a small boat yourself?"

"I'm not prepared to go quite that far," she said, turned weak at the knees by the warmth in his eyes when he looked at her, "but I'd love to see how Adrian manages."

They went to a different beach, one she hadn't visited before, with a boathouse, and a launching ramp. After strapping a life jacket on Adrian, Ethan released a small, low-slung, lateen-rigged boat down the ramp into the water.

"Sure you don't want to come with us?" he asked her, as his son dog-paddled after him and climbed into the shallow cockpit. "There's room for three, an extra life preserver on board, and we're not going out more than a couple of hundred yards."

"I'm sure," she said, chilled despite the warmth of the sun, at the thought of being out of her depth on such a flimsy craft.

"I won't let you drown, I promise. You're too important to Solange for me to take chances with your safety."

"Only to Solange?" she mocked, hearing the teasing note in his voice.

"Not only to Solange," he said. "To me, and to my son."

They were words she lived to hear, but even they couldn't persuade her to climb aboard that frail-looking little dingy. So she lifted the camera slung around her neck and said, "Go give your son his lesson, then. I'm happy to be the official photographer."

And so the remaining days spun out, with her accompanying them when they went sailing, or swimming off the beach. And willingly, foolishly, she let herself slip into a surrogate mother role, making sure Adrian wore sunscreen and a hat, and wrapping him in a towel to dry him off when he fell overboard.

She was the one he ran to for comfort when he scraped his knee on a chunk of coral. And hers was the heart he melted when he wound his little arms around her neck and told her she was pretty, and that he loved her and didn't want her to go away, not ever.

The nights followed a different theme, one of secret, searing passion between adults. With long hours stretching ahead and nothing to distract them from each other, Ethan came to her, sometimes on the beach, under a full, benevolent moon, and sometimes in her villa.

Yet at some level, she knew that he did so with a reluctance outpaced only by his raging hunger; that he wished he could rise above such carnal needs. Sometimes, she suspected he hated himself for wanting her so much, and even though, deep down, instinct told her that such self-loathing could lash out and direct itself at her, she didn't care. He swept her into a world so deeply, thrillingly sexual that she lost her sense of survival, and lived only for the pleasure of the hours they shared.

To touch him, to taste him, and to know that with her mouth and hands she could smash through his formidable reserve and connect with him at the most intimate, elemental level, became, during those star-filled nights, her *raison d'être*.

She lived for his kiss. Died a tiny death every time he brought her to orgasm. And, responsive to his slightest touch, was born again within minutes.

When foreplay tore his self-control to shreds, she loved the feel of him entering her. She loved the power and thrust of his manhood; his stamina and strength. She gloried in hearing him groan helplessly against her mouth as she teased his flesh; in feeling the muscles of his belly flex like tempered steel as he cajoled her to yet another climax while fighting to delay his own.

She loved the battle, the way the balance of power shifted between them. Relished her fleeting little victories. But in the end, he always won, hurling her beyond the limits of mortal endurance in a shattering explosion of sensation and release. After, she clung to him, sometimes weeping from the intensity of the experience, and always amazed that she'd survived so wrenching an emotional catharsis.

But unlike his son, Ethan always withheld a part of himself. He never begged her not to leave the island. Never, no matter how rich or full the passion between them, forgot himself so far as to tell her he loved her. And if part of her brain warned her that she was a temporary diversion only and was setting herself up for heartbreak by pretending otherwise, another, larger part refused to listen.

Today was all that mattered. And if she made it matter enough to Ethan, perhaps tomorrow would never come.

Sadly, though, it did, and so abruptly that she was caught completely unprepared.

"I'm afraid this is the last time we'll be able to spend the afternoon fooling around like this," he announced, hauling the boat into its covered berth, the Saturday before the wedding. "The first of the off-island guests arrive tomorrow, which means my time won't be my own between now and the day itself. Nor, come to that, will yours, seeing that my aunt still isn't up to par."

Although not a cloud marred the perfection of the sky, suddenly the sea appeared less blue, the sun not quite as bright. Unable to hide her dismay, she said, "Why so soon? The wedding's still a week away!"

"True, and most people won't arrive until a day or two

before. But for close friends flying in from halfway around the world, it's the chance to visit before the event, and make a holiday of it. We'll have a full house by Monday, with more arriving daily.''

''If the main house is full, where will the rest of them stay?''

''Some will take rooms at the Plantation Club, and others will stay with friends who live here year-round. It'll be a bit of a squeeze, fitting everyone in, but we'll manage somehow.''

''You must be wishing I wasn't taking up an entire guest villa all to myself,'' she said, hoping he'd take her not-so-subtle hint and rush to assure her that he liked her living arrangements just as they were because, that way, they could continue their midnight trysts undetected.

Instead, he replied, ''In light of everything you've done to help out, you've more than earned the right to a little extra comfort. We're all very grateful to you, Anne-Marie.''

Grateful: the word assaulted her, sharper than a blade sliding between her ribs to rip open her heart.

''And is that what these last days all come down to, Ethan?'' she cried, detesting the shrill edge in her voice, but helpless to control it. ''You're *grateful?*''

''Of course. You've been wonderful, stepping in whenever we've needed you. What else did you expect—that we'd simply take you for granted?''

Thoroughly deflated, she said, ''No.''

''But you're upset.''

'''Upset' doesn't begin to cover it, but how like a man to understate matters!''

''And how like a woman to take exception to a perfectly innocuous remark,'' he said, casting a pointed glance at

Adrian who, although he didn't fully grasp the gist of the conversation, clearly picked up on the tension underlying it.

Filled with remorse at the confusion and fear she saw printed on the child's face, she said, "You're quite right. I don't know what possessed me to overreact like that. All I can say is that, for months, I've looked forward to seeing Solange and Philippe get married, but now that the time's here, I'm almost sorry."

"Why is that? Are you having second thoughts about their chances of making it work?"

"No, not that." She drummed up a smile, even though the effort made her face ache. "I suppose, if truth be told, I'd like things to remain the same as they've been for the last little while."

It was as close as she dared come to admitting outright all that was in her heart, but it didn't elicit a similar response from Ethan. "Nothing stays the same forever, Anne-Marie," he said, averting his eyes. "We've both known that from the beginning."

Just to hammer home the message, life as she knew it at the Beaumont estate underwent dramatic change from that point on. With the growing influx of international guests, lunches became more formal, dinners more elaborate, and the social calendar more crowded.

If they weren't out sailing, or riding horses, or playing croquet, or a round of golf, the visitors lolled around the pool, a sophisticated crowd of jet-setters whose unflagging amiability set Anne-Marie's teeth on edge.

"Thanks," she said, when Ethan urged her to join in the fun while it lasted, "but I suspect Adrian's feeling a little neglected, so if it's all the same to you, I'll spend some time with him instead."

"That's very thoughtful of you," he replied.

*Oh, that's me, all right!* she thought bitterly. *Thoughtful, helpful—and stupid to a fault for falling in love with a man who's not the least bit interested in a permanent addition to his household.*

For distraction, she turned again to work, more than happy to go along with Adrian's request that she make him something special to wear at the wedding "because I'm carrying the rings and that's important," he said.

"Tell me what you'd like, then," she said.

"A space suit," he replied promptly. "A silver one, with a helmet."

"Okay, let's see what I come up with."

Fifteen minutes later, she submitted three drawings for his approval. "That one," he decided, selecting a Pierrot-style jumpsuit with flared legs and ruffled collar.

"That's my favorite, too," she said, hugging him.

The next morning, they went into town, to a little shop on the waterfront, and chose a length of fine white fabric in a silk-linen blend with just enough shine to it that it might have passed for silver if a person used his imagination. Afterward, they stood at a booth in the market and ate crayfish sandwiches, before climbing in the Mercedes and being driven back to the estate.

He was such a delight, and so happy to have her shower him with attention. Every morning, he'd show up at her door, and stand patiently while she measured and fitted the garment.

"You'll be the best-dressed man there," she told him, fashioning the underside of the ruffled collar from a scrap of turquoise silk left over from the bridesmaid's dresses. "Every lady will want to dance with you at the reception."

But, "I'm only going to dance with you," he said.

"You're my favorite lady in all the world. I love you, Anne-Marie."

"Oh, darling!" She sighed, her heart breaking for him, that he'd latched onto her, a stranger, when his mother should have been the recipient of his affection. "I love you, too."

Something of her own unhappiness must have shown in her voice because, after looking at her from his big, dark eyes a moment, he observed with preternatural insight, "Loving people is scary sometimes, isn't it? Sometimes, it's better not to, then you don't get sad if they don't love you back, but you can't always help it, can you?"

*Dear God!* she thought. *That a child so young should have learned such a painful lesson already is nothing short of criminal!*

If she could have, she'd have kept them both down at the guest villa, and stayed away from the main house altogether. She'd have hoarded every second of the time the time she had left on that magical island, and lavished him with all the love she had to give. That, though, wasn't an option.

"You need a little adult conversation once in a while, and Ethan still needs a hostess," Josephine informed her, catching her one day when she stopped by the main house on an errand for Solange. "I can do my part at lunch, but I'm too old to stay up half the night, smiling at people whose names I can't remember, and laughing at jokes I don't understand. You'll have to fill in for me, child, and that's all there is to it."

Of course, Anne-Marie agreed, but it was difficult to preserve a serene facade when she went hot all over every time Ethan looked at her, and every time she looked at him. To be so close and not be allowed to touch, made her ache. And for all his apparent willingness to let their affair lapse, there were times, when some other man in the party perhaps drank a little too much champagne and paid her too much attention, that she thought she detected in Ethan's eyes a proprietary interest that amounted almost to jealousy.

Was this how the rest of her time on Bellefleur was destined to play itself out? she wondered, as the week progressed. With her teetering on the edge of despair, and him alternating between bland indifference and covert possessiveness?

On the Thursday before the pre-wedding party at the Tourneaus, she got her answer. Pleading fatigue, she'd excused herself shortly after dinner, and was on her way out of the salon when Ethan caught up with her and murmured simply, "Later?"

Her weariness evaporated in a flash, replaced by such exhilaration that she didn't know how she remained earthbound. "Later," she breathed, her spirits soaring, and sped back to the guest villa on winged feet.

He did care, at least a little bit! And a little was better than nothing.

In a haze of euphoria, she took a leisurely bath, knowing the social hour at the main house was far from over and that she had plenty of time in which to make herself pretty for him. She shampooed her hair and rinsed it with rose water. Massaged lightly perfumed body lotion into her sun-kissed skin. Then, wearing nothing but moon shadows for a nightgown, she pulled the mosquito netting around the bed and slipped under the fine cotton sheets, to wait for him.

At last, when the music and laughter no longer drifted on the air, and the estate had sunk into a sleepy silence broken only by the occasional night sound of the jungle, Ethan emerged from the shadows.

It had been six nights since they'd made love and she, it appeared, was not the only one to have suffered from it. With a harsh intake of breath, he crossed the room, flung back the netting surrounding her bed, and reached for her in a frenzy of pent-up desire.

She rose up to meet him, and he buried his mouth against hers in a long, fierce kiss. Ran his hands up her back and down again, as if he were blind and every vertebra, every rib, every delicate muscle and tendon, spoke to him in Braille.

And when that wasn't enough to ease the ache of wanting, he ripped off his clothes and came to her in a driving rhythm so powerful that it rocked the world on its axis. So intimate that it cocooned them in a universe all their own, with neither space nor time nor wish for any other soul to share it with them.

*"Mon Dieu,"* he rasped against her mouth, as the tempo of their loving raced toward a stupendous finale, "what have you done to me, woman, that I'm so bewitched by you?"

She clung to him, desperate to halt the encroaching tremors building within her and prolong the pleasure. She turned her face to his neck and tasted the salt of his sweat as he fought his own demons of desire.

With her legs locked around his waist, she drew him deeper into her, fusing him to her so tightly that there was no discerning where he ended and she began. "I love you, Ethan," she whispered, in thrall to the convulsive pleasure overtaking her. *"I love you!"*

For a moment, he braced himself above her, his eyes wide with shock, his arms so rigid that the tendons quivered in the pale light. Then, with a groan of pure agony, he collapsed against her.

She felt his sudden gush of liquid heat, the powerful

aftershocks which shook them both, and finally, as the world outside swam back into focus, the horrified realization of what she'd said struck home.

The silence which ensued boomed with unbearable suspense and she sought desperately for words to fill it—something sane and uncompromising. Something which would reverse the damage she'd done with her impulsive confession, and return them both to that lovely, intimate place they'd shared, such a short time ago.

Nothing came to mind and, frantic to fill the void, she muttered haltingly, ''Have I ruined everything, Ethan?''

He pulled away from her, swung his legs over the side of the bed and combed his fingers through his hair. ''You've taken me by surprise,'' he said.

''Me, too. I had no idea I was going to...say what I did.''

''I know. Which is why we both need to sleep on it.'' He shook his head, as if to clear it of thoughts he didn't want to entertain, and reached for his clothes.

As miserable then, as she'd been transported, mere minutes before, she watched as he pulled on his pants, thrust his arms into the sleeves of his shirt, and tucked the tail in at his waist. That he couldn't be gone soon enough was patently obvious.

Yet, at the last, he stopped at the foot of the bed and said kindly, ''Don't look so traumatized, Anne-Marie. You're off the hook. I'm very well aware that you spoke in the heat of the moment, and will wake up in the morning wondering what in the world possessed you.''

But as things turned out, she didn't come to that realization quite so soon. Not, in fact, until the following evening.

# CHAPTER TEN

"TRULY, these friends of yours know how to throw a party!" Solange's mother, Veronique Fortier, who'd arrived on Bellefleur just that afternoon with her husband, stepped out of the Beaumont limousine in the forecourt of the Tourneau mansion, and surveyed the scene with a condescending approval which, in Anne-Marie's opinion, fell nothing short of insulting. "I confess, we had not expected such glamour and sophistication in so provincial a spot, *n'est-ce pas, mon amour?*"

*Monsieur le Consul* Maurice Fortier, suave and silver-haired, slipped an arm around his wife's fashionably thin frame and smiled apologetically at Josephine, who was glaring at the mother of the bride with fire in her eyes. How he'd managed to climb so high in the diplomatic corps with a spouse given to such decidedly undiplomatic remarks was something Anne-Marie had never been able to fathom.

"From all I've so far seen, Bellefleur appears to me to be thoroughly charming," he murmured.

In one respect, though, Veronique was quite right. The Tourneaus had spared no expense or trouble to make the evening memorable. Massive bouquets in lacquered jardinieres lined the steps and entrance hall, filled the reception rooms with their exotic perfume, and spilled down the terraces outside to join the profusion of flowers growing in the walled garden to the rear.

In the large, formal salon, a harpist plucked softly at her instrument for the pleasure of those guests seated there and at the small tables on the adjoining terrace. Down on the beach where a younger crowd gathered, the throbbing beat of a steel band filled the night.

Long, linen-draped tables in the dining hall groaned under a selection of Beluga caviar, prawns, smoked Scottish salmon, and Atlantic lobster flown in fresh that morning. A fleet of white-clad servants stood ready to serve guests. Champagne flowed like water.

The place was already crowded when the Beaumont contingent arrived, and for that, Anne-Marie was grateful. The strain of behaving as if nothing untoward had occurred between her and Ethan the previous night was taking a frightful toll, and it didn't help any that social etiquette demanded he act as her escort now.

"Please don't feel you have to stay with me," she said stiffly after, with faultless courtesy, he'd introduced her to the Tourneaus. "I'm sure there are other people here whom you'd rather socialize with, and I'm long past the age where I need a baby-sitter."

He snagged a couple of glasses of champagne from a passing waiter and pressed one into her hand. "Drink this, Anne-Marie," he ordered. "It might help sweeten your mood. And just for the record, I *never* allow myself to be coerced into spending time with someone I'd prefer to avoid."

"Not as a rule, perhaps, but you haven't been left with much of a choice lately, have you? I'm the unattached woman who can't be allowed to feel like a wallflower, and you're the one stuck with the job of keeping me entertained."

He inspected her at leisure, his blue eyes thoughtful as they swept from the top of her blond head to the tips of her strappy little gold sandals, and finally came to rest on the agitated rise and fall of her breasts. "Is that why you think I came to your bed last night?'' he asked mildly. ''To keep you entertained?''

She blushed so deeply, she was sure it was hard to tell where her rose-pink dress ended and her skin began. ''I really haven't given the matter much thought.''

''You're an atrocious liar, *ma chère*. You've thought of little else, and so, come to that, have I.'' He grasped her elbow and held her firmly to his side. ''And I think it's time we spoke frankly to one another about this elephant in the room which no one but the two of us can see.''

''You want to talk about *us* in here?'' She looked around at the crush of people, appalled. ''For heaven's sake, Ethan, I might have spoken out of turn last night, but I don't deserve to be publicly humiliated for it.''

He smiled. ''Of course not *here, Chérie!* We'll find a more private place. Did I mention, by the way, how lovely you look this evening?''

''Flattering me isn't necessary to soften the blow of whatever it is you're about to tell me.''

''What if I'm merely being truthful?'' he said, steering her outside to a quiet corner of the terrace lit only by candles hanging in delicate glass lanterns from the branches of a nearby tree.

Recalling the trouble it had landed her in the night before, she said, ''I'm not sure the truth is always such a good thing.''

''It's the *only* thing that matters between a man and a woman. How can there ever be trust, if there isn't truth?''

More agitated by the second, she twisted the pearl ring on her finger and looked away. ''You're right, of course— about everything. I'm not a good liar, never have been, and the plain truth is, I'm not feeling nearly as brave now as I was last night. In fact, I'm downright panic-stricken.''

''Then let me put you out of your misery,'' he said,

stilling the nervous movement of her hands and raising them to his lips. "You're a beautiful, generous woman, Anne-Marie, and I'd hate to think I'm too blind to recognize a gem when I see one. But—"

Sweet heaven, in trying to let her down gently, he was going to kill her with kindness! "But you're not in love with me," she babbled, unable to bear another tortured moment of uncertainty. "I understand, I really do! For some men, there's only ever one woman, one great love, and yours was your ex-wife."

"Lisa?" He laughed incredulously, and slid his hands up her arms. "Wherever did you get such an idea? She is so far from relevant to this situation that her name is an obscenity."

His touch was firm and sure, his mouth so close that she could practically taste it. For the first time in nearly twenty-four hours, a warmth chased away the chill in her blood and, against all odds, a slender thread of hope wound through her despair. Hardly daring to breathe for fear she'd shatter the mood, she whispered, "What are you saying, Ethan?"

Before he could answer, a group of four men came out of the house and when they caught sight of him, immediately headed his way. Cursing softly, he said, "I'm sorry, Anne-Marie, but it's going to have to wait. These are business associates from Venezuela, here only for a couple of days. There are matters I need to discuss with them, and if I don't do it now, I don't know when another opportunity will present itself. Will you wait for me in the garden until I'm finished?"

She nodded, swept away on a buoyant wave of optimism.

"Thank you, *mon ange.*" Cupping her cheek briefly, tenderly, he gestured to a spot beyond the immediate area.

"Hidden behind that screen of bougainvillea is a stone bench overlooking a small reflecting pool where we can talk without being disturbed. I'll meet you there."

The place was just as he described, quiet and secluded. Sprays of bougainvillea hung down from the trellis, with a few spent blossoms littering the bench which still retained the heat of the day's sun. The silver disc of the moon peeped at its image on the surface of the pool, but threw deep shadows everywhere else. Beyond the wall, the sea rolled ashore in long, lazy sighs.

Deciding she was about as close to paradise as she'd ever expected to find herself, Anne-Marie bent to brush away the papery fallen petals, and was about to sit down when footsteps approached on the other side of the screen.

"I had a wonderful time," a woman's voice, low, sultry, and unpleasantly familiar, was saying. "Miami is my kind of city and Ethan my kind of man. But we'd have had an even better time if he hadn't also brought along that tiresome child of his. I ask you, Roberto, what is the point in having more money than you can spend in four lifetimes, if you don't put it to good use? The boy could very well have been left in the care of the hired servants. Isn't that what they're for?"

"*Sí*," the man replied, his heavy Spanish accent and the mention of his name enough to clarify in Anne-Marie's mind where she'd seen and heard both him and the woman before.

Roberto Santos and Desirée LaSalle at the Plantation Club, of course!

"Do I take it then," he continued, "that you and Beaumont didn't share the same bed?"

"Alas, no."

"What a waste. The man's a bigger fool than I took him to be."

"But we had adjoining rooms." She laughed. "Once this family wedding is over and he's no longer saddled with playing nursemaid to the bride's little seamstress friend, he and I will pay a return visit to Miami. And I can promise you, Roberto, that when we do, the boy will not be coming with us, nor will there be a door separating us. I'll see to it that *nothing* comes between me and Ethan. Nothing."

"By the bride's little friend, you're referring to the Canadian?"

"Yes. Have you met her?"

"Only briefly. I found her charming."

"Then I wish you the joy of her." Desirée's voice, languid with amusement, faded as they wandered away. "I found her quite pathetic, and so, I suspect, does my poor Ethan. But he's a man of the world. He knows how to make the best of a bad situation and she's apparently very good with the child. As long as the boy's happy, Ethan will put up with a lot—too much, if you ask me! Sometimes, I think he's in danger of forgetting that there's life beyond fatherhood...."

The bench was not warm, Anne-Marie decided, realizing she was gripping its rounded edge as if her life depended on it. It was cold and hard and brutal. It cut into her hand more cruelly than a knife. Her manicure, perfect until a few moments before, was ruined. As for her heart....

She scrunched her eyes shut and drew in a tortured breath. Oh, the bench was not the only thing cast in stone! A chunk the size of her fist lay lodged behind her ribs where her heart used to be, and the pain it caused made her wish she was dead.

But that wasn't a choice. Apart from anything else,

Ethan Beaumont wasn't worth dying for, and if she hadn't known it before, she knew it now. Not only that, she'd see him in a hell to equal hers before she'd sit there in abeyance, waiting for him to show up when it was convenient, armed with more of his double-edged sweet talk!

She stalked back to the terrace, and saw at once that he was still so deep in discussion with his Venezuelan contacts that if she'd fallen in a dead faint at his feet, he probably wouldn't have noticed. Yet for all that she reviled herself for such weakness, she noticed everything about him: the pristine white jacket fitting so snugly across his broad shoulders; his dark handsome head tilted attentively as he listened to his associates; his eyes, turned navy in the candlelight, narrowed in concentration.

He leaned one elbow on the arm of his chair and propped his chin on his fist. Nodded once or twice, then gestured in response to something one of the others said. And remembering with wrenching recall how, the night before, he'd gazed at her with just the same intentness, and laid those long, clever hands on her body, Anne-Marie experienced a bolting ache of despair which made her stagger.

How naive she'd been, to think she'd ever meant anything special to him. Oh, he'd made love to her—or then again, perhaps not. Perhaps he'd merely taken her—and only now did she understand how accurate a term that was. Because he'd stolen her from herself. Robbed her of all the things which once had given her life meaning.

Blindly, she reached out, trying to regain her balance, and felt her hand grasped in a steady masculine grip. "You look pale, *señorita*," Roberto Santos murmured, bending over her. "Does the island heat not agree with you?"

Beads of perspiration broke out on her upper lip, her stomach heaved, and she was horribly afraid she might be sick. "Apparently not," she whispered, at which he slipped his arm around her waist, guided her to an empty table, and pulled out a chair.

"I will find something to revive you," he said.

"You're very kind." She fanned herself with a napkin. "Thank you."

Within seconds he returned, bearing a tall glass of water. Grateful, she accepted it and after a sip or two, rolled the side of the frosted tumbler across her heated forehead.

"Better?" Roberto Santos inquired, taking a seat opposite and watching her from heavy-lidded eyes.

She nodded. "Much. I don't know what came over me so suddenly. The heat has never bothered me before tonight."

"Then perhaps the blame lies elsewhere."

"I'm sure it does," she said, not about to admit anything incriminating which might find its way back to Desirée LaSalle's malicious ears. "I suspect I've been working too hard and not getting out enough."

"Is there anything I can do to remedy that?"

A commotion at the table in the corner caught her attention and, turning her head, she saw that Ethan had noticed both her and her companion. His glare fairly scorched the distance separating them, and he'd started up from his table so abruptly that a glass had fallen and smashed on the floor.

Deliberately turning back to Roberto Santos whose glance had followed hers, she said, "I'm actually feeling much better suddenly. If you'll join me, I'd like a glass of champagne and something to eat, and after that, I think I'd like to dance."

His teeth gleamed in a small, knowing smile. Rising, he offered her his arm. "It will be my pleasure to accom-

modate you on all counts, *Señorita* Barclay. Shall we go
inside?''

''By all means. And let's not stand on ceremony. Please
call me Anne-Marie.''

''I shall call you Anna-Maria,'' he murmured, dipping
his head to hers until his black ponytail almost brushed
her cheek. ''It flows more musically in Spanish, don't you
agree?''

''*Sí,*'' she cooed, favoring him with her most dazzling
smile, all the time vividly aware of Ethan as she swayed
past his table close enough that he could have tripped her
up if he'd had the wits to stick his foot out far enough.
But he appeared too paralyzed with rage to move.

Fine! Let him stew in his own juice, for a change!

Once inside the house, though, with no Ethan for a cap-
tive audience, the game of one-upmanship lost what little
charm it possessed. ''I'm really not up to this, after all,''
she said, begging off a third energetic samba with Roberto.
''Would you be kind enough to find *Monsieur* Beaumont's
driver and ask him to take me home?''

But it turned out that, not ten minutes earlier, Josephine
and Louis had commandeered the chauffeur for the same
task. ''Which is no problem at all, Anna-Maria,'' Roberto
assured her. ''I'll be happy to drive you there myself.''

She knew that, in accepting, she was courting trouble,
but it didn't compare to what she'd already endured that
night. If he tried to make a pass at her, she'd set him
straight in very short order.

He surprised her, though, making no effort to touch her
or engage her in innuendo of any kind. If anything, he
seemed genuinely sympathetic, an impression borne out
when, before leaving her at the villa gates, he handed her
a business card and said, ''If circumstances were otherwise, I would suggest a different way to end this evening.

But I see that you are deeply troubled and so I will say only this: if I can be of service to you in any capacity during the remainder of your stay here, Anna-Maria, you have only to ask. I can be reached at this number anytime, day or night.''

Embarrassed to find herself on the brink of tears, she took the card and said, ''You've already been of enormous help. I don't know how I would have managed tonight, if you hadn't stepped forward to pick up the pieces when I fell apart at the Tourneaus.''

He shrugged. ''I had no choice. I am not a popular figure on Bellefleur as, I'm sure, you're probably aware. I have made mistakes and will likely make many more before I die. But I am not the monster Ethan makes me out to be. I am simply a man who finds it difficult to turn his back on a woman in distress. So I say to you again, if you need me, you have only to call.''

''No,'' she said wearily. ''It wouldn't be fair, and my stay here is almost over anyway. So do yourself a favor and forget this night ever happened, Roberto. I certainly intend to.''

A midnight hush hung over the moon-dappled gardens as she made her way down to her quarters. That such calm beauty reigned all around while nothing but ugliness ate away at her, was more than she could bear. Stripping off her sandals, she ran barefoot the last hundred yards and didn't stop until, out of breath and out of emotional stamina, she gained refuge inside the villa.

''Three more days,'' she mumbled, feeling her way into the bedroom, and slumping against the wall, too weary to undress and climb into bed. ''Three more days, and then I'll be out of here. It can't happen soon enough.''

''I quite agree.'' Ethan's voice swam out of the dark,

startling her so thoroughly that she let out a shriek. And then, before she could begin to regain her composure, he turned on a lamp and, dazzled, she dropped her sandals and flung up her arm to shield her eyes.

"What's the matter, Anne-Marie?" he inquired coldly. "Too ashamed to look me in the face?"

"*Me* ashamed?" she spluttered, squinting to where he slouched in one of the wicker chairs on the verandah. "You've got some nerve, Ethan Beaumont, accusing me of that! And what the hell do you think you're doing, sneaking into my room like this?"

"You've never objected before, my dear. What's the problem, this time? Afraid there won't be room for three of us in the bed?" He hitched himself straighter in the chair and made a big production of craning his neck to scan the open doorway beside her. "Where is Santos, by the way? Lying in the weeds, waiting to be sure the coast is clear before he makes his next move?"

"I won't even dignify that remark with a reply," she informed him, "although I suppose I shouldn't be surprised that you'd try to shift responsibility for this night's fiasco to my shoulders. It's typical behavior for the abuser to heap blame on his victim."

"You're my victim?" He rose smoothly from his seat to loom, tall and dangerous, over her. "Then I must have missed something in your little performance at the Tourneaus, because I'm of a distinctly different impression. Enlighten me, please."

She turned away because, even in his present ugly mood, she was still so drawn to him that all she wanted to do was fling herself into his arms and forget every horrible thing she'd learned in the past few hours. "Just before your business associates showed up tonight, you were about to bare your soul to me, Ethan. What was it you were so anxious to tell me—that you'd taken Desirée LaSalle with you to Miami, perhaps?''

He didn't flinch. "No," he said calmly. "On that subject, there's nothing to tell."

"Oh, please! I overheard her bragging about how you had adjoining rooms."

"Yes? And your point is?"

"That you've been lying to me!" she cried. "You told me you weren't interested in her."

"I'm not."

"So why did you take her with you?"

"She wanted to go shopping. Miami has some very good shops. There are very few commercial flights from here to the mainland. I had space on my private jet. Does that answer your question?"

"She said...." What *had* Desirée LaSalle said, exactly? Pinching the bridge of her nose between two fingers, Anne-Marie shook her head. "She *said*—"

"I really don't care what she said," Ethan said softly. "What concerns me is that you set such store by it. We talked about establishing a bond of trust earlier. If finding out exactly what did or did not take place between me and Desirée was so upsetting to you, why didn't you come to me, instead of turning for comfort to a man like Roberto Santos?"

"If you had nothing to hide, why didn't you tell me of your own free will that she was with you? You've had opportunity enough."

"I am your host, not your husband, Anne-Marie. I neither needed your permission nor owed you an explanation. Furthermore, in case you've forgotten, Adrian also went with me to Miami. I'd hardly expose him to the kind of behavior you're accusing me of, and I thought you knew me better than to suppose I would."

At some level, she recognized both the truth and the logic of what he told her. But that he could remain so unmoved in the face of her obvious distress goaded her to recklessness. "Clearly, I don't know you well at all."

"Nor I, you. What a good thing we've shown ourselves in our true colors, before matters between us progressed further."

"They were never going to progress further, Ethan! Do you think I couldn't see what you were leading up to, tonight? Oh, you were being very gentlemanly, very charming, but it doesn't change the fact that you were looking for a way to get rid of me tactfully."

"Was I?" He flicked a minute speck of something from the cuff of his jacket. "Well, you certainly gave me one, didn't you?"

"And how do you figure that?"

"You made a spectacle of yourself with the one man in the world whom you know I detest above all others and with very good reason. You let him ply you with champagne, then got into a car with him, aware not only of his driving record but of his sordid morals."

"For what it's worth, he behaved like a perfect gentleman."

"Then I can only say that your concept of the term differs vastly from mine, which shouldn't come as any great surprise to me, given your own atrocious behavior."

"*Mine?*" She stared at him, outraged.

"Yes, yours." Impassively, he stared back. "You arrived at the party with me, and in full view of people I've known all my life and who've treated you with exemplary courtesy and respect, you left with him. That might be acceptable in your circles, but it doesn't wash in mine. So add all that up, my dear Anne-Marie, and you'll understand, I'm sure, when I tell you that you can save your *I love you*'s for someone who wants to hear them, because I'm certainly not interested.''

"My goodness!" she exclaimed. "And to think I deluded myself for a second into thinking you might actually care about me!"

"I did care. I'm not in the habit of sleeping with a woman who isn't important to me."

"But she'd better be perfect, just like you, or else she's history! No wonder your wife turned to another man. She probably couldn't stand living with a saint."

White with anger, he lunged out of the chair. "And you tempt me to forget I am a civilized man!"

"Well, that won't do, will it, Ethan? It might show you to be as full of human weakness as the next man."

She'd gone too far. Much, much too far!

He advanced on her with such swift, lethal grace that she found herself inching toward the door. But his arm snaked out to trap her, and jerked her up against him. His mouth sealed itself against hers in a kiss so hard and explosive that she moaned in protest. Gradually, though, his lips softened in lingering seduction, and she turned fluid with weakness, and moaned for a different reason.

When the kiss ended, he caught her chin between his thumb and forefinger so that her face remained tilted up to his. "You think I don't have my share of weaknesses? That I don't make mistakes and despise myself for them afterward?" he asked in a low, savage voice. "Then take a look at the self-loathing in my eyes right now, Anne-Marie, and think again!"

Then he tossed her aside as if she were no more than a piece of flotsam he'd found washed up on one of his precious, perfect beaches, and stalked out.

# CHAPTER ELEVEN

THE wedding rehearsal took place the following evening. At nine in the morning, a servant delivered a note from Ethan, summoning Anne-Marie to the main house.

"What have you done to my nephew?" Josephine whispered, catching her in the inner courtyard, the second she arrived. "The temperature here drops to near-freezing every time he puts in an appearance! Should I take it the two of you have had a falling out?"

Before she could reply, Ethan showed up. "In here," he said, brusquely, jerking his thumb over his shoulder to a room at the east end of the lower hall.

Josephine gave Anne-Marie's arm a sympathetic squeeze. "I pray you emerge alive, child!"

The room was set up as an office. Leaving her to trail after him like the obedient subordinate he considered her to be, Ethan strode across the floor and sat down in a black leather chair behind a massive desk made of some exotic wood. "Have a seat," he said, in the same take-no-prisoners tone.

The only other chairs faced the window. With the sun still so low in the sky, the verandahs did little to diminish its glare.

Anne-Marie had not slept well. In fact, she hadn't slept at all. But she'd done a lot of useless crying, as her puffy eyes and blotchy complexion showed. She hardly needed to have it bathed in bright morning light, while the man responsible for all her misery looked as fresh and crisp as a newly-ironed shirt.

She hadn't weathered years of coping on her own without learning a thing or two, though. Betraying hurt feelings was a weakness which invited nothing but pity from the one who'd inflicted pain in the first place, so she remained just inside the door and said, "No thanks. And I don't know why you've sent for me, but it had better be important, because I've got a hundred other things waiting to be taken care of today."

"Then I'll get straight to the point," he said and, despite herself, she shivered, the lingering hope that perhaps he'd undergone a change of heart since she'd seen him last withering under the frost of his tone. Reaching into a drawer, he pulled out the outfit she'd made for Adrian and tossed it on the desk. It landed askew, like a rag doll flung aside by a petulant child. "We'll start with this."

"Am I to assume that you have a problem with it?"

"That you even need to ask tells me how little our tastes or expectations ever coincided."

She stepped forward and smoothed her hand over the finely-textured fabric. "And I suppose it doesn't matter to you one iota that Adrian chose this over a more conventional outfit, and is thrilled at the idea of wearing it?"

"Oh, he may wear it," Ethan said scornfully. "The next time he takes part in his school's annual play, that is, or at a friend's fancy-dress Christmas party. Under no circumstances, though, will he appear at a family wedding in it. But perhaps you forgot that's the reason you're here— or else you don't know the difference between the solemn rites of matrimony and a gaudy Hollywood extravaganza?"

"He's just a little boy, Ethan, and as ring bearer, he wanted to wear something distinctive and different."

"He will wear the morning suit created for him by my personal tailor."

"He'll be stuffed into something designed for a grown man, you mean? Good grief, you'll be expecting him to shave, next!"

"It's what I expect from you that you should be concerned about."

She sighed and rolled her eyes. "And now we get down to the real reason you hauled me up before your lordliness!"

Ignoring the barb, he said, "Our respective roles as maid of honor and best man mean we can't avoid one another until this wedding is over. But however much we might wish it were already done with, this time belongs to Solange and Philippe, and I will allow nothing to spoil it for them. Nor will I permit any behavior which might draw unfavorable attention to my family's name and reputation. Do we understand one another, Anne-Marie?"

"Perfectly," she snapped. "But just for the record, I'm agreeing to your terms solely out of respect for the other members of your family and for my best friend because, quite frankly, what you might want or not want no longer matters to me."

"Appearances are all that count," he said, swiveling the chair so that his back was toward her. "As long as we're in agreement on that, there's nothing more to be said. You may leave."

She'd have preferred to make a dignified exit, but his contempt sparked an anger in her which wouldn't go unsatisfied. "Who do you think you're talking to, you pompous jerk?" she spat, glaring at the back of his handsome, aristocratic head. "I'm not one of the underlings in your little puppet empire in which you, and only you, pull all the strings, and I will not take orders from you! Nor will I submit to becoming the chattel in your ridiculous turf war with Roberto Santos. I have done nothing—*nothing* to deserve being treated like this.''

''You have shown yourself to be untrustworthy and immature,'' he said flatly.

''While your conduct, of course, has been forever above reproach.'' Despite her best effort, her voice broke. ''Somehow, no matter how hard I tried, where you were concerned, Ethan, it was never quite enough, was it? Your suspicions never quite faded away. Even when we were intimate together, you held something back. Not passion— that was beyond even your monumental self-control. You made love, but you didn't give love. You just lent it for a little while.''

''What's the point in belaboring matters now, Anne-Marie?'' he said stonily. ''Nothing you say changes the fact that I thought you were different from the woman I married, but the first time the question of integrity arose, you showed yourself to be cut from the very same cloth.''

''Did I really? Well, as a matter of interest, Ethan, would you have reacted quite as violently if I'd turned to any man other than Roberto Santos, last night?''

He swung back to face her, his features carved in stone. ''As a matter of interest, would you have bothered to turn to any other man *but* Santos to advertise your displeasure with me? Wasn't that the whole point of your little exhibition?''

''No,'' she said, past caring about pride or dignity. ''I was devastated by what I'd overheard, and he stepped in to save me from making a complete fool of myself in front of strangers. But if I'd had a choice, I'd rather it had been you who came to my rescue. Instead, you found a way to sneak ahead of me into my room, and ambushed me with recriminations before I had a chance to collect myself.''

"Only a person with something to hide needs a chance to get her story straight."

"Something to hide?" she scoffed. "I'm not the one who smuggled a companion aboard my private jet and didn't say a word about it! But since we're having a tell-all session, just how did you manage to get back here before me, last night? And don't bother suggesting it was because I took my own sweet time, because Roberto drove me straight home."

"I took a shortcut through the jungle."

"In the dark? A likely tale!"

"You forget I was born on this island. I know its terrain as well as I know my own face."

"Then all I can say is that it's a pity you didn't cut through the impromptu conference with your Venezuelan friends with equal dispatch. We might not be having this conversation then."

"A man can't base his life on might-have-been's, Anne-Marie. He has to deal with what is. You and I come from different worlds. We were fools to believe we might find enough common ground to forge a lasting relationship, and the proof surely lies in the fact that a harmless incident was enough to sabotage our efforts."

"If you're talking about Desirée LaSalle," she said, drifting to the door so emotionally depleted that she felt hollow inside, "she's about as harmless as a black widow spider, and I hope for Adrian's sake that you realize it before she has you in her clutches."

"I can survive anything Desirée throws at me," he shot back. "After all, I survived Lisa. And you."

The rehearsal for the ceremony took place at five o'clock in the church in town, and as far as Anne-Marie was concerned, it might have been a foretaste of heaven for Solange and Philippe, but it was a prelude to hell for her.

Afterward, the bride's parents hosted a dinner party at the Plantation Club. It, too, was a ghastly experience made that much worse by the memory of the last time Anne-Marie had found herself there with Ethan.

Things between them had been so much more clear-cut when her chief impressions of him had been of sheer physical beauty overshadowed by stiff formality and overweening arrogance. But they'd been surface impressions only, revealing little of his capability for passion, and to be forced to sit so close to him now that she knew the difference caused her the most poignant agony.

How could she be expected to close her heart and mind to him when the faint scent of his soap tormented her with memories of the times they'd made love; of the taste and texture of his skin, the brush of his hand, the touch of his mouth? How was she supposed to equate all that with the cool, impassive man sitting beside her now, and not find herself awash in misery?

"I thought we had an agreement that we'd put aside our differences for now," he said, looking anywhere but at her, as the main course was cleared away.

"I'm trying."

"Then I suggest you try harder," he said unfeelingly. "You're not the only one who's suffered a setback, but you don't see me visibly wallowing in self-pity."

"I'm not you, Ethan. I don't have your steely ability to cut myself off from my emotions," she replied, staring into her wineglass and struggling to hang on to her self-control. She'd have succeeded, too, but the pitiful tremble in her voice gave her away.

"You might find it easier if you stopped swilling back

champagne,'' he informed her. ''At this rate, they're going to have to scrape you up off the floor before much longer.''

She turned to glare at him, outraged by the injustice of his accusation. ''I've hardly drunk anything but water!''

''I know,'' he said, with grim irony. ''But at least now you're annoyed enough to show a little life, instead of looking and acting like a corpse. 'Pale and interesting' does not become you.''

''I'm surprised you noticed!''

''Let's hope I'm the only one who does, because I meant what I said this morning. You've created enough trouble already, and I'll be damned if I'll stand by and let you cause more. *Nothing* is going to cast a cloud over my brother's wedding.''

''Stop trying to manage me, Ethan,'' she said waspishly. ''I won't be managed by you or anyone else.''

''You don't have any choice in the matter, my dear. The most you can do is take comfort in the fact that by tomorrow at this time, it'll all be over and you won't have to put up with me giving you orders ever again.''

''That's right.'' She dared to look him in the eye again and raised her glass in a mocking toast. ''Here's to going back to being the people we were before we met.''

But the truth was, she'd never be the same again. A broken woman had replaced the heart-whole, successful business entrepreneur who'd landed on Bellefleur well over a month ago and who was now gone for good. All those things she'd once thought important had been eclipsed by love for a man who didn't want her, and a little boy who needed her but couldn't have her.

That night, as always, he stopped by Adrian's room last thing. From the beginning, it had been his favorite time of day, with the house quiet around him and his son peacefully sleeping, but it had become particularly important since Lisa had left.

During those few quiet minutes, Ethan could search the child's face without worrying that his own might give away the doubts which hounded him. Could silently convey the words he wished he could speak openly.

*Am I enough, mon petit? Do you blame me for your mother not being here? Should I have gone after her and brought her back, for your sake? Do you dream about her, miss her, cry for her when I'm not there to dry your tears? Do you worry that, one day, I, too, might leave and never come back?*

Sometimes, a great upsurge of paternal love choked him and nothing would do but that he hold Adrian close, as he had when the boy was still an infant. Curbing the urge to hug him too fiercely, he'd cradle his son against his chest and attempt to absorb into his own cold soul the warm innocence and trust that childhood was all about.

Occasionally, the boy would stir, scour his eyes with a chubby fist, and murmur sleepily, "I love you, Papa," before falling instantly asleep again. At such times, Ethan's heart would swell with gratitude and he'd steal from the room, knowing he himself would sleep in peace.

Not tonight, though. Tonight, he felt more at a loss than he had the day his ex-wife had bailed out of motherhood and marriage, and he approached the bed with a heavy heart, dreading what he might find imprinted on his son's sleeping face.

The cheeks were flushed, the eyelashes a dark sweep of color, the mouth soft as a woman's. But the dried tear tracks told of the emotional storm which had taken place earlier, as did the foolish garment lying crumpled on the floor beside the bed.

*Why can't I wear it? It's mine, and I like it!*

*It isn't suitable, my son.*

*But Anne-Marie made it specially for me. She said—*

*It doesn't matter what she said. She doesn't understand how we live on Bellefleur. She's not one of us.*

*She is so! Why do you always spoil everything? Anne-Marie will go away, the same as Mama did, and it's all your fault! I hate you, Papa!*

About to reach out and smooth the unruly spill of hair on the pillow, Ethan stopped, afraid not that his touch might awaken his son, but that he himself wouldn't be able to bear the disillusionment he might find in those dark, sleepy eyes.

*I brought this on both of us,* he thought, sick with regret. *I have rocked the foundation of both our worlds by allowing her to grow close to us. If I'd paid attention to my instincts and kept her at a distance, things never would have come to this.*

A perfect sunrise greeted the wedding day. Awake early, Anne-Marie stepped out into a morning filled with birdsong and the scent of flowers.

*I can do this,* she told herself. *I can cope with everything I have to face today. I can walk down the aisle knowing Ethan's standing at the altar, and not let myself get swept away by impossible dreams. I won't pine for what I'm never going to have.*

She held on to that thought throughout the private breakfast with Solange, her parents, and the other bridesmaid, Angelique Tourneau. She managed to laugh when they went through the ritual of giving the bride "something old, something new, something borrowed, something blue." She swallowed hard when, an hour before the ceremony began, her hours of labor were rewarded by the sight of

Solange, blindingly radiant in her cloud of white silk organza, and told herself again, *I can do this! I can!*

When they gathered in the forecourt where two horse-drawn carriages waited to take them to the church, and she saw Adrian looking like a miniature of his father in the formal morning suit, she blinked and clamped her lips together and willed herself not to think about saying good-bye to him the next day. *One step at a time, Anne-Marie!* she ordered the quivering mass of emotion hidden under the pale aquamarine silk of her dress. *You can do this!*

"You look *so* beautiful, Anne-Marie," Adrian said, running up to clasp her hand and gazing up at her as if she were the most exquisite creature ever born. "Beautifuller than Solange. Beautifuller than anybody in the whole world!"

Just briefly, she almost broke down. Then, at the last second, she wrestled the huge lump in her throat into submission and sternly repeated her mantra. *I can do this!*

"And you're the most handsome young man I've ever seen," she managed, hoping he wouldn't notice how her voice wobbled and her smile kept slipping out of place.

Shortly after, with the faint echo of church bells drifting over the island, they climbed into the carriages and set off. Half the population of Bellefleur lined the sun-splashed roads, eager for a glimpse of bride as she passed by. The other half crowded the square in the center of town.

And throughout all that followed—entry into the old stone church, the processional up the aisle, and the ancient, beautiful words of the marriage ceremony—somehow, Anne-Marie held fast to her resolve. *I can do this!*

But, in the end, when it came time to take Ethan's arm and walk beside him in the recessional march back down the aisle, she could not do it, after all. The sheer willpower which had carried her that far evaporated, and she started to shake so badly that her little bouquet of gardenias trembled as if caught in a sudden breeze.

"Hold on," Ethan murmured, his free hand reaching over to steady her. "It's almost over."

It wasn't, though. She had to pose beside him for interminable photographs. Had to join him in the carriage on the return journey to the villa. Had to sit beside him during the long, elaborate reception, and smile graciously when he toasted her and thanked her for all she'd done to make the day so memorable. Then, as the early tropical twilight descended and a thousand candles added to the moonlight spilling through the lacy iron doors of the inner courtyard, she had to dance with him. Feel his arm around her, his thigh brushing against hers, his hand warm and compelling in the small of her back.

It was too much. Too painful, too ironic, too everything!

"I can't take much more of this," she said, squeezing her eyes shut against the persistent prick of tears.

"Of me, you mean?"

"Of us."

"There is no 'us.' There never was, not really. The way I see it, having you step in as my hostess lulled us both into a false sense that we belonged together, that we were a couple, and we somehow forgot it was all just pretense."

"Blame everything on that, if you like, but what really sank us is that you lied to me by omission and didn't like being caught at it."

"By all means believe that, if it makes you feel better," he said. "The important thing is that we came to our senses before any lasting damage was done."

Oh, how she envied him his resilience! And how, for a brief, blessed moment, she hated him for emerging unscathed when she herself was wounded to the core. "Speak for yourself, Ethan, but don't ever presume to know what

I'm feeling! *You're* the one who sabotaged our relationship, and I've had about enough of listening to you trying to rationalize your way out of it.''

He swung her into one last turn as the music died, and released her. ''Then you'll be relieved to know the ordeal's almost over,'' he said. ''It looks as if the newlyweds are preparing to leave. Better join the other unmarried hopefuls milling around the bride.''

''No,'' she said, a terrible chill chasing over her where, a moment before, she'd felt the warmth of his touch.

''Yes,'' he said, taking her elbow and almost dragging her toward the grand staircase where Solange stood four steps up, ready to toss her bouquet over her shoulder. ''It's expected of you.''

She shrugged herself free of his grip. ''Fine! I'll perform this one last service, and then I'll be free of you and all your inflexible, impossible *expectations!*''

Disgruntled, disheartened, she deliberately stood apart from the women clustered eagerly at the foot of the stairs. Let one of them catch the damned flowers, if being the next bride meant so much to them! After her recent experience with love, marriage came so far down her list of priorities that it didn't rate a mention.

But either Solange had lousy aim, or the demons weren't yet done tormenting Anne-Marie, because the bouquet sailed clean over all those immaculately coiffed heads and aimed directly for her. Instinctively, she reached up and caught it—it was either that, or have it smack her squarely in the face.

It appeared to be a popular decision. Everyone cheered and applauded. Everyone, that was, but Ethan because, when she turned to acknowledge the crowd, he was no longer part of it.

# CHAPTER TWELVE

SHE was packed and ready to leave by ten the next day.
The letter to Ethan was written, she'd phoned Morton to
arrange for her luggage to be brought up to the main house
and for a car to take her to the airport. All that remained
was to pay one last visit to Josephine. At that hour, she'd
be taking coffee on the verandah outside the morning salon.

Curiously numb, Anne-Marie stopped to take one last
look around the guest pavilion. Already it wore the deserted air of a place filled only with ghosts, but they'd be
chased away soon enough, when the next batch of visitors
arrived. Would that she could be as easily rid of them!

Burying a sigh, she turned and walked slowly through
the gardens, memory after memory layering her mind.
Here was the trail where she'd ridden behind him on horse-
back, her body still sweetly singing from their lovemaking,
and here the koi pond where she'd first seen him. And
finally, as she emerged from the shade of the overhanging
greenery, and followed the winding path to the south terrace, there the big infinity pool where he'd forced her into
an impromptu swimming lesson.

As expected, Josephine sat in her usual high-backed
wicker chair, a tray on the table before her. ''What do you
mean, you're leaving?'' she demanded, pausing in the middle of refilling her coffee cup, and regarding Anne-Marie
with a mixture of surprise and indignation. ''Child, I expected you'd stay at least another week. Now that all the
excitement's over and we have the place to ourselves

again, I was looking forward to our spending some quiet time together.''

''I'm sorry to disappoint you, but I simply can't do that, Madame Duclos. I don't belong here, and now that Solange and Philippe have left for their honeymoon, there's no reason for me to stay. But I couldn't leave without first telling you how much your friendship has come to mean to me.''

''Friendship? Child, you're part of my family, and blood ties be damned!''

Family. The one thing she missed so much. Oh, if only it were possible to be absorbed into this one! But it couldn't be. She had no interest in becoming Ethan's adopted sister or cousin.

''That's the nicest thing you could have said to me,'' she sniffled, forgetting any idea she'd entertained that she might make a dignified exit, ''and I love you for it, I really do.''

''Enough to start calling this old woman *Tante* Josephine, and keep her company a while longer?''

''I'd be honored to call you Aunt, but....'' She fought a losing battle with the lump in her throat and choked out, ''I have to go.''

''Things didn't work out with Ethan, then?'' Josephine eyed her shrewdly. ''I suspected as much, the way you both behaved yesterday.''

''Were we very obvious?''

''Only to me, child. Suffice it to say, I'm very sorry.''

''The odds were against us from the beginning.''

''Isn't it possible, if you stayed, that the two of you might be able to work things out?''

''No.'' A single tear tracked down her face. Wiping it away, Anne-Marie looked out at the hummingbirds fighting over territorial rights in the garden. Such beautiful creatures, but so fiercely protective of their own! Had they taken lessons from Ethan, she wondered. "You yourself warned me, the second night I was here, that once Ethan makes up his mind, nothing changes it. And I'm afraid he's made up his mind about me."

Josephine sighed and laid her head against the back of her chair. "It would appear that you've made up yours, too."

"Yes."

"You'll be coming back you know. Often. We won't have it any other way."

"Perhaps I will. But not for a long time."

"Because of my nephew?"

"Because I'm not very good at saying goodbye. Which is why I'm going to ask you to give this to Ethan for me." She dropped the letter on the table. "I really can't face seeing him again."

"You don't have to," Josephine said wearily. "He left for Venezuela last night, immediately after the wedding was over." She hauled herself upright and fixed Anne-Marie in one of her penetrating stares. "If you're adamant about leaving, I'll do as you ask and give him your note when he returns, but I will *not* act as your messenger with Adrian. He'll be devastated if you leave without seeing him."

"I know." Anne-Marie swallowed. "I dread having to tell him. I've come to love him—to love *all* of you, dearly."

"As we have come to love you, *ma chère*—those of us with any sense, at least." She eased herself out of the chair and held out her arms. "Give me a hug to remember you by until we meet again."

Half-blind with tears, Anne-Marie went to her, kissed

her cheek and inhaled the delicate, powdery fragrance that
was Josephine.

*I'll never smell heliotrope again without thinking of her,*
she thought, as another tear slipped loose. *"Au revoir, ma
tante."*

A discreet cough from within the morning salon ended
the moment. "The car is waiting to take you to the airport
whenever you're ready, *Mademoiselle,"* Morton announced. "And I have advised the pilot that you'll be
needing the jet to take you to the mainland."

Voice cracking, Josephine murmured, *"Au revoir,* child,
and Godspeed."

Not trusting herself to speak again, Anne-Marie nodded,
pressed a last kiss to her cheek, and followed the butler
out to the forecourt. There, Adrian huddled in the shade
of a coconut palm, his little face creased with misery.

"I don't want you to go," he whimpered, the minute
he saw her. "Please, *please,* don't!"

She hadn't thought she had the capacity to endure any
more angst, but the sight and sound of him dealt yet another blow to her battered heart. "Oh, Adrian, I'd stay if
I could."

"That's what everybody always says," he cried, "but
they go anyway and leave me by myself. First Maman left,
then Papa went away, and now you're going."

"But Papa will be home again soon," she said, kneeling
in front of him and gathering him close. "He always
comes back, darling, you know that."

Adrian, though, had worked himself up into such a state
that he was inconsolable. "No," he sobbed against her
neck. "He went away because I was bad. He doesn't like
me anymore."

"You're never bad," she said, shocked that he'd even

think such a thing. "You're the best little boy in the whole world, and your papa adores you."

"Not anymore," he said again, a fresh spate of tears shaking his little body. "Nobody likes me anymore. They don't even notice I'm here."

Anne-Marie raised her eyes, mutely asking for help in coping with the situation from the nanny hovering in the background. The nanny stared back, unable to offer any. And in all fairness, how could she be expected to, when much of what Adrian said was true?

Apart from his brief role in yesterday's ceremony, he'd been shunted aside in all the pre-wedding hype of the last few days. And now that it was over, the people he most relied on were abandoning him, one by one, first with Solange leaving, then Ethan, and now she herself.

"I'm so sorry," she murmured, kissing his mop of soft, dark hair. "I'd stay if I could, but if I don't leave now, I'll miss my flight."

"No, you won't," he wept, lifting his tear-drenched face to hers. "It's Papa's jet, and it won't go 'til you tell it to. You *don't* have to go yet, Anne-Marie. You could stay a little bit longer if you really wanted to…if you really loved me the way I love you!"

If she hadn't come to know him well enough to recognize that he was the least likely child in the world to resort without cause to such a torrent of emotional blackmail, she wouldn't have caved in. But even a stranger could have seen his distress was genuine, and she couldn't turn away from him. Her bruised heart wouldn't allow it; it had taken enough punishment.

"I suppose I could stay another day or two," she conceded, "but only until Papa comes home. You do understand that, Adrian, don't you?"

His lip quivered. "Yes."

She looked over to where the ever-patient Morton waited at the car, and shrugged. "You must have heard."

He inclined his head. *"Oui, mademoiselle."*

"I'm sorry for the inconvenience—"

"Not at all," he said sympathetically. *"Monsieur's* son is more important. We all understand."

Josephine's response was much less restrained when she learned of the change in plans. "Well, hallelujah!" she exclaimed, her wise old eyes suddenly misting over. "Adrian succeeded where I failed, and managed to talk some sense into you!"

"It's only until Ethan comes back," Anne-Marie cautioned her. "Please let's all be clear on that."

"We'll take whatever we can get. *Mademoiselle* will be staying here in the main house, Morton. Put her bags in the suite beside Adrian's. The boy will feel better knowing she's close by, and so will I."

Surprisingly, so did Anne-Marie, for all that she'd been so anxious to leave before. Without the fear that Ethan might show up at any minute, the slow and easy pace of island life soothed her troubled soul, and the day drifted past, its tranquility broken only by quiet conversation, the clink of china during lunch and afternoon tea, and the sound of Adrian's laughter as he splashed in the pool.

That evening, she kept him company while he ate a light supper, then tucked him into bed, read him a story, and at his request, listened while he said his prayers.

"Make Anne-Marie stay forever, heavenly father," he ordered, closing his eyes and clasping his hands, "and that's all for today because I'm tired."

Clearly, he had a unique relationship with God!

Hiding a smile, Anne-Marie tiptoed out of the room and joined Louis and Josephine for dinner on the terrace. It was dark by then, and although the sky overhead remained clear, the usual late onshore breeze had died, leaving the atmosphere thick and breathless. By the time the meal was over, a line of cloud creeping up from the south had obscured the stars.

"We're in for a spell of bad weather," Louis remarked, leading the way inside. "Hurricane season's come early this year."

They were lingering over coffee and cognac when the tranquility came to an abrupt end—not, as might have been expected, because of the approaching storm, but by the arrival of the chief of Bellefleur's tiny police force.

"Forgive me for interrupting your evening, but I've received a report from the authorities in Caracas," he began, and his tone alone was enough to tell them he wasn't bringing good news. "*Monsieur* Beaumont left there by helicopter this morning, en route to an oil platform some seventy miles from the Venezuelan coast. However, possibly because of adverse conditions, he never arrived at his destination, nor has he been heard from since."

Josephine turned as pale as parchment and reached for Louis's hand. "Have they sent out a search party?"

"*Non, madame.* By the time anyone knew he was missing, night had fallen, but they will start looking at first light tomorrow."

"Who else was with him?" Louis asked shakily.

"No one."

"*No one?*" Anne-Marie smothered a gasp. "He flew out there alone, knowing the weather was poor?"

"*Oui, Mademoiselle,* but he is an experienced pilot." The chief backed toward the door, his expression grave. "I'm very sorry to be the bearer of such distressing news. Be assured every effort will be made to bring *Monsieur* Beaumont home safely again."

"You'll keep us informed?" Louis said.

"Of course, *monsieur*. As soon as I hear anything, I will be in touch. I am certain we will receive good news in the morning."

But they didn't, not that day, or the next, or the one after that. Instead, the weather responsible for his disappearance closed in over the island in a series of storms which left the garden littered with debris.

Not once during that time did Anne-Marie cry, because to do so would have been to admit the worst—that Ethan would never come home again. And that she couldn't bear to dwell on. A world without Ethan simply wasn't a world she wanted to be part of.

"We have to have faith," she told an increasingly distraught Josephine. "We have to believe he's coming back, for all our sakes, especially Adrian's. He needs his father."

But with the staff aware and talking among themselves of the disaster which had struck, eventually there was no keeping the news from the child. He couldn't be allowed to find out by accident that his beloved papa was missing.

No one expected he'd take the news well, but nor was anyone prepared for the way he responded. "It's my fault," he said, in a bleak, resigned little voice, when they explained that there'd been a storm at sea. "I wished bad things and now they've happened. I told Papa I hated him, and now he's dead."

"No, darling," they rushed to assure him. "Papa is just lost, and it was an accident. Nobody's to blame. Certainly not you."

But there was no moving him. "It was me. I did it," he said, and when they tried to hold him and comfort him, he wriggled free and ran up to his room.

"Let him be, child," Josephine said sadly, when Anne-Marie made to go after him. "He's his father's son, taking the blame for everything that goes wrong, and shutting himself off from those who love him, to bleed in private. That's just their way. He'll come to us when he's ready, you'll see.''

But when noon arrived and still Adrian hadn't reappeared, Anne-Marie couldn't bear it a moment longer. It wasn't natural for a child so young to be bear such a crushing burden of unfounded guilt alone. It wasn't right.

''I've come to take Adrian down to lunch,'' she told the maid she found changing the bed linen in his room.

''He's not here,'' the girl replied.

''Do you know where he went?''

''*Non, mademoiselle.* He said only that he was going to find his papa.''

A chill ran over Anne-Marie. There'd been no sign of the child for over an hour. If he'd come downstairs, it had been stealthily enough for none of them to notice.

Unwilling to heap further stress on the frail shoulders of the old couple waiting so anxiously for word of their missing nephew, she told the girl, ''We have to find that child. Help me search the rooms up here.''

But although they scoured every inch of the upper floor, and roped in other staff members to look in every nook and cranny of the main floor, all they found was Adrian's kitten curled up asleep under a chair. Of Adrian himself, there wasn't a sign.

''And why would he be here?'' Anne-Marie exclaimed, running a despairing hand through her hair. ''If he was going to look for his father, it makes sense that he'd go outside. We're looking in the wrong place!''

''But he knows that his father wasn't on the island when he became lost,'' Morton reminded her. ''He won't find him in the garden and it's not possible for him to open the main gates and escape onto the road, so he must still be here somewhere.''

A logical enough assumption, but Anne-Marie's relief was short-lived as another possibility occurred to her, one so terrifying that she couldn't bring herself to utter it aloud.

Instead, she said, "Please go about your normal business and don't say a word to alarm *Monsieur* or *Madame* Duclos. Serve lunch as usual, and if they ask where I am, tell them I've gone for a stroll and will be back shortly."

"A stroll? In this weather?" Morton raised skeptical eyebrows. "*Mademoiselle,* I doubt they will accept such an explanation."

"I'm used to wind and rain," she told him. "And that's the reason you give them, should they question you. But under no circumstance do you let them know that Adrian is missing and I've gone looking for him."

"Forgive me, *Mademoiselle,* but it is more than my job here is worth for me to let you put yourself at risk. I must insist on knowing what you plan to do."

"I think that boy's gone down to the beach," she said, looking the man straight in the eye and not even blinking at telling only half the truth. "He knows his father was lost at sea. In his mind, he expects that's how he'll come home again, and he's down there waiting for him."

*Please let that be all he's done!* she prayed, racing through the gardens, not to the steps below the guest pavilion, but to that other trail which led to a different part of the beach, and to the boathouse.

In places, the way was slippery and so thick with mud that it sucked at her feet, impeding her progress even though the hillside sloped in her favor. The return journey would be uphill all the way. If she'd guessed wrong and Adrian wasn't at the beach, it would take her another half hour to make it back to the house and raise the general alarm.

Half an hour—half a minute!—lost in the search for a

missing child could mean the difference between life and death.

But intuition was stronger than fear. He'd come this way, she was certain. And as she skidded around the last corner to where the trees thinned out and the shore came into view, she saw a sodden red running shoe, which she recognized as Adrian's, lying in the middle of the path, and knew she'd been right to follow her instincts.

Clutching at the overhanging vines to keep her balance, she fought her way over the remaining distance and, breathless from the exertion, jumped down to the sand. To her left, the boathouse rose up, its wide door standing open, its interior empty. And at the sight, everything in her hung in fearful suspension—her breathing, her heart, and the hope which had driven her this far.

With slow dread, she turned her head and looked to the right. The normally placid blue sea heaved and rolled restlessly in choppy green waves across the narrow bay. Beyond the shelter of the headland, whitecaps dotted the horizon. And some fifty yards from shore, a small boy in a red life jacket clung to the tiller of a sailboat being tossed around like a matchbox.

Until that moment, she hadn't thought matters could get any worse, that she could be more terrified or had more to lose than was already lost. Yet even as she stood there, paralyzed with horror, the boat yawed erratically, and the wind whipped the sail to one side, then slammed it back to the other with enough force to flatten the dingy so completely that the hull lifted clear out of the water.

And when the boat righted itself again, there was no longer a little boy wearing a red life jacket clinging to the tiller. There was nothing but the sail flapping limply as the vessel turned its nose into the wind.

"Adrian!" she screamed, searching the churning waters until her eyes burned.

But the wind took his name, tore it to shreds, and flung it away.

# CHAPTER THIRTEEN

THEY didn't hear him come in and he stood for a moment on the threshold, watching them. They sat close together, she with her head on his shoulder, and he with his arm around her. They'd been like that for as long as he could remember: a couple who allowed nothing to come between them, not even the grief so evident in their posture now.

A pang of regret shot through him that he should be the cause of their unhappiness, when they'd brought to his life nothing but unlimited joy and affection. "I heard a rumor that I was dead," he said, stepping fully into the room. "I hope you haven't planned an elaborate funeral. I'd hate to see it go to waste."

They sprang up from the sofa as if they were closer to thirty than seventy, and it was almost worth what he'd gone through over the last three days, just to see the way their faces lit up, and the spring in their step as they came toward him.

"I don't believe in wasting good money on funerals," his aunt said. "I planned a wake instead, and invited everyone on the island."

But Louis didn't have her stamina or resilience, and broke into choking sobs when he tried to speak.

"Now see what you've done, you fool!" she scolded Ethan. "It's a miracle you didn't give him a heart attack!"

None too sure he had as firm a grip on his own emotions as he'd have liked, he wrapped his arms around both of them. "I'm sorry I worried you. If I could have prevented it, I would have. But it's over. I'm here and as you can see, all in one piece.''

"Yes," Josephine said severely. "And you have some explaining to do. Start at the beginning and don't leave out a thing."

"I will," he said, laughing for what seemed like the first time in years. "But first I need a stiff drink. I think we all do. Morton!"

The butler came at a run, his face mirroring the same stunned amazement Josephine and Louis had shown shortly before. "Good heavens!" he exclaimed, turning a little gray around the edges.

"Relax, Morton," Ethan said. "I'm not a ghost, just a very weary man who could use a single malt Scotch, straight up. And pour one for yourself, while you're at it. You look as if you could use it."

"Scotch?" Josephine scoffed. "This calls for champagne. Don't look so woebegone, Morton! The nightmare's over."

"I'm afraid not," the butler said, and Ethan didn't like the man's shifty-eyed expression one little bit.

"What is it? What aren't you telling us?" he said sharply, the utter and unusual silence throughout the rest of the house suddenly dawning on him. "And where's my son?"

"He's in his room," Josephine said. "We kept quiet as long as we could, Ethan, but when no news of your whereabouts had come after three days, we felt we had to tell him you'd gone missing. But he'll be so happy to see his papa again. Get someone to bring him down, will you, Morton?"

The butler shuffled uneasily from one foot to the other. "I'm afraid I can't, *madame*. Young Adrian's gone missing too, you see. We've looked everywhere in the house, and he's not to be found.''

Refusing to give in to the thread of panic uncurling in the pit of his stomach, Ethan said, ''Well, he can't have gone far. We'll search the grounds.''

''*Mademoiselle* Barclay has gone already to do that. She believes the boy might have wandered to the beach to look for you, *monsieur*.''

''How long ago did she leave?'' Ethan barked, his satisfaction at hearing Anne-Marie hadn't yet left for Canada marred by the news that his son was missing.

''Nearly half an hour, *monsieur*.''

''And you've waited until now to mention it? Good God, man, what were you thinking?''

''She asked me not to say anything until she returned,'' Morton said miserably. ''She didn't want to upset *Madame* Josephine or *Monsieur* Louis unnecessarily.''

''Alert the outdoor staff,'' Ethan said, heading for the terrace at a run. ''Have them cover the entire estate, including all accessible sections of shoreline. And get a search team out on the water.''

She was out of her depth. The waves slapped at her face, stole her breath, threatened to overwhelm her. But at least the wind had lessened some, and she was closing in on the boat.

*Adrian couldn't drown. He was wearing a life jacket. The water was warm, the tide running toward shore.*

She lifted her head, searching...searching. Tried again to call his name. And was slapped again by another wave.

The salt water rushed into her mouth and up her nose. Choking, panic-stricken, she flailed her arms, and made contact with something—the hard, shiny shell of the dingy's hull. Then another wave rolled over her, and the boat slipped away.

*I can't do this,* she thought, but knew she couldn't give up until she found him, or drowned trying. She owed it to the child and to everyone who loved him. But her arms were leaden weights, her legs aching, and her lungs burning.

The boat heaved up in front of her again, and with the last of her strength she lunged for it. And missed.

It bobbed away, as buoyant as she was inept. Then, catching another wave, it floated toward her again, and this time ran over her.

Eyes wide open with terror, she went under, and bowed to the might of the sea. Green and merciless, it tumbled around her.

This was the end, and that was just as well. She could never have faced the Beaumonts again, knowing that she hadn't been able to save Adrian.

But drowning, so she'd heard, was supposed to be painless, once a person gave up the struggle. So why was her scalp hurting, and what was the dark shape looming above her? A shark? *Oh, please let me die before it attacks!* was her last coherent thought.

The tension on her hair increased, yanking her up hard toward the light. Then, like a cork popping out of a champagne bottle and with her lungs fit to burst, she resurfaced and found herself looking straight into the only patches of blue left on earth. Ethan's enraged eyes.

"How many times do I have to do this, before you learn?" he shouted over the clamor of the waves.

Oh, yes, she was dead. Even worse, she'd been sent to hell!

Warily, she opened her eyes a fraction. A late afternoon sun had broken through the leaden skies and played over the cool, cotton sheets covering her. *Hell,* she thought blearily, *looked very much like her room in the Beaumont villa.*

And the devil sounded just like Ethan! "So you're awake finally," he said, and turning her head, she found him slouched in a chair next to the bed.

She ached all over and her throat felt as if it had been put through a meat grinder. "I didn't know I'd been asleep," she croaked, struggling to reconstruct the events which had led up to the present moment.

Something dreadful had happened. She'd been afraid. Exhausted. Stricken with unbearable grief.

Then she remembered, and a great wash of misery flowed over her. "Ah, no!" she moaned, covering her face as the tears spurted from her eyes. "Adrian…!"

"Adrian's in better shape than you, you'll be happy to hear. But then, he showed a lot more sense."

It took a moment for her to absorb what he was telling her. At length, she lowered her hands and dared to look at him again. "Adrian's…*alive?*"

"He's alive."

She shook her head, wanting to believe, but afraid to. "How is that possible? There was no sign—"

"That's a very seaworthy little boat."

"And he's a very little boy!"

"But smart," Ethan said. "I'd taught him always to wear a safety line, and he knew enough to brace himself low in the cockpit, and wait to be rescued or washed ashore."

She digested that for a space. "What if he'd been carried out to sea?"

"He knew he wouldn't be. The currents in the bay sweep toward the beach. Why else do you think it's so littered with shells and driftwood?'' His voice softened fractionally. ''Relax, Anne-Marie. He really is perfectly fine.''

''And you?'' She half sat up and tentatively touched his arm. It felt reassuringly solid and warm. Still, she had to ask. ''Are you fine, too?''

''Afraid so.''

She let out a long, heartfelt sigh and flopped back against the pillows. ''Oh, thank God!'' she said hoarsely and with profound reverence. *''Thank God!''*

''Here,'' Ethan said, pouring liquid over ice cubes in a glass. ''Drink some of this. It's lemonade. It'll soothe your throat.''

She took a few sips, then glanced at him again. ''You wouldn't lie to me, Ethan, would you? Adrian really is safe?''

''Do you think I'd be sitting here with you, if he wasn't? Yes, he's safe. He's downstairs with my aunt and uncle, stuffing himself with cream cakes. If you're up to it, though, he'd probably like to pay you a visit.''

''Oh, yes,'' she said. ''Please!''

He picked up the house phone and punched in a number. ''She's awake and ready to receive company,'' he said.

He'd barely had time to hang up before the door opened to admit Adrian, Josephine and Louis. Only then, when she could see with her own eyes that things were just as Ethan had said, did Anne-Marie truly believe him.

''Well,'' Josephine said to him, when the excitement had simmered down some. ''Did you ask her?''

''Not yet,'' he replied.

''Ask me what?'' Anne-Marie said.

''Nothing that can't wait,'' he said, and lifted Adrian onto the bed.

''Tell her how you escaped, Papa,'' Adrian begged.

"Tell her how your radio didn't work and how you had to land on a deserted island and eat raw fish for three whole days."

Ethan looked at her, and she went hot all over. Whatever else had changed in the last few days, his effect on her was still the same. "He thinks I'm the reincarnation of Robinson Crusoe," he said. "Actually, I had enough supplies on board to last me a week."

"Is that why you took your sweet time coming home?" she said, basking in the warmth of his smile.

"No," he said. "Even if I hadn't managed to damage the helicopter when I brought it down, the weather didn't let up enough for me to leave."

"So how did you get away again?"

"I finally figured out how to fix the radio, and called for help."

"And they came and got him," Adrian said gleefully, bouncing on the mattress. "Now, tell her how you rescued me, Papa!"

"We'll talk about that some other time," Josephine intervened, her sharp gaze missing nothing. "I think Anne-Marie's had all the excitement she can take for now. Come along, Adrian. Let's leave her to get some rest."

"You should go with them," Anne-Marie said, when Ethan made no move to follow them. "Adrian was devastated when he heard you'd gone missing. I imagine it's going to take him a while to get over being afraid."

He paid not the slightest attention. "And what about you, Anne-Marie?" he said instead. "Were you so devastated that you turned to Roberto Santos for comfort?"

"Oh, I was pretty devastated at the time," she admitted, all her nice, warm fuzzy feeling evaporating. "But you're being so horrible now that I have to wonder why I even cared."

"I find myself wondering why you weren't already headed back to Vancouver when the news came through that I'd turned up missing."

"I stayed here to be with your son. He really needed you, of course, but you decided business was more important."

"I don't need you to tell me how to be a father."

"Well, someone has to!"

"And you think you're qualified to do that, do you? You, who've never had a child?"

"I might never have given birth, but this much I do know. You might be a prince in the eyes of your lowly island subjects, Ethan Beaumont, but to me you're just an arrogant, uncaring jerk who takes pleasure in trampling all over other people's feelings, and I hate you!"

"Oh, good," he purred, joining her on the bed and sweeping her into his arms. "You really are going to make a full recovery, *mon amour*. You had me worried there, for a while."

And then he kissed her. It was a very long, very satisfying kiss.

"I beg your pardon?" she said, when at last he lifted his mouth from hers and she got back her breath. "What did you call me?"

"You heard." He played with her fingers and she realized with astonishment that he was having a very hard time keeping his voice steady. "I called you 'my love.'"

"Oh," she said. Then, nervously, "Am I hallucinating?"

He cleared his throat. "*Non, ma très chère Anne-Marie.* It is a testament to my stupid male pride, I suppose, that only when I found myself staring death in the face did I realize how badly I wanted to live long enough to tell you that I love you. All the time I wrestled with that infernal radio, I thought of you. Remembered the smell of your hair, your skin—almond cream with a hint of tangerine. It's what gave me the strength to persevere.''

"But how much do you love me?'' she said.

He kissed her again. ''More than you can begin to imagine,'' he said against her lips.

"Enough to marry me?''

He drew back, his blue eyes wide with shock. ''Aren't you jumping the gun a little?''

"No,'' she said. ''Because I love you, too, and I love Adrian. A lot. I didn't know it was possible to feel like this—to be so full of wanting to give everything—*everything*, Ethan!—just to make someone else happy. But if that's more than you can accept, then you might love me, but you don't love me enough.''

He regarded her solemnly for a long, thoughtful minute. ''You stayed when you could have walked away,'' he said at last. ''You welcomed me into your arms, your bed, your heart. You continue to be the best thing that ever happened to me. How could I not love you enough? But when it comes to marriage—''

"It's out of the question because I'm not an island woman and you're afraid I'll turn out to be just like your ex-wife.'' She turned away, her hopes falling around her like ashes.

He caught her hands and forced her to look at him again. ''No,'' he said. ''Not that, at all. What I was going to say is that before you decide you want to be my wife, you need to recognize the baggage I bring with me. Not just Adrian—''

"Adrian is your son, Ethan. That alone is reason enough for me to love him.''

"He's also another woman's child. Can you live with the fact that, if she were to come back and want to be part of his life, much though I'd hate it, I'd have to allow it because I don't have the right to deny him his mother?''

''Can you live with the fact that, if she doesn't, I might never be able to fill her empty shoes? That Adrian will always know I'm not his birth mother?''

''It's not your job to try to replace Lisa, my love, because you're nothing like her. You're you—and you're perfect just as you are.''

''Nobody's perfect, Ethan,'' she said, ''and it's dangerous to believe otherwise. You just leave yourself open to disappointment.''

''Then let me amend the statement and say that you're perfect for me. You're beautiful, and stubborn, and smart, and unafraid to stand your ground. You're what I need. You temper my arrogance and remind me I'm as flawed as the next man. You keep me grounded. But then I look at it from your point of view, and see only the sacrifices you'd be making if you married me.''

''Well, of course I would,'' she said. ''And so would you. Loving someone doesn't come cheap. It demands sacrifice and compromise. It means caring about the other person's needs more than caring about your own.'' She stopped and drew in a painful breath. ''And that's how much I love you, Ethan. Enough to let you go, if that's what you need.''

''The hell you will!'' he said softly, stroking her face. ''I have no intention of letting you go. Ever.''

A knock came at the door and Josephine popped her head into the room. ''Forgive me for interrupting, Ethan, but we can't wait a minute longer to find out. Have you proposed to her yet?''

''No,'' he said, pressing a kiss to Anne-Marie's hair. ''She asked me first. And I accepted.''

"Excellent!" Josephine said. "I'll tell Morton to break out the champagne. Shall we have it served in the salon?"

"By all means," Ethan said, "but don't expect us to join you for a while. We have other business to conduct first and if it's all the same to you, *ma tante,* I'd like to do it in private."

"Of course. Take all the time you need," she said, and left them alone.

"I need a lifetime," Ethan said, his gaze scorching over Anne-Marie. "But I've learned in the last few days that we're guaranteed nothing except this moment. Let's make it one that lasts as long as we have the breath and strength to say 'I love you.' Let's make it last forever, my lovely Anne-Marie."

*"Oui, mon amour,"* she said, touching his mouth with her fingertip. "Let's do that."

And then they stopped talking, and got down to the other business.

# THE WEDDING DARE

*by*

*Barbara Hannay*

**Barbara Hannay**'s first romance novel was published in 1999. She lives in Northern Australia, a fascinating and beautiful location which provides a rich setting for many of her books. When she's not writing, Barbara enjoys refreshing her imagination by travelling with her writer husband to explore exciting new overseas destinations, or to revisit the awe-inspiring mystery of the Australian Outback.

She loves to hear from readers and can be contacted via email at barbara@barbarahannay.com. Her website is www.barbarahannay.com

**Don't miss Barbara Hannay's exciting new novel *In the Heart of the Outback*... out in April 2007 from Mills & Boon Romance™**

# CHAPTER ONE

THERE was really only one man in the mall who would look good taking his clothes off. Laura Goodman could tell at a glance that the fellow lounging against the letter box just outside the coffee shop was the man she'd been sent to collect.

He had all the important credentials—broad shoulders and indecently developed biceps straining the stretch cotton of his T-shirt, lean hips and long legs encased in denim.

Even from this distance she could see that his skin was tanned and glowing and, although she couldn't see his face, his bearing suggested supreme confidence.

From her parked car, Laura scanned the rest of the mall entrance. Every other male in the vicinity was pimply or pudgy, balding or under age. This guy had to be the male stripper.

She turned off the ignition and took a steadying breath as she pushed her car door open. It was all very well for Susie and the girls to delegate her to chauffeur this fellow because they knew she could be relied on to stay sober for the whole evening. But there was more than one reason why she shouldn't be sauntering into the mall to pick up a strange man.

If tonight's party hadn't been a hen-night for her best friend, and if she wasn't Susie's bridesmaid, Laura would not have ventured out mid-week at all.

Right now, she should be on the end of a telephone, trying every agent in Brisbane to find a replacement clown for tomorrow's book-reading session at the children's hospital. That was a task more in keeping with her recent promotion to senior librarian and a much more worthy cause than providing Susie and her friends with coarse entertainment.

Laura sighed as she straightened her uncomfortable dress and set off across the mall's uneven paving stones. Keeping her spiky high heels out of the cracks required most of her concentration, but one corner of her mind also tussled with the problem of tomorrow at the children's ward.

Just before she'd left home this evening, she'd had a phone call from her regular assistant to tell her he'd come down with a virus and wouldn't be able to do the clown stint.

Last week she'd promised the children she'd bring them a clown to accompany her weekly book-reading and they'd been ecstatic. Now it would be almost impossible to find a replacement in time.

She might have delayed leaving for the party while she made some calls, but Susie had cornered her at work earlier in the afternoon asking if she would "be a darling" and make a detour via the mall on her way to make an important pick-up.

A pair of faded blue jeans entered Laura's line of vision and she came to an abrupt halt. She'd reached her target.

The stripper.

He was mere inches away, still slouching against the letter box.

Time to forget about children's wards and clowns.

Never having met a stripper before—male or female—Laura pressed her lips together before smiling gingerly. "Good evening." She always made a habit of being polite, no matter whom she addressed.

"Evening."

The rich timbre of his voice startled her. In fact, its resonance was so surprising that, just for a moment, Laura couldn't think of what to say next. Especially when the man levered his noteworthy body away from the letter box and stood tall and erect, looking down at her with a distinctly guarded expression.

He crossed his arms over his chest and frowned at her.

Laura hesitated.

Up close, his face was much nicer looking than she'd expected. Maybe she'd stereotyped strippers, but she hadn't figured on finding such obvious intelligence in those wary grey eyes. His dark hair was thick and shiny and, although he hadn't bothered to shave, she could see the line of a very strong, resolute jaw through his dark stubble.

She struggled with the problem of how best to address him. It wasn't appropriate to blurt out, "Are you the stripper?"

And yet she had to say something.

Clearly she was taking too long. He was scowling at her as if she was something sloppy a bird had dropped.

"You looking for someone?" he asked suddenly.

"Er—yes!" Laura tried to cover her surprise by giving a little shrug of her shoulder.

She swung her evening bag casually from its silk string handles, hoping to look as sophisticated and cool as any of her friends who were, right at this moment, recklessly tossing down far too many champagne cocktails at Susie's party and leaving her to do their dirty work.

Laura smiled bravely. "Yes, I'm expecting to meet someone here. Actually—" she arched an eyebrow and sent him another courageous smile "—I'm pretty certain I'm here to meet you."

His eyes gleamed. "Well, I'm sorry to disappoint you, sweetheart, but my entertainment's already planned for this evening—and it's usually free."

For a long moment Laura stared at him as the full meaning of his reply sank in. Did he think she was—?

"Oh, no!" she cried. "You can't possibly imagine—" She jumped back quickly, one of her heels hit a crack in the paving and her ankle caved in beneath her.

Her arms flailed in the air and the clasp of her handbag caught him square on the chin.

He grunted a muffled curse.

Laura's heels made a noisy clatter on the paving stones as she struggled to regain her balance and to keep her handbag under control. Finally she was upright and steady.

As he rubbed his dark chin the man's frown deepened. He looked as if he couldn't believe what had just happened.

She reached out a tentative hand, but left it hovering in mid-air. "I'm so sorry."

"I'll live," he muttered, and shoved his hands deep into the pockets of his jeans. He looked around him, as if he hoped there was someone nearby who would lay claim to this annoying woman.

"I was trying to say that I'm not—what you were thinking," Laura hastened to explain. "I'm here to pick you up. Not pick you up *that* way. I'm here to take you to the party."

"Party?"

"Yes. Susie asked me to give you a lift. The mall is on my way."

"You mean Susie Thomson, Rob Parker's fiancée?" For the first time, the shadowy doubt in his grey eyes lightened a little.

"Yes."

"*She* arranged my lift? I was planning to take a taxi because we'll be drinking, but Rob insisted someone would pick me up."

Laura shrugged. "I was the lucky person commissioned to fetch you." To her relief, after he'd considered this news for a lengthy moment, he seemed to relax at last.

In fact, he shrugged his mighty shoulders and actually smiled. "Let's not waste any time, then. Take me to the party."

She looked like a feather duster on legs, Nick decided, as he followed his escort back across the mall. Of course, he had to admit they were extremely classy legs. Almost as classy as her dark auburn hair and deep blue eyes.

But that was more than he could say for her astonishing dress. It seemed to be nothing more than a long boa of blue feathers that she'd wound around her.

With her sensuous body and her vampish taste in clothes, it was no wonder he'd thought she was a hooker. Most men would take one look at that reel of feathers and think about unwinding them.

One or two feathers drifted away from her now as she deactivated the central locking system on her smart little sedan.

"Hop in and you'll be at the party in a jiffy," she said.

Nick lowered his long body into the passenger seat.

She turned the key in the ignition. "You can adjust that to give you more leg-room."

"Thanks." At a touch, the seat slid back. "Nice car."

"It's new and I'm very proud of it. I bought it to celebrate my promotion."

Her pride showed in the way she smoothly manoeuvred the vehicle out into the traffic flow. Nick enjoyed driving and he admired this woman's skill. She'd had a promotion. Maybe she wasn't a sandwich short of a picnic after all.

As she neatly switched lanes, she shot him a shy smile. "I should call you something. What er—what name do you use—at parties?"

"I beg your pardon?"

"I imagine you might like to keep your working life separate for—er—personal—for privacy. Maybe you have a pseudonym?"

"For *parties?*"

"Yes."

Nick gaped at her. "Do *you* have a special name just for parties?"

"Oh, no!" she cried. "But I told you, I'm not—" She cut off her response as she stamped down on the brake. They'd reached a traffic light.

In the glare of the overhead lights, Nick could see that this girl looked as mixed-up as she sounded. He revised his assessment of her. This was one confused cookie.

"Look," he sighed as they headed off again, "the name's Nick…at parties…at work…at home. I'm afraid I'm Nick Farrell twenty-four hours a day, seven days a week."

She cracked a brief smile. ''Hi, Nick. I'm Laura. Laura Goodman.''

''Laura,'' he repeated, and he realised that when he'd met her in the Glenwood mall he'd expected a more exotic name. Now, sitting beside her, inhaling a delicate hint of rose and jasmine and observing the prim, uncomfortable expression on her face, almost as if she were afraid of him, an old-world name like Laura Goodman made more sense.

She swung her car into a kerbside space, behind a string of other parked vehicles. ''Here we are.''

Nick frowned. ''This isn't Rob's street.''

''Rob?'' Laura frowned back. ''But we're going to Susie's. Rob's the groom.''

He stared at her. ''Rob's having his bucks' party at Susie's?''

''No, of course not. Susie's having her hen-party here. Actually, she's calling it *frocktails*.'' She rolled her eyes and gestured down at her feathers. ''That's why I'm dressed like this. Susie wanted all her girl-friends drinking cocktails in frocks. Get it? *Frock*tails? The crazier the frock, the better. Of course I don't actually drink—''

Nick interrupted her. ''I *don't* get it. What I particularly don't get is why you've brought *me* here!''

Laura's blue eyes widened. ''But you're the—the VIP guest.''

*A VIP guest at a hen-night?* Sweat broke out all over him.

Clearly Laura Goodman *had* lost her marbles. He quickly considered his options. He could scramble out of her car, run for the nearest phone box and call a cab, or he could put his nose in the door at this *frocktail* party and confront Susie, his best mate's fiancée. He didn't know her all that well, but she seemed pretty level-headed.

Surely she could sort out this mess.

Laura leaned closer and her expression showed distaste warring with sympathetic, motherly concern. "Come inside," she urged gently. "Susie organised this. She'll explain. All I know is I had to bring you here."

"She'd damn well better sort this out," he growled as he pushed the passenger door open.

On the footpath, he took deep breaths of summer night air. The sounds of hysterical girlish laughter and popular music pulsated from a brightly lit house nearby.

Closer at hand, he heard a different sound.

"Oh, *no!*"

Still standing on the other side of her car, Laura was clutching at her chest while one hand waggled in the air behind her as she tried to reach an elusive trail of feathers. Nick could see that her feathers had snagged as she climbed out of the car and her incredible excuse for a dress was coming undone. He had a clear view of a wispy lace undergarment and her super-soft, pale back shimmering in the moonlight.

"Oh, for pity's sake!" she wailed, sounding and looking panic stricken.

Nick stepped around the back of the vehicle. "Allow me."

Not giving her time to object, he picked up the offending string of feathers and drew them firmly in place across her back.

"It's OK," she cried. "Please—you don't have to bother. I can manage."

He ignored her fretful flapping. "What happens now?" he asked gruffly, walking around to the front of her and holding the tail end of the string of feathers between finger and thumb, while he did his manful best to ignore how good she looked and smelled up close.

Her flowery perfume was intriguing—both adult and innocent at the same time.

Laura snatched the feathers out of his hand. "Thank you. I can take care of this." Her blue eyes regarded him with deep suspicion. "I *said,* I can manage the rest."

Nick wasn't thick. He knew when he was being told to make himself scarce, but for a moment or two he hovered there, mesmerised by the surprising beauty of Laura Goodman's bare shoulders—marble-white and perfect like the shoulders of a Grecian statue.

"Look, I know you do this kind of thing for a living," she huffed, waving the tip of her feathery garment at him, "but some of us have different value systems."

He shook his head in bewilderment. "What do you mean? What exactly do you *know* that I do for a living?"

"Just go inside and find Susie," she snapped. "Having you here was her idea."

Somehow, Nick was getting the impression that going inside and finding Susie was going to be even less helpful than standing on the footpath with this feathered enigma—this sheep in vixen's clothing.

He didn't really know very much about Rob's bride-to-be. His mate's romance had been recklessly whirlwind.

"Look, I'll turn my back while you fix your dress," he said. "But I'd like some clarification here. I want to know who you think I am and why the blazes you brought me here instead of to Rob's party?"

Before she answered, a woman's voice called from the front gate of the party house.

"Laura? Is that you? Have you brought Nick? The girls are getting impatient."

Tall, dark and model-thin, Susie Thomson was waving to them. Nick charged down the footpath towards her. "What's this all about, Susie? I'm supposed to be at Rob's."

She beamed at him and linked a slim arm through his. "Oh, no you're not. This is exactly where you're supposed to be. Everybody's waiting." Giggling a little, she began to drag him towards the noisy house.

It occurred to Nick as the babble of female voices grew louder that some guys would find being dragged into a house bursting at the seams with tipsy single women the equivalent of being handed heaven on a plate. But a sixth sense warned him that he wasn't in for any pleasant surprises tonight.

He thought about snatching his arm away from Susie's and bolting down the street. But then his common sense reasoned that he was worrying unduly.

After all, this woman was about to marry his best mate and he was to be best man at their wedding on Saturday. Any minute now, this whole confusing evening would begin to make sense.

Susie sent him another grin over her sequin-spangled shoulder as she pushed at her front door. "These girls can't wait," she laughed.

Then the door flew open and, just as he'd feared, Nick found himself facing a room filled with laughing, shouting women. They were all clutching champagne cocktails and were dressed in costumes so outrageous they made Laura Goodman's feathers look like the last word in good taste.

"Girls," Susie yelled, and the noise died down as their eyes swung Nick's way. "Our stripper is here at last!"

*Strip—*

*Stripper!*

At first Nick thought he was choking.

Then he was sure he was having a heart attack. He was drenched by a tidal wave of adrenaline. There was a roaring in his ears, which he realised later was the massed squeal of the women in front of him.

"You've got to be joking," he finally managed to croak.

Susie's grip on his arm tightened. "Of course this isn't a joke. Rob told me what a great party trick you do."

"Huh?" he wheezed. "*Rob* told you that?"

For several puzzled seconds he stared at Susie, but as panic squeezed every last molecule of air from his lungs the penny dropped. Rob Parker, his mate, had pulled a swift one.

He and Rob shared a long tradition of practical jokes and dares dating back to their primary school days in the bush and Nick recognised this as Rob's handiwork—the ultimate practical joke.

But he hadn't thought his friend was capable of such exceedingly poor taste. In the past, their dares had been risky, but never risqué!

Feeling just a little light-headed, he gritted his teeth in an attempt at a smile. "OK, Susie, you've frightened the life out of me. Well done. Neat trick. So what happens now? Rob's arranged for someone to take me to his party, hasn't he?"

"Not yet, Nick," Susie said sweetly but emphatically. "Not till the girls have had their show." Her brows drew together. "But I do have a message for you from Rob. He said you wouldn't *dare* to chicken out on us."

"D—dare?" he echoed.

"I reckon these girls will lynch you if you even think about leaving before you *perform*."

Nick's throat felt so dry he was sure someone had lined it with sandpaper. This was the end of a perfect friendship.

Neither he nor Rob had ever refused a dare since they were eight years old when Nick had challenged his friend to run through a bull paddock. But when he found Rob, after this, his old mate would probably have to reconsider his wedding plans.

Nick looked again at Susie's determined face—at the gleeful expectation on the faces of the women pressing forward—and wondered briefly where Laura Goodman had got to. She'd be hiding and feeling very guilty, no doubt.

But he didn't have time to give her another thought as he accepted the terrible certainty that no one was planning to let him out of this dilemma.

His stomach knotted. "You're expecting me to strip?"

"Darlin'," Susie smiled silkily, "you know we are."

"Down to my jocks?"

Susie rolled her eyes as if she'd never heard such an inane question.

Frantically he looked around him. At the far end of the room stood a table laden with savouries. "I'll—I'll need some sustenance first."

"Of course!" Susie called to another woman, "Amanda, can you look after some food for our guest?"

There was a scattering of females and, within what seemed like seconds, half a dozen plates were thrust towards Nick. He took as long as he could, exchanging small talk and sampling the variety of foods eagerly offered by a circle of wide-eyed women.

"My, you eat so slowly," a sultry blonde purred. "I love a man who's not in a hurry."

He almost choked as he crammed more food into his mouth.

But a bloke could only consume so many Thai fish cakes, crudités, cheese, olives and Chinese chicken wings. He swilled down two champagne cocktails in quick succession, hoping he'd feel braver.

He didn't.

So he asked for another.

Susie appeared at his side and murmured, "Ready?"

"I—I'm going to need special music for this. I can't just perform to any old tune."

She smiled, "I have a huge selection of CDs. Come and make your choice."

In a frantic daze, Nick managed to spin out another five minutes as he sorted through Susie's collection, but all too soon she reached over and took the CD he held.

"Latin American. Good choice. This will be perfect."

He felt a surge of panic. "Oh—er—I'm not sure about that."

"I am," she said sweetly but firmly. Then she slipped it into the player and turned to her guests. "Girls, let's give a warm welcome to Nick, who has something very special to show us!"

His head pounded as the room filled with ecstatic cheering and clapping.

# CHAPTER TWO

LAURA took her time fixing her dress. She needed to stay in the darkened street and compose herself. When he'd offered to rearrange her feathers Nick Farrell had looked at her—the way a man looked at a woman when he found her—*desirable*. That wicked glint in his eye had been unmistakable.

And, to her utter embarrassment, instead of being repulsed, Laura had found his interest exciting.

*How could she?* The man was immoral. For pity's sake, he stripped for a living! But the really silly part was that a gleam in a man's eye was really nothing to get excited about.

He was only flirting. Right now he would be inside, sending each and every woman at the party a look so smouldering he would probably activate Susie's newly installed smoke alarms.

Pacing the footpath, she allowed the night air to fan her flaming cheeks and reminded herself that any of the other girls at this party would have responded to Nick's gaze with a flirtatious laugh. But she also knew she would never be like any other girl at this party.

She'd never really fitted in with her generation. Most of her friends saw her as twenty-nine going on fifty.

And that was how she was. She couldn't help it.

She was a Goodman.

From about the age of ten Laura had understood that her family was more earnest than most. The name Goodman had almost certainly been given to one of her ancestors because he had been exactly what it described—a *good* man. Since then, Goodman descendants had been both blessed and cursed with an oversupply of goodness genes.

Laura came from a long line of do-gooders.

In true Goodman tradition, she'd been born in a hut in Cambodia where her mother and father had worked as a doctor and nurse team tending orphans. Although they'd returned to Australia when Laura and her brother started school, both her parents had continued working long hours in a range of charities in addition to their jobs at the Royal Brisbane hospital.

Now they were working in East Timor, and her brother, Phil, in his final year of medical studies, was clearly following in their worthy footsteps. But, although Laura admired her family, she couldn't live up to their standards. She had been the black sheep and had turned into a bookworm instead of a caring nurse or doctor.

When she'd announced she wanted to become a librarian her parents had swallowed their disappointment and consoled themselves that at least she hadn't wanted to be anything totally frivolous like a violinist or an archaeologist.

But, even though she'd been allowed to indulge in her passion for reading, those Goodman genes had caught up with Laura. Which was why she found herself reading stories to the children's ward at the local hospital every Wednesday.

On the other hand Susie, her fellow librarian, was convinced that good works meant hunting out the sexiest romance novels and keeping them under the counter for her favourite elderly ladies.

After ten minutes or so of pacing, Laura felt calmer.

Checking once more that her feathers were firmly in place, she finally made her way inside to join the party. But when she saw Susie on the far side of the room talking to Nick, she chose to keep at a safe distance.

By the time she'd greeted one or two friends and helped herself to an orange juice *without* champagne, Nick was strolling slowly to the middle of a space that had been made for him.

The room pulsed with a sexy Latin American beat and most of the girls edged forward, clapping to its rhythm.

Laura gulped. So this was it—her first strip show.

As far as she could tell from her position against the far wall Nick looked calm, almost haughtily proud. He hardly seemed to notice the crowd of eager spectators pressing close. She guessed that keeping a mental distance from his audience was how a professional approached this kind of thing. No doubt looking bored was part of the act.

"Oh, my," drooled one of Susie's cousins. "I think I've just seen my future—my perfect match. Do you think when his eyes reach mine across this crowded room he'll realise we're made for each other?"

"Dream on, Sandy," another girl scoffed.

The bold, throbbing music filled the room and Laura noticed that Nick was beginning to move to its rhythm. Turning his back to the audience, he strutted in an essentially masculine way, shifting first one whole side of his body then the other. The girls roared as he swivelled his hips in a manoeuvre that made his jeans stretch tight across his neat backside.

Someone groaned, "What a god!"

Laura had to admit he was good at this. The girls were loving it. Now his T-shirt was hanging loose out of his jeans and, as he turned to face them once more, he slowly lifted the white cotton knit to reveal a tempting glimpse of tanned torso with an arrowing of dark hair disappearing into his jeans.

There were calls of, "Get it off!"

Laura gulped. She was shocked by how difficult she found it to drag her eyes away from those few inches of masculine flesh.

In front of her, Sandy was swooning. "You can tell he'd be good in bed just by the way he moves," she sighed.

The girls drooled in unison as Nick lifted the T-shirt higher.

Laura took an extra long sip of orange juice and her drink finished in a noisy slurp. She was beginning to feel hot and flustered again. It was a long time since she'd really paid close attention to a man, especially a man removing his clothes, and she had to admit Nick Farrell looked good.

OK make that very, *very* good. But how could these women think about jumping straight into bed with a strange man just because they liked his appearance?

She scanned the sea of eager faces. It seemed everyone at the party liked the way Nick looked.

His shirt was off now and he was swinging it over his head in big, lazy circles. Of course, his chest and shoulders were as broad as Laura had suspected when she first saw him in the mall. She wondered if his skin would feel as amazing as it looked—like bronzed silk tightly stretched over hard, man-sized muscles.

Shocked by her totally improper interest, Laura dragged her eyes upwards, away from his body, and to her dismay she found Nick's eyes meeting with hers.

From across the room they sparkled cheekily as he winked at her.

*How dared he?*

Instinctively, Laura sent back an icy glare—the sort that usually silenced the rowdiest patrons in her library—but he simply grinned and winked some more.

In one synchronised flowing movement, the heads of the women in the room swung round to see who was attracting so much attention.

Laura felt her cheeks flame. There was a buzz of feminine reaction, the unpleasant sound of catty whispers. She dropped her gaze and stabbed at the bottom of her empty juice glass with her straw. Why did this bare-chested moron have to embarrass her like this?

Nick was despicable. She'd done nothing to deserve such singling out. Embarrassed, she hurried towards the front door, but, as she did so, she saw out of the corner of her eye that Nick was tossing his T-shirt to a pretty brunette in the centre of the room.

An excited squeal erupted and she couldn't believe the little spurt of disappointment she felt. What the dickens was wrong with her? Of course she was relieved that he'd turned his attention to another woman.

This was too much! For one scary minute she'd been eyeing Nick Farrell with as much lusty interest as the rest of the girls. Thank heavens she'd come to her senses when he gave her that indecent wink.

Safely outside on the patio once more, she leaned against the front wall of Susie's house and dragged in deep draughts of air, fighting for the second time that night to regain her composure.

A loud uproar exploded inside. No doubt Nick was nearing the climax of his act.

Laura closed her eyes and refused to imagine the

scene on the other side of the wall. Thank goodness she'd left the room when she had. It would have been far too embarrassing to have witnessed the final unveiling.

How could anyone—how could *Nick* do this sort of thing for a living just because he had a great body?

Nick had kept telling himself that at any minute Rob would appear to let him off the hook. But now he was beginning to fear there'd be no reprieve. With his shirt off and his belt already gone, he was facing his darkest hour. His hands actually shook as he fingered the metal button at the top of his jeans.

The wide-eyed females before him were grinning stupidly.

"Don't worry about leaving your jeans lying on the floor, sweetheart, I'll pick them up later," someone called.

And it was about then that Nick Farrell knew he'd hit a brick wall.

There was no way he would take this charade to the bitter end. There was no way in Christendom this best man was going to show his mate's bride exactly who was the *best* man.

He let his hands drop loosely to his sides and stood still.

Perched on a stool at the side of the room, Susie was watching him carefully.

Nick shook his head at her.

Her eyebrow arched in a silent question.

"Show's over," he mouthed.

In reply, a grim-mouthed, very determined Susie shook her head.

A film of sweat broke out on Nick's forehead. For

the life of him he couldn't remember what kind of jocks he'd dragged on tonight. He inched the zipper of his jeans down a little and was relieved to glimpse solid black cotton.

OK—he'd go down to his jocks, but that was definitely the end of the line. Susie had threatened lynching. Well—that would be a character-building experience.

Nervously, he stepped out of his jeans. He knew he'd stopped performing, but, strangely, it didn't seem to matter. The room filled with even louder cheers and enthusiastic clapping. Anyone would think this was the Olympics and he'd broken a world record.

Susie was grinning and walking towards him. That grin would be wiped in a flash when he told her this was it. The finish line.

The end.

Feeling foolish, Nick stood there, holding his jeans in front of him. Susie continued to grin and clap. The whole room filled with applause.

"This is absolutely as far as I go," he warned her.

She nodded. "I know."

"You *know*?"

"Of course. You've got to turn up at church for my wedding on Saturday and most of these women will be there. We have to maintain some decorum. Besides, we can't ruin your fine reputation as Crown Prosecutor, can we?"

Nick stared at her as he felt the room sway. "So this *was* a set-up? Rob's idea?"

Susie shrugged and her lips curved in a sly smile. "You'd better ask him about that."

"These women—did they know I'm not a stripper? They weren't expecting…"

"They knew the score, but I hope you'll forgive us. You were fantastic. You're a hero, Nick."

Feeling anything but heroic, Nick clambered back into his jeans. He'd been taken for a ride by his best mate and a bunch of giggling females. This wasn't the first time he'd been at the wrong end of a practical joke and it probably wouldn't be the last, but it was taking longer than usual for him to catch on to the humour.

As he threaded his belt back through the loops of his jeans, he asked, "Laura Goodman knew I was being conned?"

"Laura?" Susie frowned.

"The chauffeur. The feather duster with the Titian hair and the long legs."

Susie smiled. "I'm glad you noticed Laura's legs. She's sweet, isn't she?"

Nick grunted and wondered why on earth he *had* mentioned Laura Goodman or her legs.

"Actually," Susie said slowly, "I didn't explain to Laura exactly what was going on. So you mustn't be mad at her. She's going to be your—"

"It's not an issue," Nick interrupted, not wanting to dwell on the matter. "I want out of here. I'll grab a cab to Rob's party. I've got a bone to pick with my humorous mate."

Suddenly serious, Susie pleaded, "Be nice to him, please, Nick. This really was just a little fun. He said you both play jokes on each other."

She stood on tiptoe and lightly kissed his cheek. "And thanks so much for being a sport about it all. You were terrific."

"Just get me back my T-shirt and I'll think about how nice I'm going to be."

\*      \*      \*

From the safety of the patio, Laura guessed that the strip show was over. The party seemed to have quietened considerably. She glanced at her watch and decided to pop inside and speak to Susie, then make her excuses before slipping away. Susie would understand her hasty departure when she explained about tomorrow's clown problem.

But the doorway was blocked by a tall, dark, bare-chested figure. Nick Farrell was coming out, dragging a T-shirt over his head.

"Oh," she said as his face emerged, "it's you." She lifted her chin, but it was hard to look down her nose at someone so much taller. "I suppose you want a lift back, do you?"

"No," he scowled. "I'll get a cab."

"I'm supposed to be your chauffeur," Laura said quickly. And then she could have kicked herself. Why on earth had she been so eager to help him?

Tucking his shirt into his jeans, Nick cocked his head to one side and studied her. He smiled slowly. "You'll take me to the groom's party this time?"

She couldn't help showing her horror. "You're not going to strip for the men, too?"

He took an age to reply. Eventually, she heard a soft chuckle. "You really do have a very low opinion of me, don't you?"

His words sent a wave of remorse coursing through her. Perhaps that chuckle was his way of covering hurt feelings. She must have sounded very judgemental. "I'm sorry. What you do is really none of my business."

Nick's mouth twitched as if he was having difficulty controlling his reaction and Laura was quite sure she had hurt him.

Beneath the bold and brassy body, he was almost certainly hiding a sensitive soul. She'd been thinking all evening how terrible it was that such a fit, well-spoken and intelligent-looking man had been reduced to taking off his clothes to make a living.

There was a red tinge staining his neck and cheek-bones and the realisation that she had embarrassed Nick was enough to activate an entire battalion of Laura's do-good genes.

Suddenly she saw the chance to do something really special. It was obvious that Nick needed help. With some tactful pressure, she could encourage him to raise his sights and find a proper job. She could even save him from further degradation.

In a flash, she decided that tomorrow would be soon enough to explain to Susie why she'd left the party so quickly. "Hop into my car," she ordered in a businesslike manner and, to her relief, he obeyed without further argument.

By the time they were halfway to Rob's party she had figured out a brilliant plan for launching Nick Farrell's rehabilitation. "You know, you have very fine entertainment skills," she began in her warmest manner.

Sounding mildly surprised, he muttered his thanks.

"Have you ever thought about using those skills for different kinds of entertainment?"

"Different?" In her peripheral vision, Laura was aware of the way Nick's big shoulders rolled as he turned to look at her. "How different do you mean?"

She swallowed and, for a moment, concentrated on taking a sharp corner. "There are nobler ways of entertaining people that could earn you just as much money," she suggested gently. "Well, maybe I should amend that—almost as much money. I'm sure stripping does pay very well, but—''

They came to a stop sign and Laura stole a glance at Nick to see how he was taking this. She was dismayed to see that he was looking very uncomfortable. ''Oh, dear,'' she whispered.

She'd hurt him again. Maybe her mother was right. She should have taken that evening course in counselling. He'd covered his face with his hands and was taking deep breaths. She thought she heard something like a hiccup.

Laura felt terrible.

But then, when Nick lowered his hands again, he looked at her very seriously and said, ''Exactly what kind of work are you suggesting?''

Laura beamed. ''I could find you a good job in no time. In fact I can organise a job tomorrow as a clown at the children's hospital. I'd pay you award rates.''

She didn't quite catch his reaction. The traffic had cleared and she had to keep her eyes on the road as she accelerated across the intersection, but, as soon as she could, she looked his way. ''What do you think?''

''A job as a clown? I'm stunned.''

''You'd make a great clown,'' she urged, hoping he couldn't guess that she actually needed him to do this job as much as he needed the work.

''I'm not sure that I'm flattered.''

''But you'd feel so good knowing you've brightened the day for all those little kids.''

''As a *clown?*''

''You'd be using your talents for something truly worthwhile.''

He frowned. ''Will you be there?''

Laura pulled to a stop outside his destination, the

Royal Hotel. "Yes, I'll be there, Nick," she said in her most reassuring voice. "I'm going to read a couple of stories to the children. I'll provide you with a costume. You just have to improvise and clown around—like you did tonight—sort of."

When he hesitated, she added, "Go on. I dare you to try it just once."

"You *dare* me?" he repeated. His hand was on the door handle and Laura could tell he was eager to go.

"Yes," she replied boldly. "Do you accept dares?"

He turned to her with a smile so slow and sexy it sizzled the blood in her veins. "OK, I'll dare to do this Beppo the clown stunt if you dare to give this big bad stripper a kiss."

# CHAPTER THREE

ASKING for the kiss was stupid, but the words had spilled out before Nick had time to rein in his wayward thoughts.

For most of the drive across town he had been hard-pressed to keep a straight face while Laura Goodman sat there sounding and acting as prissy and prim as a Sunday School teacher bent on saving his soul. She behaved as if she had no idea that her body looked sinfully sexy in those feathers.

But even if she didn't know who he was, and still thought he was a professional stripper, how could any woman with hair that rich red colour and eyes such an astonishing blue behave as if she'd never been asked for a kiss before?

What a reaction! Shock! Horror! Scandalised big blue eyes. The message was clear. Laura Goodman couldn't bring herself to kiss Nick Farrell if he was the last man on the planet.

The princess couldn't kiss the frog.

That was fine, Nick decided. A big relief! Kissing a woman who took herself as seriously as Laura would be dangerous. It had been a crazy proposition to put to her and now he had a nice simple reason to escape her ridiculous clown gig without going into complicated explanations.

He reached once more for the door handle.

"Nick." Laura's voice was just a little squeaky.

"Yeah?"

"I can understand why you asked me for the kiss. I guess you see it as a fair deal." The tip of her pink tongue made a sexy little circuit around her lips.

"Ah—a spur-of-the-moment suggestion," he mumbled. "Forget it."

"No!" she cried with a sudden urgency that startled him. Then she startled him some more by leaning closer and continuing earnestly. "I want you to do the clown job, so I'll kiss you. But..." She didn't seem to know how to finish the sentence.

And Nick was too stupefied to think of anything to say.

Seconds later, Laura edged closer, bringing again that hint of roses and jasmine—like the first hot day of spring. "I'm not exactly in the habit of kissing men I've just met," she murmured more than a touch nervously.

Out of the corner of his eye, he saw her pause and stare at him as if she were summoning up strength and he waited for her excuse to escape from this tiresome task.

"You'd make it easier for me if you could turn your head this way," she said huskily.

*Get out of this car,* Nick told himself, but he stayed, convinced the woman held a postgraduate degree in seduction. Her apparent inexperience, her bossiness and her beauty were an intoxicating mix. He'd never felt such sudden *heat.*

It was on the tip of his tongue to say, *It's OK. You don't have to do this. It was a bad idea.* But he was already turning his head her way and she was lifting her soft, lush lips towards his.

Her skin was exquisitely clear and pale, an intriguing

contrast to her vibrant hair. Strawberries and cream. He had to taste her.

Her mouth touched briefly against his lower lip and sent desire flaring and shuddering through his body.

She made a soft, apologetic sound. "I wasn't quite close enough," she whispered. "I'll try again."

*Oh, yes!* In a kind of blissful agony, Nick closed his eyes and this time Laura's lips settled firmly, softly, warmly against his. He tasted their sweetness and then he heard her rapid breathing, felt her hands on the sides of his face, sensed her lips opening beneath his.

And there was only one thing a fellow could do. He kissed her back.

It was only meant to be a gentle kiss. After all, this prudish little creature was easily shocked. But her mouth was so unexpectedly warm and welcoming and before he had time to reconsider, Nick's lips and tongue became fused in a hungry, urgent, dizzying tangle with Laura's.

And incredibly, instead of protesting, she made soft little needy sounds. Sounds that begged him for more. Sounds that drove him crazy.

He *was* crazy. He shouldn't be doing this. Not with her.

But her hands were roaming restlessly over his shoulders and her mouth was moving against his with increasing eagerness. This wasn't the time to question his sanity.

It was time to slip his fingers into her silky hair and discover if it felt as good as it looked. Damn, it felt even better. Soft. So soft. Her coppery curls wrapped themselves around his fingers. And he wanted all of her wrapped around him.

Nick couldn't remember a kiss that had sent him so

wild so fast. He needed to haul her closer, to feel all of her soft curves pressed under him, to peel away those feathers.

*Don't touch the feathers!*

He jerked his hands away from Laura's temptingly bare shoulders as if they were glowing hot embers. And the action was enough to jolt both of them back into reality. To the reality that they were still in her car and parked in a busy suburban street outside a pub full of his mates.

They were both a touch breathless. Nick was more than a little shell-shocked. He figured Laura felt the same way. But he was damned sure he wasn't going to apologise for kissing her. Best not to discuss that kiss at all.

"Well," he managed to say at last, "I'd say you won that dare, so you'd better tell me where to line up for this job tomorrow morning."

With cheeks of bright pink, Laura resumed her place in the driver's seat, took a deep breath and hooked a fiery curl behind one ear. "Could you meet me at nine-thirty at the Casey Street entrance to the Glenwood hospital?" she asked so politely she might have been issuing an invitation to dine with the Queen.

Nick nodded. Heaven help him. He had the softest heart in the country. Or was that the softest head? First a strip show, now a clown act. Twice in one night he'd let himself be conned into doing something he didn't want to do.

But he could hardly wriggle out of this agreement after Little Miss Prim had so bravely sacrificed her mouth and her high moral standards for the sake of a ward full of sick kids.

He wasn't due in court until eleven tomorrow.

"It's a done deal," he told her. "Thanks for the—er—lift." And, opening the car door, Nick dived into the pub before he could change his mind.

About anything.

"You're looking happy." Susie looked up from the pile of returned books she was processing to greet Laura. "I take it the hospital session went well this morning?"

Laura hadn't realised she was wearing such a wide grin. She reassembled her features into something more sober. "It went really well," she agreed. "The children loved it. Nick was brilliant. He's even more athletic than I realised. He can do handstands and he can juggle—well, he can almost juggle. Thank goodness he was only using oranges. He can—"

"Hey, hold it!?" Susie interrupted. "Did you say Nick?"

"Nick Farrell, the hit of your party last night. I've encouraged him to extend his repertoire."

Susie blinked and gulped in a very fair imitation of a stunned mullet. "But don't you have someone regular that you use for your hospital work?"

Laura smiled. "I didn't have time to tell you last night, but Moe's come down with a virus and he couldn't make it. Luckily, it wasn't a problem. I talked Nick Farrell into standing in for him. He was a brilliant clown."

The six books Susie had been holding thumped onto the counter top. "He was *what?*" People reading nearby looked up and frowned at them. She stepped closer to Laura and asked her again in a quieter, but distinctly strained, voice, "You got *Nick Farrell* to be a clown?"

"Yes," Laura said defensively. "I don't see why you

should look so shocked. You hired him to strip butt naked. I simply hired him to put those same entertaining skills to a better purpose. He really brightened the day for those sick kids.''

Susie was spluttering. ''But—but how on earth did you persuade him to do it?''

An elderly couple arrived at the counter to check out their books and, grateful for the excuse to avoid answering Susie's question, Laura turned away quickly to serve them. There was no way she would go into the precise details of exactly how she'd persuaded Nick to help her.

Not that she really believed that kiss had been a deciding factor for him. But she was doing her darned best to delete all thoughts of it. If she tried to analyse just how that kiss had happened her mind went into meltdown mode. She hadn't just kissed the man, she'd practically eaten him alive.

*Laura Do-good had lost her head in an outburst of uncontrolled lust with a professional strip-tease artist!*

She'd only been able to face Nick this morning because he'd been so well disguised behind clown's paint, a curly red wig, stripy pants and long-toed shoes.

But Susie wasn't to be put off. As soon as there was a lull at the desk, she was beside Laura, brimming with questions. ''I just can't believe you got Nick to do that clown gig,'' she began. ''I mean, to start with, how did he get time away from court?''

''Court?'' Laura echoed faintly. The walls of the library seemed to close in suddenly. She felt dizzy. ''He—he's on trial?'' Had she hurled herself into the arms of a criminal?

''No. Of course he's not on trial, silly.'' Susie stared hard at Laura. ''Oh, my goodness,'' she whispered.

"You don't know... Who do you think...? You don't think Nick was—a *real* stripper, do you?"

"Of course he's a real stripper. How much more real do you want? The man took all his clothes off in a room full of women!"

Again, the heads from the reading corner jerked in their direction. There were a few eyebrows raised and knowing smirks exchanged.

Laura flinched.

"Gee, Laura, I'm sorry I didn't fill you in on the plan," Susie replied *sotto voce*. "I guess I was worried you mightn't like it." She bent her head closer and outlined in clear and certain terms the exact circumstances that had led to Nick's appearance at her party— how she'd stopped him just short of baring his prime exhibits *and* exactly how he filled in most of his days in court.

"Crown Prosecutor!" Laura squeaked as she clung to the counter for support. "You mean to tell me I wasted good sleeping time last night planning ways to keep that man from the depths of moral depravity and he spends his days being a pillar of society—an upholder of law and justice?"

"'Fraid so." Susie nodded, and grimaced.

Laura stifled a shriek. This was not a good moment to be in a library. She'd made an A-class fool of herself. And Nick Farrell had let her. He'd *helped* her make a fool of herself.

This morning she'd paid him twenty-four dollars for his hour's work—and she'd impressed on him that it was six dollars over the award. And the creep had acted as if she'd done him a big favour when, chances were, he pulled in thousands of dollars in a day!

Dimly, Laura realised that Susie was still talking.

"Anyhow, you have to admit Nick's ultra-cute, isn't he?"

To her horror, Laura felt a bright red blush sweep up her neck and cheeks till it reached the roots of her crimson hair. "No way," she protested with unnecessary vehemence. "He's got nothing going for him."

*Just the sexiest mouth in the Southern hemisphere.*

Susie grinned. "You didn't notice his body? His face? His cheeky smile?"

"He's definitely not my type," Laura sniffed. *And wasn't that the honest truth?* The man was an exhibitionist and a sneaky fake. But she knew her denial sounded weak and feeble when her red face was making such an eloquent statement.

"That's a pity," murmured Susie with a sly smile.

Laura didn't want to ask, but she couldn't help herself. "Why do you say that?"

"Because you're going to have to see each other again on Saturday."

"Don't tell me he's coming to the wedding?"

"He sure is. If Rob and I hadn't decided to get married in such a crazy rush I guess you would have met him at an engagement party or something, but Nick's going to be Rob's best man. Which means, my dear, that he'll be your partner."

*G-r-r-reat!* Laura spun away abruptly and bit down on an explosive retort. *This couldn't be happening!* Grabbing an armful of books, she stacked them onto the return trolley in completely the wrong order while she wondered desperately if it would be terribly bad form to beg Susie to demote her from her position as bridesmaid.

How could she face Nick Farrell? She'd been hoping she'd never have to set eyes on the man again for the rest of her days. Meeting him had been the start of a series of disasters. She'd made one gigantic mistake after another!

First there'd been the prudish sermons about how he could better himself, then she'd locked her lips with him like a sex-starved loser. And now, this morning, she'd paid him peanuts to be a circus clown.

She tried to look and sound calm. "Nick's the best man? That's fine. It's a simple job. We'll hardly have to do anything together except follow you down the aisle. I'll—I'll be busy keeping your veil and train in order and he'll be totally preoccupied propping up Rob."

Susie picked up one of the books Laura had misplaced and slotted it into its correct position on the trolley.

"We'll see," she murmured. And to Laura's embarrassment, her friend's finger gently traced her flushed cheek. "But there are some interesting symptoms showing here. If you don't have the hots for Nick Farrell, I'm wondering why you're redder than the proverbial beetroot."

Everything about weddings was designed to make a man nervous, Nick decided as he took his place beside Rob the following Saturday. The hired suits, the unfamiliar music played on a wheezy organ, the damp-eyed relatives in the front pews and the silent, expectant hush of the rest of the congregation.

It was all a far cry from the rollicking, boozy fun of the bucks' party a few nights ago.

Rob was restless as he waited for Susie to appear. "Have you got the rings?" he muttered.

Nick frowned. "What rings?"

Rob's face blanched. "I gave them to you last night. Remember?"

"Are you sure you did?" Nick patted his coat pockets and then checked the deeper pockets in his trousers.

"Oh, my God!" Rob stared at Nick and then sank his head into his hands. "I don't believe it. This can't happen. Not now!" He looked completely shaken, on the point of nervous collapse.

With the fingers of his right hand, Nick felt his fob pocket again. "Oh," he said, withdrawing two golden circles. "You mean these rings?"

Rob's head shot up. "You rat!"

For an uncomfortable second or two the two mates eyed each other. Then a corner of Nick's mouth twitched and Rob's mouth curled in answer.

Rob shook his head and his eyes sparkled knowingly. "I knew you'd find a way to get me back for that surprise gig at Susie's party."

"Too right," Nick answered with a grin.

"Er—hem—gentlemen—" The vicar leaned towards them. "The bridal party has arrived."

Suddenly the organ launched into the dramatic opening chords of Mendelssohn's "Wedding March."

"Here she comes." Rob swung around eagerly to face the back of the church. Nick followed, wishing he didn't have to feel so choked up.

He wasn't worried that Rob was going to his doom. He was happy for the guy. Rob was head over heels in love with Susie and there was nothing to—

*Hold on!* Nick's meditation on his mate's future was arrested by the scene at the end of the flower-decked aisle. Susie was there, framed in a stone archway, looking bridal and lovely in white and smiling broadly.

But just in front of her was a redhead in blue.

*That* redhead in blue.

Something alarming happened to Nick's chest and his ability to breathe. For a second or two, there seemed to be only one woman in the church. Laura Goodman. She was moving slowly towards him, her amazing blue feathers replaced by something floaty and elegant in a paler blue.

Nick squared his shoulders and blinked. She was still there. This wasn't part of last night's dream. She was still moving slowly forward, carrying a mass of delicate blossoms. Her vibrant hair was caught at the sides of her head in clusters of tiny flowers, but from there it fell away in loose waves that shone like dark flames against her pale, perfect shoulders.

A short strand of pearls gleamed at her creamy throat. The woman was beautiful! Her deep blue eyes glowed softly with a powerful emotion. But they were fixed straight ahead of her as she preceded Susie down the aisle.

Not once did they stray in Nick's direction.

He told himself he was glad that she wasn't looking at him. He was relieved that she didn't make any kind of eye contact as she reached the chancel steps and stood to one side to make room for the bride.

In fact it would be best if they both acted as if they hardly knew each other. Dear God, they *did* hardly know one another.

And yet, despite their brief and vexing acquaintance, this uptight librarian had kissed him with a fire that had practically launched him into orbit. The impact of that kiss had stayed with Nick ever since.

By heaven, Laura's kiss had been hotter than a midsummer's night. She tasted sweeter than the freshest spring morning. Sexier than anything he'd experienced in years. He'd found getting out of her car one of the hardest exits he'd ever made.

On the strength of that kiss, his dreams had been X-rated for several nights in a row. But just how that astonishing encounter had happened so unexpectedly would probably remain one of the unsolved mysteries of the new millennium.

Of course he'd paid for it with that crazy clown caper the next morning…

The vicar moved forward and, with a start, Nick realised the man was addressing the congregation. ''Dearly beloved…''

He dragged his focus back to the job at hand. Rob and Susie's wedding day. The start of thirty, forty, who knew how many years of matrimonial bliss. Nice if you could get it. He wished them well.

He hadn't been too lucky.

But his own marriage was the last thing Nick wanted to think about today. That was territory too painful to visit.

Laura thought she was doing well. If she could keep herself mentally distanced from Nick Farrell she would be able to maintain her composure throughout the wedding ceremony.

She concentrated on Susie. In her slim-fitting satin gown and dreamy veil, her friend looked radiant and beautiful. The perfect bride. On the other side of her stood Rob. She'd never seen a guy look so happy and eager to tie the knot.

In fact Rob's happiness, his love for Susie and his quiet confidence, seemed to spread a calming aura over the whole wedding party. Laura remained aware of Nick, tall and dark and well, yes, she couldn't deny it—

impossibly handsome—on the far side of the more solid
Rob, but as the beautiful ceremony progressed his presence became less disturbing.

The hymns were sung, the vows and rings exchanged
and blessings given, and she gradually relaxed and allowed herself to become totally absorbed in Susie's
happiness.

But her serenity evaporated when it was time to follow the ecstatic couple back down the aisle. Then everything came back to her. Every embarrassing reason
why she should turn tail and flee.

Nick had already stepped forward to take the place
Rob vacated and he stood facing her with his elbow
cocked, waiting for her to link her arm with his. Unfair!
He was too tall and dark to ignore. Too dashingly handsome in his formal suit. Too darned good-looking to
forget what it felt like to—

*Stop it!* Laura lifted her head haughtily, and with the
faintest smile and minimum eye contact, allowed Nick
to take her arm. Beneath the smooth sleeve of his jacket
she could feel the solid muscle of his forearm, but she
focused her eyes ahead on Susie's veil, making sure it
was trailing neatly behind her. She smiled at the rows
of beaming faces.

Nick murmured, "Good afternoon, Laura," in his
deep, resonant voice and she dipped her head to acknowledge his greeting, but didn't look his way.

The one thing she didn't want to do was blush. With
her pale complexion, a blush was like wearing a sign
on her forehead that read: Foolish Flustered Female. But
trying not to go red meant not looking at Nick, not
thinking about him or the ridiculous mistakes she'd
made, and not getting angry with him for stringing her
along.

It was a tall order.

Progress out of the church was slow because Susie and Rob kept stopping to be congratulated and hugged by relatives and friends, but with three-quarters of the aisle covered Laura began to breathe more easily. A few more steps and they would be outside. Then she could mingle and mix with the crowd and this *togetherness* part of the ordeal would be over.

Towards the back of the church two adorable little girls were leaning forward, almost falling out of their pew as they grinned and waved madly. Laura guessed they were sisters. Although they didn't look alike, they were wearing identical dark green dresses with white lace collars and cuffs.

She smiled at them and their faces lit up, their eyes rounded with excitement. To her surprise, she realised they were looking at Nick and herself with the kind of adoration and awe that was usually reserved for the very famous. She heard Nick's soft chuckle and turned to see that he was grinning at the girls.

Her heart gave a funny little jump as she saw the way his deep grey eyes glowed when he smiled at them.

"Aren't they sweet?" she couldn't help commenting.

"Most of the time," came his surprising answer.

Then suddenly the smaller girl, a rosy-cheeked moppet with glossy dark curls, slipped out of her seat and into the aisle in front of them. "Daddy!" she called excitedly, looking straight up at Nick.

"Daddy?" Laura squeaked.

*This irresponsible jester was a father?*

She reached for the end of a pew to support her shaky legs. *She'd exchanged passionate kisses with a married man? No, she couldn't have. Not again!*

# CHAPTER FOUR

NICK watched as Laura's shocked gaze darted from his daughter to himself and back again. He knew his little girl's features were diminutive, feminine versions of his own thick, dark hair, distinctive nose and steel grey eyes. No DNA testing required to determine this paternity issue.

Bending down, he picked up the cuddly bundle in an easy, familiar movement and he dropped a happy kiss on her warm cheek. She beamed with delight. "This is Fliss," he told Laura. "My number-two daughter."

"My proper name's Felicity," the child corrected in her usual bossy manner, taking care to pronounce her name very carefully.

Laura's blue eyes clouded and Nick couldn't tell if she was stunned or angry or both. She looked as if she was suffering from severe shock, but perhaps she was just being a female—and feeling soppy about Susie's wedding.

His older daughter stepped forward. "And this is Kate," he explained, "my big girl."

He didn't feel ready to explain at this moment that the reason Kate's hair was as fine and pale as Felicity's was thick and dark was because she took after her mother.

Laura seemed to have trouble responding to Kate's shy smile, but at last she managed to speak. "Hello, Kate—and Felicity." Her stunned gaze swung to the grey-haired woman who'd been standing with the girls.

"And this is Heather Cunningham, my mother-in-law."

The two women exchanged polite greetings. "I've seen you before—at the Glenwood library," the older woman added.

"Heather brought the girls to the church to see the wedding, but they won't be attending the reception," Nick explained.

"Uhhuh," was the only answer Laura seemed capable of making.

But his daughters weren't so tongue-tied.

"I love your dress," Kate said, gazing up at Laura as if she were a fairy tale princess come to life. "And your flowers."

Not to be outdone, Felicity tightened her plump arms around his neck as she squeezed him in an excited hug. "Daddy," she cried, "I like your pretty lady. Are you going to get married, too?"

Before he could react to Felicity's question, Nick heard a helpless, choking sound beside him. Laura looked paler and more shocked than ever.

"Do you need to sit down?" he asked her.

She shook her head.

It occurred to him that she was probably feeling sorry for these poor children, who had a degenerate stripper for a father; she could even be wondering where their mother was.

Desperately, he tried to think of a simple way to explain his situation without upsetting anyone present. In court, he was famous for his sharp mind and quick, precise verbal responses.

But talking about this was different.

This was about Miranda.

There were actual tears in Laura's blue eyes. Her

mouth quivered. And damn it, Nick wanted to cry, too. Eight years ago he'd been married, just as Rob had today. He'd been incredibly young, but filled to overflowing with love for his bride. He should still be married now!

He blinked and tried to distract his thoughts by rubbing his nose against Felicity's.

"Daddy?" the little girl persisted. "Didn't you hear me? I've got a really good idea. You can marry this pretty lady."

Nick almost dropped his daughter. "Not today, Fliss," he hedged, only just managing to keep his voice steady. "It's Rob's turn to get married today." He shot Laura an apologetic grimace.

"You've quite captivated the girls, Laura," Heather Cunningham said with a cautious smile that didn't quite reach her eyes.

Nick realised his mother-in-law was right. Here was Fliss, innocently demanding that he marry the pretty bridesmaid, while Kate was standing as close as possible to Laura and looking up at her with huge brown eyes. Kate usually only looked at stray kittens with that much depth of feeling.

He'd never seen his elder daughter so impressed by anyone. If he wasn't careful the girls would start a Laura Goodman fan club, right here on the church steps.

He had to admit that Laura was looking exceptionally beautiful today with her glowing hair loosely framing her delicate face. And her gown was all filmy and feminine, the sort of romantic get-up that all little girls probably dreamed of wearing one day.

It was a pity his daughters hadn't met Laura at her library, with her fiery hair scraped back into a neat, no-nonsense knot and her feminine curves disguised by a serviceable navy shirt dress—the way she'd looked at the hospital the other day. Then the girls wouldn't have been nearly so impressed by her and there would have been no embarrassing comments.

He suggested to Heather that it was time to take Kate and Felicity home.

"Not yet!" they protested, but Nick remained firm.

"I'll give your daddy my bouquet to bring home," Laura promised the girls, and after that they went away quite happily with their grandmother, but not until both Nick and Laura had submitted to hugs and kisses.

As Nick waved the girls off Laura turned to him, her eyes shining—no, not exactly shining, he realised with mild alarm, but rather shimmering. With emotion. Negative emotion. She was angry.

"I can't believe those dear little girls are your daughters," she hissed out of the side of her mouth.

He shrugged. "I guess it does take a fair stretch of the imagination."

"They're just so sweet," she added. "They're *gorgeous.*"

"Amazing, isn't it?"

"They deserve a father who takes his responsibility seriously."

"Fair go," he protested. "I admit I'm not Father of the Year, but I'm not exactly a slack parent."

"But your morals are questionable."

"My morals?" He scowled at her.

She leaned close and whispered, "Maybe you aren't a strip-tease artist." Her tone grew chilly as she added, "And while we're on the subject, I didn't appreciate being strung along about that."

He dug his hands into his coat pockets and felt his jaw stiffen.

"But," she continued, "you can't pretend you don't know what I'm upset about now."

Nick looked around him. Luckily all eyes were on the bride and groom. Rob and Susie were posing for photos on the church steps. "No pretence," he told Laura. "I'm dead serious. I don't know what you're talking about."

"You persuaded me to kiss you."

"That's immoral? A simple kiss?" He looked around him again, worried that this ridiculous conversation might be overheard.

"It wasn't exactly a *simple* kiss," Laura muttered. "A kiss on the cheek is simple."

"Hey, let's not get tangled up in definitions."

"And don't you play fancy lawyer games with me. Any kind of kiss—and you know the kind of kiss I'm talking about—should be saved for your wife."

"My wife," Nick echoed softly, and he felt the strangeness of those words on his lips.

"I'm assuming you had enough moral fibre to marry the girls' mother."

"Oh, yes," Nick said with a sigh. He could see the blue fire burning in Laura's eyes as she gathered steam for another barrage of questions. He decided to nip them in the bud.

"She's dead."

"*What?*" she whispered.

"My wife died."

"Oh!" Laura looked stricken. She covered her mouth with a shaking hand. "Oh, Nick. I'm so sorry."

"It's OK. It happened some time back. Fliss was only a baby."

The very last thing Nick wanted was for Laura to go on saying how sorry she was. She didn't need to. He could see the remorse in her eyes. She had such an open, expressive face, it was as easy to read as a billboard.

"Those poor little girls."

He suppressed a new surge of dismay. He'd seen that dreamy, sentimental look in the eyes of many women over the past five years when they'd discovered he was a widower. It was a look that set off alarm bells.

In the past, similar comments had always been followed up eventually, one way or another, by the message, *I'd just love to mother your daughters for you.*

And, given Laura Goodman's fondness for doing good deeds, chances were she would be simply bursting with willingness to take his daughters under her wing—just as she did those children at the hospital. But he certainly didn't want another wife and his girls didn't need another mother.

He, Kate and Felicity would go on managing just fine on their own.

*However,* he thought, with a self-mocking smile, it was a damn pity that Laura was so addicted to *morality* and *good* deeds. Didn't she realise that with her fiery hair and blazing blue eyes, not to mention her sexy hot mouth and slim curves, she'd been designed for bad, bad deeds…*wicked* deeds…?

But that was a different story altogether.

Laura felt an unpleasant dizzy sensation when she joined Susie and Rob for photos in front of the church. It was as if she'd stepped off one of those scary rides at a sideshow.

At first, when she'd discovered Nick was a father, her response had been a nauseating flood of ghastly, guilty memories. Memories of the affair she'd had with Oliver before she'd found out about his wife and boys.

Five years ago she'd suffered so much guilt she'd actually made herself ill. She still felt sickened whenever she thought about Oliver's family.

After Oliver's shocking confession, she'd been so desperate for proof that she'd tracked down his home address and spied on them. She'd seen his wife drive the boys home from school, watched them laughing together as they got out of the car.

One boy, who looked ridiculously like Oliver, had been wearing football gear with soccer boots draped by their laces around his neck. Another had helped his mother carry shopping and the littlest one had tumbled on the front lawn for ages, playing with the family dog.

Such a nice, normal, happy family. *Except that she'd been making love with their father.* For four whole months! And all the time she'd known nothing of them, had believed Oliver loved only her. Had thought he was planning to marry her. What a silly, gullible little fool she'd been.

The experience had sent her scurrying back to the safe life of being a Goodman. Laura had drawn the Goodman shield around her like armour, because she knew without a doubt she wasn't cut out for anything but the security of love within a marriage.

Except that somehow Nick Farrell—who *suddenly* wasn't a stripper and wasn't married, but a widowed father and an upright citizen instead—made the thought of being an uptight, prim and proper Goodman less appealing.

It would be jolly nice if she could actually stop thinking about him completely, but ever since she'd met Nick she had been riding an emotional helter-skelter.

Even when she'd been appalled that he was a stripper she'd loved the way he looked. His amazing kiss had zapped her into a whole new level of awareness and yet she'd been embarrassed ever since about her brazen response.

And then Nick had completely charmed her with the skilful way he'd entertained the children at the hospital. And finally he'd introduced her just now to those darling little motherless girls...

And now...she couldn't pin down her feelings.

Of course she hadn't fallen in love with him or anything ridiculous like that. It was something else she felt...a nervous excitement...a puzzling need to think about him all the time.

During the photography session she was so acutely aware of Nick's presence that she was barely conscious of anyone else. She had trouble with her breathing whenever he came near. On several occasions the photographer required them to link arms and she wondered if Nick could hear her galloping heartbeats. His touch electrified her.

Somehow she managed to mingle with the wedding guests and make the usual small talk. At some point they climbed into a limousine and drove to the reception. She presumed she ate the three-course-meal that was served to her. Vaguely, she listened to speeches and toasts.

All evening people told her she looked lovely, but the only time she really took any notice was when Nick paid her a polite compliment during his speech.

She might have lingered over his words if Susie hadn't leaned over and whispered to her, "I'm so glad Nick made a straight speech. I was worried we might be in for some kind of practical joke. You know—pay-back for the hen-night.''

But Susie spoke too soon. Nick went on to read a pile of faxes and messages and his commentary was absolutely peppered with clever, teasing jokes. His comic timing was perfect and he left Rob red-faced and the guests breathless with laughter. Which is the real Nick? Laura wondered as she watched him. The tender father, the brilliant Crown Prosecutor or the daredevil joker?

Long after he'd taken his seat once more, she sat there, lost in thought. What happened to all these roles when he turned into Nick the lover? His kiss had been sensational…

''Care to dance?''

The deep voice close behind her brought Laura out of her trance and back to the reception with a jolt. She realised that Susie and Rob had completed the bridal waltz and that other couples were now joining them on the dance floor.

Everyone would expect the best man and the brides-maid to dance at least once. Feeling exceedingly self-conscious, she rose from her chair. She was intensely aware of Nick's hand at her back, gently guiding her past the other tables to the polished timber dance floor in the middle of the room.

She turned to face him, keeping her eyes lowered as she allowed him to take her right hand in his firm grasp while she placed her left hand on his broad shoulder. He tugged her a little closer and she heard the smile in his voice when he said, ''I've been waiting to dance with you all evening.''

Before she knew what was happening he hauled her

against him and held her firmly and surely as he began to guide her around the floor.

She wondered if he could feel her trembling. Her skin tingled all over, she was so conscious of the strength of him and the underlying beauty of that body moving against hers.

Her mind threw up pictures of Susie's party. The way he'd playfully shown off his tanned, silky skin stretched over taut, manly muscles. Her stomach tightened as she thought of the dark trail of hair from his chest to his navel and beyond…all that maleness…all that hard muscle and strength so very close to her now.

His broad chest pressed against her and his thigh slid boldly between her legs as he pivoted her this way and that. And Laura's electrified body felt like a time bomb. A sleeping volcano, dormant no longer. She was re-membering again what *lust* was all about.

When the music stopped, she thanked heaven that he didn't release his hold. There was every chance she would have melted bonelessly to the floor if he'd let her go. She felt his hand under her chin, lifting her face till her gaze was forced to meet with his, and her breath caught as she saw a familiar cheeky sparkle in his eyes. "Like to catch a breath of fresh air?" he asked. "I don't think anyone will notice if we're gone for a minute or two."

*Oh, yes, please.* Unable to speak, Laura nodded and allowed Nick to steer her through the tables that circled the dance floor. *How scary was this?* She was actually hoping that he was taking her outside to kiss her again.

*She couldn't be changing this fast.* What had hap-pened to all that safe and cosy Goodman goodness?

Beyond the reception room, they passed through huge glass doors opening onto a balcony that overlooked the river. Nick guided her out of the lights and into the shadows and she was grateful for the breeze coming off the water to cool her heated skin.

She tried to distract herself from the urge to stare at him by leaning against the cool stone balustrade while she admired the lights from a nearby bridge.

"This is better," she heard him murmur close beside her in his rumbling, deep voice.

Too helpless to pretend uninterest, she turned his way. And he was looking at her with hot, hungry eyes. And suddenly she needed him to haul her into his arms and kiss her. *Now.*

She wasn't sure if it was because he read the urgent pleading in her eyes, but without saying another word Nick pulled her roughly to him and, just as she'd willed him to, he kissed her.

And...just as she'd known it would be, his kiss was perfect.

Not too tentative and not too brash, he took his time, letting his mouth roam over hers in confident, unrushed, seriously sexy caresses.

Laura knew she was being kissed by an expert. With lazy but insistent pressure, his warm mouth made love to hers slowly. He kissed her till she almost whimpered with pleasure. When his tongue teased her lips apart Laura had never felt so glad she was a woman.

She'd almost forgotten how wonderful it was to feel like this with a man.

But even in the past...she had never been kissed like *this*...by a man who knew *exactly* how to ask for what he wanted.

Nick didn't just invade her mouth. The taste and the heat of him invaded her senses. As he pressed against her, his body felt so hard and strong. So male.

She didn't care that she kissed Nick back with an enthusiasm that would leave him in no doubt about how she felt. She'd been Goody-goody Goodman for the past five years and tonight she suddenly wanted to be bad.

*Gloriously, splendidly* bad.

But finally Nick lifted his lips from hers and she felt his breath on her cheek as he whispered, ''Pretty lady.''

Breathless, she looked up at him. Had any man ever looked more divine? But, to her consternation, she noticed that he was frowning and looking pensive, as if he was suddenly upset about something. He took a step away from her, shoving his hands in his pockets.

Feeling a sudden chill, Laura wrapped her arms across her chest and hugged her arms, trying to ignore an awful sense of loneliness now she was out of his embrace. ''Is something wrong?''

''Not wrong exactly,'' came his careful answer. ''But I hadn't planned to kiss you like that.''

''Oh,'' Laura replied in a tiny voice. ''How did you plan to kiss me?''

''That's the point. I didn't plan on kissing you at all.''

''I see.'' She counted a dozen thumping heartbeats while she let that news sink in. ''Do you normally *plan* such things?''

''Oh, yes.'' He reinforced his words with a strong nod of his head. ''Most definitely.''

She lifted her chin. ''That doesn't sound very romantic.''

Nick had been staring straight in front of him, but now he edged his gaze warily towards Laura. ''I don't suppose it does. But a man in my position can't afford to be too romantic.''

She swung her shocked gaze back to the river. Nick Farrell *planned* kisses? It seemed such a sad idea to her.

She planned the weekly roster for the library. She planned what she was going to cook for dinner and what she would write about in the next letter she sent her grandmother…but she never planned…romance.

Let's face it, she corrected her thoughts quickly, there had been nothing to plan. For at least five years now romance just hadn't been a factor in her life. "How do you go about planning your next kiss?" she asked, shooting him a sideways glance, but then she saw his slow grin and she felt very, very, foolish.

His lips quirked in a half-smile. "I find two volumes exceptionally useful—a telephone book and my diary."

What a fruitcake she was! A man in Nick's position, a man who was no longer married, but who found himself left with a mega-healthy, ultra-virile body, a demanding profession and an even more demanding home life…

Of course he would need to plan his…his social life. His *sex* life. She remembered with a guilty start that Oliver had been very precise about his liaisons with her.

"Of course," she said between gritted teeth. Then she tossed him a haughty glare. "So there's never any room in your life for spontaneity?"

He scratched his head thoughtfully. "What I'm trying to say, Laura, is that I don't want to give you the wrong idea. You're very lovely, and in the moonlight you look damn desirable—*heck,* it's not just the moonlight—you *are* incredibly desirable—but—"

He paused and Laura's heart seemed to shatter in her chest. She'd been buzzing with awareness of this man all evening. He'd just kissed her so comprehensively she could hardly remember her own name. He said she was desirable and she was feeling good about that.

Hallelujah! She was actually feeling good about a

man's physical desire for her. After all this time since Oliver, that was a major breakthrough. She didn't want to hear any of his *buts*.

"*But* I don't think it would be very wise if we were to repeat a kiss like that."

Laura felt her shoulders stiffen. How dared Nick kiss her and then immediately dismiss it as a mistake. "Why is it so unwise?" she asked, and she was rather pleased with the cool and haughty edge in her voice.

Nick threw his dark head back to stare at the sky and spent several seconds studying the stars before he lowered his eyes again. Her heart thumped as she waited for his answer.

He looked at her almost gently. "Pretty lady, I think if I were to kiss you for a third time I would also need to—" He stopped again and Laura felt as if she was dangling from a very fragile string. "Laura—I'm not looking for love."

She gulped as she felt a ridiculous sense of panic surge in her chest. "When did love come into this conversation?"

He frowned at her as if she'd missed something really obvious. "I think, from the little I know of you, that you're the kind of woman who would need to love the man she went to bed with. And you would prefer him to love you in return."

Laura swung away from him. She was completely shocked. She was furious. And she was mostly angry, because Nick Farrell, the clever lawyer, was three jumps ahead of her.

She felt as if she'd been left in the starting blocks while Nick was already halfway down the track. Staring at the black, silent river, she tried to keep her voice even as she asked, "How could you have the cheek to assume that just because I let you kiss me—that I would—that we would—?''

''You told me in the *way* you kissed me.''

Laura glared at him. ''It was just a *kiss!*''

Nick chuckled. ''Laura, that old song got it wrong. A kiss isn't *just a kiss.* It has a language all of its own.'' He was grinning cheekily. ''Am I right?''

''Oh, I'm sure you're always right.''

''I thought we were telling each other something just now.''

''Maybe you read me incorrectly,'' she replied. *Or maybe he'd read her dead right.*

Nick's face switched to serious mode again. ''Please, forgive me if I'm wrong, but I figured your attitude to relationships might not be particularly—*relaxed.* I don't imagine you're into casual—''

*Casual sex?* She had been on the verge of thinking she could be tempted. *No she hadn't!* Laura closed her eyes so she wouldn't have to look at Nick. She didn't want to see how gorgeous he looked while she admitted to herself painfully that he had hit right on the truth. ''I am most definitely *not* into casual,'' she said coldly.

''You see, then, we're not a good match.''

Biting down hard on her lower lip, she held back an emotional retort. She could stay cool. She could do icy. She lifted her chin and stared back at him, her mouth pursed.

''Unfortunately,'' Nick went on less calmly, ''*I'm* not into deep and meaningful.''

''I can't imagine that's an ideal situation for your daughters—to see their father having a string of casual relationships.''

''That's my business,'' he snapped. ''But I can assure

you that I'm aware of the problem. Discretion is vital, of course.''

*Discretion, planning*... Laura had never heard such a hard-headed approach to romance. She would have to make an addition to Nick's CV: Crown Prosecutor, father and...when it came to his love life, programmed robot.

He spoke again. ''I've been in love once in my life.''

She spun around, startled by his sudden admission and the depth of feeling in his voice. Her heart jerked painfully. ''Your wife?'' she whispered.

He nodded briefly. ''Miranda.''

*Miranda.* Laura repeated the name under her breath. Didn't that just sound like the name of the perfect woman? Beautiful, elegant to the core, a wonderful mother to those two little girls...

''Losing her was unbearable. I don't plan on ever loving someone that deeply again.''

She saw the stark pain on Nick's face. His mouth had twisted into a cruel sneer. In his eyes she saw a ghastly emptiness that chilled her. He was reliving the pain of his wife's death and she couldn't bear to see the agony etched into his face. How badly he still hurt!

Something hard, like a steel band, clamped around Laura's chest. It was all so very clear now. Nick would never willingly expose his heart to that kind of pain again. And why should he when there were plenty of women who would be happy to accept his take-it-or-leave-it terms?

She was tempted to point out to Nick Farrell that he wasn't the only person who'd loved and lost. When she'd discovered how Oliver had deceived her she'd done her share of grieving. But she wouldn't mention that now.

"I'm sorry you've had to suffer like that," she told him. "And thank you for making your position clear." She flashed him a brilliant smile as she added, "I'm not quite sure where you stumbled on the notion that I wanted you to fall in love with me, but there's nothing like getting things out in the open right from the start. You can rest assured I have no ambitions in that direction. Now, if you don't mind, I need to go and attend to Susie. I'm sure I should be handing out wedding cake or helping her to get changed into her going-away outfit."

Holding her head high, she swept past Nick without looking his way again.

# CHAPTER FIVE

THE following Tuesday Nick's secretary was on a tea break when he arrived back at his office and found his phone ringing insistently.

"Farrell," he answered crisply as he tossed his wig onto his desk and his gown over the back of his chair. He was glad to have the day's gruelling session in court behind him.

"Oh, good afternoon, Mr Farrell," a feminine voice spoke. "I'm Diane Forrest, Felicity's teacher."

His hand, which had been working to loosen his collar and tie, stilled. "Yes?" he asked sharply. His heart thundered. *Dear God!* Had something happened to Fliss at school? *Please, no!* Four years ago he'd received a phone call just like this from a hospital—about Miranda.

He looked at his watch, but his eyes couldn't focus on the time. "How can I help you?" he asked as calmly as he could manage.

"I was hoping to be able to discuss one or two things with you about Felicity. I'm just a little concerned about her," the teacher continued.

A wave of relief flooded Nick. He closed his eyes for a moment and wondered how long it would take before he behaved calmly and rationally about his daughters' safety?

With effort, he dragged his thoughts from disaster to the likely concerns of a first-grade teacher. "I see. Is Fliss having learning problems?"

"No, nothing like that. She's a very bright little girl," came the reassuring reply. "But there has definitely been something bothering her lately."

The teacher made a small throat-clearing sound. "I hope you don't mind my saying this, Mr Farrell, but Felicity seems to be quite disturbed about your plans to marry again."

"What?" croaked Nick. "That's impossible!"

"It might seem impossible from your perspective, but there was an incident this morning that highlighted the fact that she's been quite distressed about the whole issue."

"The reason I say it's impossible," Nick fired back, "is that I have absolutely no plans to marry again. I don't know how you got that idea, but I can assure you that such an event is simply not happening."

"Oh?"

"There's never been any suggestion, any *mention* of a wed—" Nick broke off as his mind flashed back to Saturday, to the memory of Fliss flinging her arms around him and announcing he should marry the pretty lady.

He groaned. "You said there was an incident this morning. What happened exactly?"

"The children were giving their morning talks," the teacher explained. "Felicity hasn't contributed for quite a while and so I thought it was time to encourage her to share some news. She stood out the front of the class and told us very proudly that her daddy was going to get married to a pretty lady. She seemed quite happy and excited about the news at first."

"Did she?" Nick asked grimly. "So when did she become distressed?"

"Well, you know what little children are like. The

rest of the class were allowed to ask questions and they bombarded Felicity for information about her new mother. Things like how old she is, what she looks like—if she can make chocolate cake. I could see she was getting upset and I called a halt to the questions, but I'm afraid the poor little kid broke down then. It took some time to calm her.''

Still clutching the telephone receiver, Nick dropped into a chair, stunned by the teacher's account of his daughter's morning. Of course Fliss would have been upset when she realised what she'd done. She'd told a bald-faced lie to the class and they'd all accepted it as fact. She was intelligent enough to be overcome by guilt.

He wondered why on earth the silly muffin had done such a thing. This wedding business was obviously getting way out of hand. For days now the girls had been taking it in turns to traipse around the house with a mosquito net on their heads while carrying the bouquet Laura had sent home. They were both wedding crazy.

"I had thought," the teacher continued carefully, "that there might be some unresolved issues regarding the new mother…maybe Felicity had some qualms about the changes ahead…but if you say you're not getting married then I guess we're dealing with a different issue."

Nick released a heavy sigh. "Indeed we are, Mrs Forrest. Thank you for letting me know about this, but I think I can deal with it at home. It's just that my daughter attended a wedding on the weekend and she has a vivid imagination. I don't think you'll have any more trouble with her."

"Oh, she's never any trouble."

"That's good to hear, but by all means let me know if you think she still seems unsettled."

"Certainly. I'm pleased there's not too much to concern us. Good afternoon, then, Mr Farrell."

"Afternoon and—thank you." Nick was about to drop the receiver back into its cradle, when he had second thoughts. "One moment."

"Yes?"

"This woman Felicity claimed I'm—er—marrying. Did she end up describing her?"

"Oh, yes." There was a slight chuckle on the other end of the line. "She was very definite. You were right when you said Felicity has a great imagination. She told us her new mother has lovely dark red hair and smiling blue eyes and she wears beautiful long, floaty gowns. Her classmates were very impressed."

"I see," said Nick, his voice grimmer than ever. "Thanks. That's all I need to know." This time he depressed the phone, dropped the receiver and flopped into his chair.

What the blazes was going on in his daughter's tiny mind? Leaning back, he blew out his breath as he linked his arms behind his head and stared at the ceiling.

He should never have allowed Heather to bring the girls to Rob's wedding.

"Little girls love weddings," she'd told him.

He'd finally consented because he valued his mother-in-law's opinion on the subject of what little girls liked and needed. And the girls were so fond of Rob. Let's face it, the guy had been like an uncle to them. But on the day of the wedding they'd hardly paid more than scant attention to Rob and Susie.

One look at that damn red-headed bridesmaid and they'd gone all dreamy-eyed. Then again, he acknowledged, one look at that same redhead and he'd become rather slow-witted himself.

How else could he explain the way he'd ended up out on the balcony with her, sharing that second incredible, molten kiss?

With another sigh he slumped deeper into his chair and slowly, without moving the rest of his body, stretched one hand forward and picked up a sheet of paper from his desk. It had some notes he no longer needed, so he crumpled it into a ball and tossed it towards the waste-paper basket in the corner.

It missed and rolled onto the carpet.

Nick swore. Wasn't that typical of the day he was having? He'd just finished a long session fighting one of the toughest courtroom battles he'd faced in his career so far. From the start he'd known without doubt that the accused was guilty, but it had taken every trick he'd ever learned to eventually nail him.

Now it looked as if, when he went home, he'd have an even tougher battle on his hands.

Today he'd eventually convinced the jury that the fellow in the dock was guilty of dealing in drugs. But he didn't like his chances of convincing his daughters to forget about Laura Goodman.

Laura sensed someone hovering at the desk near her, but she kept her eyes glued to her computer screen. On Wednesday evenings she always updated the catalogue files before she went home.

The person was leaning closer. "Excuse me."

Unable to avoid looking up, Laura discovered with a start that Nick Farrell's mother-in-law, Heather Cunningham, was trying to catch her attention. "Oh, hello."

"I'm so sorry to disturb you, Laura," the older woman said, "but I've brought the girls with me to borrow some books, and as I don't know much about the children's books that are available these days I wondered if I could get a little advice?"

Laura looked past Heather to see Kate and Felicity Farrell dressed in their school uniforms and standing in the children's book corner. They were staring in her direction.

Their shining eyes suggested they were brimming with suppressed excitement. Laura's heart slammed and thumped in her chest. She'd been trying so hard not to think about Nick, but seeing his girls brought a host of sensations—most of them uncomfortable.

Quickly saving the work she'd completed, she left the computer and joined Heather Cunningham at the desk. "Let's see what we can find."

"Just before we go over to the girls, Laura, I think I should warn you that they have been giving Nick rather a hard time because of you."

Laura's heart slammed and thumped some more. "What have they been saying?"

Heather took a deep breath before replying. "That bridesmaid's bouquet you sent home has meant endless games of weddings." She went on to explain that Felicity had made an embarrassing mistake at school.

Then she added, "And yesterday afternoon Kate collected all her pocket money and her birthday money and demanded that I take her to my hairdresser and have her hair dyed red."

"Good heavens!"

"Apparently Nick had to spend most of last night reassuring Kate that her light brown hair is beautiful."

"Of course it is," Laura agreed weakly. Stunned by

the woman's news, she looked across at Kate, who'd tired of waiting for them and found a book that interested her instead. Now she was sitting at a table to read it.

Her tawny hair fell in a fine silky curtain. "When I was Kate's age I was teased dreadfully because of the colour of my hair. I would have given anything for nice, quietly coloured hair like that."

Heather sighed. "Kate used to be happy that her hair was the same colour as her mother's. She is so much like Miranda."

Laura looked at Kate again, noting details. Slim and elfin-featured, the child had soft brown eyes and hair straight as a pin.

So that was what Miranda had looked like. That was the kind of quietly elegant woman Nick preferred. It couldn't be a more different look from her own fiery curls and hard-to-hide curves.

So what? Laura reminded herself sharply. What Nick Farrell thought of her appearance was irrelevant. He'd made that excruciatingly clear last weekend.

She frowned at Heather Cunningham. "If I'm causing trouble between the girls and Nick, why have you brought them here?"

The other woman looked uncomfortable for a moment. "The girls begged me to bring them, but actually I wanted to come anyhow, Laura. I wanted to warn you."

"Oh?" Laura replied, and she straightened her shoulders as she faced Heather Cunningham.

"You'd be foolish to develop any romantic notions about Nick."

Laura's eyes rounded with anger. "I don't indulge in romantic fantasies, Mrs Cunningham."

The other woman made a huffing noise. "You

wouldn't be the first woman who's made a beeline for
a widowed man, especially a handsome, well-to-do
man.''

Laura was so angry she refused to respond. A stretch
of silence vibrated between the two women, then eventually she asked quietly, ''What kind of books did you
want the girls to borrow?''

Heather turned towards the Children's Corner. With
a faint sniff, she said, ''I don't think we should be en-
couraging these two to read fairy tales. I'd like to see
them reading sensible books about animals or other
parts of the world.''

As she crossed the room Laura willed herself to ignore the spurt of affection she felt when Nick Farrell's
bright eyed, sweet little daughters turned and smiled at
her. Surely she could maintain the demeanour of a
highly professional, very efficient and impersonal librarian for the next ten minutes?

Felicity looked up at her and her grin widened. ''Hi,
Laura. Can you please help me to find a book that tells
me about where babies come from?''

Laura suppressed a groan of dismay. This was going
to be even harder than she feared.

Nick's secretary buzzed him late on Thursday afternoon.

''There's a call coming through from someone who
refuses to give his name, but he insists he must speak
to you.''

''Put him on,'' Nick sighed. He was tired, and for
the past hour he'd been fantasising about going home
and catching an early night.

When he heard the line switch through, he didn't care
that his voice sounded weary as he drawled, ''Nick
Farrell speaking.''

"Is that Mr Farrell, the famous Crown Prosecutor?"

Nick hesitated. For a minute he thought the caller was Rob, playing another prank. But Rob would hardly bother to call long distance from his honeymoon on a tropical island. He'd have better things to do right now.

And besides, the voice was a shade too thick with irony to be a joke, the tone was too sinister.

He frowned as he replied. "As I said, it's Farrell here. Who's speaking, please?"

"Never mind who I am...what I have to say is more important."

Nick thought about hanging up, but there was a chance the caller was someone with a vital tip-off...someone wanting to alert the authorities but afraid and needing to stay anonymous.

"OK," he said carefully. "Talk to me. What information do you have?"

"I hope you're enjoying your hollow victory in the Stokes case, Mr Farrell."

"Stokes? What's this all about?" Nick's eyes narrowed. Warren Stokes was the fellow he'd had convicted of drug dealing. At a guess, this would be his brother, the thug who'd hurled abuse at him as he'd left the court. "Who are you? What do you want?"

"I just want to inform you that I'm about to get even with you, Farrell. You and your family. And it will be done in a most unpleasant and painful manner."

Anger and fear gripped Nick simultaneously. "Don't you dare threaten me and my—"

But before he could finish he heard the man's laugh and then the mocking burr of the dial tone, indicating his caller had already hung up.

\* \* \*

The weekend at last! By one p.m. on Saturday Laura was grateful to be closing down the library and heading home for some peace and quiet.

Seven days since she'd seen Nick. With a little luck he would soon be a faint memory. A blip on her distant horizon.

Her post-Nick Farrell future might be looking dull, but it was definitely safe. Goodman-style safe.

Like most Saturday mornings, the library had been particularly busy, and she was nursing a faint but persistent headache.

Susie was still away and her replacement had to get home in time to transport her children to their afternoon sporting matches, so Laura had let her go early. Now she was closing windows, turning out lights and generally making sure everything was in order before she left.

As she gathered up her handbag and a thick novel to read that evening, she heard a muffled animal-like sound from behind a bookshelf nearby. Frowning, she tried to peer through the lower shelves. Without the lights on, it was hard to see, but she was sure there was a bulky shape on the floor.

She watched it for twenty seconds or so, and—*yes*—it moved. It not only moved, it grew. Someone had been crouching on the carpet and now he or she was standing.

"Who's there?" she called, trying to sound calmer than she felt.

There was another muffled squeak and the sound of whispering.

"Come out of there!" Laura ordered. If she had to face an intruder she would rather do so out in the open than in the shadowy aisles between bookshelves.

Guerrilla tactics were not her forte.

As she watched, the shape became two shapes. Two small shapes. They moved past the rows of books. But even before they rounded the end of the shelf Laura guessed who was there. "Kate and Felicity!"

Big eyes, one pair brown the other grey, looked timidly up at Laura.

"What are you doing here?" she cried, and then added quickly, "Are you alone?"

They nodded.

Laura scanned the library just to make sure. "Why were you hiding?"

"We were waiting until you weren't busy any more," Kate offered.

Shaking her head in bewilderment, all Laura could think to do was to ask more questions. "How did you get here?"

"We caught the bus," Felicity announced proudly.

"The *bus?*"

The little girl was bursting to tell of their adventure. "It was easy. We walked to the bus stop at the end of our street and waited for the bus that said Glenwood on the front. And we both gave the man a dollar out of our money boxes and he told us when to get off."

"Does—does your father know you're here?"

Suddenly Felicity's bravado evaporated. She looked sheepishly at her big sister.

"No," Kate answered softly. "We didn't tell Daddy."

"For heaven's sake, girls, he'll be worried sick. Where was he when you left home?"

"He was busy in the back garden fixing the sprinklers."

"What about your grandmother—Mrs Cunningham? Does she know anything about this?" Slowly, they shook their heads.

Laura's mouth dropped open. It looked very much as if these girls had run away from their father—to *her*. She pressed a palm against her throbbing forehead. "So why have you come here?" she asked weakly.

They looked at each other as if for help. It was a question they seemed to have difficulty answering.

"Did you want to borrow more books?" She would have been very surprised if they'd already read the pile they'd borrowed the other day.

"No thank you," Kate answered politely.

Felicity chewed her lower lip and looked worried. "We just wanted to see you again," she said in a small voice.

Laura looked down into the little girl's big grey eyes, so like her father's, and her easily softened heart melted as quickly as an ice cream on a tropical beach.

She dropped to the floor and crouched beside Felicity, taking the girl's small hand in her own. "Sweetheart," she said warmly, "it's lovely to see you." Glancing towards Kate, she added, "but your daddy will be terribly worried about you, won't he?"

Kate nodded.

"Actually," Laura said, jumping quickly to her feet again, "I should ring him straight away and tell him you're safe."

The girls followed her as she walked back to the main desk. "What's your number?"

As Laura dialled the digits Kate gave her she felt her breathing constrict. The last thing she wanted to do was to ring Nick Farrell with this kind of news. How could she start? She prayed for inspiration as she heard the ringing on the other end of the line, and her heartbeats picked up pace.

But there was no answer. She left a brief message on his answering machine.

"Your poor father is probably scouring the city searching for you," she told them as she put the phone down again. "You know you should get straight home."

They nodded.

"How about I walk you to the bus stop and you can catch a bus home?"

"We don't have any more money," admitted Kate.

Laura frowned at the child. She was only seven years old, but really! "Kate, if you're big enough to bring your little sister on an adventure like this, you should know better than to leave home with only enough money for a one-way ticket."

On cue, two fat tears spilled from Kate's big brown eyes.

*Oh, Christmas!* Laura thought. What am I thinking? I don't have any choice. I can't just throw these two onto a bus. I'll have to take them back to Nick's place.

The thought of facing the lion in his den made her head throb more fiercely than ever. "Don't worry," she quickly reassured Kate, in spite of her desire to stay as far away from Nick as possible. "I'll drive you home."

The girl breathed a huge sigh of relief and, almost immediately, her face broke into a grin. "Thank you."

"Goody!" squeaked Felicity, and the little imp almost skipped with delight.

Laura did her best to ignore the stirring suspicion that these young misses were plotting something. Suppressing a resigned sigh, she swung her bag over one shoulder and took the girls' hands.

During the trip across three suburbs Nick's daughters kept up an incessant patter—mostly information about their father. Information Laura hadn't asked for. Details she didn't want to know. Of course she didn't.

"You don't have to tell me all your father's secrets," she tried to protest.

But they ignored her.

"Daddy's favourite meal is coral trout with Thai salad," Kate told her.

"He likes to listen to boring grown-up music," added Felicity. "Sympathy orchestras."

"And he always drinks his coffee black."

When she tried to distract them by asking questions about the books they'd borrowed from the library they answered briefly then hurried on to tell her that Nick swam forty laps of their pool every day to keep his body nice and muscly.

"He cooks really yummy nachos."

"And he makes great strawberry milkshakes using real strawberries."

Their encyclopaedic account of their father's habits kept flowing and, against her will, Laura kept seeing images of Nick.

She could picture him late at night in a darkened room, listening to classical music. *She loved classical music.*

She could see him in his kitchen, laughing with his daughters as he fed them nachos dripping with melted cheese. *She loved Mexican food.*

She could picture him early in the morning, diving into a pool, looking divine in his bathers. *She loved...*

"Tell me more about yourselves," she suggested.

"Every Christmas Daddy takes us to visit Grandma and Grandpa Farrell," Kate told her.

"They live way up north on a farm," Felicity added. "They've got lots of friends."

"And does Daddy have lots of friends?" Laura asked, and then immediately wished she'd bitten her tongue. She really didn't want to know the answer to that.

The girls must have sensed the loaded nature of the question. They didn't answer straight away, and Laura was concentrating on driving so she didn't see their faces, but she knew there was a short period of silent communication between them.

"Don't worry. I shouldn't have asked that," she said quickly.

"No," responded Kate just as quickly. "It's OK. Actually," she added in a solemn little voice, "Daddy doesn't have many friends."

"He's very lonely," piped in Felicity.

"'Cos we're all he's got," Kate explained.

"And we're only little."

"He needs the companionship of a good woman," Kate added finally, with the air of a politician announcing the solution to the nation's economic crisis.

"Good grief!" cried Laura, so shocked she almost missed a turn. "Where on earth did that idea come from."

"Everyone says so," intoned the little girl darkly.

Everyone except the man in question, thought Laura. "You girls wouldn't be trying your hand at matchmaking, would you?"

Two pairs of eyes rounded with practised innocence. "What's matchmaking?" Kate asked.

"Never mind," sighed Laura. But the thought that the girls were like their father—three jumps ahead of her—left her feeling jittery and confused as she pulled up outside the address they had given.

She took a deep breath and cursed her headache, which was worse than ever now. Peering through the windscreen, she inspected Nick Farrell's house. She might have guessed it would be impressive. The contemporary timber and glass construction was set back in a beautiful natural bush garden.

"It doesn't look as if Daddy is home," Kate announced.

Laura followed her gaze to the open garage door and saw the empty parking bay. "I guess we'll just have to wait for him," she said with a sigh.

"Come and wait for him inside," Kate urged.

"You have a key?"

Kate reached beneath the neck of her T-shirt and with a triumphant cry of *"Ta-da,"* produced a key on a silver chain. "Come inside and I'll make you a cold drink." She sounded very grown up, but spoiled it when her face broke into an impish grin.

A cold drink was just what Laura needed. She could down a couple of aspirin at the same time. Without further question, she followed the girls as they led her through a slate-paved entrance into a large, beautiful living room with polished hardwood floors and pristine white walls.

At the far end of the room, floor to ceiling windows looked out into a lush green rainforest. It was a surprisingly peaceful room—spacious and airy and decorated in a minimalist style with only a few pieces of casual, but expensive-looking furniture. The high-raked ceilings were lined with honey-coloured timber and, through the far windows, a soft green light filtered through the trees.

There was no traffic noise. All she could hear were the faint sounds of birds calling to one another in the canopy outside.

Tasteful, relaxing…extremely expensive.

"You can sit here if you like," Kate said, pointing to a cane lounger lined with plump cushions covered in a navy and white batik print.

She sank gratefully onto the lounger and, with excited giggles, Kate and Felicity left the room. Laura let her head fall back against the cushions and realised that her neck and shoulders were horribly tense.

No doubt the tension had been the cause of her headache. Tension in her shoulders—tension made worse by the fact that she still had to face a certain angry thirty-something daddy she was trying desperately to avoid.

But surely no self-respecting headache would hang around in a room as restful as this.

The girls were back again very quickly. Kate carried a tray with three tumblers of bright red cordial. Felicity followed with a jug holding more of the same gaudily coloured liquid.

Painkillers and red cordial? It sounded a touch dicey, Laura thought as she reached for her handbag and sorted through the jumble of tissues, make-up, hairpins and keys till she found a packet of aspirin. As she straightened again she felt a clunk as her head hit the tray Kate held and she heard the girl's horrified cry.

Seconds later cold liquid was running through her hair, soaking into her shirt front and trickling down the back of her neck.

"Sorry!"

Laura jumped to her feet as tumblers bounced onto the timber floor around her. Thank heavens they were plastic. Kate stared at her in dismay while Felicity

stood, looking worried and clutching the jug tightly to
her chest as if she was afraid it would suddenly spill as
well.

"Oh, dear. Your shirt!" Kate cried.

Laura looked at her front. This *couldn't* be happening. Her white linen shirt was soaked pink and red. The
fabric clung to her chest in sticky wet patches. Her head
throbbed. Kate wailed dramatically.

"It'll wash out," Laura muttered. "Can I get a cloth
from the kitchen to mop it up?"

"You should have a shower."

"No. It's OK. I'll just dry it for now."

"But do you want Daddy to see you looking like
that?" the child asked, and she stared pointedly at
Laura's chest.

Laura looked down at her shirt-front again, eyeing
the way her lacy bra and—*cringe*—her nipples showed
through the damp fabric. "I guess it is a bit revealing."

"And your hair's all sticky," commented Felicity.

When Laura thought about bearding the lion in his
den with sticky hair and a decidedly transparent shirt,
she had to agree that it wasn't the most helpful armour
for a battle.

"The bathroom is this way," Kate was saying, and
she'd already covered half the distance to the hallway
door as if the matter of a shower had already been decided.

Laura snapped two tablets from the foil pack in her
hand and swallowed them with a gulp of cordial from
Felicity's jug. Ur-rgh! The mixture was way too strong.
No wonder she was sticky. She followed Kate down a
hallway and to a door at the end of the passage.

It opened into a spacious bathroom. Nick's bathroom.
Terracotta floor, white-tiled walls, nifty black fittings.

An old shirt—one he might use in the garden—hung on a hook behind the door.

In a wicker hamper she could see a jumble of masculine clothes waiting to be washed. A pair of jocks dotted with the ace of spades lay on the floor beside it as if they'd been tossed towards the hamper and missed.

Nick Farrell's underwear.

Laura dragged her eyes elsewhere.

A black and silver can of deodorant stood on the bench next to the hand basin and there was a razor with little bits of shaving cream still clinging to it next to a cut-glass bottle of expensive-looking aftershave.

A fluffy white towel, still damp from his wet body, hung on a rail nearby.

Laura could almost sense Nick here in the room. Naked. Steamy. The hair on his chest still damp and his body sleek and shiny.

*Oh, help,* she thought, and all her good work in the past week telling herself that she didn't care a fig about Nick Farrell was undone in an instant.

''Um.'' She gulped, realising that Kate was still watching her. She reached towards a stack of towels piled neatly on a shiny metal rack. ''Can I take one of these clean towels?''

''Sure.'' Kate nodded. ''And the shower's through there.''

''Thanks.''

The little girl left and Laura dropped her clothes into a heap on the floor and crossed the room to the glassed-in shower recess. She let the warm water wash over her and tried to shake off the headache and the weird feeling that she was losing her grip.

Her life seemed to be slipping sideways in a direction

way out of her control, and for a control freak it was a nerve-wracking notion.

She thought again about the way that cordial had spilt. Had she imagined it, or had Kate been leaning over her as she straightened? A seven-year-old couldn't have planned that *accident,* could she?

Surely not.

Her suspicions were getting out of hand.

Why would Kate plan to land Laura in her father's bathroom, soaping herself with the same bar of soap that had slithered over his sexy body not so long ago?

*Give it a miss!* she groaned as she reached for a bottle of shampoo and lathered her hair. *Concentrate on how you're going to explain your way out of this mess.* She stuck her head under the stream of water to rinse her hair and wondered how Nick was feeling right now.

No doubt he was scouring the suburbs, searching for his daughters. Was he frantic with worry? Would he be relieved or angry when he found them?

As she turned off the taps she heard a ferocious roar coming from somewhere within the house. Her stomach clenched as she realised her questions would soon be answered.

The lion had returned to his den!

And this was supposed to be an ordinary Saturday. What had she done to deserve being thrust into a nightmare? Her heart thudded as she dashed out of the shower to snatch up the towel.

Nervously, she quickly dried herself. But she was only halfway through the process when the bathroom door flew open and a tall, wild-looking figure rushed in.

Clutching the towel in front of her, she saw sheer panic in Nick's eyes. His face was sheet-white and his thick dark hair was dishevelled as if he'd run his hands through it many times. ''Where are they?'' he shouted.

The sound of running footsteps in the hall sent him swinging back in that direction.

''Daddy!''

When he saw the girls he slumped against the wall with relief, his breath escaping in noisy grunts. The whole sequence only took a matter of seconds, but it was enough. Those few short seconds showed Laura the astonishing depth of Nick's emotion—an insight into the love—*and fear*—this man had for his daughters.

Despite the fact that she stood naked and dripping, in *his* bathroom, her heart twisted painfully and tears sprang to her eyes.

But Nick seemed to recover quickly from his initial reaction. He gave the girls swift hard hugs before turning back to glare at Laura. ''You've got a hell of a lot of explaining to do.''

# CHAPTER SIX

NICK'S fists clenched as he willed his breathing and heart rate to slow. OK, the girls appeared to be unharmed. Thank God! But he couldn't believe that this pesky redhead was back in his life.

Not just in his life—in his *damn bathroom!* He blinked. She was wrapped in nothing but a towel.

"What have you been doing with my daughters?"

"This isn't how it looks," Laura cried, her face set in an angry scowl as if she were ready for battle. "I didn't just invade your house and your shower."

"Oh, no?" he asked coldly. He didn't believe one word.

First she'd worn feathers, now a towel. What was it with this woman? She seemed to spend half her life draped in next to nothing and then the rest of the time trying to make excuses for it.

Except today she was also damp and pink from a recent shower. Her hair clung to her head and neck and its colour was amazing when it was wet. Shining damply against her pale skin, it looked richer, darker, more luxurious and intriguing than ever. And her limbs extending from beyond the towel were distractingly shapely.

*But what the hell was she doing in his bathroom?*

"If you give me a moment to get dressed, I'll explain everything," Laura said.

"Tell me now."

"Daddy," he heard Kate cry, "don't blame Laura."

He patted his daughter's head. "You girls go and wait in your room. I just have to sort something out with Miss Goodman."

"But, Daddy," Felicity chimed in, "don't be mad at her."

Of course he was mad at her. He'd been through hell this morning. How could he *not* be mad at her? With Thursday's menacing phone call ringing in his ears, he'd spent three hours in torment, trying to trace his girls.

"Girls," he ordered coldly, "I told you to go and wait for me in your room."

"But she doesn't have anything to wear," Kate squeaked.

"I don't? Where are my clothes?" This came from Laura.

"I've put them in the washing machine."

Nick frowned. He didn't like that guilty flash in Kate's eyes. What was going on here?

"We spilt red cordial on her," explained Felicity.

"Accidentally," Kate added quickly.

*"Cordial?"* He ran desperate fingers through his hair. This was getting crazier by the minute. He looked from Laura to his daughters and back to the librarian again. "You'd better have a good excuse for this."

She glared at him fiercely and clutched the towel around her as if she feared it might be ripped away at any minute. But she sounded surprisingly cool as she said from between gritted teeth, "Is that how a Crown Prosecutor works? You yell accusations first and ask questions later?"

He dropped his voice a dozen decibels. "I'm not yelling."

"You most certainly were yelling, and before you

accuse me of a crime, Mr Farrell, perhaps you should listen to the evidence.''

He narrowed his eyes. ''The evidence? You've turned up uninvited in my home—'' He was forced to pause. He'd been about to make reference to her nakedness and her bold use of his bathroom but, for the sake of the girls, he deleted those comments. ''I find you here with my daughters after they've been missing for *three* hours. I'd say that's plenty of evidence.''

Laura's plump bottom lip stuck out as she blew a strand of damp hair out of her eyes and Nick did his best to ignore how sexy the action looked.

''Kate,'' she said softly, ''you should do what your father has asked and take Felicity to your room. I'll explain to him what happened.''

To Nick's annoyance Kate, who hadn't budged when he'd given his orders, looked at Laura with big trusting eyes and then grabbed her sister's hand and dragged her back down the hallway.

What had happened to family loyalty?

He snapped his angry gaze back to the redhead in the towel. ''This explanation had better be good and it had better be fast.''

''I can't believe you're this upset just because you think the girls have been with *me*.'' Her smooth shoulders rose and fell as she drew a deep breath. ''I'm not a convicted criminal, Nick. I'm not even a stranger. In case you've forgotten, just a week ago I was a bridesmaid at your best friend's wedding. Your girls were perfectly safe with me,'' she informed him icily and, before he could comment, she kept talking. ''They caught a bus to the library. I couldn't let them come back on their own, so of course I had to drive them. And then there was the little incident with the cordial.''

"They went to the library? Why?"

"I don't really know why they came. They said they wanted to see me."

Nick groaned. He thought he'd convinced Kate and Felicity to get over their obsession with Laura Goodman. For the past two nights there had been no mention of her—or of weddings. He'd been sure that silly phase was over.

"But don't take my word for it," she said, interrupting his thoughts. "You have two star witnesses waiting in their bedroom. Why don't you ask them?"

"Yes," he said with a rueful grimace. Of course, his daughters were quite capable of telling him what had happened. "I will check out the girls' story." He shot her another narrow-eyed glance. "You'd better get dry while I speak to them."

A wet curl flopped back into her eyes and she tossed her head sideways, trying to flick it away without letting go of the towel.

Nick shoved his hand into his pocket in case he gave in to the temptation to help her.

Looking around her and nodding towards a shirt hanging on the back of the door, Laura asked, "Can I wear that for now?"

"Sure." He shrugged as casually as he could and stepped back as she shut the door firmly in his face.

It took Nick two minutes to check out Laura's story with the girls. He returned, grim-faced, down the hall to the bathroom and she opened the door at the same moment he arrived.

Now the towel was looped tightly around her hips like a sarong and Nick's shirt hung loosely over the top, but not so loosely that he wasn't acutely aware of her naked breasts beneath the fine white cotton.

Damn!

"Fetching outfit," he said, hoping he sounded cool and unmoved.

"It's not meant to impress you," she snapped.

*Ouch! That put him in his place.* He cracked a smile as he began to walk on down the hall.

"Nick!" she called from behind him.

Slowly, he turned back her way.

"What did the girls say?"

"Your stories matched," he admitted reluctantly.

"Then I'd like an apology!"

"Oh."

"*Oh?* Is that all you can say?" Her blue eyes blazed. "Don't you think I deserve one? I know you're supposed to be a whiz-bang prosecutor, but we've told you I'm not guilty."

"You're right, I should apologise," he said softly, and he stepped towards her. Then, incredibly, of its own accord, his hand reached out and Nick found himself tucking the cutest little curling wisp of damp hair behind Laura's ear.

Her ear was exquisitely dainty. In the very centre of its lobe nestled a tiny pearl. His hand stayed there, because he suddenly needed to know everything about that delicate, soft little piece of her.

"What—what are you doing?"

He looked at her, startled. How could he answer? He didn't have a clue what he was doing. "I'm apologising," he said, dry-mouthed.

"I accept your apology," she whispered.

"That's settled, then." He pulled his hand away abruptly and was distinctly unhappy with himself.

Laura was looking unhappy, too.

He shouldn't have touched her. Why on earth had he

done that? He was in the middle of setting the woman straight.

Laura cleared her throat. ''I'd like to make something clear,'' she said. ''Perhaps you were so ready to blame me because you're worried that I'm chasing after you?''

Still feeling bewildered, he shook his head.

''You don't have to worry that I didn't understand your lecture last week,'' she continued in an excessively chilly tone. ''I'm not trying to worm my way into your life. I know perfectly well that you made a hideous mistake when you kissed me.''

Nick grunted. Had it really been a mistake to kiss Laura? It was becoming difficult to remember why. The fact that she was wearing hardly any clothes was clouding his thinking. His anger might have cooled, but in other ways he was definitely growing hot and steamy.

*''I'm not after you,''* Laura insisted. ''I'm not interested in you. If I had my way, I would never see you again.''

Nick knew a response was expected, but right now all he could manage was to shrug and to continue down the hall.

From behind him, Laura called, ''If you really want to know, I don't give a—a rat's *bum* about you!''

It dawned on Nick, then, that perhaps the lady was protesting too much.

And *that* was a sobering thought.

It forced him to remember what was really going on here. Neither of them could afford to give in to fleeting feelings of attraction. She wasn't a woman he could fool around with and he couldn't match up to the committed man of her dreams.

That was the bottom line.

That was why she'd looked so shocked and angry when he'd touched her.

As he reached the kitchen he asked over his shoulder, "How about I make us some coffee while you're waiting for your clothes to dry?"

She stormed into the room after him. "Forget coffee. I'd choke on it."

"If you don't mind, I'll make one for myself."

"Suit yourself."

The phone rang.

And in an instant Nick's lustful thoughts died and his heart rate doubled. Laura was closest to the phone and her hand jerked towards it in an automatic response.

"Leave it!" Nick snatched the receiver. "Nick Farrell."

"Mr Farrell," replied a male voice. A slimy voice that brought the hairs standing up on the back of Nick's neck. "So nice to speak again. You remember me, of course?"

It was the voice he'd come to detest.

"I know what you're up to, Stokes," Nick snarled, "and it won't work with me. Go threaten someone else or come out in the open and face me."

"Let's not be melodramatic," the voice simpered. "I just wanted to let you know what a delightful time I've been having this afternoon watching your mother-in-law, Mrs Cunningham. Would you like to know what she's doing right at this minute?"

Nick's stomach lurched. "You're spying on Heather? For God's sake, why?" He caught Laura's wide and worried eyes watching him.

"She looks after little Kate and Felicity every afternoon after school, doesn't she?"

*The girls!* Nick swore loudly. This was the first time

the caller had mentioned his daughters. His legs turned to sawdust and he sagged against the kitchen bench.

"Right now Mrs Cunningham's snipping the dead heads off roses in her front garden. She keeps a nice garden, doesn't she? I'll enjoy taking a closer look at it when I come next week for your daughters."

"This isn't going to help your brother," Nick shouted. But before he could continue he heard the click of the receiver being replaced.

With an angry cry, he dropped his phone back into its cradle. His heart pounded. Sick and shaking, he slumped onto a kitchen stool and let his head drop into his hands.

He groaned as he fought off nightmarish images of Kate's and Felicity's terrified faces as a dark, mad stranger approached them.

"Nick?"

He lifted his hands away from his face. Laura was leaning towards him, her eyes brimming with concern.

"It was a nuisance call," he told her. "There have been others. The family of a crim I prosecuted last week took exception to one of their relatives going to jail."

"What does he want?"

"He's making threats about stalking the girls and Heather."

"That's terrible," she whispered, white-faced. After a thoughtful pause, she asked, "What are you going to do?"

"I'll get back to the police." He sighed again, feeling suddenly exhausted. "But, bad as it sounds to us, as far as the police are concerned we only have a low-level threat at this stage."

"But if this man's spying on the girls?"

Nick swallowed back a wave of nausea. "What I'd

really like to do is take time off and get the hell out of
here with them.''

Laura seemed to think about that for a minute or two.
''But could you just hide indefinitely?''

''No,'' he admitted with a sigh. ''What I need is a
safe house. It looks like this guy knows the girls' daily
routine. He knows they go to Heather's. I need to find
somewhere he wouldn't know about. I'd send them up
to my parents' place on the Atherton Tableland, except
my dad's going into hospital for some tests. Mum has
more than enough on her plate, what with worrying
about him and the fact that it's almost harvest time.''

Laura nodded in silent agreement. ''Rob and Susie
get back from their honeymoon tomorrow,'' she said
slowly. ''They're setting up house at Susie's place.''

Nick rolled his eyes. ''That would be great, wouldn't
it? Rob could carry Susie, Kate *and* Fliss over the
threshold of his nuptial home.''

Laura's mouth quirked. ''I'm sure they wouldn't refuse to help you out, but OK—maybe it's not the best
option.''

She switched her gaze to a spot on the wall, and she
stood there deep in thought.

''I don't expect you to worry about this,'' he said.

''No wonder you were out of your mind when the
girls disappeared this morning.''

''Yeah. This guy has certainly put the wind up me.
That's just what he wants, of course. It's probably all
bluff, but I can't risk it.'' He grimaced and ran tense
fingers through his hair.

Still staring at the wall, Laura nodded. Then she
turned back to him. ''He'd be unlikely to know anything about me, would he?''

''No...you should be safe.'' There was something

about her expression, a kind of dawning determination in her bright blue eyes, that made Nick frown. "What are you thinking?"

He realised she was looking very earnest now—like the Laura he'd first met—the *do-gooder*. The woman who'd somehow conned him into doing a clown stint at a children's hospital. "It's not *your* safety you're thinking about, is it?" he asked.

"No," she said softly.

"Oh, no," he said. "Don't even begin to think about trying to help us."

Laura smiled faintly. "What's the use of being a born-in-the-womb do-gooder if I don't put all those helpful impulses into practice when they're really needed?"

Nick swallowed. "Are you thinking what I think you're thinking?"

"I'm thinking the girls would be safe at my place. Nobody knows we're—connected."

"But, Laura—"

"Tomorrow's Sunday and I have Monday off. That's at least two days the girls can be in a safe house with twenty-four-hour supervision while the police track this fellow down."

He stared at her, surprised at how calm and collected she sounded. "But you don't have kids. Do you know anything about looking after little girls? They can be quite a handful."

She folded her arms across her chest. "I happen to have excellent qualifications."

"Really?" Nick was aware he sounded as if he was in court as he asked, "Would you care to elaborate?"

Laura lifted her chin and eyed him haughtily. "Apart from the library work I do with children every week, I have even more useful credentials—I've spent several years of my life *being* a little girl.''

His mouth twitched into an unwilling smile, but then he frowned again. He hardly knew this woman. Half an hour ago he'd been ready to evict her from his home and his life. ''I couldn't impose on you like that,'' he began, but even to his ears his objection didn't sound strong enough.

Maybe that was because, deep down, he suspected that Laura would probably be a rather satisfactory solution to this dilemma.

''It's no skin off my nose either way. You can take it or leave it, Nick, but I wouldn't offer if I wasn't happy to help out.''

Nick looked at her and forced himself to ignore the towel draped around her hips. He noted instead the open honesty and genuine compassion revealed in her expressive face.

''This is a terrible situation for Kate and Felicity,'' Laura continued. ''My house isn't very big, but I have a spare bedroom with two beds in it. I live in a quiet street and my neighbours are very respectable.'' Her eyes flashed him a blue challenge. ''And I like your girls. I think we could get on just fine.''

Nick made a frantic mental list of his alternatives. His lawyer friends? Their wives were either career driven or ladies-who-lunched. They wouldn't have time for his daughters. There were a few stray bachelor mates, but they would run a mile before taking on such a task.

As for his female acquaintances, Nick grimaced at the thought of asking any of them to become involved in his domestic affairs. They might misinterpret his intentions and see it as a step towards the altar.

He had a sneaking suspicion that Laura Goodman was his only safe option.

Laura was standing with her arms crossed, waiting for him to comment. "I realise you'd prefer for the girls to be with someone you know better. Why don't you just think of me as a last resort?"

Maybe he was panicking and not thinking clearly, but Nick found himself saying, "I have to admit that Kate and Felicity trust you, Laura. They wouldn't be frightened to go with you." He raised an arm and rubbed the back of his neck thoughtfully. "But we'd need to think up a convincing reason."

Actually, Nick suspected there was every chance the girls would stampede to be with Laura whether he unearthed a good reason or not. Again, he ran a restless hand through his hair. "But there's another problem."

"Oh?"

"Kate and Fliss have some silly ideas about us. This past week, they've…"

"Been trying their hand at matchmaking?"

His head jerked up, startled. "Yeah. How did you know?"

"They've been working on me, too. They've made sure I know your favourite food, your taste in music, how hard you work at keeping in shape."

Nick released a low whistle. "The little devils."

"I understand that you are very lonely and need the love of a good woman."

"They said that?"

"They did." She grinned. "But I didn't believe it."

Nick managed an answering grin and found himself asking, "And you also didn't believe I have to work hard to keep in shape, do you?"

That question seemed to catch her out. She didn't

answer at first and then she said, "Look, Nick, I'd only take the girls to my place if we had a very clear understanding that I'm not in any way trying to win your affection."

"Sure."

"We probably can't stop the girls from having their little fantasies, but at least *we* know how things are."

"I guess so," he agreed. "We can both work at snapping them out of these silly ideas." He shook his head. "I never should have let them go to Rob and Susie's wedding."

"If you decide to let the girls come with me, I'll do my best to make sure they understand I'm simply a friend and that's all."

He let out a deep breath. "Thanks. That—that would be helpful. I'd really appreciate it."

"I can't see that our relationship or lack of one needs to be an issue."

Nick nodded. "You're right. It shouldn't be an issue."

However, he thought guiltily, what he didn't add was that it wouldn't be an issue once Laura was dressed properly again. It wouldn't be an issue just as soon as he stopped fantasising about her throwing off that towel and moving, naked and lovely, up close against him.

"Of course you'll want to keep in close contact. You could visit us in the evenings."

"Uh—evenings?"

"The girls will want to see you."

"Yes, of course." He struggled to clean up his mind.

Reaching over to the pen and notepaper beside the phone, Laura wrote down her contact details. "It would probably be best if you don't drive straight up to the front door—just in case anyone's watching. Heaven forbid. There's a lane at the back of my house. Come around that way. Use the back door.''

She handed him the address.

''Right,'' Nick murmured, feeling dazed as he stood staring at Laura's neat handwriting outlining her addresses and phone numbers for home and work. ''Thanks. That's terrific.''

But what wasn't terrific, he realised, was that spending his evenings at Laura Goodman's house sounded far too much like the recurring dream that had been bothering him all week.

## CHAPTER SEVEN

ON MONDAY morning, Nick looked up from his paper-work to find Rob, coffee-cup in hand, standing in the doorway of his office.

"Ah!" he exclaimed with a smile. "The worn out, glowing image of a man just back from his short but sweet honeymoon. How are you, mate?"

Rob's answering grin broadened. "I'm not feeling too bad at all. I have to admit married life doesn't seem to have done me any harm."

He settled himself into a chair opposite Nick. "But you must be feeling pretty good yourself. What's this Susie tells me about your kids moving in with Laura Goodman? That sounds very cosy. And darn quick work."

"It's not how it looks," Nick muttered, the smile dropping from his face.

"Pull the other one," laughed Rob. "Laura's a stunner. But I must admit it's not like you to be so predictable, Nick."

"What on earth's predictable about it?"

"The best man getting it on with the bridesmaid."

Nick shot Rob a withering glance. "Use your brains, Rob. You're talking about Laura Goodman. I don't know how well you know her, but think Girl Guides, Florence Nightingale—Pollyanna. The woman's simply doing me a good turn."

"Whatever you want to call it," Rob replied with a chuckle.

Nick shook his head in exasperation. "You're barking up the wrong tree."

But he could understand Rob's scepticism. Any man who didn't know Laura—who responded purely to the way she looked—would think she was one hot babe. Those fiery curls, her flashing blue eyes and come-to-me curves were so very deceptive.

It was hard to believe that underneath all that she was innocent and earnest.

Or was she?

All weekend he'd found himself thinking about Laura and it had been like deciphering a difficult but intriguing puzzle. Take the way Laura spent most of her time acting like Little Miss Never-Been-Kissed, and yet when he'd kissed her she'd known exactly what to do with her mouth.

Those sorts of thoughts had been tormenting him more and more frequently. He'd begun to imagine how things might have been if he hadn't backed off from that second kiss. If he hadn't made such a mess of trying to explain about Miranda.

Maybe he'd jumped the gun when he assumed Laura wouldn't be interested in a casual encounter...

Rob's voice cut through his thoughts. "You're not trying to tell me that Prince Charming has been turned down?"

"It's a waste of time even thinking about her that way."

His mate's smile was sly. "But you are thinking of her that way, aren't you?"

"Not worth it." Nick paid careful attention to his desk calendar.

"Yeah, well, in your case it's probably not worth

wasting time on a non-starter. Plenty more fish in the ocean just waiting to be caught by Nick Farrell.''

Rob leaned back in his chair and favoured his friend with a knowing grin. ''Problem is, you're just not used to a woman who plays hard to get. You've had far too many women throwing themselves at you. But believe me, mate, the ones who start out saying no are worth the struggle.'' He chuckled fondly. ''My Susie took an advanced degree in brush-offs.''

''Don't bore me with the details.''

But Rob wasn't giving up. ''The secret is to just lay things out in the open and see what happens.''

Nick made a point of looking at his watch and frowning.

''Treat her with respect, but put the hard word on her. You'd be surprised how many modern chicks just want you to go with your caveman instincts. And that's a fact.''

Letting out his breath on a long sigh, Nick decided it was time to put an end to Rob's endless flow of useless advice. ''Try listening to these facts, Rob.''

He leaned closer and lowered his voice. ''There's a whacko sending me threatening phone calls—the Stokes case; I think it's the brother—threatening the girls. *That's* why Kate and Felicity are at Laura's.''

In a flash Rob's grin and all mention of seduction, with or without finesse, vanished. Nick knew he could trust Rob to take him seriously on this.

''The girls are OK about going to Laura's?'' Rob asked.

''I've spun them a story that I'm getting ready for a big case and need to do a lot of extra preparation at night and their grandmother is too busy with charity work to take them this week. They don't mind. They think Laura's the cat's pyjamas.''

Rob nodded and, to Nick's relief, the two friends spent the next fifteen minutes discussing the stalker and the strategies Nick and the police had in place. They didn't mention Laura again.

As she closed the door on the girls' bedroom, Laura's telephone rang. She hurried through to the kitchen.

Nick spoke. "I've been held up at a meeting. Are the girls still awake?''

"I've just settled them," she told him, and she heard his stifled sigh. "I'm sorry you missed them, but they dropped off to sleep much more quickly this evening than last night. Tonight I only had to tell them one story. Last night it took three.''

"They were very excited when I left them last night, weren't they?''

"Yes, and they were disappointed they missed you tonight.''

"I'm really sorry." After a pause, he asked, "So what kind of a day did you three have?''

"Oh, we spent the morning baking and decorating gingerbread shapes, and this afternoon we made clothes for their teddy bears. I found some patterns in a magazine.''

There was a lengthy silence on the other end of the line.

"Nick?''

"I was just thinking what a great time they must be having—doing all that girl stuff. They don't get much of that with me.''

"It's hardly surprising, Nick, and I'm sure they don't

mind. The only complaint I heard was that you don't keep a box with scraps of fabric.''

"Well, no, I don't.''

"But they tell me you're teaching them to cook.''

"Just very simple things,'' he agreed. "When Miranda died I had to go out and take cooking lessons. I couldn't do much more than boil water. I don't want them getting caught out like that.''

Laura's fingers twisted the phone cord. She saw a sudden picture of Nick, at home alone with his daughters, dealing with his grief and struggling to learn how to cook. The thought caused a curious prickle in her throat.

After an awkward silence, she asked, "So you haven't had any more threatening phone calls?''

There was a loud sigh. "No. The sneaky devil seems to be lying low. He's probably guessed the police are taping my calls.''

"Maybe he's given up?''

"I wouldn't bank on it. Not yet at any rate. That's another thing I wanted to tell you. The girls should go to school tomorrow. I know you're due back at work, and Kate and Fliss will wonder what's up if we keep them at home any longer. I've alerted their teachers. They'll be extra watchful.''

"That's fine. I can drop them at school in the morning and I don't mind keeping them with me at night for a little longer.''

"Thanks, Laura. I really appreciate everything you're doing.'' His naturally beautiful voice sounded unexpectedly genuine. It was almost as if something deep and meaningful passed down the phone line.

Laura decided she must have been mistaken. Nick didn't do deep and meaningful. Not with her at any rate, but of course his feelings for the girls were another matter. She tried to put herself in his shoes and to imagine the strong bond he must feel with his little daughters.

"Are you calling from work?" she asked.

"Yeah. I'm just about to leave. Why?"

"I thought you might like to call by. You could take a quick peek at the girls even though they're asleep."

"Thanks, I'd like that." Nick's reply was enthusiastic. "I'll be there in ten."

As Laura replaced the phone she wondered if she'd been a little too impulsive, inviting Nick to call by. The thought of him arriving at her house without the girls around to distract him made her feel suddenly nervous.

But she decided that was a silly reaction. She'd made it patently clear on several occasions that she wasn't setting her cap at him. In her bathroom, she tidied her hair and freshened her lipstick. "I've got this situation and this man under control," she told her reflection.

Her reflection didn't look as convinced as she would have liked.

Fifteen minutes later, Nick stepped into the girls' low-ceilinged bedroom. There was just enough lamplight for him to see his daughters lying sound asleep in two little timber beds with soft white coverlets. A familiar, warm glow curled around his heart as he looked at them.

He was amazed that after just two days he missed these little rascals so much.

Fliss lay with her dark curls spread in a glossy tangle against the snowy pillow. Cuddled tightly in her chubby arms was Sir Joseph, her worn and tattered but much loved bear.

In the other bed was Kate in her favourite sleeping

position, sprawled on her back with her mouth slightly open. Her neat pink bear, Princess Tina, sat proudly on top of the little cupboard next to her.

Nick guessed that the smart white and gold satin gown the bear wore was a legacy of the day's activities.

He looked around him. The blue-carpeted room held little more than a glossy white cupboard and the beds. Everything about it was simple, fresh and clean. Between the beds was a small circular window.

It was set deeply into the white stone wall and a gauzy curtain trimmed with thin stripes of blue satin ribbon fluttered in a breeze drifting in from the garden. Through the round window he could see the silhouette of a pine tree and the evening star shining brightly. For some reason, coming to Laura's house made Nick feel as if he was stepping into a fairy tale. No wonder the girls were happy here. It would be like living in a storybook. "Looks like the girls have made themselves at home," he whispered.

Laura's eyes shone as she nodded and then quietly led him outside. She closed the door again and he followed her down a passage, past a closed door, which he guessed would be her bedroom, to her sitting room.

She indicated with a slightly awkward flutter of one hand that he should take a seat, so he lowered himself just a little uneasily into a chair upholstered in a dainty floral.

"Have you eaten?" she began.

"Yes, thanks. I'm fine. We had a snack at the meeting."

"Would you like some tea or coffee?"

"Coffee would be great. Thanks."

She hurried away quickly before he could add another comment. Not that he knew what else to say, now.

This was the second time he'd been to Laura's house but he still felt strangely self-conscious. Out of place.

He looked round him at the artistic clutter of honey-toned antiques, hand-hooked rugs and stained glass lamps. On a circular table, at his elbow, there was a collection of blue and white porcelain, and over near the window thriving plants spilled out of glowing copper pots.

Every wall was lined with bookshelves and crammed full of books. Her story book cottage was so folksy and cute it could have been photographed for one of those country-cottage magazines.

He found the house intriguing and puzzling... inexplicably attractive...adult and innocent...like Laura.

Everything here was so different from the contemporary minimalist decor of his house, it made him feel like an outsider.

Was it her feminine touch that made the difference? He felt a jab of uncertainty. Were his girls missing out on something intangible but vitally important that he could never give them?

He was still lost in thought when Laura walked quietly back into the room carrying a wicker tray, which she set down on the coffee table. As she poured fragrant-smelling coffee into two mugs and handed him one, he asked politely, ''Have the girls been behaving themselves for you?''

''They've been very good,'' she said with a warm smile that made a little dimple in her cheek, not far from her mouth.

Nick's eyes rested on her soft pink mouth.

''Honestly, they're no trouble at all. I'm enjoying having them here.'' She looked up from her task and the deep beautiful blue of her eyes almost took his breath away.

She shook her head and smiled. "But you might have warned me. I didn't know I was going to have to make up so many bedtime stories."

He sipped the coffee. "So they demanded a story about a princess?"

"How did you guess?"

"Kate always wants stories about princesses."

"Does she always get them?"

He chuckled. "As long as she's prepared to have my style of princess. One who's lost in space or climbing a snow-capped mountain."

Laura smiled. "Tonight we had a princess who lives in a castle and loves pink."

"That would have made a very pleasant change. What happens?"

"You don't really want to hear a children's story."

"Why not? I might learn something. I need to get a better handle on how small females think."

"Well…" She hesitated for a moment, but then seemed to gather courage as she told him, "This princess insists that everything in her castle must be pink. Pink carpets, pink curtains, pink walls, you name it."

"Food?"

"Oh, yes, of course," she said with a laugh. "She lives on pink jelly, pink ham and pink lemonade."

"Sounds great," he said, and he meant it. After the stories he told, where the princesses always ended battling their way through jungles or risking their necks deep-sea diving, the girls would have loved Laura's feminine slant.

Hey, he loved it. He could just picture Laura in

pink—in a pink bedroom with pink satin bed sheets. *Enough of that.* "So what happens next?"

Laura sipped at her coffee and her eyes widened. "You don't really want the whole plot, do you?"

"Sure."

She relaxed back in her chair, rested her elbow on its arm and propped her chin in her hand. Nick watched the dainty chin resting on her hand and wanted his hand there. Wanted to be touching her. Her skin looked impossibly soft.

"Well…the princess gets tired of pink and wants everything changed to blue," she explained.

He smiled. "That's typical of every princess I know."

Laura looked at him sharply, as if she was wondering exactly *which* princesses he referred to. But she didn't question him, just went on with her story. "I'm summarising, of course, but after a while she gets tired of blue. Having everything blue can become depressing."

"Indeed. So after she gets over the blues, she tries yellow? That's a happy colour."

"It is, isn't it? The girls and I decided if you could catch a laugh and put it in a jar it would be yellow."

"Did you?" Nick was suddenly spellbound by the thought of Laura and his girls capturing happiness in a jar. True happiness was such an elusive slippery emotion.

He could picture Laura laughing as she told her story in the cosy little blue and white bedroom. He could imagine her stopping patiently from time to time to let the excited girls join in and he felt something like a small skyscraper blocking his throat.

"Anyhow, you've got the gist of the plot," Laura went on. "The princess finally gives yellow the flick and then green.'' By now she was smiling broadly, but then her smile faded and he watched as she twisted the handle of her mug between two slim fingers. The gesture looked nervous, as if she was reminding herself that she mustn't relax. Mustn't let down her guard.

"So, come on," he coaxed, trying to distract her. "You can't leave me dangling. You've got to tell me how the story ends."

She rolled her eyes at him. "What happens in every good story when a princess finds herself in a mess?"

Her question caught him flat footed. Nick stared at her. "A princess in a mess?" he repeated slowly. No. He wouldn't think about the stalker or his daughters. The girls were safe here. "She hires a lawyer?" he said, and tried for a grin.

Laura shook her head. "Not this princess."

"Then obviously she relies on magic. Or failing that she uses her brains and gets herself out of the mess."

Laura let out a groan. "Blast. I didn't think of that, but now I wish I had."

"Don't tell me she's rescued by some twerp of a prince and they get married and live happily ever after?"

She looked away, pursing her mouth into a tight little pout. "It was the Rainbow Prince, actually. Kate's idea and quite appropriate, I thought."

Nick couldn't resist teasing her. "Surely you could have thought of something more—*now*. These girls are growing up in Australia in the twenty-first century after all."

Unexpectedly, her blue eyes blazed angrily. "You mean I should have left the princess happily or perhaps even miserably *single?* Avoid a married and happily ever after ending at all costs?"

"Why not?" he asked with a defensive shrug. "I don't believe in happily ever after. It's an impossible promise."

Laura looked stricken. "But they're only children, Nick. They have to dream."

Nick was very much aware that this conversation had taken a definite turn for the worse. Stepping into quicksand would be safer than discussing marriage with Laura Goodman. "Dreaming needs a touch of reality or it becomes dangerous."

Her eyes flashed with another spurt of annoyance. "I'm sure your daughters get enough realistic endings in *your* stories. I thought I did jolly well coming up with any kind of story at all. I'm a reader and a librarian, not a writer, not a story*teller*."

"You *did* do well," Nick said, suddenly contrite. "I apologise. And I'm inordinately grateful to you for taking the girls under your wing. It really is very generous of you." He sent her his warmest smile. "And, in case you haven't noticed, they think you're ace. Better than Christmas."

"I'm happy to have them here." Primly, she replaced her mug on the coffee table and folded her arms across her chest. Then she looked at him as if to say, We've had coffee, so why are you hanging around?

For some unfathomable reason, Nick felt the skin on his neck burn.

Laura didn't say anything more. She just sat there, watching him, as if she was waiting for him either to leave or start discussing international politics or the decline of the Australian dollar. He noticed that she'd begun to chew her lower lip. Why was she suddenly nervous?

Heck. He was nervous. What *was* he doing here?

He'd checked on the girls. He'd finished his coffee. It was time to go. He sat forward. He should start walking. Straight out of this cottage. Right now. The muscles in his legs tensed as he prepared to stand.

But once he was on his feet Nick found that he hated the idea of leaving. He began to walk towards Laura instead of away, and next minute he was reaching down to her and taking her hands in his. When she didn't resist, he pulled her out of her chair till she stood close in front of him.

And then he knew exactly why he had stayed.

# CHAPTER EIGHT

LAURA couldn't believe that Nick was standing so close and looking at her *that* way. That way of his...the way that made her feel incredibly female but far too melting and helpless.

His eyes were so dark and hot it was impossible to ignore their signals.

And it was dreadfully hard to ignore her own wild desire. Part of her, a very insistent part of her, wanted him to pull her close and kiss her again...and again...

But she knew it was madness and she'd made all those promises about keeping her distance. Somehow, she found the courage to hold him at bay. "Don't tell me you've written me into your diary?" she asked shakily. "Is that why you came here tonight?"

Nick frowned. "I thought you invited me."

Laura gave an exasperated shake of her head. "But last week you explained about your need for planning your social life and here you are—alone with me on a quiet Monday night and you knew the girls were already sound asleep."

"I didn't plan *this* at all. I've never yet planned to kiss you, Laura."

"I see," she whispered.

With gentle fingers, he touched her cheek. "But you keep taking me by surprise. You're so stunningly sexy."

"Sexy?" she croaked, genuinely shocked. If Nick had told her she was pretty, she might have believed him. But *sexy?* Nick *who-brought-a-room-full-of-women-to-their-knees* Farrell? How could that man think she, Laura Goodman, was sexy?

"You're incredibly sexy," he murmured, his eyes checking her out in a slow-burning appraisal. His thumb stroked her cheek. "You have such an angelic face and yet you have all this sinfully fiery hair."

His hand drew a line down her neck to her breast and she shivered. "And you have this beautiful, sensuous body. You're a deadly combination, Laura. You pretend to be so strait-laced but it's all a disguise, isn't it?"

"Of course not," she snapped.

But her response was automatic, springing out of five years of habit. When she looked up at Nick, she wasn't so sure any more. "I—I don't know," she amended.

"I think we should find out."

In sheer self-defense, Laura closed her eyes. She couldn't keep looking at Nick. When he looked at her *that* way, the man was instant temptation. No need to add water. Her will power was on the edge of total disintegration. Any minute now, he would pull her just a little closer. He would kiss her again.

And she knew that she wanted him to. She would give in. Oh, yes, she would give in to the sensational experience of Nick's mouth taking hers, of his strong arms wrapping her close.

And, yes, he was right. Whenever he was around she felt wildly sexy. He made her want to forget she was a Goodman. He made her want to forget everything except that with him she should take a few risks. Surely it would be worth it?

He leaned his face towards hers and she felt the masculine roughness of his chin against her soft cheek. One breath later and his mouth was moving over hers, tasting, and demanding. Seducing…

"You—really—are—" Nick murmured slowly between kisses as he trailed his lips over her face, "very—very—sexy." His hands slid beneath the loose hem of her shirt and she felt melting and wanton as his touch lingered over her skin. "You feel unbelievably soft. Lovely…"

*Oh, help! I'm lost,* Laura thought. But then something in her head screamed, *hold it!*

And, just in time, she remembered.

She remembered that this was Nick, The Man Who Loved Miranda. Only Miranda. The man who had explained in careful detail just exactly why they shouldn't be doing this.

With a little cry, she sprang away from him.

"What is it?"

Her mouth trembled slightly. "How could you have forgotten that I'm not interested in flings? You told me last week that you could tell at a glance I'm not into casual sex. And you explained very clearly that you're not interested in anything else. So what on earth were you thinking when you started kissing me again?"

"I—" Nick shrugged.

"How could you forget we're so different?" Laura persisted. "You shouldn't be putting all this pressure on me! You were going out of your way to seduce me!"

Nick smiled slowly. "And you liked it."

Oh, yes. She *had* liked it. She'd *loved* it. But she didn't need this ego on legs to tell her so. "That's beside the point."

"No, Laura," he said quietly, confidently. "It *is* the point. We've been driving each other crazy with this on-again off-again caper. The best thing we can do for each other is to stop all these silly inhibitions and respond to our basic needs.''

''Basic needs?'' Here he was again, talking about romance as if it were nothing more than a biological process. ''How pleasant you make it sound.''

''I'm sure it will be.''

*''Will be?''* she cried. ''Are you crazy?''

''I don't think so. I'm considered sane by most people I know.''

''This isn't a time to be smart,'' she snapped. ''You can't expect me to just say—Yes, Nick, that sounds like a great idea. The bedroom's the first door on the right.''

He had the bald-faced temerity to grin. ''Why not?''

She couldn't hold back the sudden tears that stung her eyes and burned her throat. ''You really want to make love to me just like that? Like I'm an item in your diary?'' Her voice cracked, but she forced herself to continue. ''After all that noble talk you gave me at Susie's wedding, about how sensitive you are to my— to my values—you expect me to agree to a tacky affair with no emotion, no romance and no commitment?''

He looked back at her and his eyes, his beautiful grey eyes, looked suddenly empty. Bewildered.

Laura bit back on a sob. It was a fleeting impression, but for a minute Nick had looked like a little boy who'd lost his way.

Stepping away from her, he crossed her sitting room and stood in the doorway. His grey eyes still had that empty look—like the sky when there's no chance of sunshine. ''It simply occurred to me that it really is time for some action on my part,'' he drawled. ''But I won't take up any more of your time.''

Laura's mouth drooped open. ''So you're going?''

''Of course.''

"Just like that? You mean that if I was prepared to—to fall in with your plans, you would have been happy to spend half the night here, but as I'm not you're rushing off because you're wasting your time?"

He stood looking grim but didn't answer.

Laura made an angry, shooing gesture with her hands. "You'd better go, Nick. Whatever you do, don't waste your precious time. I'm sure I can't afford your hourly rate."

"Look, calm down," he grumbled. "It was simply a suggestion from one adult to another, not a submission for a bill to be passed by parliament." He let out his breath on a sudden sigh. "But let's not start a fight now when we have much more serious things to concentrate on."

Laura grabbed the back of a chair for support. She could feel panic rising in her like liquid. She was drowning in it. Despite her protests, her mind had been running out of control—like a movie projector, flashing up images of Nick and her. Together. Making love. Hot. Happy. Loving. Love.

"Of course," she managed to say as, with a supreme effort, she pushed those pictures aside. "I'm more than willing to concentrate on serious things. As I said earlier, I'm quite happy to take the girls to school in the morning. And I can take a few minutes off in the afternoon to pick them up. They can stay at the library with me till closing time."

"It's a lot to ask."

"I've said I don't mind, Nick." Her voice sounded cracked and full of tears, but too bad. He couldn't mess her around like this and expect her to be unmoved.

"It should only be for another day or two. This rat-bag caller will probably show his hand again soon and then we should be able to nail him.'' He stepped forward as if he might touch her—or kiss her on the cheek. She tilted her cheek in his direction—just a little.

But he didn't kiss her. Instead, he frowned and stepped back again sharply, and shoved his hands deep in his trouser pockets. "I'll let myself out the back way. Goodnight, Laura.''

"Goodnight.''

She didn't watch him go. She stayed where she was in her little lamp-lit sitting room at the front of the house. And she listened to the sounds of Nick leaving. His footsteps retreated down the hall and through the kitchen.

She heard him unlock the door. There was the slight squeak of the hinge as he let himself out and the solid click of the door closing again. And she listened to his progress back down the path at the side of the house and out of the front drive and she felt tears swell in fat pools and begin to slide down her cheeks.

For a minute or two there was silence outside, but she continued to stand there listening and crying silently. And then, from some distance away, she heard a car door slamming and an engine starting up. There was the spurt of acceleration. And finally the sound of Nick driving away.

A noisy sob escaped Laura as she slumped into an armchair. What on earth was the matter with her? She should be proud of herself. She'd resisted the temptation to give in to something she didn't believe in. Nick had suggested a casual romp. A fling. Turning him down was right.

Two days ago, she and Nick had agreed that their relationship should remain strictly within the bounds of friendship. Then his testosterone had spoiled everything. Thank heavens she'd said no and saved herself from inevitable heartache. She was on the moral high ground. There was absolutely nothing for her to feel bad about.

So why did she feel so unhappy?

Why was misery soaking through her like grey, drizzling rain?

"My, what a long face!" Susie rushed up to Laura. "Nothing's happened to the girls, has it?"

"No, no, they're fine." Laura sighed and pushed a stray curl out of her eyes, and frowned at her computer screen as she scrolled through the catalogue. She had several jobs she wanted to clear before the library doors opened this morning.

Beside her, Susie folded her arms across her chest and leaned back against the counter. Her eyes narrowed and Laura could sense that her friend was studying her intently.

"And how is their daddy?" she asked slowly.

"What's that?" Laura squinted at the computer screen, paying studious attention to the location details of an obscure book she was trying to track down.

"You heard me, Laura. I asked, how's Nick?"

"How would I know?"

Susie sighed, and muttered, "I imagine you've had some kind of communication with him in the past twenty-four hours."

Laura pulled an uninterested face. "He just called to check that the girls were OK."

Susie moved to the after-hours return box and hefted out an armful of books, plonked them on the counter, and then turned back to Laura. "You and Nick must have become pals pretty quickly. You met a fortnight ago and already you're minding his kids.''

Suppressing an angry sigh, Laura took some notes about the book before closing down the screen. The last thing she needed this morning was an in-depth discussion of her relationship with Nick Farrell.

She looked up at Susie. ''You know what I'm like. I'm always a sucker for the grand gesture. As soon as I heard Nick's problem I offered to help out. It seemed logical that as hardly anyone knows I'm in any way connected to Nick, the girls should be safe with me.''

''Mmm,'' mused Susie. ''But the tiny detail you've avoided sharing with me, my dear best friend, is the precise nature of this connection you have with Nick that hardly anyone knows about.''

''The *precise* nature?''

''Yes.''

''Well, to be precise, it's a platonic connection,'' Laura snapped. ''And, Susie, I expect that should answer all your *friendly* questions in one go.''

''It doesn't answer my first question,'' Susie said softly.

''What was that?''

''Why you're wearing such a long face. You've insisted that Nick's girls are fine, and he's fine, but I've never seen you looking so miserable.''

Laura looked away. It was useless to protest that she was fine, too. She knew Susie wouldn't believe her. ''It's too hard to explain,'' she said.

''Try me.''

''Oh, Susie, you wouldn't understand. You don't have any hang-ups about the opposite sex.''

''Laura, we all get hung up about the guys we really care about.''

Laura stiffened.

"How many times have you seen Nick since the wedding?"

"A few times. Nothing—like a date. Nothing serious."

Susie smiled knowingly. "You don't have to go on a date for there to be sparks flying." Casually, she began to fiddle with the books she'd stacked in front of her, opening them to expose their bar codes. "And that's what we're talking about, isn't it? Sparks? At a guess I'd say serious sparkage."

"I'm not sure."

Susie rolled her eyes. "She's not sure," she said to the ceiling. "Laura, I saw you guys at the wedding reception. There was enough electricity on that dance floor to short circuit the wiring of the entire hotel. And that was before you went outside."

Laura's teeth clenched. "Are you going to check those books in, or are you just going to play with them all day?"

"I'll check them in," Susie replied. "Keep your hair on. But listen, honey, Rob tells me that Nick Farrell is a really great guy. I'm talking True Blue. Not just a good-looking stud, but a really nice fellow."

"I'm sure he's a monument to male perfection," Laura replied icily. "And I understand his wife was perfect, too. The perfect couple."

"His wife?" Susie frowned. "Is that what this is all about? But she's in the past, Laura."

"Try telling Nick that."

"Oh."

"Nick's heart and soul still belong to Miranda. He's not going to trust them with anyone else. All he wants from a woman is a casual fling. No emotional contact, something purely physical.''

"Oh," Susie said again.

"Now where's all your good advice?" Laura cried, flinging the words at her friend.

Susie worried her upper lip with her teeth. "I take it you haven't put him to the test?"

"I beg your pardon?"

"I mean, he's made all these claims before you two actually…" She hesitated and frowned at Laura. "Have you two—?"

"I told you it's platonic. Of course we haven't."

"So—I reckon you could change his mind."

Laura couldn't hold back a bitter laugh. "Dream on," she scoffed, shaking her head. There were certain things even a best friend could never understand. Especially not a best friend who had just come back from her honeymoon. "Just leave it, Suze. Nick and I have agreed that we're incompatible."

Laura was happy with how definite she'd made that sound, but, as she stood there, scowling at Susie, she remembered the question she'd thrown at Nick last night. *You expect me to agree to a tacky affair with no emotion, no romance and no commitment?* And she remembered that fleeting sadness she'd seen in his eyes.

"Laura, if persuading Nick that you're incompatible makes you look this sad, I think you should reconsider."

Laura let out another weary sigh. There was no doubt she had just spent a night of utter misery. She'd lain alone and thought about Nick till close on dawn. "You really think I should agree to a casual affair?"

"Darling, when a man and a woman first meet they

have to start somewhere. It usually takes time to move from casual affairs to cosy commitment.''

''Of course I know that. But Nick's different. He told me right from the start that he's not prepared to love or commit to anyone else. And as for me, after Oliver I'm much more cautious about how I hand out my—er—affection.''

''Give me a break, Laura, you've had five years of caution since Oliver.''

Wasn't that the truth? Laura thought grimly. And being cautious hadn't exactly brought a barrel of laughs—or a sense of contentment.

''And as for Nick, I still think you could change his mind,'' Susie continued confidently. ''He's only a man after all. And we all know men are dead scared about serious relationships and commitment.'' She smiled a beaming grin. ''*Until* they meet the right woman.''

Laura shook her head but Susie wasn't to be put off. ''That's why I say you should put him to the test. Go with your natural urges and then watch him try to walk away from you. My guess is he could find it a darn sight harder than he thinks.''

With a disbelieving roll of her eyes, Laura turned back to her desk. But, in spite of her outward rejection of Susie's suggestion she found it intriguing. Should she really take a risk and just grab a handful of happiness with Nick?

He'd certainly managed to rattle her safe old sense of contentment. After two heart-stopping kisses—two-and-a-half kisses, if she counted last night—she was beginning to think that when a man like Nick paid a woman attention even a Goody-two-shoes should think about her short-term happiness before all else.

If she was honest, she was getting rather tired of her

independence. Lately it had felt more like loneliness. As she riffled through an assortment of hanging files the thought lingered, teasing her.

Should she really give Susie's advice a try?

Heather Cunningham was in the library around mid-morning. She was the last in the line to check out books and she approached the desk with a serious, wary expression.

Laura pinned on a bright smile and thanked her lucky stars that Susie was in a back room, sorting new stock. "Hello, Mrs Cunningham."

"Good morning, Laura. How are my little grand-daughters?"

Despite the awkwardness of their previous meeting, Laura was determined to be pleasant to Nick's mother-in-law. She filled her in about the girls' activities and finished by adding, "You must telephone them and have a chat one evening. I'm sure they're missing you."

Heather Cunningham's eyebrows rose as if she hadn't expected such an offer. "Thank you, Laura. I shall do that."

"I hope you haven't had any trouble from the stalker."

"No, thank heavens," Heather replied, and then her face softened a fraction. "You know, I'm actually rather pleased that Nick trusts you with Kate and Felicity."

Laura hid her surprise by stacking Heather's books neatly on the counter and inserting a bookmark stamped with the due date.

"The fact that he trusts you is a good sign," Heather continued.

"It is?"

"He can't go on trying to do everything for the girls

for ever.'' Heather leant forward to confide. ''I know I was warning you off Nick last week, Laura, but if the dear boy's chosen you to help him out in this terrible situation I accept his judgement. Normally he never lets any of his women-friends near the girls.''

''Well, there's a subtle but vital difference between me and Nick's other women friends,'' Laura explained darkly. ''I'm not a—girlfriend. I'm just a friend who has a spare room and happens to be female.''

Heather nodded and her face broke into a surprisingly conspiratorial smile. ''Yes, my dear, Nick went to an extraordinary amount of trouble to explain that to me, too. In fact I was quite comforted by the way he went to such enormous lengths to make your situation crystal-clear.''

Puzzled by the knowing twinkle in Heather's eyes, Laura frowned. ''Of course, no woman could replace Miranda,'' she suggested and she tried to ignore the spiteful voice in her head that whispered, *Saint Miranda, Miranda the Mother Superior.*

''Perhaps,'' Heather sighed. ''But it's time Nick got over that.''

Laura sensed her jaw dropping so quickly she half expected to feel it hit the floor. After all, this woman was Miranda's mother. She took a deep breath and said nervously, ''Nick can't let her go, can he?''

''He's certainly finding it very difficult.'' Heather looked around the library. It wasn't very busy that morning. There was no one nearby. ''Laura, it might help if I explain something.''

Laura nodded uncertainly as she felt an embarrassingly desperate urge to hear whatever Heather could tell her about Nick.

"Nick needs very firm handling from any woman who loves him."

"But I don't—"

"My daughter set her cap at young Nick very early," Heather hurried to explain. "She decided she was going to marry him when she was sixteen. After that, she virtually never let him out of her sight. She worked very hard at being the perfect companion. Miranda even forced herself to study law—just so she could be with him at university. And, believe me, she had no natural inclination for the subject."

"That's—that's dedication."

"She was very keen to get Nick married and in the family way," the other woman said grimly.

Laura frowned.

"Kate was born just six months after the wedding." Heather's eyes shimmered as she looked at Laura. "Don't get me wrong, pet. I loved my daughter, but she was always insecure and that made her manipulative. The problem was," Miranda's mother went on, "after they were married and the girls came along, and Miranda was busy with them, Nick's career began to take off. They couldn't be together as often. Nick was working long hours and doing extra court work. He would often have to travel to trials in regional centres."

"Miranda was jealous?"

"I'm afraid so. She started going out in the evenings to make Nick jealous. Going to night clubs, of all places. I don't think she ever went out with another man. She was just making a statement. And then—" Heather sighed deeply "—one rainy evening there was an accident."

"How terrible," Laura murmured. She was shocked by this picture of Miranda—so different from the picture of sainthood she'd imagined. It sounded as if Nick's wife had been very high maintenance. "Did Nick feel guilty that he'd made Miranda unhappy?" she asked.

"Yes. The silly boy thinks the crash would never have happened if he'd paid her more attention. But I know he did his best. We all did. But Miranda needed too much."

"I must say I'm surprised that you're telling me this."

Heather's eyes studied Laura for a moment. "I've watched Nick mourning my daughter for four long years. I love that boy, Laura. He's not just the father of my granddaughters. He's the son I never had."

"But none of this has anything to do with me."

"Don't be too sure of that, Laura."

"What do you mean?"

"You're a smart girl. I'll leave you to think about it."

As Heather walked away, Laura suddenly felt she had far too much to think about.

Nick was having a bad afternoon. He couldn't concentrate on the case he was preparing. To start with, every time the phone rang he reacted badly. Stokes, the nuisance caller, had been silent for too long and that made him suspicious...edgy. Just what was the guy up to?

But there were other things adding to his edginess. Like the way he'd stuffed up last night with Laura. He was supposed to be an intelligent, clear-thinking, hot-shot lawyer, but in dealing with Laura he'd sure fused a few wires in the old brain circuitry.

So much for Rob's bright advice. *Just put the hard word on her.* What an idiot he'd been to try that! He'd known instinctively that kind of approach wouldn't work and yet he'd gone ahead and tried it anyhow.

And now, the million-dollar question was *why?* Why had he persisted in making moves on this woman when he knew she was an unlikely candidate?

The questions without answers had rolled around in his brain, driving him out of the office to seek out a coffee in his favourite Victory Street café. He wanted to clear his mind of red hair and blue eyes and pale, pale skin.

But the problem was he couldn't just ignore Laura when she was doing such a magnificent job of helping him out. He really admired her for that. It was brave and generous of her to go out of her way for a couple of little girls she hardly knew. Next time he saw her he would have to try to make amends.

He would have to apologise.

Again.

Staring mulishly at his cup of espresso, Nick wondered if it would be better to try the *actions speak louder than words* approach. But that was a challenge in itself. It called for some kind of sincere gesture. Roses and chocolates were too *ho-hum*. Obviously, he couldn't take her out to dinner. She was otherwise committed with his daughters.

But—he smiled as a new idea revealed itself—he could cook for her. He could cook her dinner at her place. Nick played with that idea for a minute or two. Yeah. That was the way to go about making amends. She was putting herself out to take care of his girls. Dinner was a practical way to help out. And to show off what a sensitive New Age guy he really was. Not that he was trying to impress her, of course. Just thank her.

He sauntered over to the café's magazine rack, picked up this month's copy of the popular *Dine-In* magazine and flicked through its pages, deciding he'd cook her something new and trendy.

He liked the sound of the Low-Stress-High-Impress section. Steamed coral trout in soy and oyster sauce…wild mushroom risotto…they both sounded rather good.

Feeling better at the thought of positive action, Nick bought the magazine and, as he marched briskly back to work, he could almost smile at the thought of surprising the librarian with something as safe as food.

His secretary looked up as he walked through the door. ''Ms Goodman is on the line. Shall I put the call through to your desk?''

Something in the region of Nick's chest did a double take. ''Thanks.'' He nodded and hurried into his private office. Swinging the door closed behind him, he snatched up the phone quickly. ''Nick here.''

''Hello, Nick. This is Laura.'' Her voice sounded tight, worried.

''What's happened? Where are the girls?''

''They're OK. They're here. There's nothing the matter.''

His sigh of relief was unavoidably noisy. He really had to stop carrying on like this. ''Sorry I jumped on you. Slight case of overreaction.''

''I—I just wanted to keep you up to date. I'm calling from the library. The girls have finished school. I was able to pick them up without any problems and they're here with me now. Kate's actually doing her homework and Felicity's in the toy corner. They've had some crackers and milk and they're both fine.''

''That's really good news. Thanks Laura.'' He sank

into his chair and leaned back, feeling the tension leave him. Well, not all the tension. Talking to Laura was never exactly relaxing.

"I'm sorry if I disturbed you," she said, sounding more nervous than ever. "I probably shouldn't bother you at work."

"No, not at all. I'm really pleased you rang."

"Right, then, I'll—er—keep in touch."

"Thanks, Laura. I'd appreciate that." Hell! She was about to hang up and he hadn't mentioned dinner.

"Maybe tonight the girls can ring you at home to have a chat?" she suggested.

"OK," he said slowly, while his mind raced. His chances of swinging the conversation to dinner were dwindling. Her suggestion didn't sound at all promising. It was Laura's way of telling him not to bother coming around this evening. He cleared his throat. "A telephone chat with the girls would be—*nice*."

"Unless, of course, you'd like to come to my place and see them."

Nick sat up straight. "Is that an invitation?"

"I—I guess so," she said, sounding doubtful. Then she laughed nervously. "Yes, it's an invitation."

"Well, I'd love to see the girls," he told her. "Maybe I could bring dinner."

"Oh?" She sounded surprised, almost shocked. "I—I thought that if you came and read the girls a bedtime story I could cook dinner. I could feed them something simple first and then rustle up something more—more adult for us."

Before he could interrupt, she hurried on anxiously. "What do you like? I was thinking about Thai-style fish. Maybe coral trout—or—um…" There was a pause and Nick heard the slight rustle of pages. "Or maybe you'd prefer something like wild mushroom risotto?"

With a sudden grin, Nick opened the magazine he'd just bought. Steamed coral trout and wild mushroom risotto. "Either of those dishes sound excellent," he told her. "My favourites."

"Your *favourites?* Really?" There was an edge of panic in Laura's voice. "Well, don't expect too much—I'm not a brilliant cook."

"Then let's make a slight change in the game plan," Nick suggested quickly, surprised at how easily the cards were falling his way. "I'll bring the ingredients and do the cooking while you read the girls their stories. They're bored with my stories anyhow."

There was a long silence on the other end of the line. "Are you sure you want to cook?"

"Steamed coral trout? You bet."

"I can give you a list of ingredients."

"I doubt that's necessary. I can manage."

"You know what to get?"

"Let me guess." He held up the magazine in front of him. "For the coral trout, I'll need soy sauce, oyster sauce, coriander roots, fresh ginger... Am I on the right track?"

"Amazingly accurate," she murmured.

"It's a cinch for a kitchen genius."

"Oh, for heaven's sake," Laura responded with more like her usual snap. "Then please don't let me stand in your way. By all means, you do the cooking."

"My pleasure."

# CHAPTER NINE

HAVING their Daddy in the house seriously disrupted the girls' usual bedtime routine, and when Laura eventually managed to bustle them off to their room for stories they took even longer than ever to settle.

By the time she headed back out into the kitchen Nick had their meal pretty much under control.

He was standing at her stove and she paused to admire the picture he made. Unmistakable masculinity—black hair, grey eyes, blue jeans and navy shirt—surrounded by the feminine buttercup-yellow of her walls and cupboards.

She had a sneaking feeling she could get used to a sight like that in her kitchen. Not that Nick was planning on hanging around.

Not yet, anyway.

*But if Susie's advice was right...*

On the bench beside him stood a bottle of wine already opened and two glasses.

"You deserve a drink," he said with a grin. "This is a light wine designed to prepare your taste buds for what's to come."

*For what's to come!*

Laura's mouth went desert-dry and she tried to wet her lips with her tongue. It didn't work. She ran her damp hands nervously down the outside of her trousers. Dry mouth, damp hands, quaking heart: she was a mess. *Nick had no idea what was to come.* He didn't have a clue that she was planning to seduce him.

Planning was the operative word. As yet, she didn't have the foggiest idea how she was actually going to pull off such a plan.

Yikes! Just thinking about the expression on Nick's face and what he would say or do when she told him she'd changed her mind lowered her communication skills to the level of a chimpanzee's. How did you tell a man that you suddenly wanted him to stay for more than a meal?

*My days as a prude are over? I just happened to turn into a sex beast overnight?*

Oh, help! It was better not to think about it. When the time came, she would find the words.

Normally she didn't drink alcohol, but when Nick handed her a glass she took it. She would need some extra courage this evening. She clutched it against her chest as she looked into the pan he was working at. "So you decided on the risotto?"

"It was more a case of risotto chose me," he replied. "No coral trout in the shops at the moment—but plenty of wild mushrooms."

She sniffed appreciatively. "Smells great. It looks—" She paused, frowning. "That's amazing. It looks just like the picture I saw today in a magazine. Good grief, Nick, it looks almost exactly like a recipe I'd been thinking about using."

"Fancy that," he said with a strange little smile. "Maybe we've got something in common after all." He raised his glass to clink it against hers. "Cheers."

"Cheers," she repeated.

"Let's drink to finding what else we have in common, Laura."

"Yes," Laura whispered, and she tried not think about the after-dinner activity she planned to share with

Nick. Just in time, she remembered not to gulp her wine.

It tasted mellow and very pleasant, but she could feel the effects of the chilled Chardonnay lighting her veins almost immediately. Best to keep her wits about her. She set the glass aside and busied herself by clearing away the remnants of the girls' meal and resetting the kitchen table with fresh place mats and serviettes.

Her cottage was too tiny to have a separate dining room, so they had to eat in the kitchen. It wasn't really practical to dim the lights, but she lit a jasmine-scented candle in the hope that it would create some atmosphere. Maybe the right atmosphere would help her to feel braver.

"I'd say this is ready," Nick reported.

He dished up the meal with easy, competent flourishes, while Laura took a seat and fiddled with the stem of her wine glass.

She figured that even if they dined at a refined pace it couldn't take them any more than fifteen or twenty minutes to actually eat this risotto. And then maybe there would be coffee, but after last night's little episode Nick would probably feel compelled to leave.

That meant she didn't have very long to develop the right mood for telling him about—her *change of heart*.

Butterflies danced in her chest. She would have to start laying some groundwork immediately. It was time to let Nick know she wasn't quite so inexperienced with men as he suspected.

Laura lifted her fork and sampled her food. "Mmm, delicious," she said sincerely. And then she decided it was best to jump in at the deep end.

She took a quick sip of wine. "I haven't dined in

this kitchen alone with a man since—since Oliver,'' she said, with what felt like a very wobbly smile.

Nick's fork froze midway to his mouth. ''And how long would that be?''

Laura could tell by the tight-lipped way he asked that it was only one of a host of questions he would have liked to fire at her, so she decided to get everything off her chest in a rush. ''It's five years since Oliver left. He used to come around for—for dinner twice a week. Most weeks anyhow.''

''Oliver was a colleague?'' Nick asked doubtfully.

''Oh, no. *No,* he was a— He was someone I met at a conference. He sold books. Actually, he represented quite a big publishing company. He was my boyfriend. Amazingly charming.''

''I see.''

''But that's not important,'' Laura hastened to explain.

Nick's wary eyes considered her. ''So what is important about Oliver besides his amazing charm and book-selling skills?''

''It's just that his visits were never quite like this. They weren't cosy.''

Nick didn't comment.

''He never cooked for me and he'd always be in such a hurry.''

''So the astonishing charm didn't last?'' He smiled faintly.

''He would come dashing in from work and he'd be so anxious to get into bed he would bolt down the meal I'd spent ages preparing. And he'd hardly notice if it was pepperoni pizza or coq au vin.''

She glanced at Nick to see how he was reacting, but his expression was too stony to interpret.

"Of course, he never offered to cook for me, and he never took me *out* to dinner."

Nick grunted something incomprehensible.

"I know *now* why we never dined out. He was frightened of meeting someone he knew. Someone who knew he was *married*."

She took a quick taste of the risotto. "Oh, Nick, this is *really* delicious." Then she heard Nick's splutter and looked up at him. "What's the matter?"

He didn't speak, but just sat there looking stony. No, she realised, he'd gone beyond stony—Nick looked stunned.

"I've shocked you," she said.

"Yes. I think you have."

"I'm sorry, Nick."

"Don't apologise. I'm just assimilating the facts. Let me see. Oliver, of the fantastic charm and incredible book-selling ability, but with an appalling appreciation for fine food, used to race you off to the bedroom although he was *married?*"

His steely grey eyes held hers. "It's rather a lot to take in. Especially coming from Laura Goodman."

"I had to say it all in a rush like that or I wouldn't have got it out."

"I see. So you had to get it out. You thought it was vital for me to know you had an affair with a married man?"

Laura winced. "Yes."

Nick placed his knife and fork very deliberately on his plate and folded his arms across his chest. "Tell me why."

"*Why?*"

"Why did you feel compelled to offload this information?"

He was looking at her so fiercely that Laura had to lower her eyes. "I wanted you to understand," she told the plate in front of her. "I felt so dreadful. I didn't know Oliver was married. I thought he was going to marry *me*. I wanted to die when I found out he had a wife and three little boys."

For a moment his voice gentled as he said, "That must have been a terrible discovery."

Laura looked up. "If there's a word that means worse than terrible, that's how I felt."

Nick nodded and took a slow sip of wine.

She downed some of her own wine. This was the hardest part. Nick would expect her to explain *exactly* why it was important for him to understand about Oliver.

Oh, dear. Now she had to make links between her past and what she hoped would be her future. She had to find a way to give him the green light to make love to her. After the king-sized fuss she'd made last night.

She'd hurried too quickly through her explanations. They were supposed to be finishing their meal by the time she got to this point, but Nick still had quite a lot of food on his plate.

She took a deep breath. "You see, Nick, you and I do have plenty in common. In different ways, we are both affected by our past relationships. You explained to me how you feel about Miranda and why you can't commit. I wanted to explain about Oliver and why I've been reluctant to—to agree to a casual relationship—" She stopped as a movement in the doorway distracted her.

Oh, Lord! Felicity was standing there, looking tiny and tousled in her crumpled nightdress. She was clutching her teddy bear.

*How long had she been listening?*

"Fliss, what do you want?" Nick asked quickly, and Laura heard the edge of impatience in his tone.

"A drink of water," the child said solemnly.

"OK. You go back to bed. I'll bring it into you." He jumped up and filled a tumbler at the sink. As he passed Laura on the way to the bedroom he rolled his eyes to the ceiling.

Nick's mind was still reeling from the conversation in the kitchen as he sat on the edge of the little white bed and met the shining directness in his daughter's gaze.

"Daddy, do you like Laura?" Felicity asked as she nestled back into bed and Nick tucked the sheets up under her chin.

Right now, his feelings about Laura were as clear as mud. "Yes, Fliss," he said. "I like her."

Like a Jack-in-the-box, Felicity sat straight up again and crossed her chubby arms over her little chest. Her dark brows drew low as she looked up at Nick sternly. "But, Daddy, do you *really* like her?" Serious grey eyes, so like his own, challenged him.

But Nick didn't spend his days asking leading questions in court simply to come home and be caught out by his five-year-old daughter. He gave her tummy a tickle as he sent her question straight back. "What about you, Fliss, do *you* really like Laura?"

Her answer was spontaneous. "Oh, yes, Daddy, I do. I *love* Laura."

He dropped a kiss on her soft, rosy cheek and suppressed a sigh. "That's good, moppet," he whispered, thinking how easy it was for Fliss to talk about *love*. The word slipped off her tongue without the slightest hesitation.

But she was talking about the no-strings love of a child. Pure, unselfish love. Unstoppable, undemanding, unfettered love.

So different from the mess adults made of it.

For a moment he felt a stab of nostalgia for the carefree days of his childhood. The love between adults was so complex.

It could stop without warning. It was extremely demanding. And it came with baggage and chains attached.

As he rose again and prepared to leave the room he fancied he caught a slight movement from Kate's bed, but when he turned her way she was lying very still with her eyes closed.

He walked back down the passage to the kitchen, reflecting that three females were more than a match for one mere male. *And, yes, Fliss,* he thought when he saw Laura standing near the microwave, *I like Laura—especially the way she looks.*

She was wearing a loose sleeveless top in a rich cream colour that made the deep cherry of her hair look more luxurious and beautiful than ever. The top was knitted and kitten-soft. She looked so *touchable.*

How could he not *like* the subtle sway of her breasts beneath that soft creamy knit as she moved? And as for the way the slim-fitting trousers hugged the delicious curve of her behind—he found it incredibly difficult not to stare.

She said, "I thought I'd zap your meal for you. It would be a shame to let it grow cold."

"Thanks." He nodded as he sat down again and refilled their wine glasses.

Laura smiled at him shyly and placed his heated food in front of him. He wasn't sure if he smiled back, he was still coming to terms with the jolting physical impact her beauty always had on him.

Added to that, he was still assimilating Laura's news.

As they ate in uncomfortable silence Nick mused over what she had told him. A woman like Laura would be devastated to discover she'd been making love to someone else's husband. It was probably enough to scare her off men for good. *For at least five years.*

*Hang on!* He sat bolt upright as he remembered the last thing she'd said. *I wanted to explain why I've been reluctant to agree to a casual relationship.* Nick felt his breathing constrict. He fiddled with his collar, which felt uncomfortably tight, but realised he wasn't wearing a tie.

*Reluctant,* she'd said. OK. Reluctant meant unwilling, but it also implied hesitation rather than absolute refusal. So, did that mean she was no longer totally rejecting the idea of a casual affair?

"Felicity's OK?" Laura asked.

"Er—yes, the little monkey has always been a bit of an attention-seeker," he said, relieved to sidetrack into safer subjects than Laura's attitude to sex.

"She's developing a very strong personality."

"She might be a handful when she hits the teen years." He smiled at her. "What were you like as a teenager?"

"Oh, what do you think?"

"Good as gold."

She grinned self-consciously. "Yes. I worked hard at school. Lived a quiet life. Didn't do anything to shock my parents." Over the top of her wine glass, her blue gaze met his. "And what about you?"

He shrugged. "I lived up north on the Atherton Tableland. You know how it is in the bush. We had a lot of freedom. Rob and I used to get up to plenty of mischief.''

''When did you meet Miranda?''

''She was there, too. We started dating when we were sixteen.''

''Childhood sweethearts,'' Laura said softly. ''So you and Rob and Miranda all grew up together?''

''Yes. And we all left the north together, when we came to university here in Brisbane.''

Laura had finished her meal. She looked suddenly nervous as she held her wine glass stiffly in front of her.

Nick felt edgy too. He suspected she was going to swing the conversation back to that *other* subject. *Sex.* Not that he usually shied away from that topic, but this was *Laura.* After last night's rejection, talking about sex with her wasn't exactly a boost to the ego.

''Nick, I've changed my mind,'' she said suddenly.

It was there again. That trouble he had earlier with his breathing. ''Dare I ask just exactly what you've changed your mind about?''

''About us.'' An incredible pink tide rose from her neck and up her cheeks till it reached her hair line. ''I think you're right. I think we need to work out what's really going on between us. I would like to—'' She swallowed some wine. ''I think perhaps we should make love.''

''Daddy.''

Nick whipped around in the direction of the girlish voice. This time it was Kate, standing in the doorway in her nightgown. ''Kate, for heaven's sake!'' he exploded.

''I'm thirsty, too,'' she whispered, looking timid, as if she wished she'd never ventured out.

Nick jumped to his feet, strode towards the sink, filled a glass and thrust it rather roughly towards his daughter. He couldn't believe her sense of timing. "I don't want to hear another peep from you girls. Do you understand?"

"Yes, Daddy," she said meekly.

He walked with Kate back to her room and watched as she drank some of the water and then climbed into bed. Felicity was lying in the other bed with her eyes squeezed tightly shut. Too tightly shut. Nick could tell that the naughty little muffin was feigning sleep.

"I'm disappointed with you girls," he told them. "Laura is very kindly looking after you while I'm— while I'm *busy* and you should be helping her by being good and going to sleep."

*What a joke!* Nick thought. Next minute the girls would be asking why he was here at Laura's place every night if he was supposed to be so busy.

He was relieved to hear replies of "Yes, Daddy," from both his daughters. His heart melted as it always did and he gave them both hugs.

Kate was looking up at him with big brown eyes that peeped from beneath her fringe. "We promise we won't interrupt you any more," she said.

"We was just checkin' on you," Felicity told him.

"*Checking* on me?"

"Yes. We wanted to make sure you ki—"

"*Fliss!*" hissed Kate. "Shut up." She glared across to the other bed.

"Oops—sorry."

Puzzled, Nick gave both girls another warning that he didn't want to see them tonight, and walked out of the room. But, from just beyond the doorway, he heard Felicity's voice.

"We should have told him he *has* to kiss Laura."

"No, we shouldn't," came Kate's loudly whispered reply. "I rang Grandma this afternoon and she said we have to let nature take its course."

"What does that mean?"

"I think it means he'll kiss her when the time is right. Maybe he has to wait till he feels like it."

"I don't think he ever will," sighed Felicity. "I think he doesn't understand that grown-up ladies like kissing."

In the darkened passage, Nick choked in disbelief. What on earth had his mother-in-law and his daughters been discussing? He wasn't sure if the emotion he swallowed was a desperate urge to cry out with rage or to chuckle wildly.

He spoke through the darkness in his sternest voice. "Girls, I don't want to hear any more talking."

There was a lengthy silence after that and, finally satisfied, he walked back down the passage, shaking his head. *Now his mother-in-law was involved!*

There were *far* too many females in his life!

When he reached the kitchen, he grabbed up his wine glass and took a deep swig. "I've made the girls promise to stay in bed." He remained standing beside the table.

Laura nodded, looking embarrassed.

"Now, where were we?" Nick continued as he tried to ignore the disturbing way his body throbbed as he looked at her. "Were you actually saying what I thought you were saying?"

She covered her face with her hands. "Do you think Kate understood?"

He frowned. "I doubt it. I'm not even sure if I heard you correctly myself."

Setting his glass aside, he reached down and drew her hands away from her face. ''At least I don't think we'll be disturbed by the girls again tonight.''

When she looked up at him, her blue eyes were filled with a bewildering mixture of emotions. She left her hands in his grasp as she rose and stood beside him. ''We should go to my room,'' she said softly, so softly he only just caught the words.

Nick's body leapt at her suggestion. ''You sure you want to?'' he whispered.

One eyebrow rose. ''Would I be suggesting it if I didn't want to?''

Without saying another word she withdrew her hands from his, turned, and walked away from him, moving silently down the carpeted passage, past the girls' closed door, past the bathroom, to her room. In the doorway she paused and looked back at him over her shoulder.

For a moment she stood there, looking slender and lovely and infinitely vulnerable and then she disappeared inside.

Nick followed.

How could he not follow?

This moment was something out of his dreams.

Since he'd met Laura, she'd haunted his nights with her soft, blue-eyed beauty. All through the meal he'd thought about lifting off that cream sweater.

So many times he'd fantasised about those pale, perfect shoulders of hers and how the rest of her skin would be the same.

White as the moon.

Round and womanly soft.

Warm with wanting—like her mouth whenever he'd kissed her.

He entered her room and shut the door firmly behind

him. There was a key in the lock and he turned it. He nodded towards the door and tried to crack a grin. "We don't want to share this with anyone."

Her bedroom wasn't frilly, as he'd expected. Not a glimpse of virginal white anywhere. Not that he was actually trying to take in details. He wasn't looking at anything except Laura.

But she was standing beside her bed and he couldn't avoid seeing it in the soft lamplight.

Her bed looked sensational—as if it was designed for a night of wild romping. A generously fat quilt in two-tone shades of antique gold and purple covered the entire bed and scattered on top of this was a decadent pile of king-sized pillows in vibrantly coloured silks.

The urge to sweep Laura into his arms and to tumble, with her long, pale legs wrapped around him, into all that richly coloured softness and silk was too much.

Nick stepped towards her.

Her quiet voice halted him. "I understand this will be a one-night stand."

"Uh-huh."

"No complications, no expectations. The way you want it."

"Sure."

"Just sex…"

*Just sex.* Sure, that was what he wanted.

Yes. He wanted to peel those clothes away from her and find her round, rosy tipped breasts and softly curving hips. He wanted to drive this woman wild. He wanted to hear her make those hungry little noises again as he kissed her. All over.

Tonight she'd learn what fun a man and a woman could have without all the clutter of emotional baggage, and he was damn sure he could be an improvement on old Oliver.

She stood very still, looking up at him, and her big eyes were huge in her delicate, pale face.

*Just sex.*

He wanted her so badly he was trembling. He could already sense the petal softness of her lips and his breath caught as he imagined the way they would open to him so he could taste the sweet, moist heat of her mouth.

Her enticing perfume fragranced the air all around him and he wondered if she'd sprinkled it on the sheets. The thought that she'd prepared her bed for him was so erotic.

*Just sex.*

Great!

She was offering herself to him.

His heart pounded and he fancied hers did too. Any second now he would lose himself in Laura Goodman. The fever of his anticipation was unbearable.

*Just sex.* This was going to be *so* good.

*So what the hell was the matter with him?*

Why was he stuffing around like a pubescent walking hormone, as if he didn't have a clue what to do?

Nick groaned.

"What's the matter?" Laura whispered.

"Laura, I'm not sure you really want this."

"How could you know what I want?" She sounded distressed.

Nick's throat was so choked up it was hard to speak. "You told me most definitely last night."

"I—I've rethought the situation."

"But are you sure?" Nick could hardly believe that question had come out of his mouth.

If word got out…

He could imagine the inter-office memo. *Gorgeous woman offers herself to Nick Farrell and is subsequently forced to stand waiting while he runs a lie-detector test past her.*

What the hell was wrong with him?

All the lady wanted was sex. *Just sex.* When had that become a problem?

Right now.

Because…because if he had sex with Laura she would start thinking about love. He was worried that she would want to own him in some way.

*No, he wasn't!*

Nick gulped. That was only half of the problem.

The real problem was *his.*

He was standing here in Laura Goodman's bedroom, with her sensational, willing body just inches from his and he was stalling. And the real reason was that he'd copped a painful kick in the guts. A bachelor's revelation.

He suddenly *knew* that touching and kissing and taking Laura couldn't possibly be *just sex*…because she wasn't just any woman.

She was Laura. She was incredibly kind and generous and way too sweet and beautiful. If he was to take her in his arms, to taste her, to give her pleasure and to join his body intimately with hers—he wouldn't be *just having sex!*

He would be making *love.*

To *Laura.*

And that was a problem. Chances were that after just one night he might fall completely *in love* with the woman.

And he couldn't risk that.

He didn't dare risk falling in love.

*What a mess!* Nick felt ill. This was physical and mental torture of the very worst kind.

"Nick, I didn't expect to have to show you what to do. I'm the one whose memory is rusty." Laura's face crumpled a little as she tried to smile. "Remember? I haven't done this for five years."

*Oh, hell!* He was a coward and she was being brave and gutsy about it. Trying to make a joke.

And her courage was killing him.

# CHAPTER TEN

LAURA felt sick.

Nick was standing in the middle of her bedroom looking as if he wanted to escape. Heavens, that was usually her role. It was the very last thing she'd expected from him. What had she done wrong?

He was actually stepping away from her and looking at her sternly, the same way he'd looked at Kate when she'd come to the kitchen for a glass of water.

"This is a mistake," he said.

She felt her knees give way. "This is *very* embarrassing."

"I know. I'm sorry."

He was *sorry?* Oh, that was a good one! Minutes, maybe only seconds ago, Nick had been anything but sorry. He'd definitely been about to take her to bed. There was no mistaking the dark heat of desire in his eyes.

It was the hungry look of a man about to get laid.

And she'd been about to give thanks for Nick Farrell, God's gift to women.

But now...

Now...he was standing in front of her, looking as if the thought of touching her was as unpleasant as petting a redback spider.

And that was unbearably embarrassing.

She'd lured him into her room. She'd planned seduction down to the last detail. *For heaven's sake!* She'd even rushed out at lunch time and spent a fortune on new sheets and pillows and a glamorous quilt for her bed. But somehow, at the last minute, she'd managed to turn Nick off.

"What's wrong?" she whispered. "I'm not wearing a danger sign, am I?"

He looked miserable. "You should be."

"Why? I'm too much of a geek?"

"Of course not, Laura."

"Did I fail a random breath test?"

"Don't be silly." He lifted a hand to his forehead and rubbed it as if his head ached. "If there was any kind of test, you passed it with flying colours."

"I don't get it."

His mouth twitched into a sad smile. "There isn't a lot to get. Look, this is nothing to do with whether or not you're a desirable woman. It's to do with me."

"I see." There was a solid block of silence while she thought about that. "I thought a casual fling was what you wanted."

"Yeah." Nick looked at the door. "Listen, I'd better go."

She shrugged helplessly. Miserably. There was absolutely nothing she would do to try to keep him from leaving. Her disappointment and embarrassment were painful in the extreme, but she would do her darned best not to show Nick how she felt. Just the same, as he walked towards the door she couldn't help muttering, "Some daredevil."

He turned. "I beg your pardon?"

"I—I don't think you're much of a daredevil."

"When have I ever been a daredevil?"

"Oh, come on, Nick, if someone had *dared* you to make love to me we wouldn't still be standing here talking."

He frowned. "You really think I'm that shallow?"

Laura dropped her gaze. "It seems to me you will do just about anything for a dare."

"Who told you that?"

"I've seen it for myself. The clown stint at the hospital. Susie's party. You could strip for a room full of women—"

She had a sudden vision of Nick at Susie's party—with his cheeky grin and his muscles rippling as he swung his T-shirt over his head. She wanted to cry.

What had happened to the bold and confident Nick, the guy who'd dared her to kiss him that night? What had happened to the man who'd stood in this cottage just last night trying to persuade her into this very bed?

Was this really the same man who'd urged her to throw aside her silly inhibitions?

What had gone so wrong?

When she looked up again, his dark grey eyes held a world of regret and Laura wasn't sure how she managed not to cry.

He spoke softly. "That room full of women at Susie's party wasn't nearly as risky as this room with just one real princess, Laura."

As he said that his eyes shimmered.

And as she stood there seeing the damp gleam in his eyes, she knew. Oh, she knew. She read the truth. "You're frightened of what this might lead to."

His smile was bleak. "You got it."

He didn't *dare* to risk his emotions. Tears burned in Laura's throat. Didn't Nick realise how unfair and cruel this was? She sniffed, determined not to cry.

"Nick, it's all very well for you to say no, but you've just been playing games with me." She was amazed by her nerve. Amazed that by some strange exchange of energies his fear was giving her courage.

"I'm sorry if it seems that way," he said.

"Of course that's how it seems. You've paid me compliments. You've been saying all these pushy things about wanting me. And when I finally weaken—when I do respond—you reject me."

"Laura, please—"

"How unfair is that?"

He frowned, but didn't answer.

Laura felt suddenly empty. Drained. She couldn't take any more of this. She crossed the room, wrenched the key in the lock and hauled the door open for him to leave.

She was proud that her voice didn't shake as she said coldly, "I think there's nothing more to be said but goodnight."

He nodded grimly. "Goodnight, Laura."

"Remember to lock the back door."

"Of course."

Just before he left her bedroom, he paused and looked down at her with dark, disturbed eyes. "I shouldn't keep imposing on you like this. I'll see if I can find somewhere else for the girls to stay."

Laura almost groaned. "I've said it doesn't matter, but—by all means do as you wish."

He nodded and she clung to the door frame for support as he stepped out of the room. But, as he brushed passed her his arm touched her breast. It was just a whisper of sensation, but a fiery flash of longing electrified Laura and she heard the harsh rush of Nick's indrawn breath.

He hesitated.

She stopped breathing. It was as if her blood stood

still in her veins for one, two, three shuddering, inde-
cisive heartbeats.

Their eyes met and Laura nearly sobbed aloud at the
longing and the sadness she saw in Nick's beautiful
face.

But then he jerked his gaze away and kept on going
out of her house.

This time Laura didn't cry when Nick left. She was
too paralysed. For ages she stood numb and dazed,
without moving. Finally she turned and stared at her
room, and the gloriously sumptuous bed seemed to
mock her.

The stupid part was, she thought miserably, she could
tell he didn't really want to reject her. It was because
he was scared of taking risks with his emotions. Nick
was frightened of falling in love with her.

She crossed the floor and flopped down onto her bed,
sinking miserably into the soft, luxurious quilt, and she
lay there, with one hand restlessly stroking the silky
fabric, while a cold, unfriendly moon leaned in through
her window to taunt her.

She had to agree with Nick that falling in love *was*
a scary concept.

Incredibly scary.

She understood that now.

There were so many things she was learning tonight.
And one of them was that at some time in the past week,
when she wasn't even trying, she'd fallen totally, no-
doubt-about-it in love with Nick Farrell.

She couldn't pinpoint when it had happened, maybe
it had been there from the moment she first saw him,
but she knew with an awful certainty that it was so.

She had never felt this deeply about Oliver. Her body
ached with her need for Nick. But it wasn't just a phys-

ical ache. She loved everything about the man. His smile, his voice…every cell in his body. The way he fathered his daughters. She hadn't known him very long, but already she couldn't imagine her life without him.

So she understood Nick's fear. Recognising that kind of love was an alarming process.

Knowing she loved him and watching him walk away from her this evening had been the most frightening experience of her life.

Complete emotional and physical exhaustion ensured that she slept surprisingly well, but when Laura woke next morning in her luxurious, sexy and ridiculously expensive bed, her first thoughts were of Nick.

She sank back into her pillow with a groan of dismay as her mind replayed in vivid detail the ordeal of the night and the embarrassing sight of his stiff, proud back as he walked away from her.

And she might have lain there for some time, wallowing in self-pity, if sounds of giggling, girlish laughter hadn't drifted down the hall from the kitchen. Kate and Felicity were up already.

Laura swung her legs out of bed, grateful for the blessed distraction of the busy morning rush required to organise the girls' breakfast and get them ready for school.

By the time she dropped them off at the school's main door she was feeling much better. She decided it was one of life's little ironies that Nick's lively, loving daughters could provide an antidote to the hurt their father caused her.

Luckily, it was a busy day in the library as well, and she could *almost* keep thoughts of Nick in the background. But shortly after lunch she answered the phone and heard his familiar baritone.

"Good afternoon, Laura."

The sickening knot of despair she'd been trying to ignore tightened in her stomach. "Hello, Nick."

"I won't keep you long. I just wanted to let you know I've been able to make alternative arrangements for the girls."

Laura jammed a fist against her lips to hold back a protest.

"We've been imposing on you for too long."

She closed her eyes. "I've never minded."

"I know you say that, Laura, and you're very kind—"

"I mean it. I've really enjoyed having the girls."

"Yes," Nick said softly.

"But maybe—" Laura's hands shook as she gripped the receiver. "But maybe it would be better if we—" Her throat closed over and she didn't think she could continue. She coughed. "I can understand that the whole situation might be getting too complicated."

"My dad's tests are completed and he's been given the all-clear so he and Mum are very keen to see the girls. I'm going to send them up there till this whole business with the phone calls and the stalking settles."

"I guess that's sensible."

"It's the only way, Laura. Stokes is bound to find out about you sooner or later. I've booked plane tickets to Cairns for this evening."

"I see." *So soon?* He really was anxious to be clear of her.

"The airline people have been very understanding. A flight attendant will keep a watchful eye on Kate and Fliss."

Laura nodded. ''It will be a big adventure for them.''
She was so glad Nick couldn't see the way she was
trembling. She would miss Kate and Felicity, but the
fact that they were leaving wasn't what was making her
feel so shaky and ill. She was glad they could get away
to somewhere right out of Brisbane. Somewhere safe.

No, that wasn't what upset her.

It was Nick and the way he sounded so calm and
definite today, so confident and in charge once more.
The uncertain, hesitant man who'd faced her last night
was a different person now that he'd found a way to
distance himself and his daughters from her.

Knowing that hurt. But the last thing Laura wanted
was for Nick to realise how miserable he made her feel.
She struggled to concentrate on practical details.
''When are you going to let the girls know about your
new plans?''

''That's a problem,'' Nick admitted. ''I'm caught up
here for the next few hours.''

''Did you want me to tell them when I pick them up
this afternoon?''

''Would you mind, Laura? I doubt they'll object to
a sudden trip to their grandparents' place,'' he added.
''They love it up there.''

She swiped at her eyes with a tissue. ''So you'll pack
their things before you come over to collect them?''

''Yes.'' There was a slight pause. ''I'll need to pick
them up around six-thirty.''

Laura could picture how it would be. Nick's car
would speed into her driveway and his daughters would
jump into it, delighted at the thought of a sudden, unexpected adventure.

In a matter of minutes they would be gone. All three
of them. Her part in their lives would be over.

Her throat tightened painfully and she had to take a deep breath before she could speak. "Sure. That'll be OK. I'll just collect the girls from school as usual."

"Thanks, Laura." After a pause he added, "You're a good sport, you know."

"Of course I am. I'm a Goodman." Laura dropped the receiver and sagged forward onto the desk.

She was a good sport.

Her head slumped onto her arms. Nick had convinced himself she meant no more than one of his mates, she thought bitterly. Of course Nick had never promised her anything, not even friendship. She could only blame herself for this wretchedness she felt. She and Nick Farrell were two people whose lives had crossed briefly and she'd been able to help him out.

And now he thought she was a sport. A good egg.

No more, no less.

The rest—the kisses, the flirtation, the strong sense of connection and attraction? Her undisciplined, wild imagination had blown all that out of proportion.

But she couldn't help her feelings. No matter how hard she tried to think sensibly, she remained awash with pain and it was all because she had made the mistake Nick had been so careful to avoid. She'd fallen in love.

And this horrible sense of loneliness, this unbearable pain was the result. No wonder Nick had been so cautious.

"Are you coming, too?" Felicity asked as soon as Laura collected the girls from school and told them their father's news.

"Oh, no, dear. I have to stay here and work at the library."

"What about Daddy?"

"He has to keep working, too."

Kate chimed in. "Will Daddy still visit you if we're at Granny's?"

Laura frowned. "I don't think so," she said carefully, wondering just what was going on in the little girl's mind.

When her reply was followed by a long silence in the back of the car, Laura asked, "It doesn't matter if your daddy and I don't see each other, does it?"

"Yes, it does!" Felicity cried emphatically, and to Laura's surprise the child sounded close to tears.

"Well, don't worry about us," Laura told her. "Just think about all the fun you're going to have with Granny and Grandpa."

They reached the library and two very solemn little girls climbed slowly out of Laura's car. She couldn't see any of their usual sparkle or eagerness. Laura sighed. This wasn't how they were supposed to react at all.

Felicity stood in front of Laura and looked up at her with steady grey eyes. "Could you tell me if Daddy has kissed you yet?"

"Fliss!" Kate glared, giving her sister a rough dig with her elbow.

"Has he?" Felicity shouted, on the very edge of tears.

Stunned, Laura looked down at the little woebegone faces. "Don't hurt your sister, Kate. I don't mind the question." She kept her voice steady as she asked, "Do you want your daddy to kiss me?"

Both girls nodded.

Laura forced a smile. "Why is kissing so important? A kiss doesn't really mean anything."

"Oh, Laura," scolded Kate, "don't you know any-thing? If a boy kisses you it means he loves you. Once Daddy kisses you, you can get married."

"No," Laura protested weakly. "It's not quite like that. Even if—even if we did kiss, we won't be getting married."

"Yes, you will. I just know you will," came the def-inite reply. "So just make sure Daddy gets to kiss you soon."

And before Laura could explain the flaws in the girls' logic the two excited sisters rushed into the library, ap-parently very pleased that they had finally imparted this very important information.

Laura followed at a more subdued pace, wondering how on earth she could set them straight and still send them off happily on the plane this evening. Nick was right, she realised. There were all sorts of dangers in telling little girls the happily-ever-after endings in fairy tales.

At five, when the library closed, Laura drove the girls home to her place for the last time. At first when she noticed the driver in a black sedan travelling too closely behind her she was merely cranky with him. But when she pulled in at the greengrocers to buy some salad items his car stopped further up the street and she felt faint stirrings of alarm.

A sixth sense warned Laura not to leave the girls in the car while she dashed into the shop.

They all piled into Joe's Fruit and Veg, and when she came out again she looked back at the black car. It was still parked in the same place and its driver hadn't moved. She couldn't see his face but she could make out the bulky shape of a man sitting behind the steering wheel.

Hairs rose on the back of Laura's neck. She made sure Kate and Felicity had their seat belts fastened and were happily munching on the grapes the greengrocer had given them before she pulled out into the traffic, but her stomach was churning.

The other car pulled out at almost the same moment as Laura. When she looked in her rear-vision mirror she could see it prowling behind her once more. It was a new model that seemed to hug the road, and it looked lower and blacker and more malign than ever.

*It isn't sinister,* Laura told herself silently. *This is just a coincidence. Your depression is colouring your thinking. You're just giving into negativity.*

But, as a precaution, she decided to vary the pace of her driving. No matter what speed she changed to, the black car stayed right behind her.

Oh, no! A surge of panic shot from her stomach straight to her throat. She struggled to breathe. This *could* be the stalker, the man who'd threatened Nick and his family.

It seemed that somehow he'd found out about *her.*

Fear drenched Laura with sweat. Her palms were so slippery she could hardly grip the steering wheel. *Not now.* Surely the stalker hadn't found them now, not when Nick had a new safety plan worked out.

Frantically, she scanned the street ahead. She had grown up in this suburb and she knew every back lane and underpass. At the next corner she took a sharp turn left and, driving as fast as she dared, she kept turning left until she was back on the main road again.

This time she headed in the opposite direction, took another swift turn to dash under a railway bridge and then another quick turn or two, and the next time she checked her mirror, the black car was gone.

But it wasn't until she'd continued for five minutes without seeing the hated vehicle that she breathed a little more easily. She wondered if she should drive to a police station, but the procedures there would be time-consuming.

She glanced at her watch. In less than an hour Nick would be arriving to pick up the girls. Too long with the police and they might miss their flight.

She decided to continue home, but she still took a circuitous route and the whole way her hands were tense as they gripped the steering wheel. Her heart thumped crazily and her stomach churned. Where was the stalker? Would he turn up at her house?

She'd thrown him off the trail for the moment, but there was a chance he already knew where she lived. She imagined him breaking into her cottage and trying to abduct the girls. The thought made her tremble. She knew she couldn't risk that happening.

The safety of the girls was paramount.

Instead of parking in her driveway, she pulled up into a little lane at the back of her house.

"Why are we stopping here?" came Kate's predictable question.

"Daddy's coming to pick you up soon. I wanted to leave a space for him in my driveway," she told them.

Hurrying the surprised girls down a side lane between her cottage and her neighbours, Laura explained, "Girls, I'm going to ask Mrs Powell, the lady next door, to look after you for a little while."

"Why?" asked Felicity.

"I—I'm expecting a visitor and I have some business to discuss with him. Don't worry, I'll come and get you very soon. You've met Mrs Powell and she's very nice.''

The urgency in her voice must have convinced them. For a minute they stood looking at her, frowning and confused, and then they happily let her take their hands and lead them to her neighbour's door.

Thankfully, Janet Powell was a kind, sensible woman, who minded her own business. She didn't hesitate to welcome the girls and immediately won their hearts by switching on their favourite afternoon television programme.

''I'll be back in half an hour,'' Laura promised.

Once inside her own cottage, she decided to ring Nick and headed for the phone in her kitchen. She took another deep breath, forcing herself to relax as she lifted the receiver to key in Nick's number.

Her fingers were pressing the third digit when she glanced across the street and froze.

Framed by her yellow gingham curtains, she could see the black car parked directly opposite her house. The driver was wearing dark glasses but she knew he was staring straight at her.

# CHAPTER ELEVEN

NICK glanced at his watch. He still had plenty of time. All he had to do was snap the locks on the two suitcases he had packed for the girls, drive to Laura's to pick them up and they would make it to the airport comfortably.

It had been a great relief to find that his parents were free to take the girls now. Kate and Felicity would love a surprise trip to visit Granny and Grandpa. Of course they had loved being at Laura's, too…

Nick tried not to think about the way his daughters' fondness for Laura had reached hero-worshipping proportions. But, to his annoyance, it was a fact that was very difficult to ignore.

Damn it, he'd been unsuccessfully trying to put Laura Goodman out of his mind ever since he'd left her house last night.

For hours he'd lain wide awake, manfully trying not to think about her…but, in spite of his best efforts, visions of her had persisted in taunting him. He hadn't been able to block out the special light in her bright eyes or the burnished sheen of her hair.

Memories of her gentle smile had come to him again and again.

What he'd fought hardest not to think about was how she'd stood there beside her bed…looking devastatingly beautiful in the lamplight…looking heartbreakingly brave as she'd offered him a night with no complications, no expectations…

What he couldn't—*mustn't* dwell on was the cowardly haste with which he'd run away from that offer...

...*or the reason he was still running away.*

He stood in the middle of his daughters' bedroom, looking at the two little suitcases, one red, the other blue, and told himself that very soon he could get on with the rest of his life. But all he could picture was an endless stretch of boring nights and empty mornings.

His mobile phone beeped and he frowned as he took it from the inside breast pocket of his suit jacket.

"Farrell speaking."

"Nick, it's Laura. You haven't hired anyone to watch me, have you?"

The stark fear in her voice shot a chill spiralling down his spine. "No, I haven't."

"Well, someone's following me. He's here now."

"You mean Stokes? The stalker?"

"I—I think so.

"Where is he?"

"Sitting in his car across the road directly opposite my house. What should I do?"

Stashing both suitcases under one arm, Nick hurried through his house as he kept talking into the phone. "Stay there, Laura. Keep the house locked."

"Should I ring the police?"

"I'll look after that. The downtown boys know me." With his elbow, Nick managed to open his front door. "Did you get a good look at this bloke?"

"No," she groaned. "I was too shocked. And he's wearing dark glasses."

Nick tossed the suitcases onto the back seat of his car and his mind whirred as he began to reverse out of his garage. "What about the girls? Are they frightened?"

"No. They don't know anything about him. I've taken them by the back way to my neighbour's just in case he tries to get in here."

"Clever girl," Nick murmured. "What about you? Are you OK?"

"I will be when you get here."

"I'm already on my way. Now you stay well and truly hidden in the house."

"But it'll take you ages to get through the peak hour traffic."

"Hang in there. I'll find a short cut and I'll contact the police right now. There'll be someone with you soon. Your job is just to keep the house locked."

"OK."

"Take care, sweetheart."

"I will. Hurry, Nick. I need you."

As he depressed the disconnect button Nick found himself whispering, "And I need you, Laura," and he was startled to hear those words coming from his lips. But, next moment, he recognised that they were true. Blindingly, obviously true.

And he was desperately sorry that she hadn't heard them.

Clasping her hands together, Laura turned away from the phone and tried to think calmly about what she must do. It was such a relief to know that Kate and Felicity were next door, happily giggling at cartoons.

As she stood there, considering her options, she heard footsteps. Footsteps moving with menacing stealth along the brick path at the side of her tiny cottage. Sharp prickles of fear broke out all over her skin.

She dashed to the kitchen window and stared in horror through the darkening twilight. The car across the street was empty. Sickening panic gripped her, squeezing the air from her lungs.

Her heartbeats boomed as her ears strained to listen for more noises, but she couldn't hear anything outside. What was happening?

Where was he?

Her imagination threw up a hair-raising image of his dark, threatening figure leaping through a doorway to attack her. She clamped a hand to her mouth, only just holding back a scream. The last thing she wanted was to terrify the girls next door.

She heard a faint click somewhere and her desperate eyes swung to the hat-stand in her hallway. Her umbrella, a pretty floral affair but quite sturdy, was the only possible weapon. It would have to do.

Grabbing it, she stood, listening, alert to the slightest sound. There was a squeak and scrape that sounded like a window opening.

*Oh, help,* Laura prayed. *I don't know if I'm strong enough for this.* Her heart pounded and she felt ill. Her hands and legs were shaking. Everything was shaking. She wasn't at all sure she was breathing.

She tried to move, but her feet were glued to the floor boards.

What could she do? Nick was on his way, and presumably the police were too, but in the meantime… *If only they would get here soon!*

And then she knew he was inside. She heard a heavy thud as his feet dropped to the floor. Terror leapt in her throat. For too long, she stood shaking with her eyes shut, clutching her umbrella, her mind frozen.

*I should get away. Out the front door!*

Once the thought took shape, Laura could move again. She hurried down the passage towards her door.

Behind her she heard heavy footsteps and harsh breathing.

He was too close!

With a cry of sheer terror, Laura spun around. She had a vague impression of a stumpy, balding man with a big nose. He was looking at her with a sickly, smug grin. ''Nick Farrell doesn't need you all to himself, Laura.''

She yelled at him and raised the umbrella high, like a gladiator wielding a sword. It made a satisfying crunch as it came down on his shoulder. She heard his exclamation of surprise, but she struck out wildly, hitting him again.

Then she grabbed the door knob, wrenched the door open and stumbled outside. Her heart raced fit to burst.

Her mind spun. The whacks from the umbrella were not enough to slow this fellow down for long. Hurrying blindly down her front path, she was sure of only one thing. She had to keep this man occupied. She had to keep on going—to lead him away from the girls at Mrs Powell's.

She scurried on down the tree-lined street, and behind her she heard the steady thump of her pursuer's footsteps. She told herself it was good that he was following her. She just had to keep him diverted until the police arrived.

But she doubted she could move any faster in the shoes she'd been wearing at work all day—just as she doubted that her heart could pump any harder. Surely her chest would explode soon?

A quick glance over one shoulder showed that the stalker was gaining on her.

She struggled to kick off her shoes. In bare feet she would be so much faster. She managed to send one shoe flying, but next moment she stumbled as the heel of her other shoe caved in beneath her, and she felt a rough hand slap at her arm as her pursuer reached out to grab at her.

Nick screeched to a halt behind the black sedan parked opposite Laura's and his headlights lit up its interior, showing him immediately that there was no one inside. He cursed loudly.

Where was Stokes? He glanced quickly at Laura's neat cottage. The front door was open, but the curtains were drawn in every room except the kitchen. On the footpath in front of her house lay a furled umbrella.

Sliding out of the driver's seat quickly, he was about to dash across to the house when movements down the street grabbed his attention.

Night was falling quickly but he could make out the form of a man running beneath the rows of spreading jacarandas that lined the street. He was gaining on a woman.

Dashing to the footpath, Nick squinted through the gathering dusk. Ahead of him, the woman seemed to be stumbling.

It had to be Laura. He could see the bright flame of her hair streaming behind her.

His breath came in grunts as he sped towards them. Keeping his eyes fixed ahead, Nick saw Laura struggling to kick off her shoes. The fellow chasing her was too damn close. Dread plunged and kicked in Nick's guts.

Laura was almost at the point where her street joined the main road now. Too far away.

Nick had been a top sprinter in his university days,

but he doubted his chances of reaching her before her pursuer did.

"Laura!" he roared, not caring how much he disturbed the neighbourhood. Vaguely, he was aware of porch lights turning on as he thundered past neat suburban hedges and white picket fences. Only one thing mattered and that was getting to Laura before Stokes did.

*Don't let her be hurt,* his mind screamed. *Don't let anything happen to her. When I get to her, I won't ever let her go.*

As he gained on them he saw Laura turn to look back over her shoulder, and he could see the flash of despair in her beautiful face when she realised how very close her pursuer was.

Nick waved his arms above his head and yelled again, hoping she would see him, but she wasn't looking his way. Her focus was purely on the man so close to her now.

Horrified, Nick saw her make a sudden shift in direction, veering behind the trunk of a jacaranda towards the road as if desperately trying to avoid capture.

*Not the road, Laura. For God's sake, watch out!*

He saw the stalker lunge onto the bitumen after her. A split second later, there was a flash of headlights and a sickening screech of brakes.

And as if everything was happening in slow motion, Nick's horrified eyes saw two figures in the ghastly glare of the yellow headlights.

He saw the impact as the car hit them, two bodies spinning in mid-air and then, like rag dolls, falling together into a crumpled heap.

# CHAPTER TWELVE

*"LAURA!"*

A horrible, tormented cry broke from Nick's lips as his legs ate up the final few metres.

He could feel his heart shattering like glass, splintering into sharp, painful spikes. By the time he reached the huddle of bodies he was praying hard.

He dropped to his knees. Laura was spread-eagled on the hard, black road next to Stokes. She was very still…too still. Her hair streamed out across the bitumen like blood. Her eyes were closed and her face was deathly pale.

*No, please no!*

Nick groaned. *He'd* done this to her! He'd asked her to care for his girls and he'd placed her at risk!

Her legs were entangled with Stokes's. Her knees were badly grazed and one of her pursuer's thick arms was flung over her chest as if he was still trying to grab at her.

Blood from a wound on Stokes's shoulder was soaking into Laura's clothes.

A couple of purple jacaranda bells fluttered down from an overhead branch to land on her pale throat as if she were simply part of the road.

With shaking fingers, Nick picked the blossoms off her perfect skin and laid them gently aside. He was dimly aware of the driver of the car leaning against the door of her vehicle, sobbing and crying over and over…
"I didn't see them. I just didn't see them…"

From up and down the street, people were running out of houses, crowding closer.

"Oh, my goodness, it's Laura from number thirty-two," someone cried.

"I've rung 000. The ambulance and police are coming," a man's voice called.

"What could have happened?"

*What happened,* Nick thought bitterly, was that this sweetheart had been trying to defend Kate and Felicity as bravely as any mother!

And this was the thanks she got.

Shaking with horror, he leant his ear close to her mouth and tried to sense the soft hush of her breath, but his own breathing was so frantic he couldn't possibly feel hers.

Desperately, he stared at her chest. Was it rising and falling? *Oh, please let her be breathing!* Why couldn't he think straight? What should he do?

God help him, all he could think of was how Laura had offered him her love and he'd rejected it as if it meant no more than the offer of a cup of coffee.

How could he have been so stupid?

Now it was too late.

*Please, don't let it be too late!*

A police car screeched to a halt and a policewoman pushed her way through the crowd. She knelt on the bitumen beside him and, with the calm assurance of someone who knew exactly what she was doing, she examined Laura. "She's breathing and there's a good pulse," she said grimly, "so that's a start. But we shouldn't move her till the ambulance gets here."

As she leant forward to examine the other body Nick found himself clinging to those words... *"She's breathing and there's a good pulse."*

Somewhere in the distance, there was the moan of a siren. And then another.

"Laura, please be all right!" he whispered as the wailing sounds drew nearer. "Hang on, please. I've something important to tell you!"

For a moment, her eyes snapped open and his heart leapt as he saw a flash of that familiar stunning blue. "Laura?"

But, too soon, her eyelids flickered and closed again. It was as if the warm, comforting dark was beckoning and she preferred it there. Nick trembled. He wanted to weep.

He needed to sweep her into his arms and run with her to the hospital.

Next moment, with a blare of sirens and flashing lights, more police cars and ambulances arrived. Nick was shoved out of the way.

A police constable he didn't recognise blocked his view of Laura and fired questions that he didn't want to waste time answering. Who cared how the accident had happened? That wasn't vital right now. Nick strained to watch what was happening to Laura.

The ambulance officers were asking her questions. He could see that her eyes were open again. He fancied she spoke a word or two…

She was being lifted onto a stretcher…

Nick waved both hands at the ambulance men. "Hey! I have to travel with her to the hospital!" he shouted, but no one took any notice.

Annoyed, he elbowed his way forward. *How could they ignore him?* He would have to explain…

Then he felt someone tugging at his coat sleeve. "Excuse me," a woman said, sounding anxious, "are you the father of the two little girls who are staying with Laura?''

His head jerked sideways and he stared at the woman stupidly.

"I think you'd better come with me," she said. "They'll be very upset by all this."

The only light came from a small lamp glowing softly on the far wall. Laura looked around the darkened room. She was in a bed with crisp white sheets.

There was a chart on the end of her bed, a plastic water jug on a table beside her. The grey linoleum on the floor was highly waxed and there was a tag on her wrist.

It was all so strangely familiar. She visited this hospital every week, but she'd never been a patient before.

It seemed like a dream. The whirling lights, the sirens…drifting in and out of sleep as she was wheeled on a trolley through endless corridors…

Voices, the continuous rise and fall of voices. Lights being shone in her eyes, fingers waved at her. Questions…too many questions.

She'd had some questions of her own. "What happened? What's the matter with me?"

And for too long, the answers had been unsatisfactory. "You've had a bump on the head."

The events of the afternoon had been coming back to her in pieces. At first all she'd been able to remember was picking up the girls from school…taking them back to the library… Had that been today or yesterday?

*And then…oh, help!* It had come back with a jolt! She remembered running…and running and… *The stalker!*

Once she'd reached hospital she'd been taken to the

X-ray department. She hadn't been able to get anyone to tell her how Kate and Felicity were. No one had known what she was talking about.

"You're a very lucky woman," a doctor finally informed her. "Not many people run in front of a moving vehicle and get away with a touch of concussion. But because you've been tired and confused we'll keep you here for observation for a day or so."

"What happened to the man who was chasing me?"

The doctor hesitated. "He's a lot worse off than you. It seems he caught up with you just at the point of collision and he took the brunt of the blow. That's why you managed to escape with so little injury."

"Where is he?"

"We have him in another ward. A police guard is waiting to question him, but he won't worry you any more."

*He won't worry you any more...* Laura let the doctor's words sink in. It was hard to accept that all hint of danger was gone, but the doctor had sounded quite certain...

Her mind kept wrestling with the horrifying narrowness of her escape. She sank back into her pillows with her eyes closed...

"Hi there." Nick's voice sounded from the doorway, low and husky, as if he were afraid of waking her.

Her eyes shot open, and next minute he was walking towards her. He looked good. His dark hair was falling softly forward and he was gazing at her with incredible tenderness. She felt the warm grasp of his hand closing around hers.

"How are you feeling?" he asked gently.

"I seem to be perfectly OK," she told him, trying to sound much calmer than she felt. "But I've been so worried about the girls. Did you get them to the airport on time?''

She tried to sit up, but the sudden movement made her head pound.

''The girls are fine, Laura,'' Nick reassured her, and she felt his hands pressing her shoulders gently back into the pillows. ''They're with Heather. There's no need for them to go away now. And you're going to be fine, too. So don't worry about a thing. Just thank your guardian angel.''

''You think I have one?''

''I'm sure you do and I'd like to shake his hand.'' Nick's smile was strange and wobbly. As he spoke he held her hands in both of his, squeezing them, caressing them, pressing his lips to them, and it felt so good that instead of insisting on more answers she relaxed.

He bent over her and she smelt the warm, spicy scent of his aftershave as his lips gently kissed her eyelids closed.

''That's *very* nice,'' she whispered. ''No one's ever kissed me on the eyelids before. I think I like it.''

''Has anyone kissed you here?'' Nick murmured, brushing his mouth ever so lightly against her temple.

''No, I'm sure they haven't.'' Laura couldn't help smiling. Nick's kisses felt so careful. He was being so sweet. And yet so stirring. Her skin was humming to life.

Her whole body was stirring. She stretched, feeling deliciously happy. Warmth was spreading through her, making her want to move close against him…and to have him kiss her and touch her and hold her…

''Do you think I should try to kiss you better?'' He was smiling as he lowered his head.

''Doctor's orders.'' Laura smiled back and his mouth

took hers in a lingering, deep kiss. A Nick Farrell special. She lifted her arms to encircle his neck and hold him close.

Everything about Nick was so special. The way he sounded, the way he looked and the way he kissed. Especially the way he kissed.

Oh, yes. Most definitely she liked his kisses. She could drown in the sensation of that beautiful mouth lovingly locked with hers. How sensational it would be to keep him here for the rest of the night—or, better still, for ever.

"Laura," Nick whispered against her lips, "I want to tell you how much I—"

The sudden clump and squeak of sensible shoes marching over the waxed linoleum cut off his words. Someone stomped into the room.

Nick looked up and his face broke into a rueful grin. "Oh, hello, Sister. I was checking our patient's vital signs. Can you give us five minutes?"

"Certainly not." The unsmiling, middle-aged nurse was clearly short on good humour or sympathy. "This patient needs to be left in peace to get some *vital* rest."

Nick murmured close to Laura's ear, "That sounds like my marching orders."

Reluctantly, she released him. "You were going to tell me something."

He stood up and smiled softly. "I won't tell you now, it's private, but don't worry, it'll keep. I won't forget."

Dismissing Nick with a sniff, the nurse set about grabbing Laura's arm and taking her blood pressure.

From near the door, he winked at her. "See you in the morning. Sleep tight."

"Goodnight," she called softly.

A moment later, he was gone.

And it was only as Nick disappeared that Laura realised with an awful suddenness that something was terribly wrong. At first she couldn't quite work out what the problem was, it was just a vague sense that things weren't really as good as they had seemed when he was kissing her.

She didn't really have the right to feel this happy.

The nurse proceeded to take her temperature, and just as she slipped the clip on her finger to check her pulse Laura remembered.

For heaven's sake! Nick had been acting like a lover and for a short while she'd been fooled. She'd been drowsy and not thinking straight.

The nurse held up two fingers. "How many do you see?"

"Two," Laura told her, and received a nod of approval.

*Oh, good grief.* She could see and think perfectly clearly now, and for crying out loud, how had she forgotten that Nick was terminally allergic to love?

She'd had a bang on the head and the first thing she'd done when she came to was to let him kiss her senseless.

*Fool!*

He was brilliant at kissing her, expertly, beautifully... But that certainly didn't mean anything significant. Nothing to get excited about.

Last night he'd rejected her Big Offer.

He'd spent the day finding ways to back clear out of her life.

The nurse frowned as she filled in Laura's chart. "That young man is not doing you any good at all," she muttered.

And, miserably, Laura had to agree with her.

She was given two small white pills in a paper cup. "These will help you to sleep."

Obediently she took the tablets. Somehow she knew that without them there would be no chance of a peaceful night's sleep.

"I want to go home," she told the doctor next morning, but he only smiled and murmured something about being a good girl and another twenty-four hours of observation.

*A good girl?* As the white coat marched out of her room Laura punched her pillow. "I've been a good girl all my life." She was tired of obeying the rules.

Her life was one long row of ticks for being a boring good girl.

If only she could break the old mould.

Tears threatened. It was time for some drastic action. She would have to start with the hardest step—exterminating any wayward, undisciplined thoughts about Nick Farrell.

She was so busy staring at the ceiling and plotting a daring, new, Farrell-free life for herself that at first she didn't notice the person who suddenly lumbered into her room.

When she did see him, she blinked. Twice.

Her visitor had a bright red nose, incredibly curly orange hair and awkward overlong shoes.

Laura raised a hand to shade her eyes. She felt a surge of dismay. Surely the doctors had made a wrong diagnosis. There was something wrong with her head after all. She was seeing things. She had to be. Nobody wandered around in a hospital dressed like a...

A clown.

Adrenaline jolted through her, making her heart leap as she peered at her visitor more closely.

In addition to the nose and the hair, the clown's face was covered in traditional circus make-up and he was wearing a red and white striped shirt with a purple and black spotted bow-tie. His overalls were bright blue with colourful patches on the knees and he wore long, black clown shoes.

"I thought you might need cheering up," the clown said in a voice she immediately recognised.

A querulous hammering started in her chest. "Nick, what on earth are you doing here dressed like that?"

Without answering, he grinned cheekily, plucked some apples and oranges from her fruit bowl and began to juggle them. Almost immediately an apple fell to the floor and rolled under her bed.

Shrugging, he returned the rest of the fruit to her bowl and scratched his orange hair. "I've been told by someone whose opinion I hold in high regard that hospital patients appreciate this sort of entertainment. Perhaps you'd prefer some acrobatics?"

Before she could answer, Nick tried for a handstand, but there clearly wasn't enough space. For a dangerous moment it looked as if his legs would end up out of the window or his whole muscle-packed body would crash-land on top of Laura's bed. He was forced to drop back to his feet very quickly.

"Sit down before you do yourself or this room some damage," Laura implored him, laughing.

With a dramatic sigh, he lowered himself into the chair beside her bed and leaned forward. "Let's do this the boring way. How are you this morning, Laura?"

"I'm perfectly fine," she said, but it was a lie. She felt as fragile as fine crystal. What on earth was Nick trying to do to her? "But for heaven's sake…" She gestured helplessly at his clothes.

He pulled a book from a pocket in his voluminous overalls. "I've also been told by someone who's an expert in this area that patients like to have stories read to them."

Laura could see his grey eyes twinkling through the clown paint. His gorgeous, dreamy eyes.

*Hold your horses, girl! Don't forget that falling for Nick is a fast track to misery.*

She turned her head away and spoke to the opposite wall. "Don't do this to me, Nick."

"Don't do what?"

"Don't play games." *Don't be charming and fun.* "Don't make me—" She'd been about to say, *Don't make me love you,* but just in time she bit the words back.

Nick dragged his chair a little closer and spoke softly. "So do you want to hear my story?"

In spite of her fears, Laura felt unbearably curious. Without risking a look at him, she asked, "Is it a story you've made up?"

"Sure."

"About a princess?"

"A prince. I thought it was time he got a story of his own."

A *prince?* Laura closed her eyes. *Why did she think this was going to be about Nick?*

The skin on her arms erupted into goosebumps as she tried to answer lightly. "I guess a prince is a new angle. Does he live in a castle or a grass hut in the jungle?"

"This one is locked away in a high tower."

"The victim of a wicked witch?"

"The victim of his own—*fears.*"

"I see," she said quietly while her nervous system switched to maximum alert. "So the prince lives in the tower by himself? No visitors? No princesses?"

After a moment, Nick answered, "The only people he lets in are jesters."

"They can be fun."

"Sure. And from time to time he does something silly and reckless and his friends cheer and clap."

Laura's tense fingers gripped at the bed sheet. Nick was definitely talking about himself. "What's the main plot development? Where's the complication?"

She braved a quick glance Nick's way and his eyes were suspiciously bright as he said, "A little redheaded bird with amazing blue feathers flew up to his window. He thought she was just a harmless bird, so…" He shrugged and slanted her a crooked little smile. "So he chatted to her."

Laura couldn't bear this. What game was Nick playing? Couldn't he guess what this was doing to her?

She sank back into the pillow and closed her eyes again, but hot tears slipped beneath her eyelashes and ran down her cheeks. She dabbed at her face with the sheet. "A harmless bird?" she croaked. "Where's the threat in that?"

"Laura," he murmured, and suddenly his voice sounded as choked and raspy as hers. She felt his knees nudge the bed as he leaned even closer. "If she was really a harmless little bird there'd be no problem at all."

Laura couldn't reply.

After some time, she heard Nick clear his throat. "Problem was…" he began, and then there was another pause. Three long seconds…four…five agonising seconds of silence.

"Problem was," he said at last, "she was in disguise. She was really a gutsy, big-hearted, dragon-slaying, perfect-in-every-way princess."

Now she definitely couldn't take any more of this game-playing. Laura turned towards Nick and sobbed, "Cut the story. Just give it to me straight, Nick. What are you trying to tell me?"

He reached for her hand. "I'm here to say thank you. The risk you took yesterday…"

Just in time Laura stifled her cry of disappointment. *He was here to say thank you.*

That was what all this was about! Heck, if he only wanted to say thank you, she would have preferred a quick phone call. Maybe a box of chocolates.

But Nick had gone to all this trouble just to offer his thanks.

What kind of soft-headed fool was she to have been thinking about something more? She'd been nursing a ludicrous hope that at some time in the past twenty-four hours this man had changed. No matter how hard she tried to be sensible she kept thinking about how she actually wanted to spend the rest of her life with him.

"There's no need to go to so much trouble to thank me," she replied dully. "I can't take too much credit. That kind of do-good stuff comes instinctively to me. It's in my genes."

"Then I'm in debt to your ancestors."

Her lips pursed into a tight little circle. Then she shrugged and suddenly felt terribly, unbearably tired.

Nick cleared his throat. "Actually, there is something else I want to tell you."

"You'll need the keys to my house to pick up the rest of the girls' things?"

"No. Well, I guess I might do that at some stage, but what I wanted to say was a touch more personal."

"Oh?" When she saw the shimmer of deep emotion in Nick's eyes, the tiredness left her in a flash. "I'm listening."

He suddenly dropped his gaze to the floor and shook his head. "I—I stand in court all day and spout all kinds of nonsense, and quite often it has serious implications for other people's lives. And now I want to say the most important sentence of *my* life and I'm stagestruck. Shaking in my boots."

*Just one sentence?*

Laura felt as if her heart was tripping down a long flight of stairs. She could feel each painful bounce. It hurt so badly.

"One little sentence?" she whispered, and a corner of her mouth lifted into the bravest of tiny half-smiles. "I *dare* you to say it."

"Dare?" He looked at her quickly, then suddenly his eyes flashed and he grinned as he pulled off his clown nose. His own nose looked tanned and decidedly noble amidst all the white clown paint.

"OK, here goes." He took a deep breath. "Laura Goodman, I love you—I never knew it was possible to love another human being as much as I love you."

"Oh, Nick," Laura cried.

His eyes shone damply.

She couldn't help asking, "Do you really mean it?"

"Ouch." He flinched. "I guess I deserve that." With long brown fingers, he prised her hand from its death grip on the bed sheet and massaged her fingers gently. "I'm very sure I love you, Laura. You know how hard I've fought against falling for you. But I couldn't help it; it happened anyhow."

He pressed his lips to her hand. "You're just so inescapably lovable."

Laura could hardly see Nick through her own tears.

"Is that OK?" he asked. "If I tell you I love you, is that a problem?"

"No problem," she whispered. "No problem at all." She sat up a little straighter. "But what made you change your mind?"

His mouth quirked into a lopsided grin. "It finally sank in to my slow brain that I was game enough or stupid enough to strip off my clothes, but I wasn't prepared to strip away my emotions—to discover how I really felt about—you."

Deep inside, Laura was singing. She could feel happiness pushing its way to the surface. Only one thing was holding it down. She needed to be sure Nick wasn't confusing love with guilt. "Was last night—like Miranda's accident all over again?"

Nick's face grew tight and he looked away for moment. "Yes and no."

In heart-hammering silence, she waited for him to explain.

"You must understand that I'm not the same bloke who developed a crush on the prettiest girl in Atherton High at the age of sixteen."

He moved to sit beside her on the bed and tucked a stray curl behind her ear. "I did love Miranda with all the zeal of immaturity, and I was sad when I lost her, but so much of that was tied up with guilt."

"It's not like that now?"

"Laura, after I dragged myself from your house the other night I was utterly miserable, but I kept telling myself that my feelings were simply lust. But yesterday, when you phoned to tell me Stokes was tailing you, I suddenly realised the truth. I've been falling in love with you ever since the night we met when you were wearing those ridiculous feathers.''

He touched her cheek with shaking fingers. "Last night, when I thought I'd lost you, I wanted to lie down and die right next to you. I was completely destroyed. You have no idea how much I need you in my life.''

She had things she wanted to say but her throat was blocked by tears.

"So what do you think?" Nick asked shyly.

Laura snuffled and coughed and fiddled with his clown's bow-tie. "I think you know that I've been pretty much in love with you since the first time I saw you in a clown suit.''

He looked relieved and amused. "It took you that long? So you want me to stay in this kind of get-up for ever?''

With a slow grin, she asked, "You really want to know what I'd like?''

"Of course.''

Grabbing a handful of tissues from the pack on the bedside table, she wiped the make-up from his mouth.

Nick was a bright boy. He could take a hint. And, without a word, his make-up-free lips settled over hers and once again Laura was experiencing Nick Farrell style magic. Bliss.

When they came up for air, she whispered, "I really like you as a clown, but I think I fancied you even more as a stripper.''

His eyes widened with amused surprise.

"You wouldn't strip for me now, would you?''

"What?" Nick looked incredulous and sent an anxious glance over his shoulder. "Here in this hospital?''

"You're not the only one who's changed, Nick. I'm

often in a daring mood these days. We can close the door. Anyhow, medical people see naked bodies every day. I rather like the idea of all those bits of clown costume coming off one by one..."

"The whole way?"

She smiled and raised a questioning eyebrow and he shook his head and chuckled. "You're daring me again, aren't you? How about a guaranteed private performance at home?"

The very thought made Laura sizzle, but she pretended to think it over. "I guess I could settle for that."

"OK. You're on, but there's one condition."

"What's that?"

"Marry me."

"Oh..."

Laura stared at Nick. His handsome features were covered in messy, smudged paint, but his eyes... His eyes were full of love and longing and they told her everything she wanted to know.

"You see, that's another thing I've found out about myself," he said with a warm smile. "I need to let the whole world know you're mine. I really want to get married, Laura."

"Yes," she whispered.

"Yes?" he repeated. "Is that yes, you'll marry me?"

"What did you expect, Nick? Look at me. I'm positively drooling at the thought of being your wife."

She was rewarded with another of Nick's seriously expert kisses. As he nuzzled her sexily, he asked, "You haven't forgotten that my daughters are a kind of permanent attachment?"

"Of course I haven't. I love your little girls almost as much as I love their daddy." And, just to prove it, she reached up to kiss him again. A deep, hungry kiss, full of seductive promise.

"Can you hang on just a tick?" Nick eventually muttered. Without waiting for her answer, he stood up and crossed the room. Ducking his head around the door, he gave a thumbs-up sign to someone down the hall.

The next minute there was a scurry of running feet and two little bodies hurtled into the room.

"Did she say yes?" Kate and Felicity shouted simultaneously.

Nick beamed at them. "She did."

"What's been going on?" Laura cried. "A conspiracy?"

Kate rushed to hug Laura while Felicity danced around the room with excited skips accompanied by war hoops of delight.

"You're going to marry Daddy!"

"You're going to be our mummy!"

"I'm so relieved," Kate whispered to Laura. "I told Daddy you would never want to marry him if he asked you while he was dressed up like a clown."

Laura laughed. "Your father happens to know I'm rather fond of clowns."

"Do you think you will need a flower girl at your wedding?"

Laura hugged Kate with one arm and reached out towards Felicity with the other. "I think I'll definitely need two flower girls."

"In pink dresses," crowed Felicity.

"No, blue," corrected Kate.

"One of each?" suggested Nick. He winked at Laura and her heart did a weird little duck dive from feeling so much happiness all at once.

Felicity looked at Laura intently. "Has Daddy kissed

you yet?'' She studied Laura's glowing face. ''Oh, goody, he has. You've got clown paint on your nose.'' Letting out a happy, relieved sigh, the little girl sent a beaming smile around the room to her father, her sister and Laura. ''Everything is going to be perfect now.''

''Yes,'' agreed Laura. ''Everything will be perfect.''

She smiled up at Nick. She loved these little girls and she was going to marry their father—the sexiest clown-cum-stripper in the world.

What could be more perfect than that?

# THE WEDDING CHALLENGE

*by*

*Jessica Hart*

**Jessica Hart** was born in West Africa, and has suffered from itchy feet ever since, travelling and working around the world in a wide variety of interesting but very lowly jobs, all of which have provided inspiration on which to draw when it comes to the settings and plots of her stories. Now she lives a rather more settled existence in York, where she has been able to pursue her interest in history, although she still yearns sometimes for wider horizons. If you'd like to know more about Jessica, visit her website www.jessicahart.co.uk.

# CHAPTER ONE

'GO AND work in the outback?' Bea stared blankly at her friend. 'Why would we want to do that?'

'*Why?*' Emily echoed, equally uncomprehending. 'How can you even ask that, Bea? *Everybody* wants to work in the outback. It's beautiful!'

'It's not beautiful, it's brown.'

'It's full of hunky men riding around in hats and dusty boots.'

'It's full of flies,' said Bea, unimpressed.

'Don't be like that, Bea.' Emily abandoned her customers and pulled out a chair so that she could sit down opposite her friend. 'This is the chance of a lifetime! I've always wanted to go and work on a cattle station.'

'What on earth for?'

'Because it's different and romantic and wonderful,' enthused Emily, gesticulating wildly. 'Besides,' she went on, clearly grasping at straws by now, 'it's part of my heritage.'

Bea goggled at her. To her certain knowledge, Emily had been born and brought up in London, about as far from the outback as you could get. 'Since when?'

'My mother's Australian,' said Emily loftily.

'From Melbourne. It's not exactly the red heart of Australia, is it?'

'Well, *her* mother grew up on a cattle station,' Emily conceded with an edge of defiance.

'My grandmother grew up in Leamington Spa, but it doesn't mean I want to go and work there!'

'Leamington Spa isn't chock-a-block with men who know how to throw a lasso and wrestle bulls to the ground

5

single-handed, though, is it? *Real* men, Bea, not like this lot here!'

Emily glanced disparagingly around the bar where she was a waitress. She was wearing a long, white apron, and ignoring customers on nearby tables who were trying to catch her eye.

Bea followed her friend's gaze. It was a Sunday night, and the bar was buzzing, packed with young people enjoying the end of another great Sydney weekend. As far as Bea could see, every single man there seemed to be tall, broad-shouldered and eminently fanciable. That's if you weren't still recovering from being dumped from a very great height and therefore not inclined to fancy any of them.

'What's wrong with them?' she asked.

'They're all city boys,' grumbled Emily. 'We might as well be in London.'

Through the plate glass window, Bea could see the Opera House, its famous roof lit up against the night sky, and the harbour clustered with yachts bobbing at anchor.

Like London? Bea didn't think so.

'You've changed your tune, haven't you?' she said. 'It's only a week or so since all you could talk about was Marcus, and he was as smooth as they come.'

'Too smooth,' said Emily, remembering Marcus with a scowl. 'And I've learnt my lesson! I'm sick of guys like him. I want a man with a bit more grit to him.'

'Well, if it's grit you want, maybe the outback is the right place for you.' Bea grinned as she picked up her drink. *She* wasn't on duty. 'I hear it's very dusty out there!'

'I'm serious, Bea.' Emily leant forward persuasively. 'It's not as if this is just a whim. Even before we left London, I said I wanted to see the outback while we were over here, didn't I?'

'I thought you meant a trip to Alice Springs and a quick whiz round Ayers Rock or Uluru or whatever it's called now, not stuck on a cattle station!'

'I don't want to be a tourist,' said Emily, lower lip sticking out stubbornly. 'I want to experience real life in the outback, and what could be better than spending a few weeks on a cattle station?'

Bea could think of quite a few things. In fact, just about anything.

'Em, we haven't got long before we have to go home,' she said reasonably. 'There's still so much to see, I really don't want to spend the rest of my time stuck out in the middle of nowhere. You go if you want to, and I'll meet up with you later. We did agree that we wouldn't have to stick together all the time.'

'I know, but I won't get the job if you won't come too,' Emily wailed. 'They want two girls, and if you won't come with me, I won't even have a chance.'

'Why can't they give you a job and find someone else?' Bea objected.

'Because the station is a squillion acres and so isolated that they don't want to risk having two girls who might not get on. Apparently it's a very famous property in Australia.' Emily perked up, remembering what she'd been told. 'Someone told me it was the size of Belgium—or was it Wales? Anyway, it's big, and it's got a beautiful old homestead…it's like your perfect outback property. They're used to people not staying very long, though, but this time Nick says that they've decided to take two friends.'

'Who's Nick?'

'Nick Sutherland. He's the owner—*very* attractive,' said Emily with a dreamy sigh. 'All blonde and rugged and square-chinned…just my type! And if you won't come with me, he'll just find another two girls—I know loads of people who'd jump at the chance of working in a place like Calulla Downs,' she added with a resentful glance that bounced off Bea, unnoticed. She was used to Emily.

'Maybe they'll find two girls who would actually be some use in the outback,' she pointed out. 'I can't see that we'd be much good to them, anyway. We don't know the first thing about riding or cows or whatever else it is they do out there!'

'They don't want jillaroos. They've got stockmen to do all that kind of stuff. They need a cook and a governess.'

'A *governess*?' Bea laughed. 'You're kidding! I thought governesses went out with Jane Eyre!'

'Well, I thought it was a bit odd, too,' Emily confessed, 'but I gather it just means a nanny really. The little girl's only five, so it's not like she's going to need intensive coaching. I think it's more a question of looking after her and keeping her amused.'

Bea began to look alarmed. 'We don't know the first thing about children!'

'It can't be that hard.' Emily gave an airy wave of her hand. 'Read her a few stories, make sure she doesn't lose her teddy bear...it'll be a doddle.'

'Well, I don't want anything to do with her,' said Bea firmly. 'Children make me nervous.'

'It's all right, I'll deal with the kid,' Emily soothed her. 'You just have to be the cook. You know I can't cook to save my life, and you're brilliant,' she went on, laying on the flattery with a trowel. 'When I told Nick that you were working for a catering company, he sounded really keen. He said they hardly ever get a qualified cook and—oh, *please* say you'll come, Bea! It's sounds so perfect, and I can't do it without you. It'll be fun!'

'But we're having fun in Sydney,' Bea objected. 'We've got jobs, friends, somewhere to stay...you can't help but have an excellent time here. It won't be like that in the outback. We'd be stuck in a house with a small child. It'll be boiling hot and there'll be nowhere to go and nothing to do. We don't even know how to ride!' She shook her head. 'You'd hate it. *I'd* certainly hate it.'

'Just like you were going to hate Australia?' countered Emily unfairly. 'You said you didn't want to come and that you'd be miserable, and now you're talking about emigrating! I *said* you would love it, and I was right, wasn't I?'

Bea had to concede that. 'Yes,' she said.

'So why won't you believe me when I say you'll love the outback too? You know what your trouble is?' Emily went on, and Bea sighed. She knew that an answer wasn't required, and that Emily was about to tell her anyway.

Sure enough, Emily was leaning forward, all earnest amateur psychologist. 'I blame Phil,' she said. 'He hurt you so badly that now you're afraid to try anything new.'

'That's not true,' Bea tried to protest, but Emily was on a roll and refused to be interrupted.

'You've got no self-confidence any more. As soon as anyone suggests doing something a bit different, you start making excuses. You wouldn't even buy that dress the other day because it was a tiny bit shorter than you usually buy.'

'It made me look fat.'

'You looked fantastic in it, but you couldn't have that, could you? Because if you looked fantastic, some bloke might get interested in you and you'd have to risk getting involved again.'

Bea took a defiant slug of wine. 'Rubbish!'

'And now I'm offering you the chance of excitement and adventure, and all you want to do is stay safely where you are.'

'I've done adventure,' Bea said, glad that Emily had got off the subject of her ex-fiancé. 'I went trekking, didn't I? Adventure means no loos and no showers and no hairdryers, and you know I have to wash my hair every morning.'

'And that means Calulla Downs will be just perfect for you,' said Emily, seizing the advantage. 'It'll be a lot more luxurious than where we're living now, I can tell you. It's supposed to be a fabulous old homestead—people pay through the nose to go and stay there—so there'll be adventure in just being somewhere so isolated, but with the added bonus of hot water and somewhere to plug in your hair-dryer. What more could you ask for?'

'Shops, bars, clubs, theatres, lights, music…'

'You can have those any time. This might be our only chance to go to a place like Calulla Downs. You can't just throw away opportunities when they come your way. Seize the day, and all that.'

'I don't know…'

'It's not as if it's for ever,' Emily wheedled. 'I'm sure Nick would agree if we said we could just do a month, and then we can spend the rest of the time travelling, the way we'd planned. We could go straight on to the Barrier Reef. What do you say?'

Bea hesitated, aware that she was running out of arguments. This was typical of Emily. She just went on and on and on until it was easier just to give in and do what she wanted.

Sensing that Bea was weakening, Emily pressed home her advantage. 'Please, Bea,' she said again. 'I really, really want to go, and I can't do it without you. I *need* you…and I was there for you when you needed me, wasn't I?'

It was true. She had been. It had been Emily who had come straight round when Phil had told her that he was leaving, and who he was leaving her for. Emily who had dealt with everything while she was too numb to do anything more than lie curled up on the sofa, too wretched even to cry.

Bea sighed. 'Come on, Emily, you can do better emotional blackmail than that,' she said. 'Why not wring out a few tears while you're at it and accuse me of ruining your life if I don't agree?'

'That's my fall back position,' said Emily, grinning.

Bea gave in. 'For a month,' she said, a warning note in her voice. 'But I'm not staying a moment longer!'

Emily gave a whoop of delight. 'You're a star!' she said, jumping up to hug her. 'I knew I could rely on you. I'll go and ring Nick right now—and yes, I promise I'll tell him we can only stay a month. But I bet you anything that by the end of that time, you're going to want to stay for ever!'

'It looks like being a very long month,' grumbled Bea, dragging her suitcase across to where a row of orange plastic chairs were ranged uncompromisingly against the wall in what passed for a terminal at Mackinnon airport. 'I'm bored already, and we've only been here ten minutes.'

Ten minutes was all it had taken for the plane to land, to let off six passengers and pick up two, and to take off again. The other four passengers had departed for town, the man who had pushed out the steps, unloaded their cases and checked the joining passengers onto the plane had disappeared, and Bea and Emily had been left alone to watch the plane climb up into the glaring blue sky until it vanished into the distance.

Bea slumped into one of the chairs and put her feet up on her suitcase. 'I suppose you did tell this Nick Sutherland person when we were arriving?'

'Of course I did,' said Emily. 'I told him when the plane got in, and he said he'd send somebody called Chase to pick us up.'

'Chase? What kind of name is that?'

'I think it must be his surname. Nick said that he was the one who ran the station anyway, so I guess he's some kind of manager.'

Bea sniffed. 'Not a very efficient one if he's forgotten that we're coming.'

'He won't have done that. Reliability is these guys' middle name,' said Emily confidently. 'He just won't be rushing.'

'Evidently!'

Emily ignored her sarcasm. 'The strong, silent types

don't bother with clock-watching. That's what makes them so attractive. They've got all the time in the world, so they never hurry or get flustered. Bet you anything this guy rolls up in a checked shirt and a battered hat and says g'day in a slow drawl that'll go with his slow smile and his slow hands—'

Starting to hyperventilate, she broke off and fanned herself with her plane ticket. 'I can't wait! He'll be all brown and rangy, and his eyes will be crinkled at the edges from all that time he spends squinting at the far horizon.' Her eyes narrowed thoughtfully. 'He might be a bit shy, but he'll be famous for his way with horses and don't get me started on the things he can do with a lasso…! He can rope me in any day!'

Bea couldn't help laughing at her friend's famously rich fantasy life. 'Aren't you thinking of cowboys?' she said. 'In which case, you're in the wrong country.'

'Same man, different hat,' Emily declared authoritatively. 'In the States, cowboys wear those hats which curl up at the sides, but an Australian stockman will wear an Akubra.'

'A what?'

'It's like a cowboy hat, but not so curly.'

Bea was pretty sure that Emily didn't have a clue what she was talking about, but she knew from bitter experience that there was no point in arguing with her.

'I'm surprised you haven't got a hat of your own to go with your outfit,' she said instead, eyeing Emily's pristine jeans, blue checked shirt (clearly specially selected to match her eyes) and the red and white spotted neckerchief. 'I didn't realise we had to come in fancy dress. If you'd told me, I'd have brought along a Stetson and a fringed jacket!'

Emily tossed her blonde curls. 'You can mock, but at least I'm appropriately dressed, unlike some people I could mention! I can't believe you're wearing a dress and those stupid shoes!'

'You love these shoes,' Bea pointed out, twirling her ankle so that she could admire them properly. They couldn't really be called shoes. Shoes was much too prosaic a word for fantasy on heels. 'You were furious when they told you they didn't have any in your size.'

'That was in Sydney. I'm prepared to admit that in their right context, they're fab, but they look absolutely ridiculous out here. I don't know why you couldn't wear jeans at least,' Emily grumbled. 'It's going to look as if you don't know the first thing about the outback, and I'll be associated with you.'

'I don't like travelling in jeans. Anyway, this Nick of yours didn't specify a uniform, did he? He's employing me to cook, not to sit around on fences looking like something out of a cowboy film.'

'Well, don't blame me when this Chase turns out to be a gorgeous hunk who dismisses you as a real city girl,' said Emily with the air of one washing her hands of the matter. 'You'll be left gnashing your teeth and cursing your kitten heels while I'm out learning just how good he is with his hands!'

'I don't care how attractive he is, I wish he'd just turn up.'

Swinging her legs off her suitcase, Bea got up to prowl impatiently around the terminal.

It didn't take long. The terminal wasn't much more than a hut with glass doors looking out onto the runway. A couple of single-engine planes were parked to one side near a water tank, and a windsock hung limply against its pole. The sky was a relentless blue, and even cocooned in the air-conditioned comfort of the terminal, Bea could practically feel the heat beating down outside.

Beyond the runway, there was nothing, just an expanse of flat, brown earth covered with sparse spinifex grass stretching out to where the horizon shimmered hazily. It seemed to go on forever. Bea had been appalled flying over hundreds of miles of the same, unchanging scenery that morning. For a boring landscape, it was hard to beat. She couldn't understand why Emily was so thrilled with it.

A fly buzzed against the glass, but apart from that the silence was crushing. Bea sighed and looked at her watch again.

'Perhaps Nick Whatsisname has changed his mind and employed someone else,' she suggested hopefully.

'It's Nick Sutherland, and I'm sure he wouldn't do anything like that.' Emily leapt to his defence. 'He sounded really pleased when I rang and told him that you'd be coming with me. I wish you'd met him,' she went on. 'He was gorgeous, and nice with it—and we know what a rare combination that is!'

'If he's so nice, why isn't he coming to pick us up himself?'

'He's not here.' Emily sounded distinctly regretful. 'His wife's working overseas, and he's gone to be with her. That's why they need someone to look after the kids on the station.'

'Wife?' Bea shook her head in mock sympathy. 'It must have been a bit of a blow when you heard about her!'

Emily sighed. 'I know...but I suppose he was a bit old for me. And he did say something about a brother,' she added airily.

'Younger brother?'

'I think so.'

'Married?'

'No. I'm pretty sure Nick said he wasn't.'

All was now becoming clear to Bea.

'Name?' she asked.

'I don't know,' said Emily regretfully. 'I couldn't ask too many questions. I didn't want to look *too* obvious, and Nick didn't say very much, just that he would be keeping an eye on things. I got the impression he might have his own property.'

'Shame. Bit of a waste of your country-girl outfit if he's not even going to be there!'

'Oh, well, there's always this Chase person. I know a manager isn't quite the same but I bet he's to die for.'

'He might be married.'

'I shouldn't think so. These guys don't get out much,' said Emily hopefully. 'I've always fancied having a wild affair with a strong, silent farmer type. Anyway, with any luck we'll have the brother and the manager, so we can have one each!'

'Thanks, but I've always thought the appeal of the strong, silent type was overrated. I like a man who can talk about something more than cows. I'm going outside to see if there's any sign of him.'

Retrieving the sunglasses from the top of her head, Bea settled them on her nose and pushed open the door. The heat hit her like a blow, and even behind her glasses she had to screw up her eyes against the glare.

At least there was no chance of missing anyone on a road like this, she thought, squinting first one way and then another along an absolutely straight, absolutely empty, road. She hoped one of Emily's fantasy figures would turn up soon, as the only alternative was clearly going to be to walk into town, and it looked like a very long way.

It was a relief to get back into the air-conditioning, but both girls were soon thoroughly bored and fed up. They took it in turns to go outside and check on the traffic, but in an hour and a half counted only three road trains rumbling past.

Eventually Bea remembered a copy of *Cosmopolitan* in her suitcase, and she had just lost herself in an article about the joys of city living when a dull drone overhead made them both look up.

A tiny plane with wings that seemed to be propped up

on long poles dropped lightly onto the runway and taxied towards the terminal, its propeller still blurring. As the girls watched, the plane came to a stop, the propeller faltered and slowed, and a man jumped out and set off towards the terminal at a brisk pace.

'Do you think this is him?'

Emily sounded disappointed, presumably because of the absence of a checked shirt. He wasn't giving a very good impression of being unhurried either. In fact, even from a distance, he looked distinctly impatient.

On the other hand, he was definitely tall and rangy, thought Bea. Nice broad shoulders, too, she couldn't help noticing. As far as build went, he was everything Emily could want.

'Can't be,' she said. 'He's not wearing a hat.'

Emily was obviously struggling to make the best of things. 'He can fly a plane,' she said. 'That's good.'

If the man noticed the two girls studying him through the big plate glass windows, he gave no sign of it. Instead, he stiff-armed the swing door in a manner worthy of the most harried city executive and strode into the terminal.

Bea gave Emily a sympathetic glance. His body might be good—actually, it was even more impressive at close quarters—but the rest of him was a distinct disappointment. He was just a very ordinary-looking man, with an irritated expression.

She judged him to be in his early thirties, but something about him made him seem older than that. Obviously ignorant of the sartorial codes Emily found so romantic, he was wearing jeans and a dull brown shirt. In fact, dull brown seemed to be something of a theme. He had a brown face and dull brown hair, and Bea fully expected to meet dull brown eyes too but, as his gaze swept over them, she was taken aback to discover that they weren't brown at all, but an icy, almost startling, blue, and very unfriendly.

As the cold eyes encountered hers, she felt something

like a tiny shock, and an odd feeling shivered down her spine. Putting her chin up, Bea stared back at him. She wasn't about to be intimidated by a cowboy in a brown shirt.

Chase's heart sank as he took in the two girls before him. So much for Nick and the 'suitable' girls he had found. 'They'll be perfect,' he had enthused before getting on the plane and no doubt forgetting all about them.

Chase didn't think they looked perfect at all. There was a very pretty blonde one, dressed for some reason in a cowgirl outfit, and a brunette who looked as if she was off to a party in a skimpy dress and high heels, for God's sake. She had a wide, lush mouth that sat oddly with the snooty expression she was wearing. Chase was hard put to decide which of them looked more ridiculous.

Suitable? Perfect? Thanks, Nick, he sighed inwardly. Personally, he had them down as nothing but trouble.

Which was all he needed right now.

Outwardly, he looked from one to the other, trying to guess which one was Emily Williams. He picked the brunette with her nose stuck in the air. Emily sounded a prissy, old-fashioned name, and she looked the type.

Or maybe not, with that mouth.

'Emily Williams?'

It came out brusquer than he had intended, and the brunette was clearly not impressed.

'This is Emily,' she said, gesturing at the blonde girl, who smiled a little uncertainly. 'I'm Bea Stevenson.'

Her voice was very clear and English, and Chase wondered whether she expected him to bow.

'Bee?' he repeated. What kind of name was that? 'As in buzzing and honey?'

'As in Beatrice,' she said coldly. 'You must be Mr Chase.'

He raised an eyebrow. 'Most people just call me Chase.'

Bea ignored that. She probably didn't like being associated with 'most people', Chase decided.

'Didn't Mr Sutherland tell you that we were coming?'

'I wouldn't be here if he hadn't,' Chase pointed out
crisply. 'I've got better things to do than hang around at
the airport on the off chance that a couple of cooks are
going to turn up.'

'We've all got better things to do,' she snapped, 'but it
hasn't stopped *us* from having to hang around all afternoon.
The plane got in two hours ago!'

'Sorry about that,' said Chase, not sounding at all sorry.
'We've been putting a mob of cattle through the yards, and
I couldn't get away any earlier.'

'Are we supposed to be grateful that you could spare the
time to come and get us?'

'*Bea…*'

Bea pushed her hair defiantly behind her ears and met
Emily's pleading blue eyes. She knew it was a bit soon to
get into a stand-up argument, but something about this man
rubbed her up the wrong way.

'You should be grateful I remembered, anyway,' he said,
unmoved by her tone. 'I need to get back as soon as possible,' he added briskly, 'so if you're ready, I suggest you
get your things and we'll go.'

'In the plane?' Emily revived magically at the prospect.

'It's the quickest way.' Chase glanced at her. 'It's not a
problem, is it?'

'Oh, no, I've always wanted to go in a small plane,' she
assured him. 'It's all so exciting!'

Chase suppressed a sigh. One who was keen, and one
who was obviously going to hate every minute of it. They'd
had both types before, and it was a toss up as to which was
the hardest to deal with. The keen ones, probably. The girls
who hated it usually burst into tears and insisted on going
home the very next day. Perhaps Bea Stevenson would be
the same.

Although she didn't look like a girl who would cry easily. Too proud for that, Chase guessed, taking in the stubborn set of her chin.

'Where are your things?'

They indicated two huge suitcases in the corner of the
room, and he raised one eyebrow. 'Brought your ball gowns
and the kitchen sink, have you?' he asked sardonically.

Bea bristled. 'We thought we'd bring a few books and
things to keep us occupied,' she said in a cool voice. She
wasn't about to tell him about the hair-dryer. 'We didn't
want to be bored.'

'You won't have time to be bored at Calulla Downs,' he
said, unimpressed by their forethought.

Bea opened her mouth to tell him that she would be the
judge of what bored her or not, but Chase was already
striding over to the cases. 'Is this yours?' he said to Emily
as he took hold of the blue one.

'Yes, it's a bit heavy, I'm afraid...'

Emily trailed off as he picked it up in one hand and
glanced from the red suitcase to Bea. 'Want me to take this
one for you?' he asked.

Bea lifted her chin proudly. 'I can manage, thank you.'

'OK.'

To her fury, he took her at her word and headed for the
doors, carrying Emily's suitcase as if it was empty. He
didn't even have to put it down to open the door. Bea was
left to struggle after him across the tarmac. Her case had
wheels, but it was so heavy that it kept toppling sideways
and snagging at her ankles, which did nothing to improve
her temper.

'So much for slow smiles and slow drawls!' she said
bitterly to Emily who was doing her best to help keep the
case upright. 'This guy makes that lot you see jumping up
and down at the Stock Exchange whenever there's a finan-
cial crisis look laid-back!'

'Perhaps he's just having a bad day,' said Emily.

'He's not the only one!' grumbled Bea, stopping to wipe her forehead with the back of her arm. The heat was pouring down and then bouncing back off the tarmac until she thought she was about to expire, but she made herself carry on. Frankly, she would rather collapse into a sweaty puddle than ask the sneering Mr Chase for help!

Reaching the plane, Chase threw the case into the hold and turned to watch the two English girls trailing across the tarmac. The brunette, Bea she called herself, was clearly struggling, but just as clearly would rather die than ask him to help.

Well, if that's the way she wanted to be, let her. It was no skin off his nose, Chase thought, but he couldn't help noticing how tired she looked when she finally hauled her case up to the plane. Her face was a bright, shiny pink and her smooth brown hair was pushed wearily behind her ears.

Chase indicated the hold. 'Do you want to put the case in there, or shall I do it for you?'

Bea shot him a fulminating glance. There was no way she could lift the case six inches off the ground, let alone all the way up there.

'Thank you,' she said stiffly, and perversely hated him for the ease with which he tossed the case into the plane.

As if she hadn't been humiliated enough, she still had to get into the plane, a process which made Bea regret taking such a stand about refusing to dress the part. Of course, they couldn't have anything easy like steps. The wings were set high on the body of the plane, and you had to climb in underneath by setting your foot on the strut and hauling yourself up. In her jeans and boots, Emily managed it without any difficulty and settled herself in the front seat, swivelling round to watch Bea's efforts with a smug grin.

Gritting her teeth, Bea tried to follow her example, but the soles of her shoes kept slipping off the smooth strut and she couldn't find any purchase to pull herself into the cabin.

She heard Chase sigh behind her, and the next moment found herself set brusquely aside. He stepped easily up into the cabin and reached down a peremptory hand.

'Here, I'll pull you up,' he said.

Bea would have given almost anything she possessed not to accept his help, but it was a question of taking his hand or being left on the tarmac. She was very conscious of the cool strength of his fingers as they closed around hers and he lifted her effortlessly off the ground.

Already scarlet with the heat and humiliation, she flushed a deeper and even more unbecoming shade of red as she scrambled up and collapsed in an inelegant heap beside him. Somewhere along the line, her dress had got rucked up and Chase was subjected to an eyeful of her thighs in all their lack of glory. If he had been hoping for a glimpse of slender golden legs, he must have been sadly disappointed. Bea's thighs were absolutely not her best feature.

Serve him right, thought Bea, hastily covering them up. She wished she had taken the tarmac option.

Her only comfort was the thought that he probably wished she'd stayed behind, too.

As it was, it looked like they were stuck with each other for the duration.

# CHAPTER TWO

APART from a faint lifting of his eyebrow, which was somehow worse than an open sneer, Chase gave no sign that he
had even noticed her legs. He dropped her hand pretty
quickly, though, pulled the door to, and went forward to
fold himself easily into the pilot's seat.

Bea was left to brush herself down and get herself into
one of the small passenger seats behind Emily, who grinned
knowingly at her. She glared back.

Chase was flicking buttons above his head, ignoring both
of them. Bea just hoped that he knew what he was doing.
She had never been in a plane this small before, certainly
not one with a propeller. It looked pretty flimsy, too. She
tapped the side panel dubiously. Oh, for a jumbo jet, four
massive engines, and a pilot in a navy-blue uniform with
multiple rows of gold braid!

'Seat belt?'

She started as Chase turned abruptly to fix her with that
unnervingly cool blue stare.

'Oh,…yes…' She fumbled for her belt, but her fingers
were clumsy under his icy gaze and it seemed to take forever to snap it into place.

'Are you secure?' he asked with an edge of impatience.

'I'm a bit neurotic about my weight and I've got a massive complex about my hair, but on the whole, yes, I'd say
that I was as well-balanced as the next person.'

'What?' Chase stared at her as if she had suddenly
sprouted tentacles and turned into an alien, which was probably how she seemed to him.

Bea rolled her eyes. 'Yes, I've fastened my seat belt.'

With a final hard look, Chase turned back to the controls,

and they were soon speeding down the runway, the propeller a blur on the plane's nose. The sound of the engine
reverberated deafeningly through the cabin. Bea's stomach
dropped alarmingly as they lifted into the air, and she
closed her eyes and clutched at her seat. If she survived
this trip, she was never, ever, *ever* going to let Emily talk
her into doing anything else.

When she felt the plane level off, she opened her eyes
cautiously and risked a glance out of the window, and
promptly regretted it. The ground looked very far away, a
flat, reddish-brown expanse that stretched out interminably
in every direction. Bea could see the tiny shadow of the
plane travelling along the ground below them, and wished
that she were down with it, instead of suspended in mid-
air.

In the front seat, Emily was chatting away, apparently
unperturbed by the fact that she was sitting a thousand feet
up in a flimsy tin can powered by little more than a rubber
band. She had obviously recovered from her initial disappointment and was doing her best to flirt with Chase, although she wasn't getting very far, judging by his mono-
syllabic replies. After the way he had pulled her into the
plane, his strength couldn't be denied, and no one could
call him chatty, but Bea didn't think he was quite what
Emily had in mind on the strong, silent front.

She hoped not, anyway. She had a nasty feeling that
Chase was not the kind of man to mess with. He certainly
didn't look the type to put up with much nonsense. Still, it
was odd that he was so unresponsive. Very few men were
immune to Emily's sparkling blue eyes and spectacular
lashes, but Chase seemed impervious to her many charms.

Maybe he just didn't like women, Bea thought. It would
be a shame with that mouth. Or maybe he was married after
all. There was no reason why he shouldn't be. The thought
made Bea frown for some reason, and she leant forward

casually, as if to get something from her handbag so that she could check out his left hand on the joystick.

No wedding ring. Nice hands, though.

Bea relaxed slightly and sat back, only to realise that the lack of a ring probably didn't mean much. She couldn't imagine outback men going in for jewellery in a big way. If Emily's description was anything to go by, they were all macho in the extreme and would consider wedding rings something only city boys wore.

Not that Chase seemed particularly macho, but there was something spare and uncompromising about him. Definitely a no-frills type, she thought.

So he *might* be married.

Bea's eyes rested on him speculatively. She couldn't see his expression, just the edge of his jaw, his ear and the side of his throat. He had a good, strong neck, she couldn't help noticing. She'd always had a thing about men's necks. It didn't bother Emily, but Bea couldn't bear thin, scrawny ones. She liked her men strong and solid all over.

How did Chase like his women? Bea found herself wondering. It was pretty obvious that he didn't have much time for brunettes with a stylish shoe sense! No, he'd probably go for a robust, no-nonsense type, she decided. Blonde, probably, with short sensible hair that didn't require washing, moussing and blow-drying every day, and a minimal beauty routine.

Oh, well. Each to his own. It wasn't as if she cared.

Although it did seem a waste of a neck like that.

Bea looked away with a tiny sigh.

If only there was anything else to look *at!* Looking down at the ground made her feel ill, and the sky was just a blue glare that made her feel dizzy. Bea tried looking at her hands, but that was just boring, and it was impossible not to let her mind drift towards imagining how Chase would be with his wife. Was he always this chilly and forbidding, or did he relax with a woman he liked enough to marry? He might even smile. Imagine what *that* would be like!

Closing her eyes, Bea was alarmed to find that she could imagine it all too clearly, and the picture of that stern mouth relaxing into a smile left her with such a queer feeling inside that her eyes snapped open again.

Nerves, she told herself.

'Are you OK?'

Chase's brusque voice made her jump, and she jerked her head round to find him regarding her with a frown. His eyes were uncomfortably keen, and in spite of herself Bea flushed, remembering the wayward trend of her thoughts.

'I'm fine,' she said stiffly.

He had turned right round in his seat to look at her. 'You seem a bit nervous,' he commented.

'I'm not in the least nervous,' lied Bea in a brittle voice, adding pointedly, 'I might feel better if you were looking where you were going, though.'

A half-smile quirked the corner of his mouth. 'This old girl can fly herself. It's not as if there's anything to bump into up here, anyway.'

'Maybe not, but there's plenty to bump into down there,' she said, pointing at the ground.

'Relax, Bea.' It was Emily's turn to swivel round in her seat. 'I tell you what, why don't we change places? You'll get a much better view up here.'

'No,' said Bea, a little too quickly. The plane felt unstable enough as it was without them all playing musical chairs. 'I mean, I'm happy where I am.'

'Are you sure? It's a fabulous view!'

Of what? Bea wondered. Brown, brown and more brown? She could see more than enough from her side window.

'I'm sure,' she said, thinking longingly of Sydney. She could be in the kitchen, preparing for the evening ahead. The catering company had been a great place to work, and no two days were the same. One day they might be doing a five-course dinner for eight, and the next canapés for eight hundred. It had been hard work, but Bea loved it. It had been good experience too, and had given her plenty of ideas for when she branched out on her own.

Remembering the atmosphere of controlled chaos and the surge of adrenalin that somehow made everything come together at the last moment, Bea sighed. Afterwards they would all go for a drink in a noisy bar and then she'd get the ferry across the harbour to the house she and Emily had shared with two friends. Sydney seemed part of a different world from this interminable journey.

The noise and the vibration and the smell of fuel was making her feel queasy, and she clamped her lips together as her stomach churned. Excellent, being sick was all she needed to complete the good impression she had made on Chase so far. She could just imagine his expression if she chucked up in his plane.

At least on proper planes they gave you a sick bag. Bea hunted surreptitiously through her handbag, but couldn't find so much as a tissue. And she certainly wasn't using the bag itself! She had bought it in Italy, and it was one of her favourites.

Oh, God, please don't let me be sick, she prayed silently, pressing her lips together as her stomach gave another alarming lurch. Hadn't she been through enough humiliation today?

Clearing her throat, she leant forward. 'Um…how much longer will it take us to get to Calulla Downs, Mr Chase?'

'Only another twenty minutes or so,' he said, glancing over his shoulder. 'And you can call me Chase.'

Where did he think they were? In the army? Bea had no intention of barking his surname at him, but she was damned if she was going to be interested enough to ask for his first name either. 'I'd rather stick to Mr Chase for now,' she said coolly as she sat back in her seat.

Chase glanced at her again, and then shrugged. 'If that's what you want.'

In fact, it was nearly half an hour before the little plane began its descent. Somehow Bea got through it without throwing up, but it was a close run thing. She was so relieved at the prospect of landing that even the flat scrub below them looked inviting. She didn't care how brown and boring it was, as long as it was firm beneath her feet.

The plane had barely touched down before she was out of her seat belt and waiting by the door like a dog sensing the prospect of a walk. Chase gave her an odd look, as he bent to push the door open.

'Hang on a minute,' he said irritably when Bea made to clamber out. 'You'll break your ankle if you try and jump down in those shoes.'

Evidently exasperated, he swung himself down in one fluid motion and turned to hold up his arms. 'Well, come on,' he ordered, as Bea dithered, torn between her longing to be back on terra firma and an acute attack of shyness at the thought of touching him.

In the end, she didn't have much choice. She leant forward and took hold of his shoulders as he grasped her firmly by the waist and lifted her bodily onto the ground. It only took a second, but that was quite long enough for Bea to register the rock-hard body and the warmth of his hands searing through the flimsy material of her dress. It might even have been that rather than the heels which made her stumble slightly as she landed and fall against him.

'Sorry,' she muttered, flustered by his closeness.

Chase wasn't flustered. He simply put her aside like a parcel and held up a hand to help Emily jump down before unloading their suitcases.

'You look a bit funny,' said Emily to Bea. 'Are you all right?'

Before Bea could answer, the sound of an engine made them turn to see a pick-up truck bumping along a track towards them, red dust hanging in a cloud in its wake. It stopped beside the plane and a man got out.

And not just any man. Emily drew a deep breath, her concern for Bea forgotten. Here was her fantasy at last!

He was tall and lean and incredibly handsome, with just the right hint of toughness. Here was a man who could ride the bucking bronco, and wrestle bulls to the ground before breakfast. He didn't actually have a lasso in his hand, but you could just tell that it was looped onto his saddle.

In fact, thought Bea, the only thing that was missing was that trusty horse. By rights he should have ridden up and swung easily to the ground. A pick-up truck didn't have quite the same effect, but she could see that Emily didn't care. In every other way he was perfect. The dusty boots, the checked shirt rolled up to reveal powerful forearms…he even had a hat tilted over his eyes.

'Maybe this is Nick's brother,' Emily whispered hopefully to Bea and sent him a dazzling smile.

He gave a slow smile in return, outback man incarnate. It was like watching Emily's fantasy come alive, so much so that when he actually tipped his hat, Bea almost laughed out loud. Any minute now he would whip off his hat and bend Emily back over his arm for a kiss before tossing her over his saddle and galloping off with her into the sunset. At the very least, he would call her ma'am, surely?

Instead he spoke to Chase. 'I brought the ute out when I heard you coming in. I thought you might want a lift back in case the girls here had some luggage to bring in.'

Oh, yes, even the right Australian drawl. Emily was starry-eyed. 'I think I've just died and gone to heaven,' she sighed to Bea.

'I don't think he's Nick's brother, though.' Less dazzled, Bea was watching the two men together. They were of a similar age, and Chase was shorter and more compact, but in some indefinable way you could tell that he was in charge. 'If you're planning on becoming mistress of a million acres, I'd hang on and check out the brother first.'

'What do I care about acres?' Emily was well gone. 'Did you *see* the way he smiled?'

Bea was more concerned about the way the men were throwing their suitcases into the back of the ute. She hoped her hair-dryer would stand up to all the rough handling.

'This is Baz,' said Chase, belatedly remembering to make the introductions.

'Hi,' said Emily before he could go any further. Her eyes shone as she smiled at Baz. 'I'm Emily.'

'Welcome to Calulla Downs, Emily,' he said in his deep, delicious voice.

Chase eyed them sardonically. Here they went again! He'd lost count of the number of girls he'd seen swoon at Baz's feet. The little blonde was clearly a romantic like all the others. Baz barely had to open his mouth and they were besotted. Chase was surprised that he never seemed to get bored with all that uncritical adoration. For himself, he preferred a bit more of a challenge.

Involuntarily, he glanced at Bea. A smile was tugging at the corners of her lush mouth as she watched her friend gazing dreamily at the stockman, and the snooty expression that had so riled him had been replaced by a gleam of amusement. Chase was taken aback to see how different she looked, and even more disconcerted to discover that he was pleased that she was apparently immune to Baz's legendary charms.

She wasn't as pretty as her friend, but her face had more character with its dark brows, firm nose and stubborn chin. And that mouth. Her straight brown hair was cut in a bob that he guessed was normally immaculately shiny but which right then was looking rather the worse for wear, with her fringe sticking to her forehead and the rest hanging limply around her pale face. She had been nervous in the plane, and probably more than a little sick, but she hadn't been going to admit it, and Chase thought she was probably still feeling a bit queasy.

She turned her head suddenly, as if becoming aware of his gaze, and their eyes met for a tiny moment. There was a funny little jolt in the air, and he found himself remembering the warmth of her body between his hands as he lifted her down from the plane.

'And this is Bea,' Chase said to Baz almost roughly.

'G'day, Bea.'

'Hello.' Her voice sounded comically high and brittle after Baz's deep, slow tones, but something in the way Chase had been watching her had put her on edge. Retrieving her sunglasses from the top of her head, she put them on and hoped they would hide her expression.

'Where's Chloe?' Chase was asking, all briskness, as if he hadn't even noticed that odd frisson in the air as their eyes had met.

Perhaps he hadn't, thought Bea. Perhaps she had imagined it.

Baz was talking about somebody called Julie, while Emily hung on his every word. And there was plenty of time to do that. Bea had never heard anyone speak quite so slowly.

'We may as well pick her up on the way, then.'

As if the hierarchy wasn't already obvious, Chase strode over to the ute and opened the driver's door, while Baz climbed into the open back with the suitcases.

Emily gave Bea a nudge. 'You get in,' she said, obviously hoping that she would be able to get in the back with Baz, but her plan was foiled when Chase leant over the bench seat and opened the door.

'There's room for three,' he said drily.

Which meant, of course, that Bea was stuck in the middle. The gear stick was set into the column of the steering wheel, so there was nothing to stop her sliding across the shiny leather seat against Chase. She kept edging back towards Emily, who used her bottom to shunt her back into the middle.

'Budge over, Bea,' she said. 'You're squashing me.'

Bea clung to the bar across the dashboard and concentrated on not brushing against Chase's arm, but it was hard when the ute was lurching and bumping over the rough ground.

'Who's Julie?' she asked to distract herself from the solid length of his thigh on the seat next to hers.

From the fine hairs at his wrist glinting in the sunlight.

From his hands on the steering wheel and the tingling where his touch seemed imprinted still on her skin.

Bea shivered, and Chase shot her a curious glance. 'Julie's married to one of the stockmen,' was all he said. 'He's known as the married man, which means he gets a house on the property. Julie's got two kids of her own, but she's been keeping an eye on Chloe until you got here.'

He pulled up outside a low house which looked to Bea as if it had been plonked down in the middle of the bush with an arbitrary fence thrown around it to create a yard otherwise indistinguishable from the surrounding scrub. Three children were playing in the shade of the long veranda, but when they saw the ute pull up at the gate, a little girl detached herself and came tumbling down the steps.

'Uncle Chase! Uncle Chase!'

Glad of the excuse to get out of the car, Bea had slid out after Chase, just in time to see him smile at the child who threw herself at him.

It gave Bea a horrible fright. For one terrible moment she thought that her heart had actually stopped beating, but the next instant it had slammed back into action, thudding painfully against her ribs and sucking all the oxygen from her lungs so that it was difficult to breathe properly.

For God's sake, she scolded herself. It was only a smile! You've seen a man smile before, haven't you?

Not like that, an inner voice answered.

She was so taken up with breathing again that it took a minute to realise just what she had heard. *Uncle* Chase?

Bea swallowed. 'Uncle?' she repeated in a hollow voice.

Chase looked at her over the top of the cab. There was no mistaking the glint of mockery in his eyes. 'Uncle Chase,' he confirmed, the little girl hanging off one hand.

Even Emily was diverted from Baz for a moment. '*You're* Nick's brother?' she said, staring.

'I'm Chase Sutherland,' he agreed.

'We thought you were the manager!' Emily put her hand to her mouth and giggled. 'You must have thought Bea was weird when she insisted on calling you Mr Chase!'

Bea gritted her teeth. 'I'm sure *Mr Sutherland* knew perfectly well what we thought,' she said tightly, glaring at Chase. 'Why didn't you tell us Chase was your first name?' she demanded.

'I told you to call me Chase,' he pointed out with what she was sure was a smirk. 'But you seemed pretty set on calling me Mr. I thought maybe things were more formal where you come from.'

He hadn't thought anything of the kind, Bea thought savagely. He had just enjoyed seeing her making a complete idiot of herself.

Chase put one hand on the shoulder of the little girl in her denim dungarees. Her blonde hair was tied up in bunches and she had an angelic face belied by the expression in her sharp green eyes.

'This is Chloe,' said Chase. 'Say hello to Emily and Bea, Chloe. Oh, I'm sorry!' He caught himself up and looked at Bea in mock apology. 'Would you prefer her to call you Miss Bea? I know how keen you are on formality!'

'Bea's fine,' she said grittily and forced herself to smile at the child as Emily was doing. 'Hello, Chloe.'

Chloe eyed her warily. 'Hello,' she said without enthusiasm.

Bea and Emily exchanged a glance. Even inexperienced

as they were, they recognised the mutinous set to that little mouth.

'Emily and Bea are going to look after you until Dad comes home,' said Chase.

'Emily is going to look after you,' Bea put in firmly. She knew absolutely nothing about children, and she had no intention of getting roped in to looking after one. 'I'm just the cook.'

Chloe studied her with suspicious green eyes. 'Why do we have to call you Miss Bea?' she demanded.

'That was just your uncle's idea of a joke,' said Bea.

'Why?'

'I've no idea. It wasn't very funny, was it?'

A smile twitched at the corner of Chase's mouth as he went over to speak to Baz. To Emily's dismay, the stockman nodded, tipped his hat again in their direction, and walked off.

'Don't panic,' said Chase drily, correctly interpreting the look on Emily's face. 'You'll see him again this evening. If you get in the ute, I'll be back in a minute,' he added. 'Chloe, you get in too.'

The three of them squeezed into the front seat and, when Chase reappeared, they set off down a fork in the track. Bea could feel the dust gritting her skin already, and her hair felt awful. She couldn't believe why anyone would choose to live out here. There was nothing but scrub, a few spindly trees and the bare earth, cracked and baking in the heat.

And then Chase swung off the main track, and they suddenly found themselves in an oasis of green. It was so unexpected that Bea actually gasped. Tall trees cast fractured shade over a lawn where a sprinkler flickered. There were lemon trees and great clumps of pink oleanders and purple bougainvillea, and set amidst it all the homestead, a solid, stone building with a deep veranda running around all sides and an air of gracious calm.

'Oh, it's beautiful!' Emily cried.

Bea said nothing, but she had to admit to herself that things might not be *quite* as bad as she had feared.

Chase drove round the back to a big, dusty yard and parked the ute under a gum tree. From this view the homestead was less impressive. Nobody was wasting water on the working side of the house, with its collection of sheds, its water tanks and windmill.

Inside, though, the homestead was cool and quiet. The floors were of polished wood and the furniture was a comfortable mixture of the antique and the modern. Someone, thought Bea, had a lot of style.

And a lot of money.

Chase dumped their cases in a room with twin beds and looked at his watch. 'I'll show you the kitchen,' he said to Bea, 'and then leave you to get on with it.'

Leaving Emily to cope with Chloe on her own, he strode back down the corridor, with Bea forced to trot to keep up with him.

'This is the kitchen,' he said, opening a door into a large room equipped, to Bea's relief, with what looked like the latest technology. He pointed through a door on the other side of the room. 'We eat on the veranda through there.'

'What, outside?'

'It's cooler out there.'

'Yes, but what about the flies?'

'It's screened in,' said Chase impatiently, as if she was supposed to know that everyone in the outback ate on their verandas. 'Now, you should find everything you need over there,' he went on, pointing at a wall of steel fridges and freezers. 'There's a larder and a cold store as well. I suggest you keep opening doors until you find what you need. The stockmen will come over for supper at seven o'clock, so you'll need to have a meal ready by then. Any questions?'

'"What am I doing here?" springs to mind!' sighed Bea.

Chase frowned. 'I understood you were a qualified cook.'

'I am. That doesn't make me a mind reader!'

He glanced irritably at his watch, impatient to be gone. 'What do you need to know?'

'How many I'm cooking for, for a start.'

'Oh.' It was a reasonable enough question, Chase allowed grudgingly. 'Nine of us, plus you two. Chloe eats separately in the evening. She should be in bed by seven.'

'I'll tell Emily,' said Bea sweetly. 'Any special dietary requirements?'

She was looking straight at him, and Chase saw her eyes properly for the first time. They were golden, the colour of warm honey, and very clear.

'Meat,' he said gruffly, annoyed with himself for even noticing. 'Nothing fancy.'

'Well, I should be able to cope with that.'

She didn't even bother to disguise her sarcasm, and Chase shot her a look as he took a hat from the hooks by the door.

'You're not much good to me if you can't,' he said, and went out, letting the screen door bang behind him.

He didn't reappear until six o'clock. Bea looked up as the screen door creaked and then went back to slicing carrots vengefully.

The door clattered back into place and Chase hung his hat on a hook. 'Is everything OK?'

The casual note in his voice infuriated Bea.

'Oh, yes, everything's fine!' she said, tight-lipped, her knife flashing dangerously as it demolished the carrots. 'We've been dumped in the middle of nowhere, with no idea of where anything is or how anything works...and you disappear and just leave us to get on with it!'

'I thought you wanted to come and work on a cattle station?'

'*Emily* wanted to come. Personally, I appreciate a more professional set-up!'

Chase eyed her cautiously. She seemed tense, and he knew from past experience that the last thing you wanted was a tense cook at this stage of the evening. If they wanted to eat tonight, he would have to be careful not to provoke her.

'You seem to have managed, anyway,' he said pacifically. 'Something smells good. Did you find everything you needed?'

'Eventually,' said Bea with something of a snap. If she had, it was no thanks to him!

There was a tiny pause.

'Where's Emily?' Chase tried again.

'Giving Chloe a bath.'

'Has she been all right?'

Bea reached for another carrot, her edginess at the sight of Chase easing slightly. 'She seems a bit…wary,' she said.

There had been a definite sense of wills being measured and in Chloe's case at least, some calculation as to how much she could get away with. It hadn't taken her long to realise that the answer was 'a lot' as far as Emily was concerned.

Still, it wasn't her problem, Bea told herself firmly. She had enough to do as it was. Finding your way around a strange kitchen and producing supper for eleven with no warning was problem enough for her!

She had changed, Chase realised. She had replaced those ridiculous shoes with flat sandals and the dress with cotton trousers and a sleeveless top beneath a practical apron. Her hair was pushed behind her ears, and her lashes were lowered as her eyes followed the rapid slicing movements of the knife in her hand.

For some reason Chase felt awkward. 'She's a nice kid when she gets to know you,' he said after a moment. 'She's had to get used to a lot of different people passing through, and she tends to take her time before deciding whether she likes you or not. I don't blame her.'

'Nor do I.' Bea looked up from her knife and he was struck again by how clear her eyes were. 'I do exactly the same.'

Although that wasn't quite true, was it? She had decided she didn't like Chase straight away.

There was another pause. Bea reached for another carrot.

'It must be difficult for Chloe with her mother being away as well as her father. When is she coming back?'

Chase had gone over to the beer fridge, but he stilled with his hand on the door and turned to face her, his brows drawn together. 'Didn't Nick explain the situation?'

'I've never met him,' said Bea. 'I gathered from Emily that his wife was working in the States and that he'd gone to join her.'

Chase's hand fell. 'It's a bit more complicated than that,' he said slowly.

Bea paused in mid-slice, and something in his expression made her lay the knife down. 'What?'

'Georgie's left Nick.'

'Oh, I see,' she said uncomfortably. 'And Chloe?'

'She doesn't know. She's too young to understand.'

Chase pulled a beer out of the fridge and wrenched off the top before belatedly remembering to offer Bea one. She shook her head and he sat down at the table, turning the bottle between his hands. It went against the grain to pass on Nick and Georgie's private business, but she and Emily really needed to know the situation so that they didn't upset Chloe unnecessarily.

'Nick's gone to try and persuade Georgie to come home,' he said.

To his relief, Bea didn't offer sympathy or sit down next to him and encourage him to tell her the whole story. Instead she swept the carrots off the board into a saucepan and picked up an onion.

'Why has…Georgie?…gone to America? Is she really working?'

'Oh, yes, she's working all right. That's part of the problem. Georgie's an actress. She's making a movie somewhere in Texas, and she's got a starring role.'

Bea froze and put down her knife very carefully. 'We're not talking about Georgie Grainger by any chance, are we?'

'You've heard of her?' Chase took a pull of his beer. 'Georgie would be pleased.'

Bea opened her mouth and then closed it again. Georgie Grainger was not yet in Nicole Kidman's league, but comparisons were already being made. She had had a small part in a film that had turned into the unexpected success of the previous year, breaking all box office records, and for a while the media couldn't get enough of her.

Bea remembered seeing her being interviewed on a television chat show, and how envious she had been of her creamy skin and swinging chestnut hair and spectacular green eyes.

'She's gorgeous, isn't she?' she had said to Phil, but he had only grunted and said that he preferred blondes.

That should have been a warning.

# CHAPTER THREE

'I DIDN'T realise that she was married,' she said after a moment. Georgie Grainger had seemed so young and so glamorous that it was hard to imagine her as a wife and mother, let alone in a place like Calulla Downs!

'Not many people did. She was told to keep it quiet. Apparently a husband and a baby aren't the right image for an up and coming star.' There was a bitter edge to Chase's voice. 'Once you've made it, a baby is the ultimate accessory, I understand, but when you're still trying to hit the big time...no, much better to hide them away. They kept telling Georgie that she had a great future. They talked about Hollywood and dazzled her with hints of multimillion-dollar deals. You can see why cooking a roast for the stockmen would lose appeal, can't you?'

Only too well, thought Bea, but it didn't seem tactful to say so. She had never wanted to be a movie star, but she could certainly understand the lure of Los Angeles after Calulla Downs. She'd been here less than half a day and already she couldn't wait to head back to the bright lights.

On the other hand, she didn't have a husband and a small child to think about.

She went back to chopping onions. 'Why did Georgie marry your brother if she wanted to be an actress?' she asked. 'She must have known there wouldn't be much scope for her career out here.'

For a moment she thought Chase wasn't going to reply. He was brooding over his beer, frowning down into it as if it held the answer to her question.

'She was very young when she met Nick,' he said eventually. 'She was just out of drama school and the play she

was in folded after a couple of weeks. It seemed then that
her career wasn't going anywhere, and Nick can be very
persuasive. He swept her off her feet.'

When Bea glanced at him under her lashes, his face was
stern and set. He obviously disapproved of his brother's
romance. It was hard to imagine Chase sweeping a girl off
her feet, she thought. Tapping his watch and telling her to
make up her mind would be more his style.

Unaware of her thoughts, Chase was still talking about
his sister-in-law. 'I think marriage for Georgie was just another role she could play. She saw herself as mistress of a
famous cattle station, and was carried away by the romance
of it all. She should have known better,' he added drily.
'She grew up on a property down south, but I guess she
thought it would be different here. It wasn't, of course. It
was just more isolated.'

He looked at Bea, but she was busy chopping onions and
it was impossible to tell what she thought.

'Georgie did try,' he went on, almost as if he had to
convince her. 'She used to love having parties, and the
homestead was always full of her friends, but then we had
a bad drought and things were a bit tight for while. Georgie
decided that we should get into the tourist business, and
spent a fortune we couldn't afford on all this.' He waved
a hand at the gleaming array of kitchen equipment.

'She redecorated the homestead, built a new wing with
extra bedrooms, and insisted on employing a chef, all with
the idea of taking paying guests who wanted to experience
life on a station, but without getting their hands dirty or
sacrificing home comforts.

'It's been popular, too,' Chase had to acknowledge.
'We've never advertised, but Georgie had so many friends
that word of mouth was more than enough. And then a
friend of a friend from her acting days turned up. He'd
made it big in Hollywood and he decided Georgie was just
the fresh face they needed. Before we quite knew what was

happening, he'd persuaded her to fly out to LA and audition for a small part and the whole circus took off from there.'

'Didn't Nick want her to go?'

'Have you ever seen a picture of Georgie?' Chase countered.

'Yes.'

'Then you'll know how beautiful she is.'

His voice softened imperceptibly, and Bea sent him a sharp look. He had sounded as if he disapproved of Georgie before, but now she wondered how he really felt about his beautiful sister-in-law.

'Nick was jealous?'

'Of course he was. Any man would have felt the same.'

Including him? Bea wondered.

'He could see that she was getting bored out here, though,' Chase was saying, unaware of her mental interruption. 'He encouraged her to go back to acting at first, but none of us expected that her career would take off the way it has. Suddenly Georgie's a star, and everything's changed. When this new part came up, Nick didn't want her to take it, and he told her she would have to choose between him and the movie.'

'Oh, dear,' said Bea. She could just imagine how *that* had gone down.

'Quite. Georgie's not the kind of person to give in to an ultimatum like that, and of course they had a huge argument which ended up with her demanding a divorce. She wanted to take Chloe with her, but Nick said that she wouldn't be able to look after her properly while she was filming, and I think Georgie knew herself that she'd be better here until everything was sorted out.'

'Is that why Nick's gone to the States? To arrange the divorce?'

'No, he wants Georgie back. He was devastated when she left, but a lot of hard things were said on both sides, and it won't be easy. He didn't even tell Georgie he was coming. I'm not sure he even knows exactly where to find her, but he was determined to track her down and persuade her to give him another chance.

'He asked me if I would keep an eye on Chloe while he was gone, but it's a busy time on the station, so I said I'd do it if he found someone to replace the cook and the governess who'd both left in a huff. They couldn't cope with the rows. I told Nick we'd had enough prima donnas around here and to make sure that he got someone suitable.'

Chase looked at Bea. 'So he gave the job to you and Emily,' he said drily.

Bea bridled. 'Is that what you think we are? Prima donnas?'

'I don't know about that, but you're definitely not what I had in mind when I asked for someone suitable!'

She lifted a chin in what he already thought of as a familiar gesture. 'How do you know?'

Chase finished his beer and set the bottle back down on the table. 'I knew the moment I saw those shoes you were wearing,' he said. 'They didn't look very suitable to me!'

'Why do I let you talk me into these things?' Bea threw back the sheet and climbed into bed. '"*You'll love it,*" you said. "*It'll be an adventure,*" you said.'

'Well, it is,' said Emily, still brushing her hair.

'What's adventurous about getting up at four-thirty tomorrow morning?'

'Think of the romance, Bea! Feeding the men before they saddle up, waving them off to a hard day's work as they ride into the dawn…it'll be wonderful.'

'If you think it's so romantic, *you* can get up and cook breakfast for them!'

'You know I can't cook,' said Emily, 'and there's no point in both of us getting up, is there?'

She put down the hairbrush and began slathering moisturiser into her face and neck. She was always very strict about her beauty regime. Bea often thought it was the only area in which Emily had any discipline.

'I'm so glad we came, aren't you?' she was saying, rather muffled. 'It's even better than I thought it would be! You can practically feel the possibilities of romance buzzing in the air!'

Bea stared glumly at the ceiling. 'The only possibility I can see is the chance of being heartily bored for the next month.'

'You're not looking in the right place.'

'The stockmen's quarters, I suppose?'

'You've got to admit it looks promising!'

'*It?*'

'OK, he,' Emily conceded with a grin. 'Baz is to die for, isn't he?'

Bea considered the matter. 'I can see he's good-looking,' she said slowly, 'but he hasn't got a lot to say for himself, has he?'

Not that anyone round the table that night had had much to say much for themselves. Emily hadn't given them a chance. Thrilled with everything, and especially with Baz, she had been on sparkling form, flashing her bright blue eyes at the shy young men who had trooped in at seven o'clock and stood around awkwardly, mumbling names. They had all been dazzled.

All except Chase, thought Bea. She had a feeling that it would take a lot to dazzle him.

'Baz doesn't need all that superficial chatter,' Emily was saying as she got into bed. 'He just needs to sit there and I go all squirmy inside.' She heaved a dreamy sigh.

'I thought the governess always had a passionate affair with the master,' said Bea. 'What happened to your plan to be mistress of a million acres?'

'Oh, well, Nick's off the market if he's steamed off to Hollywood to fetch his wife, and that just leaves Chase, and I can't imagine having an affair with him, can you?'

The worst thing was that Bea could. 'Why not?' was all she said.

'He's a bit of a cold fish, isn't he?' said Emily, settling herself in bed. 'I tried to chat to him in the plane, but it was like trying to flirt with a brick wall. I don't see him having a passionate affair with anyone. He doesn't look like he knows what passion means!'

'No,' agreed Bea after the tiniest hesitation. She had thought much the same herself, but when she remembered his mouth, she wasn't quite so sure.

'He's too dour for me,' Emily went on. 'You'd never guess he was related to Nick. With a name like Sutherland he must be a throwback to some Scottish ancestors. He could do with lightening up a bit, if you ask me. It might make him less intimidating.'

'I wouldn't say that he was *intimidating,*' said Bea, thinking about the way Chase had sat at the kitchen table and told her about his brother's marriage. He hadn't been friendly exactly, but he hadn't been quite as dismissive either.

'That's because you don't intimidate easily,' said Emily. 'Anyway, I think he likes you.'

Bea sat up and stared across at her friend. 'How do you work that out?'

'I noticed him watching you at dinner.'

So Emily had noticed too. Bea had wondered if she was imagining it, or if it had just been chance that whenever she looked up her eyes had encountered Chase's cool blue ones. His expression had been impossible to read, but she didn't think it had been one of liking.

'He was probably just wondering how soon he could get rid of us,' she said with an unsuccessful laugh.

'He'd better not have been,' said Emily, reaching out to switch off the bedside light. 'I've just found the man of my dreams. I've got no intention of leaving on Chase Sutherland's say so!'

When the alarm went off at four-thirty the next morning, Bea sat bolt upright. She had been sleeping uneasily, dreading the moment when it would go off, and now she groped for the clock and switched it off quickly.

Rubbing her eyes, she switched on the little lamp by her bed. There had been no need to worry about waking Emily. She was sound asleep, one arm flung above her head. You could have conducted a rousing rendition of the 'Hallelujah Chorus' under spotlights without her so much as stirring.

It was pitch dark outside and the early morning air was unpleasantly chilly. Bea dressed, shivering. Nobody had told her it could be cold in the outback, and she hadn't brought a jumper with her. The best she could do was a T-shirt and chinos. Hugging her arms together, Bea cast a last, longing glance at her warm bed and crept down the darkened corridor to the kitchen.

The overhead lights were very bright when she switched them on and she had to screw up her eyes until she got used to them. It didn't stop her feeling any less of a zombie, though. Her body kept insisting that it had missed out on a good four hours sleep to which it was accustomed, and refused to co-operate as Bea moved blearily around the kitchen, putting on the kettle, laying the table and setting out cereals, and jams for toast.

Chase appeared just before five, and something about the sight of him jerked Bea abruptly awake. His presence seemed to fill the kitchen. Under the harsh overhead light, his features were stronger and more definite than she remembered, but his eyes were as cool and keen as ever.

As they swept over her, Bea was suddenly acutely conscious that her hair was rioting uncontrollably around her head, that she hadn't so much as washed her face and that she was bug-eyed from lack of sleep. She eyed him with resentment. He made it look as if it was perfectly normal to have breakfast in the middle of the night.

Chase was glad to see that she was up and appeared to

have breakfast under control, although she looked less than her usual immaculate self. There was a cross, tousled air to her this morning, and he had a sudden, disturbing awareness that she had just got out of bed.

So had every cook that had ever got up to make breakfast for the men, he reminded himself, but he had never been able to picture any of the others waking and stretching and throwing back the covers with such unsettling clarity. The thought made him frown.

'You're shivering,' he noticed abruptly.

'Of course I'm shivering,' snapped Bea, beginning to slice bread for toast. 'It's absolutely freezing in here!'

Chase was relieved to be irritated by her wild exaggeration. It was easier than picturing her getting out of bed.

'If you're cold, put a sweater on.'

'I haven't got a sweater.'

'You must have something. What was in that enormous suitcase you dragged with you yesterday?'

'I was *told* that the outback was hot,' she grumbled. 'Nobody said there was a danger of frostbite when you got out of bed in the morning.'

Chase sighed irritably and went out. He reappeared a couple of minutes later with a faded sweatshirt. 'Put that on,' he said, shoving it into her hands.

Taken aback by the brusque gesture, Bea stood holding it. 'Whose is this?'

'Mine,' he said curtly. 'It'll be too big for you, but at least it might stop you shivering like a whippet!'

He lifted an eyebrow when Bea hesitated. 'What's the matter? Isn't it your colour?' he asked sarcastically to cover his mixed feelings about the thought of her wearing his clothes.

Bea flushed. She had been thinking how intimate it would be to put on something of his, but she couldn't tell him that.

She pulled the sweatshirt over her head. It was clean and

warm, and smelt oddly familiar, as if she wore his shirts every day. As Chase had said, it was much too big for her, but she rolled up the sleeves, very conscious of how many times he must have pulled on the same sweatshirt, of where the material he had worn against his skin was now brushing against hers.

Don't be ridiculous, she told herself. It's just a sweatshirt.

But she still felt stupidly shy as she glanced up from rolling the second sleeve. 'Thank you,' she said belatedly. 'I'll let you have it back when I've washed it.'

'You'd better keep it,' said Chase brusquely. 'We can't have you freezing to death every morning.'

They looked at each other, then away, and then, as if their eyes had a will of their own, back again. Bea was very aware of the noise of the kettle coming up to the boil, of the faint hum of the fridges in the background, which only seemed to emphasise the odd silence between them. It was broken, to her intense relief, by the sound of boots clumping up the wooden steps onto the veranda, and she turned away to busy herself putting on the toast as the stockmen came in.

Breakfast was a largely silent affair, with conversation restricted to what needed to be done that day. The men were taciturn at the best of times, Bea guessed, and she was glad of it at this time of the morning. It was bad enough having to fry eggs for a bunch of hungry men and serve it with grilled steak without having to cope with cheeriness as well.

'We'll be back for smoko at ten-thirty,' said Chase as they trooped out.

Who was Smoko? Bea wondered. One of the stockmen? They all seemed to have funny names like that. But surely they had all been there, eating their way stolidly through steak and eggs. Maybe it was a dog?

'Smoko?' she echoed cautiously.

Chase looked at her baffled expression. 'Smoko,' he repeated very slowly and clearly as if talking to an idiot. 'The men come back for a cup of tea and a smoke in the middle of the morning.'

'Oh, a *break!*' Her face cleared.

'Right,' said Chase drily. 'If you could make some biscuits or a cake for "break",' he said, putting inverted commas around the word and mimicking her English accent, 'that would be good.'

Bea had been planning to go back to bed and baking was the last thing on her mind, but when she looked at her watch she saw that there was still hours to go before half past ten. With any luck she would be able to catch up on some sleep, have a shower, do her hair and still have time to knock up a quick batch of biscuits.

'Fine,' she said, catching herself on a yawn.

'We'll see you later then.'

Chase took down his hat and stood with it hanging from his hand for a moment as he glanced back at Bea. She was holding an armful of plates, and had succumbed to another huge yawn. Her brown hair was messy, and smothered in his sweatshirt she looked a completely different girl from the one who had stuck her nose in the air at Mackinnon airport.

'Thanks for breakfast,' he said abruptly.

The screen door clattered shut behind him.

Bea was still staring after him, trying to work out what that odd expression on his face had meant, when a suspicious voice behind her made her jump.

'What are you doing?'

It was Chloe, looking deceptively angelic in pink pyjamas covered in teddy bears.

'I'm not doing anything,' said Bea, eyeing her with equal wariness. She carried the plates over to the sink and dumped them down.

'You had a funny smile on your face.'

Even though she knew it was nonsense, Bea felt a flush creeping up her cheeks. That was the trouble with children. They always made you feel such a fool.

'Can I have a drink?' Chloe went on without waiting for a reply.

Bea's heart sank even further. Where was Emily when she needed her? When she looked at the clock on the wall, it wasn't even six o'clock.

'Do you always get up this early?' she asked.

Chloe looked at her as if she didn't know what she was talking about, which she probably didn't. No doubt six o'clock counted as a lie-in around here.

Now what was she going to do? She couldn't go back to bed and leave the little girl on her own. She couldn't even have a shower until Emily woke up, she realised.

In the end, she made Chloe some breakfast, and sat down to drink a cup of coffee with her. It was light by then, and Bea was beginning to feel that she had been up for hours.

'Why are you wearing Uncle Chase's jumper?' Chloe demanded suddenly.

Bea had forgotten the sweatshirt. She looked down at herself a little self-consciously. 'He lent it to me because I was cold.'

Chloe digested this, trailing her spoon in her cereal. 'Are you Uncle Chase's new girlfriend?'

*New* girlfriend? Hmm, thought Bea.

'No,' she said, putting her mug down, carefully casual. 'What makes you think that?'

'You're the cook.'

'Yes?' Bea suddenly realised that Chloe thought that she had answered the question. 'Is the cook always his girlfriend?' she laughed.

'Sometimes.'

Bea stopped laughing abruptly. 'I see,' she said, inexplicably ruffled.

She picked up her mug again, determined not to show

any more interest, and Chloe went back to her breakfast, apparently satisfied.

'So, was the last cook his girlfriend?' Bea heard herself ask.

'Who?'

Bea sucked in her breath. 'Uncle Chase. Was the cook who was here before me his girlfriend?'

Chloe frowned with the effort of memory. 'I think so.'

Somehow this wasn't the answer Bea wanted to hear. 'Well, I'm not,' she said as if Chloe had accused her of something.

'Is Emily?'

'No!' Bea didn't want to explain even to herself why the thought of Emily and Chase together was out of the question. 'No,' she said again, more quietly, 'she's not his girlfriend either. I'm afraid Uncle Chase is going to have to do without a girlfriend for a while.'

She got abruptly to her feet. 'You finish your breakfast. I'm going to clear up.'

Unaccountably cross, she began to clear the table with much clattering of plates and cutlery. She was about to scrape the last pieces of toast savagely into the bin when Chloe stopped her, shocked.

'We can give those to the chooks!'

She insisted on taking Bea down to see the hens in their run as soon as she had finished her cereal. At the sound of the gate being opened the hens came running, tumbling over themselves in their eagerness to find the scraps that the little girl scattered for them.

Bea calmed down as she watched the chooks, and waited for Chloe to collect the eggs. Really, she must be even more tired than she thought. What did it matter to her if Chase was used to the kitchen staff throwing themselves at his feet? If he wanted to be that undiscriminating, that was his problem! As long as he didn't expect her to fall in with tradition, he could do what he liked.

Chloe found five eggs and presented them proudly in the bowl for her to admire. 'We could make something for smoko,' Bea suggested. 'What do you think the men would like?'

'Chase likes rock cakes best.'

'Then let's make those,' she said, thinking that rock cakes would be an easy place for Chloe to start.

Chloe was thrilled at the idea of helping Bea to cook, and she chattered all the way back to the homestead, her wariness vanquished.

By the time Emily appeared, yawning, the rock cakes were in the oven and Bea and Chloe were both liberally dusted with flour. Bea was desperate to have a shower and wash her hair, and she was taking off her apron and leaving instructions about when to take the rock cakes out when Chase came in.

'You're early!' she said without thinking and then was furious with herself. It sounded as if she had been watching the clock, waiting for him to return. 'I mean, it's only quarter to ten. I didn't think you'd be back until half past.'

She was just making matters worse. Chase raised a faint eyebrow, but said only that he had come back to make a couple of phone calls. 'The men will be back at ten-thirty.'

'Chase! Chase!' Chloe was tugging at this hand. 'We made rock cakes! I said they were your favourites, so Bea said we should make those.'

'Oh?' Chase looked at Bea, who was still half in, half out of her apron.

'Aha!' said Emily wickedly. 'Trying to curry favour with the boss, eh, Bea?'

Bea set her teeth and finally managed to wrench the stupid apron over her head. 'I just asked what everyone would like.'

'Chloe's right, I do like rock cakes.' The keen gaze rested on her face and Bea was horribly conscious of her dirty hair. Involuntarily, she lifted her hand to a smudge of flour on her cheek and wiped it off. 'I'll look forward to smoko,' Chase said in his cool way, and disappeared in the direction of the office.

Leaving Emily in charge, Bea had a shower, washed her hair and dried it carefully. When she had finished, it fell straight and shining, swinging below her jaw the way she liked it.

Bea and her hair had a complex relationship. It was so wildly curly that it had to be washed and blow-dried into shape every morning or it looked awful, and Bea had long ago established the intricate connection between her hair and her well-being. Endless people had mocked her for the time she spent forcing her curls into a neat style, but she was used to it now. If her hair was out of control, so was her life, and that was all there was to it. The whole process took hours out of her life every week, but Bea told herself it was worth it.

At least now she felt human again, and would be once more the calm, composed person she knew herself to be the next time that she saw Chase.

Although, as things turned out, she might as well have spared herself the effort, Bea reflected as she carried a big metal pot of tea out onto the kitchen veranda where the men could have their smoko without taking off their dusty boots. Chase took a rock cake that Chloe handed carefully round on a plate, but he hardly seemed to notice Bea as she poured out the tea. He talked about bores and dams and fences and when they would start to muster, and gave her absolutely no opportunity to impress him with her cool control.

Aggrieved in a way she couldn't begin to explain, Bea sat down as far away from him as possible but, although she tried to ignore him, her eyes kept sliding towards him as he sat on the bench, leaning his elbows on his knees, his mug clasped lightly between his hands. He was listening to one of the stockmen, his expression intent. Their conversation was unintelligible to Bea, but it seemed to mean something to Chase, for he nodded every now and then, or put in a quiet word.

His sleeves were rolled up above his wrists and his shirt was open at the neck. Bea could see the strong column of his throat, the firm set of his mouth, and she found herself wondering about the girls who had made smoko for these men before her. How many of them had been carrying on a relationship with Chase? He obviously hadn't ignored *them!*

Chase drained his tea and stood up. It was the signal for all the other men to get up as well, and they headed back out into the heat and dust. Chase went down the wooden steps, too, but he turned at the bottom to look back up at Bea as he settled his hat on his head.

'Good rock cakes,' he said with a smile.

Quite without wanting to, Bea found herself smiling back until she caught Emily's interested eye and stopped abruptly. 'Thanks,' she said in a curt voice, and began collecting up the mugs. By the time she looked up again, Chase had gone.

'I told you he liked you,' said Emily.

Her hands full of mugs, Bea hooked the screen door open with her foot. 'He likes my rock cakes,' she said dismissively. 'And that's all.'

It took more than a smile and a tossed compliment about her baking to win her over, she reminded herself. If Chase thought she was going to be like all the other cooks who had apparently fallen into his arms, he would soon discover that he was mistaken!

By six o'clock, Bea was exhausted. She was used to hard work, but she certainly wasn't used to getting up at four-thirty, or to the heat, or to the constant background noise of Chloe asking unanswerable questions.

Why is your hair straight?

Why is England far away?

Why, why, why, until Bea wanted to scream. It was a huge relief when Emily, having taken a typically relaxed view of her duties all day, finally roused herself to take Chloe off for a bath. Bea contemplated sitting down to savour the blissful silence, but she was afraid that if she did she might never get up again.

'Chloe is desperate for you to read her a story,' Emily announced coming into the kitchen a bit later. 'Is everything under control in here?'

'Yes, but—'

'Oh, good. I'll just nip and have a shower, then. Baz is taking me out in his ute this evening.'

Bea undid her apron with a sigh.

Chloe was sitting up in bed in her pink pyjamas, books strewn around her. 'I'm only reading one,' warned Bea, sensing danger.

Of course Chloe chose the longest, and she was unimpressed when Bea sat down on the other bed. 'Don't you *know* how to read a story?' she demanded witheringly. She made Bea sit on her bed, and tucked herself comfortably in beside her. 'This is how Mum reads me a story,' she confided.

Bea glanced down at the small shining head. Chloe was extraordinarily self-possessed but she must miss her mother. What would it be like, having a mother like Georgie Grainger? she wondered. Georgie would always be warm and beautiful, and she probably smelt of expensive perfume and not of roasting meat and onions.

She probably read wonderful stories too, Bea thought glumly. An actress like Georgie would be able to do all the voices properly.

Oh, well, she would just have to do. She had never said that she was Mary Poppins.

She was doing all right, too, until Chase came in, and she faltered in mid-sentence.

He had had a shower, and his brown hair was slicked back against his head. He wasn't a particularly big man, but he seemed enormous amongst the little furniture in Chloe's room.

'I'll wait till you finish,' he said, and sat down on the spare bed to listen.

Bea immediately lost the thread of the story and started stumbling over the most basic words. Clearing her throat firmly, she started the page again, but it was hard to concentrate with Chase sitting opposite her like that. He wasn't exactly smiling, but the creases at the edges of his eyes had deepened and one corner of his mouth looked as if it might be about to twitch upwards.

It was very distracting.

She tried skipping a few pages to get to the end, but Chloe was having none of it.

'You missed a page!'

'Did I?' Bea gritted her teeth and let Chloe turn the page back. 'Silly me.'

Chase's eyes rested appreciatively on Bea's face. She looked a little pink, although whether from cooking or frustration with the slow progress of the story he couldn't tell. It was pretty obvious that she wasn't used to children, but Chloe seemed to have taken to her for some reason. Chase would have expected her to have preferred Emily, who was pretty and lively, while Bea was wary and utterly out of place.

Not that she was exactly plain, Chase allowed to himself. She was attractive enough if you liked your women smart and tense. His gaze rested on her face. The straight brown hair was hooked behind her ears, and long lashes shielded the strange golden eyes. She absolutely wasn't his type, he decided. Too uptight and British for him.

In spite of that mouth, which wasn't uptight at all.

At last Bea struggled to the end of the story and closed the book with relief.

'More! More!' cried Chloe, but Chase was firm.

'No, you're going to sleep now.'

For a perilous moment, Chloe's bottom lip stuck out rebelliously, but a glance at her uncle's implacable face made her clamber reluctantly into bed. Chase bent to kiss her goodnight, tickling her until her cross little face dissolved into giggles.

Getting to her feet in relief, Bea was surprised at how much Chloe obviously adored him. He didn't seem like a man who would be good with children. He wasn't exactly the cuddly type.

Even if he did have a nice smile.

Just the thought of Chase's smile gave Bea an odd feeling inside, and when she saw him grin down at Chloe, she turned abruptly for the door.

'I'd better go and check on supper.'

# CHAPTER FOUR

'I HAVEN'T kissed you yet!' Chloe protested. 'You haven't kissed me goodnight.'

Chase moved out of the way, but Bea still had to brush past him to bend down to Chloe. He smelt really nice after his shower, and something tightened inside her as Chloe wound her arms around her neck and planted a smacking kiss on her cheek.

'Goodnight.' Absurdly flattered, Bea kissed her back.

She made as if to straighten, but Chloe's grip tightened. 'Another one!'

'No, we've all had a kiss now. Your uncle's kissed you, and you've kissed me.'

'You haven't kissed Uncle Chase,' Chloe pointed out with devastating logic, and stupidly, Bea felt herself colour.

'We're not going to bed,' she heard herself say. 'I mean, not yet.' God, that was even worse! 'That is we will go to bed, but not together,' she said firmly.

Chloe was doing her best to follow. 'Will you kiss him later, then?' she asked.

'Go to sleep, Chloe,' said her uncle calmly, and held the door open with what Bea was sure was mocking courtesy. 'Never get into an argument with a five-year-old,' he said, and, yes, that was *definitely* mockery in his voice!

Bea stalked past him, burningly conscious of what an idiot she must have sounded. What one earth had possessed her to start wittering on about going to bed, with or without him? It was all Chloe's fault for putting the idea of kissing Chase into her mind. It wasn't that she wanted to kiss him—God forbid! No, it was just that the thought had thrown her there for an instant.

Chloe could whistle for a story tomorrow, Bea decided.

Coming into the kitchen to make himself some coffee later that evening, Chase found Bea wearily drying a saucepan. Her hair swung forward to hide her face as she bent to put the lid away in a lower cupboard, and gleamed in the harsh overhead light. She was wearing a red dress with tiny little straps that left most of her shoulders bare, a distraction that had irritated Chase throughout supper when he had found it hard to concentrate on anything else.

Bea had to be the only cook they had ever had who dressed for dinner, he thought, exasperated. It was as if she was determined not to fit in. Chase could have told her she didn't need to put on a dress to look out of place. Everything she did made it obvious not only that she didn't belong, would never belong, but that she had absolutely no intention of belonging in the outback. If she hated it so much, why didn't she just leave? Chase wondered crossly.

But then she straightened as she saw him, pushing her hair behind her ears in what was already a familiar gesture, and he saw how tired she looked. She might be snooty, but she was a hard worker, he had to give her that.

'Why isn't Emily giving you a hand?' he asked roughly.

'She's not here as a cook.'

In spite of the fact that she had been furious when Emily had slipped out with Baz and the other stockmen the moment Chase had disappeared into his office, Bea felt obliged to defend her friend. It was a matter of loyalty, she told herself. Or habit.

Chase frowned. *She* wasn't there as a governess, but it hadn't stopped her spending time with Chloe, he found himself thinking. Now guess who was going to have to help her?

Picking up a big pot, he began drying it crossly with a tea towel. 'Where is Emily, anyway? Or need I ask?'

'I think she's with Baz,' said Bea with restraint, although

she wasn't sure why she was bothering to be careful. It wasn't as if Emily had made any effort to disguise her obsession.

'I hope she doesn't mind being the latest in a very long line.'

The dismissive note in his voice made Bea's hackles rise. 'Oh?' she said sweetly. 'I understood that it was you who was used to working your way through the long line!'

To her annoyance, Chase looked amused, rather than embarrassed, or guilty or defensive. Instead of the way he *ought* to have looked, in fact.

'Who told you that?' he asked.

'Chloe seems to think that being a cook here automatically confers me with the position of your girlfriend!'

'And you're basing all your assumptions on the word of a five-year-old?'

Bea's lips tightened. She hated the way Chase always made her feel stupid. 'Is it true?'

'That you're my girlfriend?' Chase lifted a mocking eyebrow. 'Don't you think you'd know if you were?'

'It might be such a horrible thought that I've blocked it out,' snapped Bea, but to her fury, he only laughed.

And that made him look disconcertingly attractive, which made her even crosser.

'I think Chloe might be thinking of Kirsty,' said Chase.

Kirsty? How very cute.

'Or possibly Sue,' he went on, still drying his pot. 'Or do I mean Sophie?'

Bea stared suspiciously at him. Was he pulling her leg? 'Or Sara?'

'I'm surprised you can remember the names of all of them,' she said, more than a little piqued.

'I can't,' said Chase, still with that unsettling glint in his eye that made it impossible to know whether to take him seriously or not. 'Do you have any idea how many English girls have come out to Calulla Downs over the past few years? They're all just like you and Emily, thrilled with the whole idea of the outback and even more thrilled with the idea of marrying a million acres.'

'*Not* like me then!' said Bea, ruffling up immediately. 'I've felt lots of things since I arrived yesterday, but thrilled is not one of them!'

'Like Emily, then,' amended Chase. 'I could tell as soon as I saw her that she was going to be like all the others. She thinks it's all going to be so romantic, doesn't she? They all think that. They think they're going to ride around on horses, and lend a hand with mustering every now and then, and most of all, they think they're going to land themselves a guy with an Akubra and a property half the size of England that they can write home and boast about.'

*Exactly* what Emily had thought, in fact.

'Why not get an Australian girl to cook if we're such a terrible problem for you?'

'Easier said than done,' said Chase. 'Most Australian girls have got a more realistic idea of the outback, for a start. They know how hard life can be out here, and how lonely sometimes. It takes nearly two hours to drive to the nearest pub, and that's not exactly buzzing. If you're looking for night life, this isn't the place to come.'

'No kidding,' said Bea glumly, looking at the tea towel in her hand. Half past nine. She could be tucked up in a bar, right now, or at a movie, or planning a party. And instead she was washing dishes a hundred miles from anywhere.

'English girls are so bound up in their romantic ideas that they don't think about things like that,' Chase went on as he reached for another pot. 'And as soon as they clapped eyes on Nick, that was it. He's not just the eldest son, he looks the part, and they'd all have a little fantasy about being the next Mrs Sutherland.'

'No doubt Nick was just fighting them all off!' said Bea sarcastically.

'Oh, it had its advantages for him, all right. It was worse for us. The quality of the food would go down dramatically as the girl in question realised that Nick wasn't serious, then we'd have tears, and the next thing, she'd have left and then another one would have taken her place.'

'It must have been a great relief for you when Nick got married,' commented Bea drily.

'It might be a relief for Nick, but not much else has changed. The girls still come, but now if they want to be Mrs Sutherland there's only one option...'

'They fall in love with *you?*' She stared at him with unflattering incredulity.

'Who said anything about love?' said Chase with a slight edge.

'So now you're the one who has to beat off hordes of eager women?' Bea hoped that she sounded suitably amused, as if she couldn't care less about all those girls throwing themselves at him.

Hold on, that 'as if' wasn't right and, come to think of it, 'sounded' wasn't that convincing, either. Bea back-tracked mentally...she *was* amused because she *couldn't* care less. Yes, that was better. No 'as if' about it.

Anyway, it looked as if Chase had got the right message. He was looking quite nettled, she noticed smugly.

'It's not always a question of beating them off,' he said.

Bea's smugness vanished abruptly. 'You sleep with them?' she said, and then winced inwardly at the note of outraged missionary in her voice. Of *course* he slept with them! What did she think, that he was saving himself for the right woman?

Chase raised an eyebrow. It was his turn to be amused now. 'Only the pretty ones,' he said.

Bea turned away and wrung out the cloth she had been using to wipe down the surfaces with unnecessary vigour. 'How discriminating of you!' she said tartly. 'How long do you give them before you dump them? A month? Six weeks?'

'It's not a question of dumping anybody. I've always made it clear that I've got no intention of marrying someone who'd be bored stiff before a year was out. It's been bad enough for Nick with Georgie, and she grew up on a station and should have known what she was getting into when she married him.'

Chase hung his damp tea towel over a cupboard door. 'No, I'm not tying myself to an unsuitable woman. I like a lot of the girls who come here. Most of them are good fun. It's not as if I've taken a vow of celibacy, or any of them are unwilling, so we have a good time while they're here and then they go. Six weeks is usually more than enough for them to realise not only that I'm not going to come through with a ring, but that they're not really cut out for the outback after all.'

'It must be a disappointment to you this time, then. Emily isn't the slightest bit interested in you!'

'No, life has been a lot easier since Baz arrived,' Chase agreed infuriatingly. 'Of course, he doesn't come with a property attached, so he tends to have better luck with the romantics like Emily. It's a pity he's leaving,' he went on, leaning back against the worktop and folding his arms. 'We'll have to make sure we get someone just as handsome to replace him.'

Bea was outraged at his cynical attitude. 'I hope Baz is leaving soon,' she said tight-lipped.

'In a couple of weeks. Why?'

'Because then Emily will want to leave too, and we can go back to Sydney. I hate to break with tradition,' she went on sarcastically, 'but I can tell you now that I have absolutely no intention of sleeping with you, falling in love with you or wanting to marry you!'

'Now that sounds like a challenge.' Chase straightened and walked across the kitchen to Bea, who found herself backing into the corner. He put one arm on either side of her, not touching her but effectively pinning her against the units. '*Is* it a challenge?' he asked softly.

Bea's heart was pounding. He was very close. She could see the lines fanning out from his eyes, the rough, masculine texture of his skin, the cool set of his mouth.

Oh, dear, she wished she hadn't noticed his mouth. Now she couldn't drag her eyes away from it.

She knew that all she had to do was to push his arm away and step past him, but somehow she couldn't move. Moistening her lips surreptitiously, she managed, 'I'd call it a promise rather than a challenge,' but her voice was uneven and her knees felt ridiculously weak.

And she still couldn't take her eyes from his mouth.

Unfairly, Chase smiled. 'Let's see, shall we?' he said, and his mouth came down on hers.

Bea just had time to brace herself for a hard, ruthless kiss which never came. Instead his mouth was warm and tantalising and so shockingly persuasive that the breath caught in her throat, parting her lips beneath his even as she closed her eyes against a startling jolt of response.

Before she quite knew how it had happened, she was kissing him back, and when Chase pulled her into his arms, she didn't even resist. His body was hard and exciting, and her hands slid over his shoulders as if they had a mind and a will of their own. More than she had, anyway. Bea's bones were dissolving, her head spinning, any will she had once had lost to the wicked excitement of his kiss, to the taste of his mouth and the strength of his hand sliding up her spine.

When Chase's lips left hers at last, Bea gasped with a mixture of protest and pleasure, only to shiver as they travelled deliciously along her jaw to the lobe of her ear.

'That was definitely a challenge,' he murmured, nibbling it gently, 'and what's more, I think I might accept it.'

Still drifting in the shivery excitement of his kiss, it took

Bea a few seconds to assimilate this. The languid smile was wiped from her face as she realised what he had said, and she jerked herself out of his arms, her mind reeling.

What was she *doing?* Well, she knew what she had been doing, but not why. How on earth had she ended up kissing Chase Sutherland? She didn't even like the man…although who would have guessed that someone so brusque and businesslike could kiss like that?

Bea wrenched her drifting mind back to reality and pulled herself together with a huge effort. Great kisser he might be, but she certainly wasn't planning on falling into his arms like all of her predecessors. Well, not again, anyway.

'I wouldn't,' she said unsteadily. 'You'll lose.'

'Maybe, but it might be fun trying,' said Chase, and he smiled one of those smiles that had such an alarming effect on Bea's legs. 'Want some coffee?'

'What?'

Thrown as much by the smile as by the complete change of subject, Bea stared at him as he filled the kettle, clicked it on, and resumed his position leaning back against the units as if absolutely nothing had happened.

'I could make you some tea if you prefer,' he offered.

'Nothing, thank you,' said Bea stiffly.

She was still tingling from that kiss, and wondered if she was in shock. She certainly felt very odd. Almost like flinging herself back into his arms and begging him to kiss her again. Which must mean that she was unhinged. Or coming down with a very nasty virus.

'I think I'll go to bed,' she said. 'Alone,' she added, just in case he thought that she was inviting him along too. The worst thing was that she wouldn't be able to blame him if he *did* think that, not after the way she had melted into him and kissed him back.

Chase's eyes rested on her face, light, amused, unsettling

as hell. 'Suit yourself,' was all he said as he turned away to make his coffee.

Now look what she had done! Bea tossed and turned irritably in her bed. She was exhausted, but she couldn't sleep. How could she sleep after being kissed like that?

If only it hadn't felt quite so good. Why couldn't Chase go in for wet, slobbery kisses, or be one of those guys who set about your mouth as if they were vacuuming it? Then she wouldn't be lying awake like this, wondering about all those other girls he had kissed in the same kitchen, girls who would know what else he might be surprisingly good at…

Bea rolled over and punched her pillow into shape. It wasn't that she was interested in the idea of sleeping with Chase. She wasn't. Not in the slightest. *Especially* not knowing that for him she was just a challenge.

It was just that now that she had started to think about it, she couldn't *stop* thinking about what it might be like.

The more Bea thought about it, the more she liked the idea that she might be going down with a virus. It would explain the dizziness and the trembling legs and the fact that she hadn't been thinking clearly. So, really, she wasn't responsible for kissing Chase back like that at all. She wasn't attracted to him at all, she was just sick.

Oh, yes, it was definitely a virus.

Bea had just dropped off to sleep at last when Emily came in and woke her up. 'Are you asleep?'

'Yes,' mumbled Bea.

'I just had to tell you…I'm in love!'

'Great.' Bea turned over to bury her face in her pillow.

'Baz is everything I've always wanted!' Oblivious to Bea's attempts to go back to sleep, Emily chattered on about Baz as she undressed and jumped into bed. 'I'm sorry I had to leave you with that grumpy Chase all evening, though,' she went on as an obvious afterthought. 'Was it really boring?'

Bea was lying with her back turned pointedly to Emily, but at that her eyes snapped open and she stared unseeingly at the wall. Chase, boring? She thought about the feel of his hands, the touch of his lips, the way he had smiled against her mouth as he pulled her closer, the glint in his eyes as he had let her go.

'No,' was all she said.

'Oh, good.' Emily snuggled down into bed and switched off the light. 'Then you won't mind if I spend tomorrow night with Baz again, will you?'

Breakfast was at five thirty the next morning, which meant that Bea got a whole half hour extra in bed. Not that it made much difference. It was still dark, and still a completely unnatural time to wake up as far as Bea was concerned. When the alarm clock went off, she had to force herself to throw back the covers and stumble into her clothes.

It was still cold, too.

Bea's eye fell on the sweatshirt hanging over the back of the chair where she had left it yesterday when the sun was beating down outside and she hadn't been able to imagine ever being cold again. Chase's sweatshirt. The sight of it was enough to bring back the memory of that kiss the previous evening in a rush that did more than the chill night air to wake her up.

She hesitated for a moment, and then pulled it over her head, tugging it down crossly as she tried to ignore the tiny shiver of familiarity at the scent of him that still lingered in the fabric. She was not going to freeze to death just because Chase had kissed her.

In fact, she wasn't going to dignify what had happened with any comment at all. The last thing she wanted was for Chase to imagine that she had spent half the night reliving the entire experience, even if she had. No, far better to just ignore the whole topic.

It was a good decision, but it didn't stop Bea's heart

giving a tiny jerk when Chase walked into the kitchen. Quickly, she lifted her chin and turned her head away, although she needn't have bothered. It was pretty obvious that Chase had decided to ignore the entire issue too.

He was talking about some e-mail he had had from Nick, something about visitors, and making beds, but Bea wasn't listening. She was considering the possibility that perhaps Chase wasn't ignoring the kiss at all. Perhaps he had kissed so many cooks in the kitchen that she had just blurred into the memory of all those others.

Bea stabbed at the steaks under the grill, distinctly disgruntled at the thought. OK, so she had wanted to ignore the fact that they had kissed in this very room the night before, but not if it meant Chase simply wiping the whole incident from his mind! It was his fault, after all. She might have kissed him back, but he had kissed her first. By rights, he should be on his knees with a grovelling apology.

For a moment, Bea let herself imagine it. It would be a perfect opportunity for her to pretend that she couldn't understand what he was making such a fuss about, and that she was the one who had forgotten all about it. 'Kiss? What kiss?' she would say, and then she might even laugh. 'You don't really call that a *kiss,* do you?'

She could picture her own expression of amused superiority perfectly. Chase was the trouble. Try as she might, she just couldn't imagine him on his knees, grovelling, or making a fuss about anything.

Shame.

'So is that OK with you?'

Chase's voice broke into her thoughts, and she looked up from the grill. 'What?'

He sighed. 'Have you heard a word I've been saying, Bea?'

'Something about an e-mail?' she tried.

Chase controlled his irritation with an effort and started again. 'Nick e-mailed me last night. He does all the arrangements for Georgie's paying guests, and he'd forgotten to remind me that another lot are due to arrive today. Two couples, apparently, so there'll be four more for supper. Can you cope with that?'

'Of course I can cope,' said Bea, offended.

'At least they're driving themselves, so they won't need to be picked up, but I could have done without them today,' Chase went on. 'I want to check the bores out at Kilungra, and we'll be gone all day. Which reminds me, can you put together some sandwiches? Oh, and something for smoko.'

'Oh, sure, it's not as if I've got anything else to do, just cook breakfast for nine, plan supper for thirteen and now you want sandwiches and biscuits as well!'

'You just said you could cope.'

'I can cope,' said Bea. 'I just appreciate a bit of notice.'

Chase was unmoved. 'You can do the sandwiches while we're having breakfast,' he said.

Bea was glad to see the back of them for the day. She sent them off with a big packet of sandwiches made with leftover roast, and the last of the rock cakes, which meant that she would have to make something else for the guests when they arrived. In spite of her grumbling, she even had time to offer to make up a Thermos of tea, but Chase shook his head.

'We'll just boil up a billy,' he said, and Bea wasn't about to give him the satisfaction of asking what *that* meant.

As soon as he had gone, though, the homestead felt strangely empty. Even when Chloe, and later Emily, appeared, Bea couldn't shake off the feeling of absence, and she kept listening out for the sound of his boots on the veranda steps, or the tell-tale creak of the screen door.

It wasn't that she was missing him, of course. It just seemed like a long day without the men coming back for smoko or lunch, and the three girls felt lost and a bit silly sitting at one end of the big table.

And it wasn't as if she didn't have anything to do. Bea

hardly drew breath all day. She ran around making beds, cleaning bedrooms, picking flowers, knocking up a cake and a supply of flapjacks, feeding chickens and dogs, sweeping the veranda, and preparing the meal for that night. Chloe and Emily offered occasional help and advice, but they had identically low boredom thresholds, and in the end Bea found it easier to do most things herself.

The paying guests arrived in the late afternoon. All Americans, they were initially thrown to be greeted at the archetypal Australian homestead by the unmistakably English Bea, but by the time she had shown them to their rooms and given them tea on the veranda, they were ready to be charmed by everything. They told Bea that they were fulfilling a lifelong dream to drive around Australia, but that this was the first time they had ventured into the outback.

'I was nervous about camping,' Joan confided with a guilty laugh. 'Ben laughs at me about it, but you hear so much about spiders and snakes in the outback, don't you?'

Bea gulped. She hadn't thought about spiders, let alone snakes. Why hadn't she remembered them when she was trying to convince Emily that she didn't want to come?

'Then a friend of a friend who knows Georgie Grainger recommended Calulla Downs. It sounded just what we wanted, to stop travelling for a few days and share in life on a cattle station but in comfort, and I must say everything is even better than we expected.' Joan beamed. 'It's certainly worth that long drive. We have plenty of isolated ranches in the States, but this place is something else again, isn't it?'

'It certainly is,' said Bea drily, marvelling that anyone would actually pay to come out there.

Supper that night was a noisy, jolly affair with so many people around the table. The Americans were as chatty as Emily, and so pleased to be there that Chase didn't have to do much to keep the conversation going.

It meant that he was able to watch Bea at the other end of the table instead. She wasn't *that* pretty, he told himself. She had a fine-boned face, with strong features and clear skin that flushed easily, but the most distinctive thing about her was those strange golden eyes.

There was something odd about her hair too. Chase frowned slightly, trying to work out what it was, but then shrugged mentally and pushed the problem aside. She was resting her chin on one palm, smiling at something Joan's husband saying to her, and Chase marvelled again at how a smile transformed her face, lighting it up in a way that made his heart tighten strangely.

She was dressed up as usual, still pretending that she was in Sydney, no doubt, but it was a different dress to-night, something cream and classy with a demure neckline. Chase was glad of it. He had spent most of the day trying to forget how she had felt in the red dress the night before.

His palms felt twitchy, as if he could still feel the silky material slipping over her body beneath his hands, and he swallowed. She looked so cool, but last night her mouth had been warm and soft, and she had felt so good...

It had been a mistake, Chase told himself firmly. He shouldn't have kissed her, but something about her had got under his skin in a way none of the other girls he had known had. He didn't want Bea going the same way as them. They needed a cook at Calulla Downs and, with Nick away, he couldn't afford the time to replace her. If Bea threw down any more challenges like the one last night, he would ignore them.

Well, he would try.

'Here.' Chase handed Bea a mug of coffee and sat down beside her in one of the wicker chairs.

'Thanks.'

Bea wasn't quite sure what was going on. After their long drive, the guests had opted for an early night, but Chase had caught Emily just as she and Baz were hoping that they could do the same. He had insisted that she help Bea with the washing up, and had stood over them until the kitchen was spotless, much to Emily's disgust. She had spent most of her time rolling her eyes behind his back until Bea wished that she had been left to do it all by herself after all.

At last, Chase had let Emily leave, and then he had announced gruffly that he would bring Bea coffee on the veranda if she wanted to go and sit down.

It was still relatively early and, in spite of the busy day, Bea wasn't tired enough to go to bed. Nor could she admit that she was nervous about being alone with him, even to herself. So she took the mug Chase handed her and cradled her hands around it, trying to forget just what they had been doing when they had found themselves alone together the night before.

'What's brought all this on?' she asked.

'I thought I owed you a cup of coffee at least,' said Chase. 'Joan and the others have been telling me how impressed they were with the welcome you gave them today. They really liked the bush flowers in their rooms and the tea on the veranda. I don't think any of our other guests have been treated as well.'

He glanced at Bea. 'It could have been awkward with me being out all day, and not here to welcome them, but it's obvious that they're going to be happy with everything because of you. I guess I just wanted to say thank you. I know how hard you must have worked all day.'

Bea shifted uncomfortably, uncertain like most people as to how to deal with gratitude. 'I always wanted to have my own hotel,' she said as lightly as she could. 'Think of it as me living out my fantasy!'

'That's your fantasy?' said Chase incredulously.

It did sound a bit tame, Bea had to admit. 'Well, one of them,' she said.

'What are the others?'

It was dark on the veranda, and the night air was blissfully cool. Below, the blue light crackled as flying bugs blundered into its trap, but otherwise it was absolutely quiet. Just the kind of background to start blurting out things that you would regret the next morning.

'They're private,' said Bea.

Chase's smile gleamed through the darkness. 'Very sensible,' he commented in a dry voice.

'That's me, sensible Bea,' said Bea with an edge of bitterness. *You're so sensible, Bea,* Phil had used to sigh. *You don't know how to let yourself go.*

'You surprise me,' said Chase honestly. 'Sensible is the last word I'd use to describe you.'

Bea wasn't sure whether to be pleased or offended. She turned her head to look at him. 'Why not?'

He hadn't been expecting that, and had to think for a moment. 'Well, you don't wear sensible shoes,' he said, and she forgot any thought of being offended and laughed instead.

'Why, Mr Sutherland, that's the nicest thing you've ever said to me!'

'You're welcome,' said Chase, and because she looked so different when she was smiling, he smiled back.

As soon as their eyes met, Bea knew that smiling was a mistake. It changed something in the air, and made the dark veranda intimate, as if they were friends and not two people with completely different lives who didn't even like each other very much.

Biting her lip, she looked quickly away and stared out into the darkness with a kind of desperation. Now was absolutely *not* the time to start remembering that she hadn't disliked the way he had kissed her!

There was a short, strained silence, broken only by the regular zap and crackle of the blue light, and eventually by Chase clearing his throat.

'Why aren't you running a hotel now, if that's what you

want?' he asked, sounding reassuringly like someone who had found the silence as uncomfortable as she had.

'Money,' said Bea, grateful to him for the change of subject. 'I haven't got any capital, and at the current rate, I never will have. Anyway, the kind of hotel I'd always imagined would be out in the country somewhere, and as you know, I'm not a country girl. You've got to be realistic about these things. I'd go mad if I lived in a place like this the whole time. I need to be in a city, the bigger and busier the better.'

No harm in reminding Chase that she at least wasn't in the running for the coveted position of his wife.

'Doing what?' he asked. 'Or is that one of your private fantasies?'

'I want to set up my own business,' said Bea. 'I've planned it all. I'm going to specialise in catering for social events like PR launches or smart parties. If you want to make a splash nowadays you've got to provide more than a bowl of nuts and a warm glass of white wine. The food can set the tone of the whole occasion. I can do clever canapés, new twists on finger food, imaginative nibbles…you know the kind of thing.'

'No,' said Chase, 'but I'll take your word for it.'

'I'll still need a loan, of course,' she went on, warming to her theme, 'but not nearly as much as I would need if I wanted to take over a hotel. It might take a little time to build the business up and make contacts, but I know I can do it,' she added determinedly.

Chase wasn't so sure. He'd seen enough of her to know that she was organised and efficient and a hard worker, but that mouth of hers gave her away. It wasn't nearly ruthless enough to belong to a successful businesswoman.

'Is there enough call for that kind of thing in Sydney?' he asked.

'Oh, yes, there's always something happening in Sydney. They have the best parties there.' Bea sighed nostalgically.

'I wish I could stay, but my visa runs out soon, and I'll have to go back to London.'

To London. To Phil and her family and all those humiliating memories.

Chase heard her voice change. 'You don't sound very enthusiastic about it.'

'No.'

'Don't you like London?'

Once, she had loved it. 'It's not that. It's just the thought of leaving Australia and never seeing Sydney again.'

'Come back, if that's the way you feel.'

'I can't afford it, especially not if I'm going to set myself up in business, and even if I could, I'd be too old for a work permit by the time I got here. If I was a brain surgeon or something useful, I'd be able to apply to emigrate, but as it is being able to make miniature Thai crab cakes or caper flower garnishes doesn't count for very much.'

Bea contemplated her future glumly for a moment, and then squared her shoulders. There was no point in whingeing. That was the way things were, and she was just going to have to get on with it.

'Anyway, what about you?' she asked, turning to him, determinedly cheerful. 'What's your fantasy?'

Chase raised an eyebrow. 'Do we know each other well enough for me to tell you that?'

'I'm talking about making a living,' said Bea with a frosty look. As if he didn't know perfectly well what she had meant. 'Haven't you ever wanted to go to a city?'

'You think I've never been beyond Mackinnon?' said Chase drily. 'I've been to plenty of cities.'

'I meant to work.'

He shrugged. 'I worked in London for a bit when I was travelling, but it wasn't my kind of place. I like to be able to see the horizon.'

'But don't you ever get bored? It's all so…so empty!'

'That depends what you're looking for,' said Chase.

'What about shops and bars and restaurants and cinemas and art galleries and museums and concerts…?'

'No, we don't do those,' he said, unfazed. 'We just do space and stillness and silence. And the bush. You never get bored of the bush.'

That's what he thought. Bea glanced at him. 'Looks like we're incompatible,' she said.

'Looks that way,' Chase agreed, although he didn't sound very bothered by the fact. 'Lucky you don't want to marry me, isn't it?'

'Very lucky,' said Bea crisply.

A little *too* crisply, perhaps.

# CHAPTER FIVE

BY SATURDAY, Bea was starting to get used to getting up in the dark and cooking steak and eggs at a time when most normal people were still asleep. Getting used to it didn't mean that she was enjoying it, though. She told herself that the experience would prove useful in another life, although it was difficult to imagine what that life might be.

It was increasingly hard, in fact, to imagine anything other than being at Calulla Downs. Her life in Sydney already seemed to belong to someone else altogether, while London was unimaginably distant.

Wryly, she remembered telling Emily how boring it would be in the outback. She never had any time to be bored, just as Chase had forecast that first evening. She was working harder than she ever had before. Exhausted by her passionate encounters with Baz, Emily had yet to wake before eight, by which time Bea felt as if she had been up for half a day, cooking breakfast, baking for smoko and tidying up the kitchen while Chloe ate hers, listening with half an ear to her chatter.

Together, they would take the scraps down to the chooks and collect the eggs. The trip across the yard and down a short, dusty track was the furthest Bea had been from the homestead. She liked the light then, before the sun started to glare and dazzle, and while the air was still flushed with the memory of dawn, and the birds squawked and wheeled above the trees.

Sometimes they would come across a wallaby on the track. It would freeze when it saw them, bounding off into the bush at the last minute as they approached. The mere sight of a wallaby or a kangaroo was so Australian that it always gave Bea a little thrill, but Chloe was less impressed.

'Chase says they're a pest,' she informed Bea. 'We should call the roo shooter.'

'Oh, but they're so pretty!'

Chase rolled his eyes when this conversation was reported to him by Chloe. 'I don't care what they look like, they're still pests! I need the grass for my cattle.'

At least the Americans tourists were on Bea's side. They were having a wonderful time. Chase took them out in his big four-wheel drive to show them some of the station, and another day they all got on horses to help muster the near paddocks.

'You should have come with us,' Joan enthused to Bea at dinner one evening when they got back from a drive along the creek. Bea had given them a packed lunch, and they were full of excitement when they came back. 'It's so beautiful!'

'The bush isn't Bea's thing,' said Chase before she could answer. There was an odd edge to his voice. 'She likes cities, don't you, Bea?'

'Yes, I'm an urban chick,' she agreed brightly. 'Give me a café and a newspaper and a crowd of people to watch, and I'm happy.'

But the truth was that she wasn't missing the city nearly as much as she had expected. She liked the cooking, she liked picking lemons straight off the tree, she liked the cool, quiet homestead and sitting around the big table every evening.

And then there was Chase.

Every evening, Emily disappeared off with Baz, and it wasn't long before she was spending the entire night in the stockmen's quarters. It meant that Bea had a room to herself, and although she could have gone there after supper, it seemed unsociable to leave Chase to entertain the guests on his own. So Bea stayed, and somehow they had fallen into a routine of sitting on in the dark after the others had gone to bed.

After a rocky start, they knew where they were with each other. Now that they had established that they were incompatible, it was easier to talk. They both knew that the other was not what they wanted, so they could relax.

Bea hardly ever thought about that kiss now. Only sometimes, when their eyes met across the table, or when she looked at his mouth, or watched his hands brushing the dust off his hat.

Only every now and then.

'Oh, but you must see more of the outback since you're here,' Joan was saying, unconvinced by Bea's assurance that she wasn't interested. 'You'll fall in love with it!'

'Bea doesn't do falling in love either,' said Chase.

There was a tiny, awkward silence.

Bea smiled as if he had made a joke. 'I'm leaving soon, anyway,' she said. 'There's no point in me falling in love now.'

It was probably just as well she was going, Chase thought. He was glad that she had reminded him. He was getting too used to coming home and finding her there.

She had seemed so uptight at first, but sometimes she would forget that she was supposed to be practical and efficient, and she would relax and smile. Sometimes Chase wished she wouldn't. It made it harder to forget what it had been like to kiss her, how warm and good she had felt in his arms.

He watched her now, laughing with Joan, her face all lit up and that mouth as disturbing as ever. Her hair curved straight and gleaming beneath her chin. When she was unsure, she would tuck it behind her ears, but at other times it swung around her face and she would shake it back in a gesture that never failed to dry the breath in his throat.

She wasn't his type, of course. She was too much of a city girl, too sharp and too strained. She cared too much about appearances and every time he turned round she seemed to have a different outfit on. She certainly wasn't interested in *him*.

It was just that she was a hard worker, Chase told himself. A hard worker and a great cook. If it hadn't been for her, the Americans' visit would have been a disaster. He hadn't had time to look after them properly but Bea had made sure that everyone was comfortable. Chloe was happy, too—no thanks to that Emily, who as far as Chase could make out lazed around all day while Bea did all the work.

So while Bea still wasn't his type, he found himself looking forward to coming home at the end of the day. Too often in the past, the atmosphere when he walked up the veranda steps had been fraught with tension. Nick and Georgie were rowing, or the latest cook, in love with Baz, or disappointed in him, was tearful.

There was none of that with Bea. Chase liked sitting on the veranda with her when the Americans had gone to bed. He could talk to her in the darkness without her mentally choosing a wedding dress, and if once or twice he thought about how close she was, and how easy it would be to reach out and kiss her again, well, that didn't mean anything.

It didn't mean that he would miss her when she went back to the city. She was just another temporary cook.

The Americans left the following Saturday, with many kisses and promises to stay in touch. The homestead seemed very quiet after they had gone. When Chase came back at five o'clock, he found Bea giving Chloe her supper.

'Where's Emily?' he asked, hanging up his hat with a frown.

'She's gone with Baz and the others into the pub in town.'

'Didn't you want to go?'

Bea was washing up a saucepan. 'Someone's got to keep an eye on Chloe,' she said mildly.

'Why?' said Chloe.

Chase scowled. 'You should have told me. I would have come home earlier. I always let the boys go off early on a Saturday.'

'It doesn't matter.' Bea wiped her hands on a tea towel. 'I don't really fancy driving for a couple of hours along a dirt road to go to a noisy pub, drink myself stupid and then drive all the way back again.'

*You know your trouble, Bea?* Emily had said. *You've got no sense of adventure. You should relax, learn to live a little.*

She smiled crookedly. 'Emily says I'm being boring.'

'What does Emily know?' Chase bristled. 'As far as I can see, she hasn't lifted a finger all week, except to deprive Baz of sleep. He's not exactly chatty at the best of times, but he's been walking round like a zombie since you two arrived. He used to be a good stockman, but he's useless to me at the moment. It'll be a relief when he leaves.'

'I'd forgotten he was going,' said Bea slowly.

'I thought you were counting the days,' said Chase, trying and failing to keep the note of jealousy from his voice.

She *had* said that, Bea remembered. She had told Chase that she couldn't wait to go back to the city. It felt like a lifetime ago.

'Emily's going to be upset,' she said, as if excusing herself. 'She's absolutely besotted with Baz.'

Personally, she couldn't see the attraction. Baz was handsome, sure, but he hardly ever opened his mouth. You couldn't sit and talk to him the way you could with someone like Chase, say.

Just for an example.

'Stop worrying about Emily,' Chase ordered roughly. 'She can look after herself.'

'I'm not worrying,' lied Bea. 'I'm just tired.'

'Well, tomorrow's your day off. You can have a lie-in.

Nobody turns up for breakfast, and we just have a barbecue in the evening, so you won't have to do any cooking.'

'What about Chloe?' asked Bea, glancing at the little girl who was following their conversation with intense interest.

'I'll look after Chloe,' said Chase. 'You do what you want.'

'Great,' she said, but she couldn't help wondering what on earth she was going to do with herself all day. She wouldn't be able to buy the Sunday papers and sit reading them. There were no markets to potter round out here, no cafés where she could have a long, lazy breakfast, no galleries to visit, or cinemas showing double bills. There wasn't even a friend to ring up and suggest that they spent the day together, doing nothing.

There was Chase, of course, but he wasn't really a friend, was he? He was her employer, to all intents and purposes, and he hadn't shown any interest in spending the day with her.

Not that she wanted him to, of course.

Perversely, Bea woke without the alarm at five the next morning. When she saw what time it was, she willed herself to go back to sleep, but it was hopeless, and it was only as matter of principle that she made herself lie there until six.

Thoroughly awake by then, she decided to go and make herself a cup of tea. She would take it back to bed, and that would be her treat.

Tea in bed? Was that the best she could do? Bea shook her head and threw back the bedcovers.

It was just light as she made her way along the corridor to the kitchen, the wood cool beneath her bare feet. She could hear the counterpoint of Chase's deep voice with Chloe's light one, and she hesitated in the doorway, suddenly shy.

'Bea!' cried Chloe, spotting her, and Chase turned from the sink where he was filling the kettle to see Bea standing there, bare-legged and tousled in a baggy T-shirt. It didn't take much stretch of the imagination to guess that she wore absolutely nothing underneath.

Chase's throat tightened and he swallowed with some difficulty. 'You want to be careful wandering around in bare feet,' he said, hoping that she wouldn't notice how odd his voice sounded.

'Why?' That was Chloe, of course.

'Spiders,' he said briefly. 'You don't want to tread on a redback.'

Bea leapt onto a chair, tucking her legs up beneath her, and stared down at the floor in horror as if expecting to see it heaving with creepy-crawlies. Her expression was so apprehensive that Chase couldn't help laughing, and somehow the awkward moment when all he could think about was her warm, naked body had passed.

'Chloe will go and get your shoes for you, won't you, Chloe?'

Chloe ran off obligingly and the two of them were left alone in the kitchen. Chase turned his attention firmly back to the kettle.

'I keep forgetting about things like spiders,' said Bea. 'Just when you think you're starting to get used to it, you realise you're in a foreign country.'

'They're not too much of a problem. You just have to be careful.'

When he switched the kettle on, the click sounded very loud in the silence.

'I thought you were having a lie-in,' he said after a moment.

'I tried,' said Bea. 'I never thought I'd see the day when it felt lazy to be lying in bed at six in the morning!'

'You must be adapting to the outback.'

'I must be.'

Bea couldn't look at Chase. Last night had been bad enough, when the easy atmosphere on the veranda had evaporated in the consciousness that the two of them were utterly alone apart from Chloe sleeping inside. They would talk stiltedly for a while, and then the conversation would dry up without warning, leaving them marooned in an ever-tightening silence. In the end, Bea had muttered something about being tired and had escaped to her room.

She had thought it would be easier in the daylight, but somehow it wasn't.

'Here you are!' Chloe came running back with Bea's sandals, and thrust them into her hand.

'Thank you, sweetheart.'

Bea slipped the shoes on, but it didn't stop her feeling burningly conscious of her nakedness beneath her T-shirt. Why hadn't she got dressed before she came along to the kitchen?

'Your hair,' said Chase suddenly.

'What about it?'

'It's been bothering me all week, and I've just realised why. It's always curly in the mornings, and straight in the evenings.'

Involuntarily, Bea's hand went to her hair. 'I haven't washed it yet.'

'It goes straight when you wash it?'

Chloe cast him a pitying look. 'She dries it with a *hair-dryer*,' she said, rolling her eyes at his ignorance.

'What, every day?'

A flush rose in Bea's cheeks. 'Yes.'

There was a pause. 'Why?' said Chase eventually, unable to think of anything else to say. He sounded just like Chloe, he realised ruefully.

'Because I hate it like this.' Bea plucked resentfully at her wild brown curls. 'It's bad enough at home, but when it's hot like this it goes even kinkier.'

'I like it,' he said, considering her. 'You should leave it. Think how much time you'd save every day.'

'I can't carry off the natural look,' said Bea, on the defensive. She hated any discussion of her horrible hair. 'I like to keep my hair and my life under control.'

'Control freak,' said Chase as he made a pot of tea.

'That's what Emily says,' she said glumly. 'She's always telling me I should learn to live dangerously.'

Chase put the teapot down on the table, but he was careful not to come to close to her. 'Start by not washing your hair on Sundays,' he suggested lightly.

'I like it when it's curly,' announced Chloe. 'Don't make it straight today, Bea.'

'Come riding with us instead.' The offer was out before Chase quite knew what he was saying. Just what he needed, a whole day of trying not to let Bea distract him! Why hadn't he kept his mouth shut?

Chloe was thrilled at the idea. 'Oh, yes, come with us, Bea!'

'I don't know how to ride, Chloe.'

She had given him the perfect let-out. Instead of taking it, Chase heard himself offering to find her a quiet horse.

'It's easy,' Chloe assured her. 'Isn't it, Uncle Chase?'

'We'll take it slowly,' he promised, pouring out two mugs of tea.

Bea couldn't take her eyes from his fingers curled around the teapot handle. The sight of them did something funny to her insides. Last night had been awkward enough. How would she manage a whole day in his company?

Chloe was jumping up and down by Bea's chair. 'Say you'll come, Bea!'

Chase could see Bea chewing her lip indecisively. 'Maybe Bea wants to have some time to herself,' he suggested.

That would be the safe option, Bea thought, but she was getting a bit sick of the safe option. Maybe Emily was right and it was time she lived a little. A day with a five-year-old and a horse would hardly qualify her for membership in the extreme sports club, after all. They weren't suggesting that she jumped out of plane or threw herself off a cliff. It would just be her and Chloe.

And Chase.

Even she couldn't be pathetic enough to be nervous about that, could she?

'No, I'd like to come,' she said, making up her mind. 'If I leave my hair as well, this will really be my chance to live dangerously!'

She almost lost her nerve when she saw the size of the horse Chase had saddled for her. Suddenly the idea of a bungee jump didn't look so bad.

'How am I going to get up there?'

'Put your foot in the stirrup,' said Chase, holding it for her. He gave her the reins to hold in one hand and made her hang onto the saddle with the other, and before Bea had time to panic, he had boosted her up into the saddle.

Bea swallowed. It looked a long way down to the ground. 'Don't let him run away with me,' she said nervously.

'I thought you wanted to live dangerously?'

He was grinning up at her, his eyes beneath his hat light with amusement, and the breath clogged in Bea's throat as she looked down into his face, suddenly very glad of the sunglasses that hid her expression.

'Not that dangerously,' she managed with difficulty.

'Don't worry.' Chase slapped the horse's neck affectionately. 'Old Duke here won't go faster than a walk, and even if he went wild and broke into a trot, I've got you.' He showed her the leading rein he held in his hand.

'Well, please don't let me go,' said Bea, trying to make a joke of it, but somehow it came out all wrong, and Chase looked up at her.

'I won't,' he said.

Chloe was already on a fat little pony, looking quite at home. Chase settled his hat on his head and swung himself up onto an even bigger horse than Bea's. Emily would have appreciated the sight, thought Bea, trying not to think about the look in his eyes.

At first it took all her attention just staying on the swaying horse, but as soon as it became obvious that Duke was happy to plod along and not do anything alarming, Bea let herself relax a bit and even to look around her.

The sun was already high in the sky, but it was pleasantly shady under the trees along the creek. There had been no need for Chase to insist that she wore one of his old hats, she thought, remembering the sharp little argument they'd had when she proposed going out without one. He had won, of course, and now her hair was going to look even worse than usual.

Chloe was trotting confidently ahead. As she passed under a branch of a great ghost gum, a flock of cockatoos erupted into flight, screeching indignantly at the disturbance. Bea's gaze followed them as they wheeled and darted through the trees and, turning her head, she found Chase watching her.

Something about the way he smiled made her put up her chin. 'Don't tell me, you have to teach all your cooks to ride!'

He shook his head. 'You're the first.'

'I find that rather hard to believe,' she said as coolly as she could.

'It's the truth.'

Bea regarded him uncertainly, not sure whether he was joking or not. 'Why me, then?'

'Maybe I like the idea of you not being good at something,' he said. 'Maybe I like the idea that for once you won't know what you're doing. You're always so practical and competent in the homestead, but out here you're going to have to rely on Chloe and me. It wouldn't kill you to let someone else look after you for once.'

He was teasing…wasn't he? Bea stared at him, her heart beating uncomfortably, and then just when she had decided

that he might be serious, he smiled. He was so clearly outlined against the bush, and his teeth were so white and his
eyes so light that she felt suddenly giddy.

Wrenching her gaze away with an effort, she gripped the
reins in her hands and stared resolutely between Duke's
flickering ears. That disturbing lurch of her heart didn't
mean anything. For a moment there she had felt suspended
in time and space, but it had just been the heat and the light
and the silence making her dizzy, playing tricks on her.

Nothing to do with Chase.

Nothing at all.

The bed of the creek was bone dry and littered with the
bleached branches of fallen trees. Chase told Bea how it
flooded in the wet season, but she couldn't imagine the
churning water or the way the grass grew with the rain. She
had grown so used to the brown, bare landscape that she
exclaimed with surprise and pleasure when they came to a
waterhole so deep that it survived the searing heat of summer.

'Fancy some tea?' Chase asked Bea, who was so thirsty
by then that her face lit up as if he had offered her champagne.

Dismounting, Chase tied up his horse with Bea's and
moved to help Chloe down. She was having none of it. 'I
can do it!' she said stubbornly, kicking her feet out of the
stirrups and slithering to the ground.

'What about you?' Chase smiled up at Bea, and her heart
gave a breathless little somersault. 'Can you get off on your
own?'

Bea would have given anything to have been able to
manage by herself as Chloe had done but, short of a ladder,
there was no way of getting down.

'I think I'd better have my lunch up here,' she said, and
then Chase destroyed all her resolve by laughing.

'Put your hands on my shoulders,' he said, and held up

his arms. Taking her by the waist, he lifted her down and set her on the ground.

Clumsy with sudden shyness, Bea stumbled against him. His body was strong and rock solid, and her mouth dried with lust. Even when she had pulled herself away with a muttered apology, she felt boneless and light-headed.

Too much sun, she told herself.

She sat on a warm, worn rock in the shade and watched Chloe scrambling happily around the waterhole. Behind her, the horses stood patiently, shaking their heads every now and then against the flies. Their harness chinked softly and they exchanged an occasional whicker, while all around them the cicadas scraped and sawed in a raucous symphony.

With quick, deft movements, Chase made a fire among some stones, and fetched what looked like a large can with a handle on top of it from his saddle.

'What's that?' asked Bea as he set it over the fire.

He looked up at her over his shoulder. 'How long have you been in Australia?' he asked.

'Nearly a year.'

'And you've never had billy tea before?'

Oh, so *that* was a billy. Bea had often wondered. But the derisive note in Chase's voice made her put up her chin. 'No, I'm glad to say it's always been possible to pop out for a cappuccino wherever I've been before.'

'Right,' said Chase drily, and went back to poking the fire with a stick.

Bea eyed him almost resentfully. It wasn't her fault she hadn't grown up in the outback. There was no point in her pretending that she was anything other than a city girl. Chase didn't seem to realise how alien all this was to her. Emily might appreciate the startling light, and the hot, dry scent of the bush, but she was a girl who liked a pavement beneath her feet, and was used to grabbing a cab, not throwing herself on a horse.

Emily would love the idea of riding along a creek and drinking tea out of a billy. She would be thrilled by the sight of Chase, hunkered down by the fire, the brim of his hat pulled down over his eyes, looking utterly at home even without a checked shirt.

Bea's eyes rested on him, on the curve of his back, on the lean length of his thigh, on the line of his jaw, and heat flooded through her without warning. She had a terrible urge to go and crouch next to him and put her hand on his shoulder, to lean into him and breathe in the scent of his skin. To let him pull her down onto the ground and to hell with the dust and the dried leaves and even the insects if only he'd touch her...

Gulping, Bea tore her gaze away. If she wasn't careful, she'd end up like Emily, carried away by a fantasy that had no basis in reality. The reality was that she and Chase might as well come from different planets, and that she would be leaving soon in any case. So there was no point in even *thinking* about finding him attractive, was there?

*Was* there?

No, Bea answered herself firmly. None at all.

Chase was throwing some tea leaves into the billy and stirring it with a stick. He let it steep for a while, then poured the tea into a couple of battered enamel mugs and handed one to Bea. As she reached out for it, her fingers brushed his and she snatched her hand back without thinking.

If Chase had felt a similar jolt of electricity at the touch of her skin, he gave absolutely no sign of it. All he did was look exasperated. 'Careful!' he said, and offered her the mug again. 'Now, have you got it?' he demanded, much as he might to a child.

'Yes,' muttered Bea, humiliated. She took the mug very carefully, trying to avoid his fingers, and then, just when she thought she'd got herself under control, Chase sat down on the rock beside her, and all her senses jerked into a state of full alert.

Chase misunderstood her expression. 'Sorry it's not a cappuccino,' he said.

'It's fine,' said Bea, searching wildly for an excuse. 'A bit hot, that's all.'

She made a big deal of blowing on her tea, keeping her eyes firmly away from Chase's jean-clad thigh that was disturbingly close to her own, and took a cautious sip. To her surprise, it tasted more than fine, it tasted delicious.

It must be because she was so thirsty, Bea decided. It was nothing to do with being out here with the light and the gum trees and the drifting fragrance of the bush, or with the fact that Chase was sitting beside her, still and self-contained.

She was a girl who liked champagne and cocktails, or if it had to be tea, would insist on Lapsang Souchong. She wasn't a girl who would ever be happy with a few coarse tea leaves shoved into a tin can and stirred with a stick. So it had to be thirst that was making it taste so good.

In spite of herself, Bea's eyes slid sideways. Chase was leaning forward, drinking his tea, apparently absorbed in watching Chloe playing by the waterhole. His body was lean and compactly muscled, its quiet strength obvious in his wrists and his neck and the breadth of his shoulders, but his face was shaded by his hat and, when he glanced up at her from beneath its brim, the lightness of his eyes stopped the breath in Bea's throat.

'Can I ask you something?' he said.

What was he going to ask? If he could take off her hat and run his fingers down her throat? If he could unbutton her shirt? If he could kiss her again, the way he had kissed her in the kitchen? Bea's mind span with the possibilities.

'Yes,' she managed on a gasp. 'Of course.'

'What are you doing here?' he asked, as if he really wanted to know.

Oh.

Bea stared down in her tea, horrified at her own disappointment. 'What do you mean?'

Chase turned back to watch Chloe, his hands clasped loosely around the mug. 'You don't like it here. You don't belong. Why come in the first place?'

'Emily wanted to come,' said Bea, trying not to think about the pang that had gone through her when he had told her that she didn't belong. It was true, but he didn't have to make it sound so…so *definite*. 'Nick told her that you wanted two friends.'

Chase nodded. 'That's right. We've had problems in the past. The cook and the governess end up spending so much time together that if they don't get on, it makes it difficult for everybody.'

'That's what Nick said. Anyway, Emily can't cook—she can barely open a tin of beans—so she asked if I'd come with her.'

'Hasn't she got any other friends she could have asked?'

'None who can cook like I do, and none who owe her like I do,' said Bea wryly.

She saw Chase glance at her in frank disbelief. 'Emily's a bit scatty, I know, but she's been a good friend to me. I always envied her,' she went on after a moment. 'She's so outgoing, and such good fun, and…well, you've seen what she's like. Everybody loves Emily.'

Chase looked sceptical, but he didn't say anything.

'Emily's always got a plan,' Bea tried to explain. 'It's usually romantic and more often than not completely impractical, but at least she knows what she wants, and she isn't afraid to go for it.'

She swirled the tea around in her mug with a sigh. 'I feel such a coward compared to Emily. I don't like change, and I never take risks.' She glanced at Chase. 'You saw what I was like today. Not washing my hair is about as brave as I ever get. Pathetic, isn't it?'

'You came out to Australia,' he pointed out.

'Only because Emily bullied me into it. I'd never have given up my job and my home and my life if it had been up to me. I was quite comfortable as I was. I had a great job doing something I loved, I had a flat I loved, and I was engaged to a man I loved. Why would I want to give up any of that?' she said defensively, as if Chase had accused her of something.

'No reason,' said Chase calmly, but his eyes had narrowed at the mention of Phil.

'I liked my life,' said Bea. 'I didn't want to change anything about it, but it all changed anyway,' she remembered bitterly. The pain was less raw now, but the memories still had the power to hurt her.

Chase wasn't looking at her, and he wasn't probing or exclaiming or demanding to know what had happened. He was just sitting there, listening quietly, and suddenly Bea found herself wanting to tell him anyway.

She took a deep breath. 'Phil and I had been going out for years. We were living together in London, and we'd decided that we'd get married. We had a big engagement party, invited everyone, and started planning the wedding. I was looking at wedding dresses when Phil came home one day and told me that he couldn't go ahead with it.'

'He'd met someone else?'

'My sister.'

A double betrayal. No wonder she was a bit spiky sometimes, thought Chase. 'I'm sorry,' he said after a moment.

'These things happen,' said Bea. She even managed a careless shrug. 'It was probably all for the best, although it didn't feel like it at the time.

'They met at our engagement party. Anna had been away at university, and Phil hadn't seen her for years. Phil said it was like a bolt from the blue for both of them. Now, I think it was brave of him to tell me, and far better then than after we'd married, but at the time I was devastated. I'd had no idea that anything was wrong.'

She shook her head at her own stupidity. She still found it hard to believe that she hadn't been able to read the signs.

'I'd always been the one who had life under control,' she said. 'I was good old Bea, sensible Bea, you can always rely on her, but when I found out about Phil and Anna, I just fell apart. I'd always been close to Anna...' She trailed off, unable to put that particular pain into words.

Chase admired the courageous tilt of her head, the defiant press of her lips. 'What did you do?' he asked quietly.

'Oh, it was all very civilised,' said Bea with a sardonic, sideways look. 'Shouting and screaming wouldn't have changed anything, although Phil and Anna might have felt better if I had. I was just...numb.'

She paused, remembering those terrible days. 'It was Emily who saved me,' she told Chase, getting back to the point. 'She'd been planning to come out to Australia for years. Her mother's Australian, so she doesn't have any visa problems, but she changed all her plans so that I'd be able to come too.

'I didn't have much say in the matter,' said Bea, smiling slightly at the memory of Emily who had come round, or phoned, every day to make sure that she was all right. 'I didn't think I'd like Australia, but Emily insisted. She made all the arrangements, and in the end I was too miserable to care one way or the other. It was Emily who got me on the plane, and out here...and it was the best thing that ever happened to me.

'I fell in love with Australia the moment I stepped off the plane. Coming here changed my life, and I owe that to Emily. That's really why I came out to Calulla Downs,' she told Chase frankly. 'I did it for her.

'And maybe I was hoping that being somewhere I didn't expect to enjoy would make it easier when it came to going home,' she added honestly. 'I've only got another month, and then I have to leave.'

Her mouth turned down at the corners. 'I'm not looking forward to going home. Phil and Anna are getting married soon, and I'm going to have to smile and be nice and pretend I don't mind. It's not going to be easy, is it?'

'I guess that depends whether you *will* be pretending or not,' said Chase. '*Do* you still mind?'

# CHAPTER SIX

BEA thought about it, a tiny frown of concentration between her brows. 'I thought I did,' she said slowly, as if it was only just occurring to her. 'I suppose I just got used to the idea of being broken-hearted but...no, I don't think I am any more. I think I mind more about my sister than about Phil, which probably means that it wasn't that great a relationship to start with.

'Emily always said that I was never really in love with Phil,' she went on. 'She thought I was just playing safe, and maybe she was right, but it won't make it any easier to see him with Anna.'

'You know, you'll get used to it,' said Chase, and she turned to him with a sudden surge of bitterness.

'Easy for you to say! You don't know what it was like, discovering that your fiancé is in love with your own sister!'

'Don't I?' he said evenly.

Bea stared at him, and he looked back at her with a crooked smile. 'How do you think Nick met Georgie?' he said.

'*You* were engaged to Georgie Grainger?'

She was so frankly incredulous that Chase couldn't help reflecting that it was just as well he didn't have any false hopes about her opinion of him. He shrugged.

'It wasn't as bad as that. We weren't engaged, but I was in love with her, yes.'

Bea shook her head to clear it. She was still having trouble believing that Chase had ever been involved with anyone as gorgeous and glamorous as Georgie Grainger. 'How...?' she said simply.

'Georgie and I were at school in Brisbane at the same time,' he said, understanding Bea's less than flattering reaction. 'She comes from a station like this one, not so isolated, but still remote enough for the kids all to be sent to boarding school. There were a lot of country kids there. Georgie was a couple of years younger than me, and we used to see each other at school dances, sports, that kind of thing.'

He chucked the dregs of his tea into the dust. 'Georgie wasn't as glossy in those days. She was always really pretty, but she hadn't learned how to dress or how to be a star. She had to be centre of attention, though.'

He grinned affectionately, and Bea was conscious of a sharp pinch of jealousy. 'No one was surprised when she announced that she wanted to be an actress and took herself off to drama school. We'd see each other as often as we could, but it wasn't easy with me out here, and her in Sydney.

'I used to try and get down there every other weekend,' he said, 'and one time I took Nick with me. He's four years older than me, and had been away travelling. We went to see Georgie in some play. I can't remember what it was, only that it was terrible and she was lousy, but Nick couldn't take his eyes off her. We went backstage afterwards and…well, I'm not the most sensitive man on earth, but even I could see what was happening. Three weeks later, Georgie threw in her acting career and married Nick.'

He sounded so matter-of-fact that Bea eyed him curiously. He didn't *seem* broken-hearted, but it was hard to tell what he was thinking sometimes.

'How did you feel?' she asked, and then winced as she realised how fatuous her question must have sounded. She knew better than most people how he must have felt. 'Sorry,' she said inadequately.

'It's OK,' said Chase. 'It was a long time ago. No, it wasn't the best time of my life, but I think I always knew that Georgie was out of my league. I couldn't feel bitter with her, anyway.'

His voice always softened when he talked about Georgie, Bea noticed, and then caught herself up. That wasn't her feeling *jealous,* was it?

'I went off travelling for a couple of years,' he was carrying on, unaware of her mental interruption. 'When I got back, Nick and Georgie were established in the homestead, and I just moved back in with them.'

'Wasn't that awkward?' asked Bea. She couldn't imagine calmly moving in with Phil and Anna.

'It's hard to feel awkward with Georgie, or with Nick, come to that. They can both charm the crocs out of the creek. She's great, Georgie,' said Chase. 'You'd like her.'

Bea wasn't so sure about that.

'You would,' he insisted. 'You think you're not going to, but then you do. Sometimes she drives you wild, of course, but you can never stay cross with her. It's impossible not to like Georgie,' he assured a still unconvinced Bea. 'She's just…irresistible.'

'You sound like you're still in love with her.'

Uh-oh, that *definitely* sounded like jealousy! And what was worse, Chase obviously thought so, too. He did that business with his eyebrow that never failed to make Bea feel about six inches high.

'Georgie's a very special person,' he said carefully, 'but she isn't easy to live with. I've seen what a dance she leads Nick. Georgie wants everything. She wants Nick, but she wants her career too. She needs applause, and she doesn't get enough to keep her happy in the outback, which is what Nick needs. I'm glad I didn't have to deal with that.'

Obviously he *was* still in love with Georgie, thought Bea, ruffled in a way she couldn't explain. He hadn't denied it anyway, had he?

'So you're not looking for a substitute?' she said, more sharply than she had intended.

'No,' said Chase. 'I'm holding out for a suitable girl.'

*Suitable?* Hadn't he heard the twentieth century was over, let alone the nineteenth? 'What's a suitable girl?' asked Bea derisively, knowing even as she asked that the answer wasn't going to be anyone like her.

Sure enough, it wasn't.

Chase appeared to take her question seriously. 'A girl who belongs here, who understands the outback,' he said. 'A girl who isn't going to be bored or complain when times are hard. A girl who's prepared to work as hard as I am.'

'You're asking a lot,' said Bea. 'Don't you think that's a bit demanding?'

'I think it's realistic,' said Chase flatly. 'Calulla Downs is home, but I want my own place eventually. I've heard rumours that a property on the other side of Mackinnon is coming up for sale. It's been run down for years, so it would mean starting again, and it wouldn't be easy. Someone who spent her time hankering after shops or movies or smart restaurants would be no use to me.'

*Someone like you.* He might as well have come right out and said it, thought Bea peevishly. She was the opposite of what he wanted.

Which was just as well, she pointed out to herself as she lay in bed that night. The isolation of Calulla Downs must be going to her head. She had an uncomfortably distinct memory of sitting by the waterhole and wanting him to kiss her, and really, what would have been the point of that?

What would be the point of getting over Phil only to fall for someone who not only had nothing in common with her but was obviously still in love with someone else? And not just any old someone else, but a beautiful, glamorous, talented, charming actress. Your rival from hell, in fact.

So, no, she absolutely, definitely was not going to do anything stupid like that. *I've got no intention of sleeping with you, falling in love with you or wanting to marry you,* she had told Chase, and she meant it. A relationship involving any of the three would be doomed to disaster from the start, and Bea had been hurt enough.

Baz was leaving on Monday, so Bea wasn't surprised when Emily didn't turn up that night. She presumed that they were saying their goodbyes, and hoped that Emily wasn't going to get too tearful.

But when Emily appeared the next morning after Chase and the remaining stockmen had left, she was all smiles.

'I've come to say goodbye,' she said hugging Bea.

Bea pulled back and looked at her friend with foreboding. 'Goodbye?'

'I'm leaving with Baz. He's taking me home to meet his parents!' Emily twirled Bea ecstatically around the room. 'I'm so happy!' she cried. 'I knew that coming here would change my life. It's as if it was *meant* to be! Oh, thank you, thank you, thank you, darling Bea, for agreeing to come! If you hadn't, I'd never have met Baz, and think how terrible that would have been!'

'But, Emily, what are you going to do?'

Emily flung her arms wide. 'I'm just going to be with Baz. What more do I need?'

'What about your job here?'

'Baz is more important,' Emily declared. 'I thought you'd be pleased, Bea,' she went on, hurt by Bea's lack of enthusiasm. 'It means that you can go back to Sydney straight away. You never wanted to be here in the first place.'

'Who would do the cooking? And what about Chloe? I can hardly walk out and leave her to look after herself,' Bea pointed out, having checked that Chloe was out of earshot.

'That grumpy old Chase can get someone new,' said Emily airily. 'Baz says he turns over girls every month or so, so he's bound to be able to replace you really easily.'

Somehow, this wasn't what Bea wanted to hear.

Emily's mind had already flitted back to Baz. Beaming, she sat on the table and swung her legs. 'Oh, Bea, I'm so happy I can't tell you! I wish you could be in love like this, too.'

'I'm not sure I want to be if it means losing my mind,' said Bea crisply. 'I can't believe you're seriously talking about taking off with Baz. You hardly know anything about him!'

'I know I'm in love, and that's all that matters.' Emily jumped off the table, too excited to keep still. 'Now, don't fuss, Bea. Go back to Sydney and I'll contact you there when I know where we're going to be. If you're still around, I'll invite you to my wedding.'

Bea goggled at her. 'Baz has asked you to *marry* him?'

'Well, not in so many words,' Emily admitted, which was no surprise to Bea. Baz wasn't big on words. 'We don't need things cut and dried like you do. We just know each other instinctively, and I just *know* this is right and Baz is The One.'

There was no point in trying to argue with Emily when she was in this kind of mood, as Bea knew to her cost. She sighed, foreseeing just how well this was going to go down with Chase.

'When are you planning to leave?'

'This morning. Baz is just putting his things in the ute, and we'll go as soon as I've packed my stuff.'

'I don't think Chase will be back until lunchtime,' said Bea, but even as she opened her mouth she knew what Emily was going to say.

'You'll explain how it is for me, won't you, Bea?' she pleaded. 'I find him a bit intimidating, and I know if I try to explain about Baz and falling in love, he just won't understand.'

Chase wasn't quite such a stranger to love as Emily seemed to imagine, but Bea didn't think there was much point in explaining that. He was still unlikely to be very sympathetic when he found that Emily was leaving.

'It's not as if Chase cares whether we're here or not, as long as there's someone to cook the meals and keep an eye on Chloe,' Emily was saying.

She was probably right, Bea thought, depressed, as Emily flitted off to throw her clothes in her suitcase.

A few minutes later, Baz tooted his car horn at the bottom of the veranda steps. Emily gave him her suitcase to throw in the back, hugged Chloe and Bea, climbed in beside Baz and drove off with a cheerful wave.

Chase was furious, just as Bea had known he would be. She had to break the news when he came back at lunchtime, and she hadn't enjoyed the experience. She had never seen him lose his temper before.

'I suppose you're going to want to go now, too?' he said in a savage voice as he paced angrily around the kitchen.

'I won't go until you've found someone to replace us,' said Bea, quailing but trying not to show it.

'Too right you won't!' Chase glowered at her as if Emily's irresponsibility was all her fault. 'You can look after Chloe as well, and if Emily thinks I'm going to forward her wages, she can think again.'

'I'm sure she won't,' Bea tried unsuccessfully to placate him. 'She may be a bit thoughtless, but she's doesn't care about money at all.'

'Just as well, if she's thrown her lot in with Baz,' he said with a snort. 'She's a fool if she thinks that relationship will last the month!'

Bea had her own doubts on that score, but she thought it would be better to keep her mouth shut for now. Saying anything would only antagonise him even more, and he looked thunderous enough as it was. His brows were drawn together in a ferocious line and a muscle jumped angrily in his tense jaw, which made it all the harder to understand why she should have this inexplicable longing to put her arms around him and assure him that everything would work out fine and kiss the last of his fury away.

Unsurprisingly, Chase showed no sign that he would appreciate such a gesture, even if she had given in to such a bizarre urge. He was striding around the kitchen, oblivious to Chloe's wide-eyed stare, ranting and raving about Emily.

'I'm sick of you girls coming out here and playing at being in the outback. You think you can turn up, enjoy our quaint little ways for a while and then swan off again as soon as you get bored or are panting after some man. You don't seem to understand that this isn't a game for us. We've got work to do. I've got ten thousand head of cattle out there to get through the yards, but I don't suppose Emily gave that a thought!'

The chances of Emily knowing or caring about Chase's cattle were zilch, Bea thought privately, but it didn't seem tactful to say so.

'It's bad enough losing an experienced stockman like Baz without having to run around after governesses and cooks,' Chase was storming. 'I haven't got time to find a replacement right now, so I don't care how much you're pining to get back to your precious city, you can just stay here and do the job you're being paid to do until I have!'

And with that, he slammed out. The screen door clattered alarmingly in his wake, and the wooden steps from the veranda reverberated with the angry strike of his boots.

Bea didn't blame him, but when she turned back to Chloe, she saw that the little girl was looking upset. She wasn't used to seeing her uncle lose his temper like that.

'Uncle Chase is cross,' she said, and her little mouth wobbled.

Bea took her on her lap and gave her a cuddle. 'Don't worry about it, Chloe,' she said. 'He's not cross with you.'

'Is he cross with you?'

'A bit.'

'Why?'

She should have known *that* was coming. 'Because he's cross with Emily, but she's not here, so I'm the next best thing. He has to be cross with somebody, otherwise he might burst!'

Chloe giggled, her wobble forgotten. 'Would he go pop?'

'He would. And we don't want that, do we?'

Bea wished she could be reassured as easily as Chloe. She might understand Chase's anger, but that didn't mean that she had liked being on the receiving end of it.

The implication that she was like all the other girls who came out here had hurt. She wasn't playing at being in the outback, she didn't find him or his way of life the slightest bit quaint, and *she* hadn't left him in the lurch! Chase only had his cows to deal with; now she had two jobs to do.

It was a long afternoon. Bea hadn't appreciated before just what a difference Emily had made. It wasn't so much that Chloe was difficult but, without Emily, Bea had to be constantly aware of where she was and what she was doing. If Chloe wasn't there, she had to keep checking on her to make sure she was all right, and if she was, she talked constantly, which made it extremely difficult for Bea to concentrate on what she was doing. The meal that night was not going to be up to her usual standard, she thought, resigned.

When Chase came back, Bea and Chloe were on the veranda. Chloe had insisted on having her hair washed, and Bea was combing out the tangles. She was sitting on the wooden bench where they had smoko every morning, Chloe pinned between her knees, and ignoring her vociferous complaints. 'If you stand still, I won't need to pull,' she said.

Chase watched them from across the yard. It had seemed a very long afternoon to him, too. He knew that he had overreacted to Emily's departure, and he had a nasty feeling that part of the reason for his fury was the thought that Bea would take the opportunity to leave too.

And part was anger with himself for caring whether she did or not.

The thing was, he'd got used to Bea being there. Chase had spent the afternoon trying to convince himself that it would better if she went sooner rather than later. There was no point in getting used to her. She had made no secret of the fact that she was a city girl, through and through. She didn't like the outback. She was uptight and prickly and she wasted a ridiculous amount of time on her appearance every day. She was the last person who would ever belong out here.

So why did his stride increase as he got closer to the homestead? Why did his heart feel lighter when he went into the kitchen and saw her standing at the cooker, stirring gravy, her face pink from the heat, or moving around the long table, setting out knives and forks, that hair that was such a bother to her tucked behind her ear?

Why did he hate the thought of sitting out on the veranda in the dark without her?

Chloe saw him first. 'Uncle Chase!' Wriggling out of Bea's grasp, she ran down the steps towards him and let him swing her into the air. 'Bea was pulling my hair,' she complained.

'Don't tell tales,' said Chase, carrying her back up the steps. 'And anyway, it didn't look like she was pulling it to me.' He put Chloe down and pushed her gently back towards Bea. 'You let her finish combing your hair.'

After that first heart-stopping moment when she caught sight of him, Bea was doing her best to appear normal. She went back to untangling Chloe's hair with unnatural concentration.

'You were very cross before,' Chloe told her uncle.

'I know,' he said.

'Bea says you had to shout at her or you would have gone pop!' She stuck out her tummy and mimed it bursting with so much of her mother's dramatic flair that Chase laughed, albeit ruefully.

'As usual, Bea was quite right,' he said.

He sat down on the bench next to Bea and placed his hat between them. 'I'm sorry about earlier,' he said.

'It doesn't matter,' said Bea, who had fully intended to remain aloof. 'You were entitled to be angry.'

'I shouldn't have taken it out on you, though.' He cleared his throat. 'I know you'll want to get back to Sydney as soon as you can, but would you mind staying until I can find someone else?' It was what he should have asked her before, instead of ordering her to stay.

'I said I'd stay a month, and I will,' said Bea, not meeting his eyes. She gave Chloe's hair a last comb and let her go. 'I'm used to things now, and I'm fond of Chloe,' she added hastily in case he started getting the wrong idea. 'It's only for another couple of weeks in any case. I don't mind staying as we agreed until Nick comes home.'

Chase was taken aback at how relieved he felt. He studied her profile, reluctant to exploit her guilt about Emily. 'I thought you were desperate to get back to Sydney,' he said.

'I am, but I'm running out of time on my visa. It's not worth me getting another job, so I may as well stay here where it's cheap. There's nothing to spend my money on, so I could use my wages to spend my last two or three weeks travelling.'

Put like that, it sounded quite convincing, Bea congratulated herself. It sounded as if she was staying for purely practical reasons, and not because she particularly wanted to.

'Are you sure you're not saying that because you feel responsible for Emily?' Chase asked suspiciously. 'There's no need for you to stay that long if you don't want to. I could probably arrange to get someone here by the end of the week.'

What did he want her to do? Beg him to let her stay? 'Look, if you'd rather get someone more suitable, just say so,' snapped Bea. '*I* don't mind,' she lied.

'No, no,' said Chase hurriedly. 'I want you to stay, if you really don't mind.' He paused and looked at Bea, whose head was tilted at a characteristic angle. Her cheeks were flushed and her eyes were bright with an edgy sort of defiance.

She would be here for another fortnight. Another two weeks of not having to think about who was going to cook the meals or worry about who was looking after Chloe. Two weeks of not having to deal with Georgie's guests.

Two weeks of coming home and finding her here at the end of the day.

How did he thank Bea for that? A simple thank you would sound hopelessly inadequate, but in the end it was all Chase could think of, so he said it anyway.

'Thank you,' he said.

*I'm not having anything to do with children.* Wasn't that what she had insisted to Emily? Look at her now, thought Bea as she tucked Chloe up in bed that night. She was turning into a regular Julie Andrews. She would be bursting into song next.

'Sleep tight,' she said as Chloe wrapped her arms round her neck in one of her throttling hugs.

Watching from the door, Chase was aware of something alarmingly like jealousy. He wished that he could pull Bea down to him the way Chloe could, and feel her hair swinging softly against his skin. When he bent to kiss Chloe's cheek in his turn, he could smell the lingering traces of Bea's perfume.

'Bea smells nice,' said Chloe, reading his thoughts with uncanny accuracy.

'I know,' said Chase.

He found Bea moving briskly around the kitchen. 'Thanks for looking after Chloe today,' he said.

'That's OK,' she said, carefully casual as she turned the potatoes. 'It's a new experience for me, being with children. I've never had anything to do with them before.'

'I wouldn't have guessed. Chloe likes you.'

'Chloe likes everybody,' said Bea, forgetting how wary Chloe had been when they first arrived.

'I don't know about that,' said Chase. 'She's made life very difficult for some of the girls who've been here.'

Had Chloe been difficult for Kirsty and Sue and all those other girlfriends whose names Chase had struggled to remember? Bea was ashamed of herself for hoping so.

'It can't be easy for her with people coming and going all the time,' she commented instead. 'She must miss her mother.'

'You've got to remember that Chloe's never had her mother there the whole time,' said Chase. 'It's not that Georgie doesn't love her—she does—but they decided that it would be better for Chloe to stay here with Nick rather than be dragged around hotel rooms and film sets.'

He looked at Bea with a kind of baffled frustration as she stood at the cooker with her back to him. Why were they talking about Nick and Georgie's childcare arrangements? he wondered wildly, when all he wanted to do was go over and kiss the back of her neck, to put his arms around her and tell her how glad he was that she was staying.

But Bea was busy lifting lids on saucepans and stirring things, and there was tension in her spine. She wasn't taking any notice of him, probably wasn't even looking at him, Chase realised. She wouldn't lean back against him with a shudder of pleasure, or turn in his arms and smile.

She was much more likely to be horrified, and he wouldn't be able to blame her. Bea was doing him a favour by agreeing to stay on for a while. After the way he'd shouted at her earlier, he was lucky she hadn't walked out there and then. As it was, if he made a move now, she'd just think that he was taking advantage of the fact that they would be alone together in the homestead tonight, without even Emily's nominal presence.

She might even be nervous about the possibility, Chase thought, appalled. It would explain why she held herself so tensely, her body language practically screaming, Keep your hands to yourself!

So he kept his hands to himself and, muttering something about a shower, he left Bea to her cooking.

They had coffee as usual on the veranda after the stockmen had left that night. Bea thought about going straight to bed, but that would look as if she was nervous about being alone with Chase, which she definitely *wasn't*.

She was just wondering why she hadn't accepted his offer to find another cook by the end of the week and gone while she had the chance. Now she had let herself in for another fortnight of sitting edgily next to him and trying not to think about that time he had kissed her.

She hadn't even managed to maintain a cool distance after being shouted at like that. She should have held out for a grovelling apology, but oh, no! all Chase had had to do was sit down next to her. It was pathetic, thought Bea, despising herself. Anyone would think that she *wanted* to stay!

The silence stretched awkwardly between them. Bea was acutely conscious of Chase beside her, very still and self-contained and somehow definite in the dim light. Beyond the veranda, it was very dark. The blue light in the yard went *psst, psst, psst* with each doomed insect. The faint crackling noise made Bea think of the way her nerves jumped whenever Chase lifted his mug, or leant forward to rest his arms on his knees and look out into the night.

The stiller he sat, the more Bea fidgeted. The silence might not bother him, but it was making her twitchy.

'It's quiet without Emily,' she tried at last.

'Yes.'

'Not that she was ever here at this time.'

'No.'

It was like trying to make conversation with one of the cattle dogs that lay panting in the shade all day. Worse, in fact. At least the dogs wagged their tails and looked pleased when she stopped to give them a word.

Sipping her coffee, Bea racked her brains for something else she could say that wouldn't make him think that she was even aware of the fact that he was a man and she was a woman and that to all intents and purposes they were quite alone in the dark.

'Look,' said Chase suddenly, making her arm jerk and spilling coffee down her front.

He stopped.

'What?' said Bea as she brushed ineffectively at the drops.

'You seem a bit tense,' he commented.

'I'm not the slightest bit tense!' she said tensely.

'OK, great,' said Chase. 'But if you *were,* I just thought I should say that you don't need to worry about…well, the two of us being alone together.'

Bea managed an unsuccessful laugh. 'We're hardly alone. There's Chloe, four stockmen, the married man and his wife…it's a positive crowd.'

At least Chase didn't point out, as he could have done, that most of the 'crowd' was well out of earshot.

'If you're not worried, that's fine,' he said.

'Of course I'm not worried,' snapped Bea, and then spoilt it by adding childishly, 'I know how you despise us English girls!'

Chase turned to stare at her. 'I don't despise you. I'm very grateful to you.'

*Grateful?* What self-respecting girl wanted a man to be *grateful?*

His reasonable tone only made Bea feel even more child-ish. 'Good,' she retorted. 'So I'm not worried about you, and you *certainly* don't need to worry about being alone with me!'

Chase had known that all along.

It was a relief to both of them that more guests were booked to arrive the next day. Chase flew to collect them from the airport in Mackinnon, and Bea threw herself into preparations for their arrival and tried to forget the restless night she had spent, wondering what it would have been like if Chase hadn't made it crystal clear that he had no intention of laying a finger on her.

Wondering what it would have been like if he had given her reason to be worried, if he *had* suggested that they could make the most of the fact that they were alone in the quiet outback night. What had kept Bea awake most of the night was the fear that the only thing that would have really worried her would have been her own ability to resist.

Which was stupid. She had already decided, very sensi-bly, that there was no point in getting involved with a man like Chase. This wasn't the time or place to get tired of being sensible.

The guests were boisterous and good-humoured and deter-mined to enjoy every minute of their stay. They liked to help in the kitchen and to sit out on the veranda at night, which meant that there was no opportunity to be alone with Chase any more.

Bea told herself that she was glad. She was busy enough what with cooking and cleaning and Chloe, and running around after five guests. That was what she was here for she reminded herself sternly. She wasn't here to listen out for the sound of Chase's step outside, to wait for him to come and join them at table, or to look out for his rare illuminating smile.

She knew that he regarded looking after the guests as a

chore he had been landed with in Nick and Georgie's absence, but the guests themselves would never have guessed that he was anything less than an eager host. He could be charming when he wanted to, Bea observed somewhat jealously. He was never like that with her. She might as well not have existed for all the attention he paid her now.

Not that she cared, of course.

# CHAPTER SEVEN

ON THE third day of the visit, Chase had succumbed and agreed to let the guests take part in the muster. Bea got up even earlier than usual to send them all off with a big breakfast and, while the stockmen were saddling up the horses, Chase gave Bea instructions as to how to reach the stopping place. 'Can you bring lunch out to us? We should be there just after midday.'

He drew her a map on the kitchen table, but Bea was distracted by his deft brown fingers moving over the paper in swift, sure movements, marking out paddocks and creeks and dams. He was leaning on the table next to her chair, his arm very close to hers, his shirt carelessly rolled up. She could see the fine, flat hairs at his strong wrist and the frayed strap of his watch.

Bea could feel herself being drawn irresistibly into the hard body so close to hers, a terrifying feeling, and the image of giving and simply suckering against him was so vivid that she had to lean right over the other way in compensation. Chase cast her a curious look.

'Have you got that?'

'Um…yes,…over the third cattle grid…'

Chase sighed and straightened. 'Don't forget to bring this with you,' he said, pushing the paper towards her. 'If things get really bad, Chloe can probably show you the way.'

It was a huge relief when he moved away.

Outside, the horses were ready, shaking their heads up and down and jingling their harness, as the guests milled excitedly around. Bea took out some flapjacks for them to have at smoko, and they commiserated with her for being left behind.

'I don't mind,' said Bea, not entirely truthfully. 'Musters aren't really my thing.'

They weren't, of course, but it didn't stop her feeling left out when she eventually found them all sitting round a fire with Chase and the stockmen, waiting for the billies to boil. The horses were tethered nearby, and wherever Bea looked there were cattle browsing, grateful for a pause in being herded headlong through the bush.

'Here they are!' cried Janet, and waved as Bea drew up and parked Chase's big four-wheel-drive in the shade.

Chase turned to see Bea jump down from the driver's seat and reach back inside for a basket of sandwiches. She looked gloriously out of place as usual in tailored shorts and a pale pink shirt, with pearls, for God's sake. He was surprised she wasn't wearing high heels.

Her hair was dried into a neat, conker-brown bob that swung as she walked towards them, Chloe running ahead. When she got closer, Chase could see that she had her aloof expression on, the one which meant that she was more un-sure of herself than she wanted to admit.

He got up to take the basket from her. 'I see you found us.'

'Eventually,' said Bea a little tightly, and Chloe tugged at his arm.

'Bea got lost. She said your map was stupid!'

They all laughed, although Bea's smile was decidedly frayed at the edges. She had been driving around for what seemed like hours across flat, brown paddocks that all looked exactly the same as the last one. In the alien land-scape, she found herself getting hot and panicky, and she had turned the map round and round on the steering wheel, trying to make sense of it.

In the end it had been Chloe who had pointed her in the right direction. She was the one who was stupid, not the map, and getting here to find Chase looking lean and easy and utterly at home hadn't made her feel any better.

Forcing a smile, she sat on a worn log next to Janet and tried not to watch Chase as he passed the sandwiches around. Janet was full of the morning they had had. Bea only listened with half an ear until Janet heaved an envious sigh. 'You're so lucky to have a guy like Chase,' she said.

Bea sat abruptly upright. 'Sorry?'

'You and Chase...May and I were just saying this morning how lucky we think you are.'

'That's right.' May joined in the conversation, leaning across Chase and beaming at Bea. 'We were wishing we were twenty years younger!'

Appalled at the misunderstanding, Bea stared from one to the other. 'Oh, but we're not—' She broke off, not sure how to put it.

'You're *not?*' Janet looked back at her, evidently unable to decide whether Bea was joking or not.

'No! I mean, I just work here.'

'You don't mean it?' Janet shook her head in amazement. 'Hey, did you hear that?' she said to the others sitting round the fire. 'Bea and Chase aren't a couple! We were so sure, too, weren't we, May?'

May nodded vigorously. 'We've noticed the way you look at each other.'

Bea was poppy red by now, not even daring to look at Chase. 'No, there's nothing like that.'

'Well, why not?' May's husband, Ron, a big, jovial man, dug Chase in the ribs with his elbow. 'A great little cook like Bea! I'd snap her up if I were you!'

Chase's eyes flickered to Bea, who was sitting bolt upright on her log, scarlet-cheeked and clearly wishing that she was anywhere other than here. He managed a thin smile. 'I think Bea has other plans,' he said.

'Oh, come on! What girl's going to turn down the chance of a fine man like you? You make sure of her while you've got the chance. You'll be sorry if you let her go.'

It went on like that for the next two days. For some

reason, May and Ron and their friends had decided that
Bea and Chase were meant for each other, and if they
weren't already carrying on secretly then they ought to be.
They thought it was a great joke, and missed no chance to
tease Bea with sly references to their supposed passionate
affair or to josh Chase about what a lucky man he was,
while Bea and Chase's smiles grew more and more fixed.

Having welcomed their arrival as a distraction, Bea now
couldn't wait for them to go. She waved them off at last,
feeling sorry for Chase who was doomed to another couple
of hours of winks and nods and pointed comments as he
flew them back to Mackinnon.

At least the atmosphere between the two of them had
improved, she thought, walking back into the homestead.
Not that they'd spent any time together. If they'd so much
as bumped into each other on the veranda, Ron and the
others would have pounced on it as evidence of an assig-
nation! But she'd caught Chase's eye once or twice, enough
to know that they were united in the gritting of their teeth
if nothing else.

'Thank God they've gone,' she sighed that night as she
threw herself down next to Chase and savoured the silence.

'I know. No more demands to be invited to the wedding!'

'No more laboured jokes, or heavy hints about what a
great couple we would be!'

'No more wondering aloud what we got up to the moment we left the room.'

'Or why we were pretending to sleep in separate rooms.'

Chase smiled as he shook his head. 'They were terrible,
weren't they?'

'Honestly, you'd think there was something wrong with
us for not tearing our clothes off at every opportunity,'
complained Bea. 'I think they were amazed that we could
keep our hands off each other!'

There was a sudden pause.

Bea could have bitten her tongue out. See how easily it

happened! A few careless words, and without warning the shared laughter had turned into something else, something deep and disturbing, something that tightened the air between them and made her heart slam in slow, painful strokes against her ribs.

'Just out of interest,' said Chase conversationally, 'why aren't we tearing each other's clothes off?'

'Because…we're not interested in each other that way,' said Bea with difficulty.

'Oh. Right.'

'And because you're not my type.'

He turned to face her. 'I see.'

'And I'm not yours.'

This time Chase didn't say anything. He just looked at her mouth.

'And…and because I'm leaving next week.'

Silence. Bea's heart was booming and thudding and breathing was strangely difficult.

He was going to kiss her. Oh, please, please let him kiss her.

'Look at me, Bea,' said Chase softly at last, and it took every ounce of Bea's will not to turn her head.

She was thinking about all the other girls who had sat here in the dark with him. *Look at me, Kirsty,* he had probably said then, too. *Look at me, Sue. Look at me, Sara.* She didn't want to join the end of that particular line.

Or did she?

Bea was uncomfortably aware that it might be *exactly* what she wanted right then. For some reason an old cliché was running round her head, 'a taste of honey is better than none at all'. Or should that have been 'worse than none at all'?

Bea was still trying to remember when all her senses snarled as Chase reached out and smoothed a strand of hair behind her ear, very gently.

'Remember your challenge?' he asked.

She swallowed, distracted by the burning of her skin where his fingers had grazed her cheek. 'Wh-what challenge?'

'You said that you weren't going to sleep with me,' Chase reminded her. 'You weren't going to fall in love with me and you weren't going to marry me.'

'Oh, yes.' Bea remembered now. She couldn't help wishing she hadn't been quite so dogmatic about it. She moistened her lips. 'Well, not much has changed. I'm certainly not going to marry you,' she said bravely.

'No, that wouldn't be a good idea at all,' he agreed. 'You'd be a very unsuitable wife for me.' But there was a thread of laughter in his voice and his hand was drifting tantalisingly in her hair.

She forced her mind back with an effort. 'And I'm not going to fall in love with you,' she said.

Not very much, anyway. Deep down, Bea had a nasty feeling that she *might* be a little bit in love with him already. Only a very little bit, though. The bit that would be satisfied if he would just take her to bed and make long, sweet love to her right now.

But that wasn't the same as being really in love with him, was it?

'I'm not going to fall in love with you, either,' Chase said, moving closer along the bench and telling himself that he believed it. 'So that just leaves sleeping together, doesn't it?'

'Yes,' she said, ridiculously breathless. She couldn't manage anything else.

If she was sensible, she would get up and go right now. The trouble was that she didn't want to be sensible, not here, not now, not with Chase so close beside her, smiling in a way that made her skin shiver with anticipation.

'Do you think you might be up for negotiation on that one?' he murmured, and Bea couldn't stop an answering smile tugging at her mouth.

'I might be.'

'We-el,' he said slowly, pretending to consider, 'since you're not going to fall in love, I wondered how you felt about a meaningless, short-term relationship?'

That ought to reassure her that they didn't need to take this too seriously, Chase told himself. If he was honest, a meaningful, long-term relationship didn't sound too bad right then, but Bea might back off if she felt that he was too keen. Being involved was too close to being in love, and neither of them wanted that.

And, in the meantime, a meaningless, short-term relationship with her was better than nothing.

A lot better.

'Would it involve some tearing off of clothes and not being able to keep our hands off each other?' she said a little shakily.

'Oh, yes,' Chase promised, his hand tightening at the nape of her neck to pull her towards him. 'There'd be lots of that…just to please our late guests, of course!'

'In that case,' Bea smiled against his mouth as she succumbed to temptation, 'I think I might change my mind about the first part of my challenge.'

And then she stopped smiling as his lips claimed hers, and she was lost beneath a warm, rolling tide of sheer, wicked pleasure that went on and on as he pulled her onto his lap and they kissed and kissed and kissed again, the way Bea had been trying not to think about kissing him all this time.

How could she have resisted something that felt so good? she wondered, but it was her last coherent thought for a very long time.

'I think it's time we tore off some of those clothes, don't you?' said Chase unevenly at last.

It took them a while as they kept stopping to kiss on the way, but at length he was able to pull her into his room and swing her back into his arms, pressing her back against the door. They kissed with increasing urgency until Bea was gasping and giddy with excitement. She fumbled with the buttons of his shirt, tugging it from his trousers so that she could slide her arms around his bare back and kiss his throat, while Chase's hands moved insistently over her.

He was trying to find a way to unfasten her dress, and finally located the zip under her arm.

'Ah!' he murmured with satisfaction, kissing his way along her shoulder, and slid the zip down after a brief, frustrating struggle to undo the hook at the top. But at last he was able to push the dress down over her hips until it fell into a puddle of material at Bea's feet.

Then they were moving across the room, kissing and shedding the last of their clothes as they went, falling together onto the bed. Bea was lost, and she didn't care. There was only the feel of his body and the taste of his skin, only his strong, sure hands unlocking her, his mouth making her arch against him. The differences between them were forgotten in the pounding excitement as they moved together in a timeless, throbbing, relentless rhythm that ended only when Bea felt her senses explode in a joyful release.

Afterwards, they lay breathless, Bea's body still twitching and tingling with pleasure. 'I think we just made May and Ron very happy,' she said when she was able to speak.

'Who cares about them?' said Chase lazily into her throat. 'We just made *me* very happy.'

*Careful,* thought Bea as her heart turned over. This was just a short-term romance. It wouldn't do to forget that. But still she couldn't stop her hands smoothing over his back, loving the feel of his firm, sleek body and the way his muscles flexed in response to her touch.

She stretched luxuriously beneath him. 'I've been thinking about this for quite a while,' she confessed, and Chase raised himself up on one elbow to look down into her face with a slow smile.

'So have I. Since the day I walked into the airport at Mackinnon and saw you standing there with your high heels, and your nose in the air.'

'I don't believe you!'

'Well, maybe not right then,' he conceded, smoothing the hair from her face, 'but it wasn't long after that. Definitely since that day at the waterhole.'

'I wish you'd said something sooner.'

Chase rolled onto his back. 'You said you weren't interested,' he reminded her.

Oh, well, if he was going to be put off *that* easily…!

'I didn't want to be just another cook to join the queue.' Bea told the truth, and he turned his head on the pillow. In the starlight, she could see that his expression was serious.

'You would never be that, Bea.'

'It's all right.' Bea was suddenly afraid that she might have given too much of herself away. It would be awfully easy for Chase to misinterpret the way she had cried out his name, for instance. The way her hands had moved hungrily over him. The way she had kissed him just as if she had been in love with him.

It wouldn't do for Chase to think that. It would spoil everything.

'I don't want you to tell me I'm different,' she insisted. 'I'm leaving soon, and this is just a physical thing, right?' If she said it often enough, she might even believe it.

'Right,' said Chase after a tiny pause.

'This is me living dangerously at last!'

'Not that dangerously. We were careful.'

'I don't mean that. I mean doing something without thinking about the consequences and what might happen in the future, and you know what?' said Bea, shifting over so that she could spread her hand over his hard stomach. 'It feels good. In fact, it feels more than good. It feels fantastic!'

Chase pulled her back against him as her fingers drifted

tantalisingly. He wouldn't think about the future now. For now she was here in his arms, and that was enough. 'It certainly does!' he murmured.

Bea floated through the next few days, adrift in a tingling, satisfied glow. She wouldn't let herself think about the future. She couldn't think about anything but the night to come, and Chase with his hard hands and his hard body and his cool, firm mouth. All she had to do was look at him and her bones dissolved with desire. It was hard to believe now that she had once disliked him or dismissed him as ordinary.

'Why don't you dry your hair any more?' Chloe demanded one morning.

'I haven't really got time now that Emily's gone,' said Bea, but she didn't meet Chloe's eyes. The truth was that Chase loved to tangle his fingers in her wild curls and so she left it for him.

Chloe was still suspicious of Bea's uncharacteristic behaviour. 'You're always humming now,' she said accusingly.

'That's because I'm happy.'

It was true. There was a lot to be said for a short-term meaningless relationship, Bea told herself. No complications, no anguished wondering about how Chase really felt. They weren't asking anything of each other which meant they could just enjoy the way their differences dissolved in the heart-stopping excitement of the long, sweet nights they shared.

If, once or twice, Bea's thoughts touched on what would happen when her time at Calulla Downs came to an end, they veered quickly away before she had a chance to imagine it, and she closed her mind firmly to the prospect of saying goodbye.

Chase never mentioned it either. Why should he? It wasn't as if they were in love, Bea reminded herself. Their relationship was a purely physical one, they both knew that, and for now that was enough.

And things just kept getting better. Bea was in thrall to the touch of Chase's hands, of his mouth, to the feel of his body. He made her feel beautiful and sexy and exciting in a way Phil had never been able to do. Every evening she would sit across the table from Chase, her body thumping with the promise of the night to come, and she would will the poor stockmen to finish their pudding and leave.

By the middle of the next week, Bea had lost all track of time as the days and nights drifted lazily into each other. When she met Chase's eyes, over supper that night, she wondered how she could ever have thought of them as cold. Had there really been a time when she had been nervous about being alone with him, and the stockmen had seemed to bolt their food and disappear all too soon?

Now the meal seemed endless. It was gratifying that they appeared to enjoy her cooking so much, but Bea longed for them to go. At last it was over, and she leapt to her feet to clear away while Chase had a word with the men outside.

She was already washing the pots at the sink when she heard the screen door creak behind her. She didn't turn round. She knew that Chase was watching her, knew that he wanted her, and she smiled down into the soapy water.

When he came over to brush her hair aside and press his lips to the nape of her neck, she went weak at the knees but somehow managed to carry on washing up.

'Leave it,' he murmured, untying her apron.

'I can't,' said Bea unevenly. 'It's a matter of principle with me to always leave the kitchen clear for the morning.'

'We can wash up later,' said Chase. His lips drifted down her throat as he turned her to face him, unwinding her resistance as she went.

Bea held up her hands in her rubber gloves to stop them dripping on him while he pulled the apron over her head and discarded it. 'I can't leave the kitchen until it's done,' she said provocatively, just to prolong his delicious assault on her senses. They both knew that she was going to succumb in the end.

'We don't need to leave.' Chase smiled as he kissed his way back up her throat to her mouth. 'We can do it right here.'

Breathless, Bea let him tug the rubber gloves from her hands. 'On the kitchen table?'

'Why not?'

With a grunt of satisfaction, he peeled the second glove off and dropped it to the floor so that he could pull her against him. Bea wound her arms around his neck and sank into his kiss.

'It doesn't look very comfortable,' she murmured.

Chase's hand was already sliding up her thigh. 'You won't know until you try it,' he said, and Bea was just about to give in, unable to put up more than a token struggle, when the phone in the office down the corridor started to ring, and they both froze.

They had so few calls that the sound of the phone was startling at the best of times, and now it rang insistently, jarringly, in the silence, impossible to ignore.

Chase cursed under his breath. 'That'll be Nick. No one else would call at this time.'

'You'd better go,' said Bea reluctantly. 'It might be important.'

He kissed her hard, once, and released her. 'Don't put those gloves on again,' he said. 'I'll be back as soon as I've got rid of Nick.'

In fact, Bea had had time to finish the washing up and wipe down the surfaces before Chase reappeared. He had been on the phone for so long that she was afraid that it might be bad news, and it was a huge relief to see that his expression was odd rather than grief-stricken.

'Sorry I was so long. I had Nick and Georgie on the line, and I couldn't shut either of them up.'

'Has something happened?'

'They're back together again,' said Chase. 'They've sorted everything out, are blissfully happy and Georgie tells me that they're going to live happily ever after.'

'That's good news, isn't it?' said Bea doubtfully, confused by his tone, while a cold voice inside her wondered whether it hurt him to hear that his brother was happy again with the woman he had once loved.

'Oh, yes, it's good news. Good for them, anyway.'

Chase raked his fingers through his hair. He felt irritated and unsettled, and more than a little frustrated at having been dragged away from Bea to listen to Nick raving on and on about Georgie. He was glad that they were both so happy, of course, but it had brought home to him that his own relationship with Bea was all too temporary. There would be no living happily ever after for them. Bea would go back to her city and he…he would miss her.

But he couldn't tell her that. Meaningless, short-term, no commitments and no demands…that was the way they had agreed it would be.

'They're so happy, in fact, that they can't bear to be separated again,' he went on. 'They've decided Nick will stay over there until Georgie has finished filming, and then they'll come home together.'

'When will that be?' asked Bea, pulling off her gloves on her own this time.

'A couple of months. They're going to make it a second honeymoon.'

'Two *months?*' She stared at him in dismay. 'What about Chloe?'

'They wanted to know how she was, and I said that she seemed perfectly happy, so Georgie asked if I would carry on as things are rather than uprooting her at this stage.'

Georgie again, Bea noted jealously. 'What did you say?'

'What could I say? I can hardly put Chloe on a plane to LA and ask her to find her parents herself.' Chase looked at Bea. 'I suppose you wouldn't consider staying on a bit longer, would you?' he asked, carefully casual.

'I can't, Chase.' The full realisation of how little time they had left hit Bea like a blow to the stomach. 'My visa runs out in less than a month.' She took a deep breath. 'You would have to get someone new anyway for the rest of the time. Maybe it's better for you to do that sooner than later.'

'Yes, sure. You're right,' he said bleakly. 'I'll contact the agency tomorrow.'

There was a heavy silence. 'I wish I could stay,' said Bea wistfully, understanding now that it was too late just how much she was dreading having to leave.

'It doesn't matter.' Chase couldn't bear the thought that she might be trying to spare his feelings. He forced a smile. 'We've had a good time, haven't we?'

'Yes,' said Bea. 'We have.'

He came over and took her by the waist, needing to touch her, to hold her, while he could. 'We might as well make the most of the time we've got left, don't you think?'

Suddenly terrified that she might be about to cry, Bea put her arms around him and buried her face in his throat. 'Yes,' she said unsteadily, 'let's do that.'

Bea pressed her mouth into Chase's shoulder and spread her hand over his stomach. She could feel his chest rising and falling with each slow, steady breath. They had made love with a kind of desperation, losing themselves in touch and taste and the wild surge of sensation, making the world go away for a while.

But the world was still there when their heartbeats returned to normal at last. The world where at some point soon they were going to have to say goodbye.

She didn't want to go. Bea admitted it to herself as she lay entwined with Chase. She wasn't ready to be sensible again, not yet.

*I'm not going to fall in love with you.* How confidently
she had said it! She had meant it, too, although now it
seemed incredible that she hadn't known that of course she
was going to fall in love with him. How could she *not* fall
in love when her heart seemed to stop every time she
looked at him? When his smile clogged the breath in her
throat and the merest brush of his hand was enough to set
her senses zinging and singing with delight?

So, yes, she'd fallen in love in spite of her best intentions. It wouldn't last. Bea could see that already. She
wasn't a fool. They were too different, and they wanted
different things. They had both made that clear from the
start. *I'm looking for a suitable girl,* Chase had said. *I don't
want to marry you. You don't belong, and you never will.*

No, this was just a holiday romance, a consuming passion that would burn out eventually in the face of humdrum
reality. But, while it did last, shouldn't she make the most
of it, as Chase had said? If she left now, while things were
so good, she might spend the rest of her life regretting it,
and turning Chase into a fantasy figure that would bear little
relation to the real man. Wouldn't it be better to stay until
the excitement had worn off and practicalities had taken
over, until she could kiss and say goodbye without her heart
breaking, and they could both walk away without regret?

There was only one way she could stay long enough for
that to happen.

'Chase?'

He was quiet, thinking too. 'Yes?'

'Chase,' said Bea slowly, 'how would it be if I stayed
until Nick and Georgie came home?'

Chase lifted himself up on one elbow and looked down
at her. Her skin was luminous in the moonlight and her
eyes were like dark, gleaming pools.

'I thought you had to leave Australia?'

'I would have to,' said Bea, 'unless...' She stopped,
wondering how best to put it.

'Unless what?' he asked, and she took a breath.

'Unless we got married. Wait!' she hurried on, flinging out a hand to stop him before he could react. 'Wait, I know what you're going to say, but it wouldn't be like that. I said I didn't want to marry you and I don't. It would just be a temporary arrangement. We could divorce as soon as your brother came home.'

Chase's eyes narrowed. 'What would be the point of getting married, then?'

'It would mean I could stay in Australia.'

'Ah,' he said, his voice empty of expression.

He could see it from Bea's point of view, of course. No more visa hassles, no need to go back to London with its bitter memories and its awkward encounters. She could set up her business in Sydney, just the way she had wanted.

'What would I get out of it?' he asked after a moment.

'You wouldn't have to look for someone else to look after Chloe,' said Bea.

'Not much of a reason to get married, is it?'

'No.' Bea swallowed at the hard edge to his voice. She had gone about this all wrong. 'No, it isn't. I just thought…we've got something good,' she tried to explain.

'We both know it's not going to last,' she stumbled on. 'I'm a city girl. You want a country girl, and I'm never going to be that, just like you're never going to live in Sydney and do the kind of things I want to do. I don't want to stay for ever, Chase, but I don't want to go. Not yet.'

'I don't want you to go, either,' he admitted.

'There's no pressure,' Bea said, gaining confidence. 'If you don't want to risk marriage, I'll quite understand, and I'll go as soon as you find another cook.

'I don't want you to think I'm getting involved or anything,' she added carefully, suddenly nervous in case she scared him off by appearing too keen. She had heard enough about Chase's reaction to the English girls who built him up into a romantic figure and then fell for him. As she had done. 'It's just…'

'Just sex?'

Bea hadn't been going to put it quite like that, but wasn't that what it boiled down to? 'Yes,' she said. 'It's the same for both of us, isn't it?'

Chase lay down and stared at the ceiling. 'Right,' he said.

'Getting married…it wouldn't mean anything. I wouldn't touch any of your money. We could make it a proper agreement, if you wanted. There'd be no question of commitment…' Bea trailed off unhappily.

Well, what had he expected? Chase asked himself. A passionate declaration of love? She was being straight with him. She was right, too. They did want different things. Their relationship would never work in the long-term…but it was working so far. It was working fine.

If he married her, Bea would stay. Only for two months, perhaps, but that would be two months when he wouldn't have to come home to an empty house and an empty bed, two months when he wouldn't keep turning his head and expecting to see her, or reaching out in the morning and finding that she wasn't there.

Bea bit her lip as the silence lengthened.

'Look, forget it,' she blurted out at last. 'It was just an idea. I just thought it might be a convenient arrangement, that's all.'

Chase turned towards her, and when Bea saw the smile curling the corner of his mouth she nearly wept with relief. 'Convenient?' he repeated as he swept a possessive hand over the contours of her body, his smile deepening as she shifted in instinctive response to his touch. 'Who for?'

'For both of us,' said Bea, hope trickling into her heart at the undercurrent of laughter in his voice.

'I can see it would be convenient for *you*.'

'For you, too,' she said as her breath shortened. 'You won't have to waste time seducing a new cook!'

'Good point,' said Chase, pinning her beneath him and kissing the curve of her shoulder so that she shivered and squirmed deliciously. 'And then there would be other compensations, wouldn't there?' he suggested.

Bea wrapped herself around him, her hands moving hungrily over his warm, solid back. 'Oh, yes,' she sighed against his mouth, 'there would definitely be compensations for both of us!'

'I think you might have talked me into it,' he murmured back, and that was the last talking they did for a long time.

Much later, Bea was lying in his arms, her body throbbing contentedly. 'Are you sure?' she asked.

'I'm sure,' said Chase lazily. 'We'll get married with no commitments and no messy emotions, and we'll get divorced before we have time to drive each other mad. You get what you want, a visa, and I get to behave badly with an unsuitable girl before I settle down with someone sensible.' He turned his head on the pillow and grinned at her. 'The more I think about it, the more I think it's just what I want!'

# CHAPTER EIGHT

CHASE found Bea picking lemons in the garden when he came back to the homestead the next morning after setting the men to work.

'I've been making a few calls,' he said as he came across the grass towards her, stopping to ruffle Chloe's hair on the way. 'We can get married in Townsville.'

'I know too many people in Mackinnon,' he answered Bea's questioning look. 'It would turn into a circus if we tried to get married quietly there. Before we knew what had happened there would be parties, and questions about why we hadn't waited for Nick and Georgie, and it could get awkward when they find out we're getting divorced just a couple of months down the line.'

'Townsville sounds fine,' said Bea. She knew that she was the one who had first suggested a divorce, but Chase didn't need to go on about it.

'We should get the next mob of cattle through the yards by the end of the week, and there are no more guests booked in for a while, so we might as well go on Monday,' he was saying.

His eyes rested on his niece who was playing happily on the grass. 'We'll have to take Chloe with us,' he added, 'but it can't be helped. We might as well stock up on a few things while we're there, too. There's more choice than in Mackinnon. Make a list of anything you need—and don't forget toothpaste and more beer,' he remembered.

It was a new slant on a wedding list. 'Very romantic,' said Bea a little tartly, and he glanced at her, his pale eyes as startling as ever beneath his hat.

'It's not about romance, is it?'

'No,' she said, looking down at the lemons in her hands, 'of course not.'

She couldn't help remembering how she had planned her wedding to Phil. They hadn't got to the stage of issuing invitations, thank God. Phil had mocked her for wanting a traditional wedding in the local church, with a marquee in her parents' garden. It would have been a family affair, and that's what it had been in the end, although not exactly the way she had planned. The affair had been between Phil and her sister.

It had been obvious then why Phil had shown so little enthusiasm for her suggestions. He had kept saying that there was no hurry, that they were living together, and there was no point in rushing into an expensive wedding until they could afford it. Looking back on it, Bea could see that these had just been excuses, and that he hadn't been ready for marriage—at least, not to her.

And now she was contemplating marriage again. There would be no traditional wedding this time, just a brief ceremony, with no marquee, no guests, no family.

'What's the matter?' Chase was watching her more closely than she realised.

'Nothing. It's just not going to be how I always imagined my wedding, that's all.'

'It's not too late to change your mind,' he said.

Bea looked at him. He was standing a few feet away, every line of his body overwhelmingly distinct against the dazzling light. His shirt was open at the neck and, as her eyes drifted downwards, she imagined undoing the buttons, touching her lips to his bare chest, and she was shaken by a wave of lust that left her feeling dizzy and disorientated for a moment.

'Bea?'

Bea blinked the giddiness away. 'I don't want to change my mind,' she said.

'Sure?'

'Sure.'

'Come here.' Her hands were full of lemons, so Chase took her just above the elbows and drew her towards him to kiss her.

Bea felt the world shift beneath her feet. She had the strangest sensation, as if her whole life had been arrowing into the intensity of that moment, standing in the garden at Calulla Downs with the huge outback sky arching over her head. Chase's shirt smelt of hot, dry dust and sunlight and horses, mingled with the scent of the lemons in her hands.

'It will be worth it,' he said as he let her go.

Bea felt ridiculously close to tears, but she managed a smile. 'I know.'

They flew to Townsville four days later. Being in the plane again felt very strange to Bea. The last time, she had been nervous about entrusting herself to the grim stranger Chase had been, and she felt a very long way from home.

And now...now Chase was her lover, soon to be her husband, and she felt utterly safe in his hands. True, the outback still didn't feel like home, but at least it was not quite as alien as it had been. It wasn't really her kind of thing, of course, but if you liked starry nights and silence and spectacular sunsets, then there was no doubt that the outback was the place for you.

Not for her, of course. She was still an urban girl through and through, Bea reminded herself. She liked the bustle of the city, not the hush of the creek at dusk, but it didn't mean that she couldn't appreciate the bush...for a little while.

The truth, however, was that Bea didn't enjoy being back in a town quite as much as she had expected. It felt odd to be walking along pavements again, and she felt over-whelmed by the noise of the traffic, by the number of people, by the height of the buildings. And Townsville, busy though it was, was hardly Sydney or London. How on earth was she going to get on in a big city now?

But she didn't have to face the big city yet. She had two more months in the outback, two more months with Chase. And tomorrow she was getting married.

Bea felt her spirits rise as they left their things at the hotel and went out to lunch. Chloe clamoured to have a hamburger and chips, and although Bea was longing for some fish after the Calulla Downs diet of beef, beef and more beef, the little girl was so excited at the prospect that she gave in. They found a fast-food joint, where they were served a flaccid hamburger in a polystyrene box with dry, tasteless French fries.

Chloe thought it was delicious. 'I wish we could have this every day!'

Bea laughed. 'You'd soon get bored of it if you did.'

'I wouldn't!'

'Well, I'd get bored cooking it,' Bea told her.

'Will you make me a hamburger for my birthday?' Chloe asked.

'That depends when it is.'

'July the fifteenth. I'm going to be six,' she said proudly.

Bea's eyes flickered to Chase and then away. Chloe was thrilled at the idea of the wedding, and it seemed a shame to spoil her pleasure by telling her the truth, which was that Bea was unlikely to still be around on her birthday. The thought was like a cloud passing over the sun.

'We'll see,' she said, carefully non-committal.

'I guess you won't be serving hamburgers when you set up your catering business,' said Chase when Chloe was absorbed in sucking up the last of her milkshake.

He thought he had better reassure Bea that he hadn't forgotten her ambition. It was too easy to forget when she was sitting there with the sunlight in her golden eyes and glinting off her cloud of brown hair, when her face was warm and vivid, and the beautiful mouth was curved upwards into the smile that never failed to make his throat tighten.

Right then, Bea couldn't imagine cooking anywhere other than the kitchen at Calulla Downs, let alone setting up a business, but she didn't want Chase to think that she had forgotten their agreement. 'No, I'm strictly a canapé sort of cook,' she said lightly. 'The fiddlier the better.'

That ought to convince him that she had no intention of outstaying her welcome. There was no call for canapés at Calulla Downs.

After lunch, they went to buy a ring. Bea felt very awkward in the jeweller's shop, and selected the first plain gold band that fitted, but when she tried to pay for it herself, Chase wouldn't allow it.

'I'll dock it out of your wages,' he joked, handing over a credit card.

Short of having an unseemly tussle, Bea didn't see much option but to accept with good grace. 'Thank you,' she said, vowing to find some way to repay him before she went. She would be getting far more out of their marriage than he would, and it didn't seem fair that he should have to pay for everything, too.

There was a short silence while the assistant busied himself with the card. Bea picked up the ring in its box and pretended to admire it. 'It's lovely.'

'Want a diamond one to go with it?' said Chase.

Bea glanced at him uncertainly. Was this another joke? It was hard to tell from his expression. She attempted a laugh. 'Not if it's coming out of my wages too!'

'The diamonds would be on me.'

His voice was casual, but when their eyes caught, the look held, and for some reason Bea's heart started to slam uncomfortably against her ribs. She wrenched her gaze away with an effort.

'I had a diamond ring when I was engaged to Phil,' she told him. 'It didn't do me much good. I never made it to the wedding I planned then, so perhaps if I skip all the trimmings, it'll be second-time lucky.'

Chase's eyes rested on her averted face. 'I hope it will,' he said.

Chloe was in a fever of impatience to go and buy the dress she had been promised for the wedding, so Chase went off to deal with station business and left them to it. Bea had never shopped with a five-year-old before but, for a child who rarely saw more than the general store in Mackinnon, Chloe had a remarkably clear idea of what she wanted.

She set her heart on a pink, frilly confection that was so patently unsuitable for the outback that Bea looked at her with new interest.

'I think you might have the makings of a city girl,' she said, and bought her hairclips and a plastic necklace to match.

'What do you think I should wear?' she asked Chloe.

Chloe was keen on a long, white dress with a skirt like a meringue, which came complete with a tiara and a veil, but Bea didn't think Chase would appreciate the joke if she turned up in that.

'I suppose I *could* wear one of the dresses I've got with me,' she said. She didn't want to look as if she was making a big deal out of the wedding. On the other hand, she didn't have anything that would really be suitable, and it might look a bit odd if Chloe outshone her as the bridesmaid. It *was* her wedding, after all, and it might be the only one she ever had.

Fortunately, Chloe vetoed the suggestion that she should make do with what she had, and they had the perfect excuse to carry on shopping. In the end, Bea found a sleeveless raw silk dress in an unusual bronze that brought out the colour of her eyes, which she thought was suitably stylish without looking as if she was trying too hard. With it, she bought a straw boater and wonderful peep-toe shoes with perilous heels to remind herself of the girl she had once been.

The girl she still was, Bea corrected herself hurriedly.

Each secretly glad that they didn't have to wear the other's outfit, they decided to go and have a drink to celebrate their successful purchases. They found a café in the centre of town, and sat at a table outside under a parasol, where they could watch the world go by.

'What can I get you?' their waitress asked above them in a cheerful voice.

Cheerful, and very familiar.

Bea did a double take. 'Emily!'

'Bea!' Emily stared, just as surprised, and then, being Emily, homed in on a complete irrelevance. 'What's happened to your hair?' she demanded, eyeing Bea's curls with astonishment. 'Don't tell me your hair-dryer broke!'

Bea didn't feel like going into her changed attitude to her hair right then. 'Emily, what are you doing here?' she asked severely.

'What am *I* doing here? You were supposed to be in Sydney by now!'

'I thought *you* were setting up home with Baz!'

'Oh, that didn't work out,' said Emily with an airy gesture that dismissed Baz to the past. 'I was heading back to Sydney—to you!—and I stopped here on the way. I liked it, so I thought I would stay for a few weeks, earn enough money to learn to dive and then maybe head out to the reef.'

She tucked her order book into her apron pocket and fixed Bea with a beady look. 'So that explains why I'm here, but not why you're sitting here with your hair all frizzy!'

'It's not frizzy! It's just…easier to look after…like this.'

'Emily?' Chloe tugged at her apron, ignoring Bea's warning look. 'Bea and Chase are getting married tomorrow, and I'm going to be bridesmaid!'

'Sorry, I don't think I can have heard that right,' said Emily, shaking her head as if to clear her ear. 'I know you couldn't have said *Bea* was getting married—unless you mean another Bea? Because I used to have a friend called Bea, who wouldn't dream of getting married without telling me, so maybe you've muddled her up with someone else?'

Her sarcasm went over Chloe's head. 'No,' she said earnestly, 'it's this Bea.'

'*Bea?*' said Emily awfully.

'Well, you haven't been here to tell,' said Bea, on the defensive.

Emily was outraged. 'You mean it's true?'

'It's not quite how it seems—'

'*You* are marrying *Chase Sutherland*? When did this happen?'

'It's a bit difficult to explain at the moment,' said Bea, harried, indicating Chloe with her eyes. 'Why don't I meet you later?'

'Where are you staying?' Emily whistled when she heard. 'He's not paying for you, is he?'

'Is it expensive?' Bea looked anxious. She hadn't even thought about how much the hotel would cost. Perhaps she should have offered to pay for that instead of the ring?

'It's the best,' said Emily. 'Look, I finish here at six, so I'll meet you in the bar there at half past—and you'd better be ready to tell me *everything*! Now, how about some ice cream?' she said in a different tone, and winked at Chloe. 'It's on the house!'

Chase was unsurprised to hear that Emily had moved on from Baz, and being ignorant of the rules of female friendship, didn't understand why Bea was in a tizzy about Emily discovering that she was actually getting married without having discussed it with her.

'She had to find out some time,' he pointed out reasonably. 'How else were you going to explain that you'd managed to stay in Sydney and set up a business out here?'

Bea didn't bother explaining to him that being reasonable wasn't the point of her friendship with Emily.

'I'll put Chloe to bed,' he offered. 'You go and have a drink with Emily.'

Emily was waiting for her at the bar. 'So, tell,' she ordered.

'There's not much to tell,' said Bea, slipping onto a stool next to her. She explained about Nick staying on in the States with Georgie, and her visa running out. 'Getting married is just a way of getting round regulations. It's all right for you, you can stay as long as you like.'

'But I thought you hated the outback!'

Bea's eyes slid away from Emily's. 'I'm not planning to stay. Chase and I have agreed, it's just a temporary arrangement. As soon as Nick and Georgie are back, I'll be off, but this time I will be able to stay in Sydney.'

'I can't believe it,' grumbled Emily. 'You're living my fantasy!'

'I thought your fantasy was living with Baz. What happened?'

Emily sighed. 'You were right, I got bored. At Calulla Downs, he was out all day, and we'd just have the evenings, but as soon as we were spending twenty-four hours a day together, we drove each other mad. Baz couldn't talk about anything except horses and cattle and when the next rodeo was.'

'So he didn't take you home?'

'Oh, yes, I met his parents, but they didn't have much to say for themselves, either. Where they lived wasn't romantic at all. It wasn't like Calulla Downs. It was just... boring. I didn't fit in at all. His parents thought I was weird for talking the whole time, and I think Baz was relieved in the end when I said I was leaving.'

'What are you going to do now?'

'I think I'll be a beach bum for a while,' said Emily gaily. 'Not that it stops me being insanely jealous of you!'

'You've got no need to be,' said Bea, fiddling with her glass. 'It's not as if we're really getting married.'

'You're getting a ring on *your* finger, aren't you? How much more married do you need to be?'

'Well, let's say we're not going to be living happily ever after,' said Bea with an unconscious sigh.

'That's up to you,' said Emily. She glanced at Bea. 'Are you sleeping with him?'

Bea's eyes wandered vaguely around the bar, and Emily sat back on her stool.

'Aha! You are! I always *thought* there was something between you and Chase!'

'It's not a big deal,' said Bea hastily.

'Well, make it a big deal!' said Emily. 'Come on, Bea! He can be a bit forbidding, I know, but he's not bad-looking, and he must be worth a bit. Imagine being mistress of all those acres!'

'He's not really my type,' muttered Bea.

'You wouldn't be sleeping with him if he wasn't your type,' Emily pointed out, and then her eyes narrowed in sudden comprehension. 'You're in love with him, aren't you?'

'No!' Bea almost shouted it. 'OK, I find him quite attractive,' she added more calmly, 'but it's just sex.' She was desperate to convince Emily that she wasn't serious about Chase, or perhaps she was desperate to convince herself. 'I've got no intention of being stuck out in the outback for ever,' she said loudly. 'I can't wait to get back to Sydney.'

'There's no need to shout, Bea, we all know that.' Chase spoke quietly right behind her, and she spun round on her stool. His expression was closed, his eyes shuttered. 'I'm sorry to disturb you, but Chloe's insisting you go up and say goodnight.'

Bea hesitated. She wanted to explain what he had heard, but what could she say? He wouldn't want to hear that she was in love with him. They were getting married the next day. It would be hard to find a surer way of making him feel trapped.

'I'll go up now,' she said awkwardly. 'See you later, Emily.'

But when she went down again, Emily had gone, and Chase was sitting on his own looking bleakly into a beer.

'Where's Emily?' she asked.

'She had to meet some diving instructor who I guess is Baz's replacement.'

'Did she say how I could get in touch with her?'

'No, but she's coming to the wedding tomorrow.'

Dismayed, Bea sat down next to him. She loved Emily, but she didn't trust her an inch. 'Didn't you tell her we didn't want to make a fuss?'

'I tried, but she insisted on coming to be your witness. I couldn't think of a good reason to refuse.'

His voice was pleasant, but distant and Bea's heart twisted. 'Chase—' she began impulsively, but he stopped her before she could go any further.

'You don't need to say anything, Bea,' he said. 'We both know what we agreed. We'll get married for two months, and where you want to go and what you want to do after that is entirely up to you.'

*We're married!* Bea looked at the ring on her finger, and tried to take it in. The ceremony itself had been a blur, and all she remembered was holding tightly to Chase's hand.

Chase had brought a posy of bush flowers for Chloe to give her that morning. Where the more usual roses would have been insipid with Bea's dress, the bouquet with its outback colours and dramatic shapes looked wonderful.

Bea was delighted. 'How did you know?' she asked him.

'I didn't,' said Chase. 'I just chose the ones that made me think of you.'

'They're beautiful,' she said and, as she kissed him on

the cheek, she felt his arm close around her. The distance between them had dissipated in bed the night before, and they had reached a tacit agreement to make the most of the time they had together, without thinking about the future.

'Thank you,' she said softly in his ear.

Observing this, Emily had rolled her eyes. 'Oh, yes, *sure* you're not in love with him,' she muttered in an aside, but Bea chose not to hear. It was her wedding day, and she could do whatever she wanted.

It turned into a surprisingly happy day. Emily had brought her diving instructor with her. He bore a startling resemblance to Baz, and was so laid-back that he was practically horizontal.

'As soon as I saw him I fancied the pants off him,' Emily confided to Bea.

In spite of Chloe's pleas to return for hamburgers, they had lunch in a restaurant on the waterfront, and sat all afternoon in the dappled light of a pergola. Emily ordered champagne, and insisted on making a toast.

'To convenience!' she said ironically.

Bea was very aware of Chase beside her. Her husband. A temporary husband, maybe, but hers for the next two months.

Her hands twitched with the longing to reach out and touch him, and she had to clutch them together at times to stop them moving towards him of their own accord. She knew that she could touch him if she wanted to—he was her husband, after all—but she was afraid that the moment she laid a finger on him she would lose all vestiges of control, which might not go down too well with the other diners.

So she sat, smiling and chatting and simmering with desire, and longed for the night to come.

When Emily got reluctantly to her feet and said that she had to go, Bea put up only a token protest. Now all they had to do was get Chloe to bed.

Easier said than done. Chloe was thoroughly over-excited by the time they got back to the hotel, and refused point blank to take her dress off at first. 'I'm not tired,' she said mutinously. 'I don't want to go to sleep.'

When Bea finally persuaded her into bed, her eyelids were drooping with exhaustion. Bea kissed her goodnight and tiptoed through into the adjoining room, closing the connecting door softly behind her.

Chase was lying on top of the bed, his hands behind his head, and for a moment they just looked at each other. Then he smiled and lifted an arm invitingly.

Kicking off her shoes, Bea crawled onto the bed beside him and snuggled into his side.

'Well, we did it,' she said.

Chase lifted her hand and fingered the gold ring, picking his words with care. 'Was it hard for you today?' he asked. 'Thinking about what it would have been like if you'd got married as you planned?'

'No, it wasn't hard,' said Bea honestly. She rested her head on his chest, tired now that the day was over at last. 'If I'd married Phil, I would have spent my wedding day in a frenzy about place settings and food and whether the relatives were going to behave. As it was, we didn't have to worry about anything.

'It was the perfect wedding, in fact,' she told him, only half joking. 'Just the two of us, and no pressure.'

'No pressure...' Chase repeated thoughtfully. 'That had better be the motto of our marriage.'

'We could do worse.'

Rolling Bea beneath him with a smile, he bent to kiss her. 'Some things we could do better,' he said. 'If we prac-tise...'

Bea's honeymoon, if it could be called that, was spent stocking up on fresh fruit and vegetables that they couldn't grow at Calulla Downs, loading it all into the plane and unloading it at the other end. By the time she had put every-thing away, she barely had five minutes to unpack before she was back in the kitchen, preparing the evening meal.

Her wedding ring seemed very shiny and obvious on her finger. Every time Bea moved her hand, it winked and gleamed in the light. She waited for the stockmen to com-ment on it, or to mention the fact that she and Chase had actually got married, but no! It was horses and cattle and how many points of rain they'd had, just as usual. Bea wondered whether they'd even noticed that she and Chase hadn't been there.

'Do they know we got married yesterday?' she asked Chase incredulously when the stockmen had trooped out to their own quarters.

Chase shrugged. 'I think so. I told Doug, anyway, when I explained that I'd be away for a couple of days.'

'I can't believe they didn't even acknowledge it!'

'What did you expect?' said Chase. 'A welcome home party with champagne and canapés?'

'A word of congratulation might have been nice,' she said a little sulkily.

'If you're looking for social skills, you've come to the wrong place,' he pointed out, dumping plates in the sink. 'Why do you want congratulations, anyway? It's not as if it's a real marriage.'

'Yes, but they don't know that!'

Chase sighed. 'Bea, what is the problem?'

What *was* the problem? Bea didn't know. She just knew that she felt grouchy and obscurely hurt by the stockmen's indifference, by their air of having seen girls like her come and go a thousand times. She wanted to shout at them and remind them that Chase hadn't married any of the others, he had married *her*.

It wouldn't have killed them to have welcomed her back, or at least pretended that she was more than just one in a very long line, would it? Bea thought, washing up huffily.

Another reason, if she needed one, why she would probably be delighted to leave at the end of two months. She belonged in a city, with the kind of people who would throw a party for you if they heard you'd just got married, and yes, there *would* be champagne and canapés! What was so wrong with that?

It didn't occur to Bea that the men might simply be shy, or intimidated by her assurance. She saw their lack of response as a challenge. They obviously thought that she would never belong in the outback, and that there was no point in wasting any of their rare words on someone who would inevitably leave, wedding ring or no wedding ring.

Now Bea was on her mettle. She might not be intending to stay in the outback for ever but, as she had pointed out to Chase, the stockmen weren't to know that.

Her chin lifted, and her eyes held a militant sparkle. She would show those men that she wasn't just the silly city girl they so obviously thought her, and that she was quite capable of belonging if she wanted to. And when she *did* leave, she vowed, they would miss her!

Determined to get the hang of this outback business, Bea made Chase take her riding again that Saturday, and bravely refused the leading rein. She even managed a brief, and exceedingly uncomfortable, trot, and when Chase suggested a canter, she was so excited and pleased with herself for not falling off, that he laughed.

'We'll have you rodeo riding next!' he said, helping her out of the saddle.

'I think I'll leave the bucking broncos to you,' said Bea, but she couldn't help feeling thrilled by his approval.

Pathetic, really. She was glad Emily wasn't there to see how a mere word of praise from Chase made her quite light-headed with pleasure.

Of course, trundling a few yards on placid old Duke wouldn't be enough to get her accepted by these hard-riding men, but it was a start, wasn't it?

Encouraged, she began to listen intently to their talk about mustering and bull-catching and horse-breaking in the hope that she might be able to join in one day without Chase having to act as an interpreter, but it was all pretty baffling still, she had to admit.

What she needed, Bea decided, was go down to the cattle yards and see the men at work. She had only the haziest idea of what they actually did down there, but she could see herself leaning on the rails, perhaps slapping the rump of a cow every now and then.

'Fattening up nicely!' she would call out to the stock-men.

Or would that sound a bit heartless?

Maybe it would be better if she noticed that someone had forgotten to close a gate or something? She wouldn't make a fuss, she would just shut it quietly, but Chase would notice, of course. He would smile his thanks, and after-wards he would say what a good thing it was that she'd been there.

'You'd better come down to the yards more often,' he would say. 'The boys were just saying how nice it was to have you around.'

After this pleasant daydream, the reality of the cattle yards came as a terrible shock. Bea managed to pick a day when they were dehorning calves. There was blood spurting everywhere, and the press of cattle bellowing and milling around in clouds of dust made her nervous. She hadn't realised that cows could be that big or look that wild.

She certainly wouldn't be slapping any rumps, thought Bea, edging away. So much for her daydream!

On the other hand, wasn't that a gate over there, standing wide open? If they didn't watch out, all those cattle in the holding paddock would be making a break for it. Bea trot-ted over.

'What the hell are you doing?' Chase came galloping up through the dust on a huge, snorting horse. 'We're just about to drive that lot through here!' He wheeled the horse around with an iron hand. 'Get out of the way!' he shouted over the sound of the bellowing animals. 'And don't come out again without a hat!'

Mortified, Bea beat a hasty retreat to the homestead. Sometimes it seemed that the more she tried, the less she fitted in. When they ran low on flour, she decided to drive into Mackinnon with Chloe and go to the local store rather than wait for the weekly delivery. Because that was the kind of thing country girls did, right?

She forgot that country girls knew how to use the four-wheel drive. The track was far rougher than Bea had imagined, and she was about halfway between the homestead and the sealed road—in other words, a long way from anywhere—when she drove into sand and was promptly bogged. She had to get Chloe to show her how to use the radio and call Chase up for help.

He came, but he was in the middle of a particularly busy day, and not best pleased, to put it mildly.

That night, they went to bed in grim silence. Chase lay very still, but Bea knew that he wasn't sleeping either.

'I'm sorry,' she said miserably into the darkness at last.

There was a pause, and then he sighed. 'It's my fault,' he said. 'I can't expect you to know about driving on these roads. You've probably never been off a sealed road before.'

He made it sound extraordinary, as if there weren't millions and millions of perfectly good drivers like her who never needed to venture off tarmac. Bea knew that he was trying to comfort her, but it just made her feel even more of an outsider.

'No,' she agreed dully.

'I'm sorry I shouted at you.'

When she didn't respond, Chase rolled over and kissed her shoulder, working his slow, seductive way along to her throat. Even depressed as she was, Bea couldn't prevent an instinctive shudder of response and, without meaning to, she lifted her arms to encircle his back and pull him closer. 'We've both had a bad day,' he murmured against her warm skin. 'Let's make it a good night, and forget about

still until the only place she belonged, thought Bea later, couldn't spend tmplete in Chase's arms. With her body had discovered. Chase might want hed, as Emily and Baz he was a tough, shrewd man with a strong practical streak, and he had never pretended to be anything else. A wife who couldn't even drive into town to do the shopping without having to be rescued was no use to him. He needed a woman who would be a partner, not a liability.

She had better not forget that, Bea told herself sternly, because Chase certainly wouldn't.

# CHAPTER NINE

AND just in case he needed remind~~~~ two days later.

Erin, it turned out, ~~~gie's cousin. She and her husband ran a pl~~ in New South Wales, Chase explained when he came back from answering the phone with the news that there would be another two for supper the following night. They would be spending a couple of days at Calulla Downs on their way to buy bulls' semen or something at a station near Tennant Creek.

Bea never understood exactly what they were doing, and she was damned if she was going to ask. From the moment Erin arrived, stepping out of their big four-wheel drive in jeans and an authentic Akubra, she made Bea feel utterly inadequate.

She might have been designed to show Chase the kind of woman he really needed. Out all day with the men, at supper she joined in their discussions about bore holes and salt licks and the price of feed, and was instantly accepted as someone who knew what she was talking about.

Tall and slim, she looked wonderful in jeans and a shirt, and raised her eyebrows at Bea's habit of changing into a dress every evening.

'You can tell *you* didn't grow up in the outback!' she said with a light laugh.

It was clear that she herself wouldn't have been seen dead in anything so frivolous and impractical. Eyeing her sourly, Bea guessed that no lipsticks cluttered Erin's bathroom. She couldn't imagine Erin squeezing her feet into high-heeled shoes and convincing herself that they fitted just because they were the only size available, or beginning her packing with a travel hair-dryer.

Why would she bother, after all? Her hair was cut short and stylishly practical, and with those sickeningly long legs she had no need of any extra inches. She was annoyingly attractive as she was, with healthy skin, good bones and beautiful green eyes that held a distinctly chilly expression whenever they rested on Bea, who took to drying her hair in its sleek, time-consuming style again out of sheer contrariness. There was no way she could compete with Erin in the suitability stakes, so she might as well not try!

That was obviously Erin's opinion too. Her attitude to Bea was amused and faintly patronising. She spotted the wedding ring on Bea's finger straight away—she wasn't *that* unfeminine—and when Chase introduced Bea as his wife, she didn't bother to conceal her amazement.

'You're *married*?' She didn't actually add *Why*? but she might as well have done.

'I'm sorry if I seemed surprised,' she explained to Bea later, when she had deigned to offer her some help in the kitchen. 'We'd all given up on Chase getting married. We never thought he would get over Georgie marrying Nick.

'Oh!' Erin put a hand to her mouth in a bad pretence at dismay. 'I haven't said anything I shouldn't, have I?'

Bea, chopping onions, set her teeth. 'It's all right, Chase told me all about Georgie,' she said evenly.

'Then you'll know how much he adored her?'

Bea's fingers tightened around the knife. 'Yes, but then I've always thought that it's better to be a last love than a first love.'

'You're a brave woman then.' Erin offered a bright, insincere smile. 'Georgie's a hard act for any girl to follow.'

Bea appreciated the slight stress on that 'any'. No need for Erin to add, 'especially one like you.'

'I remember how jealous I was of her when we were kids,' Erin was saying. Bea had given her some tomatoes

to slice, and it was an eye-opener to see what a botch someone could make of such a simple job. 'Georgie wasn't just
pretty, she was a fantastic rider. You'd never think it to
look at her now, but she could ride before she could walk.'

Erin paused delicately. 'Do you ride, Bea?'

'Occasionally,' said Bea with defiance, thinking of her
ambles on Duke. And she *had* cantered. Cantering was riding, wasn't it?

'Oh.'

It was perfectly judged, managing to suggest just the
right level of polite disbelief mingled with regretful bewilderment. Why on earth, Bea could practically hear Erin
thinking, had Chase tied himself up with a girl like this?

Erin reached for another tomato. 'I gather you're a very
good cook,' she said, managing to make just as much of a
botch up of that one too.

Bea had no trouble in interpreting this. Chase had only
married her because of her way with gravy and apple pies.

Her smile glittered quite as falsely as Erin's. 'Yes, Chase
loves my cooking,' she said soulfully, 'among other things,
of course!'

Erin looked down her nose with distaste. Evidently real
outback women didn't go in for suggestive remarks.

'He says you're from London.' She made it sound like
Pluto. 'You must miss the bright lights.'

In other words, get back to where you belong, Bea trans-
lated sourly.

'Not at all,' she declared, lifting her chin.

But, much as she hated to admit it, Erin's barbed comments had had an effect.

Why was she wasting her time trying to be accepted out
here? It was obvious that she was never going to belong.
Chase had told her that himself not so long ago. She could
spend a lifetime learning how to lasso calves and wield a
branding iron, reflected Bea, but the likes of Erin would

always think of her as a London girl in a dress, out of place and out of her depth.

She didn't even know if Chase wanted her to stay. When he made love to her, it was hard to believe that he didn't feel something, but he was careful to let no words that might smack of commitment past his lips. He seemed happy to accept the situation as it was, and not think about the future.

She should do the same.

Bea thought about it as Erin went off to join the men on the veranda for a beer, obviously considering that she had done enough woman's work in the kitchen.

Had she fallen into the classic trap of confusing lust with love? Bea paused in the act of scraping Erin's ruined tomatoes into a pot to make a sauce and frowned.

She had often accused Emily of doing the same thing, and now it was looking suspiciously as if she had fallen for the same romantic dream. Why else would she have started dreaming about helping out in the yards or galloping confidently around the outback?

Did she really think Chase could be that easily fooled into wanting to spend the rest of his life with her?

Bea cringed inwardly when she thought of how obvious her attempts to fit in must have seemed to Chase. She had let herself get carried away by the intensity of their physical attraction, forgetting that they had little else in common.

The sensible side of Bea's nature reasserted itself with relief after weeks of being ignored. Really, what had she been thinking of? Had she honestly imagined that she could be happy boiling billies and chasing cows around the outback?

The only trouble was that now she couldn't imagine being happy without Chase.

Well, there was no hurry, Bea told herself sensibly. Nick and Georgie weren't due back for another three weeks at least. Time enough to think about whether her feelings for

Chase were real or just romantic dreams dressing up plain, unadulterated lust.

In the meantime, she should relax and enjoy what she and Chase had without trying to pretend that she was someone she wasn't. She would be herself and if Erin and the stockmen didn't like it, that was just too bad.

'How would you like a day out?'

It was nearly a week later when Chase came in from the office and found Bea studying a recipe for apple cobbler. A thousand ways to cook stodge, she and Emily had called it when they found the cookbook, yellow with age, tucked away on a shelf in the corridor, and Bea was a little embarrassed to find herself poring over it for inspiration more and more often.

'A day out?' she repeated blankly, images of ice creams and funfairs chasing bizarrely around her brain. 'Where?'

'I've just been talking to the land agents in Mackinnon,' said Chase. 'There's a property for sale on the other side of town.'

Bea sat back, putting a finger in the book to keep her place. 'Are you thinking of buying it?'

'I might go and have a look,' he said. 'I just wondered if you wanted to come with me.'

'Me?'

The sensible side of Bea, having recovered its ascendancy over the last few days, instantly urged caution. Things had been much better between them since she had stopped trying to pretend that she would ever fit in, but it might also have had something to do with the fact that Chase had been so busy outside that they had hardly spent any time alone.

Except when they were in bed, where there was never any problem about getting on.

'I wouldn't know the first thing about buying a station,' said sensible Bea, even as the reckless romantic who had

emerged so alarmingly recently was thrilling at the mere
thought of going anywhere with him.

'That doesn't matter,' said Chase. 'We could make a day
of it. I'm sure Julie wouldn't mind looking after Chloe, just
this once, and it would make a change for you,' he went
on, uneasily aware of how much he wanted Bea to come
with him.

And, uneasily aware of how she wanted to go, Bea said
that she would. Only because she couldn't think of a good
reason to refuse, sensible Bea justified it to herself.

The other, dangerous, Bea, didn't bother with reasons or
excuses. She was just standing there and smiling, while her
body cheered at the prospect of a whole day alone with
him.

Sensible Bea was firmly back in control, however, by the
time they flew over to look at the station Chase was thinking of buying. She was getting used to jumping into a plane
the way most people got into a car.

'What's this place called?' she asked, settling into her
seat.

'Wilbara.' Chase eased the joystick back as the plane
levelled off. 'I can just remember it being a fair-size station
before it was gobbled up by a conglomerate with two other
properties. They ran cattle on the land, but abandoned the
homestead and the yards. Nothing much has been done on
the property for years. It's a shame, because it's good grazing land over there.'

They had been flying for about three quarters of an hour
when Chase swooped down to have a closer look at the
ground. 'This ought to be Wilbara now,' he said.

Bea peered out of her window, wondering how on earth
he could tell. It looked exactly the same to her, a bit rockier
maybe, but otherwise indistinguishable from the land,
rough and red with a sparse scattering of grey-green scrub,
that stretched out in a dizzying expanse to the curve of the
earth.

'*That* is good grazing ground?' she said before she could help herself.

'We don't do lush green fields like you do in England,' said Chase with a sardonic look.

'You can say that again!'

'You should see it after the Wet,' he told her, banking the plane so that they flew along the line of the creek. 'If we get good rains, the grass will be over your head.'

Bea tried to picture the cracked red earth covered with a mantle of long grass, but she had to shake her head in defeat. 'I can't imagine it.'

'It's beautiful then,' said Chase warmly. 'You've never seen anything like it.'

'It sounds amazing.'

That was his chance to say that she could see it for herself if she wanted to stay for a few months longer, or to suggest that he would like to show her the miraculous transformation of the landscape but, if Chase was aware of his cue, he missed it.

Studying the ground below, he only grunted absently. 'It is,' was all he said.

Bea was furious with herself for being disappointed. She was supposed to be living for the present, enjoying their relationship while it lasted, and not wondering why he wasn't planning on spending the Wet with her.

'You'll have to send me a photo,' she said in a brittle voice.

Chase glanced at her sharply, but she had turned away and was making a pretence of watching two kangaroos loping through the scrub below them.

'Sure,' he said flatly.

Wilbara's airstrip was little more than a rough clearing in the bush. A bumpy landing in more ways than one, thought Bea, feeling as if she had been brought abruptly down to earth by Chase's blunt reminder that her time as his wife was strictly limited.

JESSICA HART                                    155

A wild-looking character who introduced himself as Wal
was there to meet them.

'The agents said you'd be coming to have a look today,'
he said laconically, and jerked his head in the direction of
a battered ute. 'They thought you might want a vehicle, so
I said I'd show you round.'

The three of them got into the front of the truck. Chase
stretched an arm along the back of the bench seat and
turned slightly so that he could talk to Wal, who set off at
a cracking pace across the rough ground. Stuck in the middle on the slippery seat, Bea was lurched and jolted between the two men.

'Sorry,' she muttered, having been flung against Wal.

'Don't apologise,' he leered. 'I haven't had a pretty girl
throwing herself at me for a long time!'

Edging back towards Chase, Bea could believe it. Wal
might have been keeping an eye on things since the station
closed down, but washing was evidently not high on his
priority list.

She was appalled when she learnt that he had been left
on his own. 'Don't you get lonely?' she said, wincing at
the sound of her prim, prissy voice next to Wal's slow
drawl. It was as if everything today was conspiring to remind her how English and out of place she was.

'Nah,' said Wal.

'But what do you do all day?'

'Shoot roos mostly.' He gave her a gap-toothed grin. 'I
just *love* killing wildlife!'

Bea smiled nervously. She wasn't quite sure what to
make of Wal, and it was obvious that the feeling was mutual.

'You two been married long?' he asked, with a curious
look at Chase. He might as well have wondered out loud
what Chase was doing with a wife like Bea.

'No, not long.'

Bea wished Wal would look where he was going. They

were careering across the bush with a fine disregard for the
fact that the ground was littered with rocky outcrops,
scrubby trees and bleached wood. Wal would drive straight
towards whatever was in his way, only swerving at the very
last second.

'I was married once,' he said, avoiding a towering ter-
mite mound by inches. He screwed up his face in an effort
of memory. 'What was her name now?'

By the end of the afternoon, Bea had been jolted and
jarred over miles. Every now and then, Wal would pull up
with a screech, and they would get out. Bea stood rubbing
her aching bottom and waving the flies from her face while
Chase and Wal inspected dams or studied the stray cows
that had evidently escaped the last muster and were now
running wild. They lifted their heads to eye the humans
warily before turning and blundering off into the bush, just
in case.

The cattle looked all right to Bea's inexperienced eye,
but even she could see that otherwise Wilbara was in an
appalling condition. The fences were broken and the dams
and bore holes badly neglected. Still, she stared in disbelief
when they returned to the airstrip and she saw Chase shaking Wal's hand in an unmistakable gesture of farewell.

'We're going?'

'I thought you'd be pleased,' said Chase, having heard
her muttering under her breath every time they bounced
over a particularly deep hole.

'You haven't even looked at the homestead!' Bea
pointed out incredulously, and his heart sank. He had been
afraid that she would think of that.

'I don't think it'll be up to much,' he said, taking her
arm and urging her towards the plane.

Bea shook herself free. 'But that's where—' she stopped
herself from saying 'we' just in time '—where *you'll* be
living if you buy Wilbara. I can't believe you wouldn't
even bother to look at it!'

'Want to see the homestead?' Wal offered obligingly.

'I don't think we'll bother,' Chase began, but Bea spoke firmly over him.

'Yes, please, Wal. We *would* like to see it.'

Wal beamed and opened the door of the ute. 'Hop in, then.'

He drove them down a rough track and pulled up with a flourish outside the homestead. 'There you go,' he said. 'Welcome to Wilbara.'

For several minutes, Bea could only stare in appalled silence. Once, perhaps, it had been a fine, solid building with a wide veranda, but now it was crumbling and neglected. The corrugated iron roof was hanging off the veranda in sheets, and the doors stood broken on their hinges.

To Bea, used by now to the gracious homestead at Calulla Downs with its polished wood and cool, luxuriant garden, it looked dismal and depressing, standing in a bare, dusty yard with a clutter of ramshackle huts behind it and not a blade of green to soften the view.

Inside, it was even less inviting. As they walked through, they left footprints in the thick layer of dust that lay over everything. Wal led them down a long corridor, enjoying his new role as a real estate agent.

Flinging open a door, he nudged Bea so hard that she nearly fell into the room. 'The passion pit!' he announced.

'What?'

He grinned. 'Master bedroom to you,' he told her with a lewd wink. 'All you need is a bed in here and you'll be well away!'

Bea coloured but Chase only asked how many bedrooms there were altogether.

'Six or seven, I reckon,' said Wal, having given the matter some thought. 'They had big families in those days, and no shortage of space. You two planning on having children?' he asked with frank curiosity.

'Not right at this moment,' said Chase, with a glance at

Bea's hot face. No prizes for guessing that having a family was the *last* thing on her mind just then!

'Plenty of time for practising, eh?' Wal chuckled dirtily and ambled off down the corridor.

'Who *is* this guy?' hissed Bea at Chase as they made to follow him.

'He's just trying to wind you up,' said Chase dismissively.

'Well he's doing a very good job!'

'Ignore him.'

Easy for *him* to say. He hadn't been leered at all afternoon, and if Wal dug his elbow into her ribs one more time, she would punch him. Her side was black and blue as it was.

Bea peered into another gloomy room. 'God, what a dump!'

'You were the one who wanted to see it,' Chase pointed out irritably.

'Yes, and it's just as well I did, isn't it?' She flicked a switch on the wall to see if a little light might improve matters, but nothing happened.

'There's no electricity,' Wal informed them, popping up behind her. 'You could fix up the generator if you wanted,' he added, managing to suggest that needing electricity ranked somewhere up there with bathing in asses milk or peeling grapes as far as priorities went.

'Oh, we'd need the generator, darling,' said Bea naughtily. Wal wasn't the only one who could do winding up. 'You *know* I have to be able to plug in my hair-dryer!'

Wal thought that was a great joke. 'Hair-dryer!' he repeated, laughing wheezily, and Bea could hear him still chuckling as he took Chase outside to look in the tumbledown sheds around the yard.

Bea wandered back along to the kitchen. Having a wife who actually dried her hair probably counted as a guilty secret around here. She hoped Wal told everybody and ruined Chase's reputation. She wasn't invited to hang around and see the Wet, so what did she care?

She stood in the middle of the dusty floor and looked around the kitchen. It was a shame everything was so filthy, because now she looked at it properly, she could see that it had quite a lot of potential. Swept and scrubbed and with that dreary paint stripped off the walls, it would be a pleasant, decent-sized room. You could even knock through to the dining room next door and screen off the veranda there to make an eating area as at Calulla Downs, and if you put in some plants and a pergola it would make the whole kitchen a light and airy place to work.

Bea turned slowly in the dust, picturing herself there. It would need to be gutted completely, of course, and you'd have to get rid of those units and replace the sink... Her eye ran along the worktop, mentally replacing it with something cool and clean, and then came to a jarring halt.

What was that?

What *was* that?

'Oh—my—God!' croaked Bea.

A spider so enormous that her gaze had travelled over it uncomprehendingly at first before jerking back in disbelief was squatting evilly by a rusty old breadbin. It was the size of a man's hand, at least, with feet like boxing gloves.

All eight of them.

Horror gripped Bea by the throat and the hairs rose on the back of her neck. For a long moment she could only stare at the spider, paralysed by panic, and then as if sensing her fear, it scuttled forward.

Bea's scream would have done justice to any horror movie.

The spider stopped on the edge of the unit. Bea couldn't actually see its eyes, but it seemed to her that it was regarding her with a cold, unwavering stare. Very, very slowly, she began to edge backwards towards the door—there was no way she was turning her back on that thing!—

only to scream again as she bumped into Chase who came running into the room.

'What is it?' he demanded urgently.

Bea clutched at him. 'S-s-sp-pp...' was all she could get out, and Chase followed the direction of her shaking finger.

'For God's sake, Bea, it's just a spider!'

Chase was clearly not in the mood to play the comforting hero. He took Bea's hands off him impatiently.

'He's a big fella, though, isn't he?' Wal had appeared now, and was studying the spider with admiration. 'Take a look at those paws on him!'

'Don't touch it!' shrieked Bea as Wal peered closer.

'Stop making such a fuss!' said Chase shortly. 'It's not going to hurt you.'

'It might go for Wal! Look at it, it's getting ready to jump.'

'Don't be ridiculous! Spiders don't attack without provocation.'

'Sometimes they do,' Wal joined in the argument. 'I knew a fella once opened a drawer and a big monster like this jumped up and bit him on the face.' Wal spread his fingers and clapped a hand over his face in graphic illustration. 'Spoilt his weekend,' he added with masterly understatement.

Bea moaned. 'I feel sick.'

'Pull yourself together,' Chase ordered, propelling her outside. 'You're being hysterical.'

He was so unsympathetic that Bea, who had been on the verge of tears, pulled herself free and glared at him. Whatever happened to love and protect? Any decent husband would have swept his wife into his arms and begged her to tell him that she was all right, not marched her outside and told her to stop making a fuss! He would have tackled the monster himself just to prove his love for her, instead of letting Wal—Wal!—be the hero.

Of course, any decent husband loved his wife, and Chase didn't do that. She kept forgetting.

From inside the kitchen came sounds of banging and thumping. It sounded as if a huge fight was going on. Bea looked nervously at the door.

'Do you think Wal is all right?'

'What, you think the spider's into kung fu?' asked Chase sarcastically.

'You can't tell with something like that. This is how horror films start, you know.' Bea hugged her arms together, feeling twitchy. 'Three people and a spider, alone, miles from help, and the next thing you know there's only two...'

Her imagination was leaping ahead, already seeing the spider, grotesquely enlarged, poking one of its assorted huge, hairy legs around the door, raking the veranda in frustration as it tried to drag her and Chase into its gaping fangs. All they would find later would be a few crushed bones. No one would ever know what had happened to her.

'Oh, God,' she whimpered, heedless of Chase's look of disgust, and when a moment or two later Wal appeared in the doorway, she was so relieved that she practically threw her arms around his neck.

'Are you all right, Wal?'

'Yeah, I'm all right,' he said, grinning broadly. 'The spider's not feeling too good.'

'Oh, *thank* you!'

'No worries,' said Wal. 'I told you I liked killing wild-life!'

Bea couldn't wait to get back to the plane. 'Are you sure you don't want to come with us?' she asked Wal, who looked surprised at her concern.

'Nah, I'll be right,' he said, apparently unperturbed at the prospect of sleeping and eating with spiders lurking all around him.

He waved at Bea as she climbed into the plane. 'See you next time,' he called after her.

'*Next time*?' said Bea to Chase as they strapped themselves in. 'He's got to be kidding!'

'Why?'

She gaped at him. 'You're not seriously thinking of coming back here?'

'I don't see why not. It's good land.'

'It's heaving with monstrous creatures!'

Chase sucked in his breath irritably. Why did she always have to exaggerate? 'It was only a spider,' he said, holding on to his temper with difficulty.

'That was not a spider,' said Bea. 'That thing had a starring role in *Arachnophobia*!'

'In what?'

'It's a film, a horror movie.' She sighed. 'But of course, you won't have seen it. You don't have cinemas, and anyway, why would you need to go and see a horror movie when you can live the horror right here at home!'

Chase swore under his breath. He should never have taken Bea to Wilbara. He had known that she would be horrified by the state of the house. It was one of the reasons why he hadn't wanted her to see it. He'd *told* her the homestead had been abandoned. Why had she had to insist on seeing it for herself?

And then that bloody spider had turned up.

She would never consider living there now.

Perhaps it was just as well. The whole idea had been stupid, Chase realised, scowling at the controls.

Even before she reacted so hysterically to that spider, it had been obvious that there was no way he could ever take a girl like Bea to Wilbara. A girl who fussed with her hair and wore ridiculous shoes and scattered garnish on her stews. It would have been a disaster.

It was just that he had wanted to take her to Wilbara, so that he could imagine her there when she was gone.

And she would go. Chase had known that all along. He had kept thinking, hoping, that she would adapt and learn to love the outback, and then he would go home and she would be doing something bizarre like painting her toenails.

At Wilbara she wouldn't even have a cooker she could switch on without the generator, and that was broken like everything else.

He could have Wilbara, but if he did he would never have Bea.

'You're not really thinking of buying that place, are you?' Bea broke into his thoughts.

'It's Wilbara, or stay on at Calulla Downs with Nick and Georgie,' he said curtly.

'But you can't live at a place like Wilbara on your own,' she objected.

Chase wished she would stop rubbing in the fact that she wouldn't be there to help him. He had already got that particular point.

'I won't be on my own,' he said shortly. 'I'll have stockmen who aren't so fussy about conditions. They don't need to wash their hair every day—unlike some people,' he couldn't resist adding.

'You should offer a job to Wal, then. He certainly doesn't wash every day!'

'I was going to do that anyway,' said Chase. 'He knows the land and he knows cattle. He'd be a useful person to have around.'

*Unlike her.* Why didn't he come right out and say it?

Bea hunched a shoulder angrily. 'Well, if you want to spend your life in a dump being stalked by giant spiders, I should go ahead and put in an offer. Wilbara's perfect for you!'

'What is it to you, anyway?' retorted Chase, nettled. 'You're not going to be there,' he reminded her brutally.

'No, I most certainly won't be there,' she told him. 'I'll be in Sydney, enjoying quaint little features like running water and telephones and electricity at the flick of a switch, and as I garnish my canapés I'll think of you cooking in that kitchen—because it *will* be you doing the cooking. You'll never get anyone to work for you in those conditions!'

There was a tight look around Chase's mouth. 'Maybe I'll get married,' he said unpleasantly. 'I'll find someone who's not afraid to get her hands dirty, and wants to work with me to build something good together, someone who doesn't go to pieces at the sight of a spider and wants to do something more with her life than fiddle around with fancy food for people who've got nothing better to do than stand around at parties bitching about each other.'

'Good idea,' said Bea, white with anger and hurt, 'except for the minor matter that you're already married!'

'Not for much longer,' he practically snarled back. 'Nick and Georgie should be back soon. We agreed that we would divorce then.'

'There's no need to panic, I'm not going to contest it in the hope that you'll sweep me off to Wilbara and hand me a dustpan and brush!'

'I never thought you would.'

'The sooner we get a divorce the better as far as I'm concerned.' Bea was too hurt to think about what she was saying. 'You might have to be a little less picky when it comes to a wife for Wilbara, though. Perhaps you should try advertising?' she suggested bitterly. '*Wanted: a wife, preferably spider lover, likes cleaning houses but not self.* I'm sure Erin could put you in touch with someone suitable!'

'Funny you should say that,' said Chase, baring his teeth. 'Erin said when she was here that she knew a girl she thought I'd get on with. That's one of the reasons she was disappointed to find that I'd married you. Apparently the girl is the daughter of one of Erin's neighbours, so she's grown up on a station.'

'She sounds just what you need,' said Bea with a glittering smile. 'Don't mind me, give her a ring when you get back!'

'Maybe I will.'

They didn't say a word to each other for the rest of the flight. Chase had left the car parked in the shade, and Bea banged the door behind her as she got in. Chase hated it when she did that.

Serve him right.

They were both so angry that neither noticed a spanking new vehicle parked by the veranda at the homestead. Bea jumped out and slammed her door again childishly before stalking towards the steps without a backward look. Chase was left to vent his fury on the car by slamming his door even louder.

'Bea, Bea!' Chloe danced out onto the veranda to meet her. 'Guess who's here?'

Bea halted. Wasn't Chloe supposed to be with Julie?

'What are you—' she began, but Chase was already looking behind her to the woman coming out of the homestead with her famous wide smile.

'Georgie!'

Ever afterwards, Bea only retained snapshot impressions of the next few minutes. She remembered looking at Chase and seeing the way the bitter, closed expression he had worn with her was lit by a smile that tore at her heart. Georgie, throwing herself into his arms for an uninhibited hug. Chloe's excited face.

And the stain on the side of the corrugated iron water tank that she stared at, her anger swamped by sudden desolation. Georgie was back, and now she would have to leave.

# CHAPTER TEN

I'M NOT ready, she thought in panic. Of course she wanted to go, especially after today. Just not yet.

'And you must be Bea!' Georgie seized her hands with a dazzling smile. 'I can't thank you enough for looking after Chloe so well!'

Somehow Bea found herself swept into the homestead on the tide of Georgie's warmth. She hadn't wanted to like Georgie, and mentally dug in her heels to resist her charm, but it was no good. Georgie was simply impossible to dislike, just as Chase had said.

Disorientated, Bea shook her head to try and clear it. One minute she and Chase had been in the middle of a bitter fight, and the next they were being hugged and kissed and greeted excitedly.

Now Georgie was introducing her to Nick, who was every bit as attractive as Emily had said. He had twinkling eyes, a deep lazy voice, and a way of looking at you that made you feel that he had waited his whole life to meet you.

In short, he wasn't anything like Chase. Bea sneaked a glance between the two men. It has hard to believe that they were brothers. Next to Nick's effortless good looks and easy charm, Chase looked grimly reserved. A muscle was jumping in his clenched jaw and there was a tight look around his eyes.

'So you're my new sister-in-law,' said Nick, grinning as he held Bea at arm's length to study her. 'We've been hearing *all* about you!'

His warm appreciation seemed to annoy Chase, who turned to Georgie with a frown. 'What are you doing here?'

Georgie looked surprised at his tone, as well she might, Bea reflected, given the way Chase had been hugging her only a minute ago.

'I'd finished filming, and Nick and I were just about to leave for the second honeymoon we'd promised ourselves in Mexico when I had the most extraordinary phone call from my cousin Erin. She said you'd got married!' Georgie's green eyes widened. 'Well, we knew you wouldn't have done that without telling us unless something was wrong, and I was afraid it might be something to do with Chloe.'

'Why didn't you ring?' said Chase irritably. 'We could have told you Chloe was perfectly all right.'

'We did try and call you, but we couldn't get a reply, and then I got into a panic and insisted that we came straight back. I was in a fret all the way! I nearly had a fit when we got here and there was nobody around,' Georgie confided, 'but then we found Chloe when we went to find out whether Julie knew what was going on, and Chloe told us that you and Bea were in love, which was a huge relief, I can tell you, after some of the things Erin had been saying!'

Whoops, Chase wasn't going to like *that!*

He didn't. 'Chloe said *what*?'

'I told Mum I saw you and Bea kissing,' said Chloe pertly. 'And I showed her my bridesmaid's dress.'

'Why don't I go and put the kettle on?' said Bea, finding her voice quickly as Chase's mouth tightened ominously.

'This is no time for tea!' said Georgie gaily. 'Nick put some champagne in the fridge to chill as soon as we knew everything was all right. Go and get it, darling,' she added to her husband. 'We've got so much to celebrate!'

As Nick disappeared obediently, Georgie tucked a hand through Chase's arm and kissed him on the cheek where a muscle still jumped furiously. 'I have to say we were both a bit hurt you didn't let us know,' she said reproachfully.

'You must have known that we'd want to be there for your wedding.'

'I didn't tell you because it wasn't important,' said Chase, biting the words out in an effort to restrain his temper.

Charming! thought Bea bitterly.

Startled, Georgie took her arm out of his and stared at him. 'What?'

'Chloe doesn't understand the situation, I'm afraid,' he said curtly. 'Our marriage was a purely practical arrangement so that Bea could stay in Australia. Your busybody cousin could have saved herself a phone call and you and Nick could have had that holiday in Mexico!'

Georgie looked from him to Bea with a puzzled expression. 'Is this true?'

'Absolutely.' Bea bared her teeth in a smile. Since Chase was being brutally honest, there was no need for her to pretend, either, was there? 'Marriage was just a way for me to get round visa restrictions, and we agreed to get a divorce as soon as you came home. In fact, we were discussing that just now, weren't we, Chase?'

'We were,' he agreed with something of a snap. 'Neither of us can wait!'

'Here we go!' Nick reappeared, flourishing champagne and glasses, but he stopped as he picked up the tense atmosphere and looked from Chase to Bea to his wife. 'Have I missed something?'

'Bea and I were just explaining to Georgie that we only married on the understanding that it wouldn't be permanent,' Chase told him tightly. 'Bea's only stayed here to look after Chloe until you came home, and now that you *are* home, she's going to be heading for Sydney as soon as possible.'

'Are you really going to Sydney?' Georgie asked Bea later when she joined her in the kitchen after putting Chloe to bed.

'That was the deal.' Bea had herself well under control now. 'I want to set up a catering business.' If she said it often enough, she might even remember why.

Georgie sat down at the table. 'What about you and Chase?'

'It was only ever a temporary thing,' said Bea, managing a careless shrug. 'I'm very grateful to Chase. If he hadn't married me, I would be back in London by now.'

'So it really was just a practical arrangement?'

Bea thought about the nights she and Chase had spent learning each other's bodies, the joy and the laughter and the rocketing excitement. 'Yes.'

'You wouldn't think about staying a bit longer?' Georgie suggested delicately.

'There's no point,' said Bea, lifting the casserole out of the oven and making a show of tasting it. 'It's not as if either of us have planned a future together.'

'Why not?'

'I'm sure Erin told you how unsuitable I am!'

'Oh, Erin!' Georgie rolled her eyes. 'What does she know? She's spent a lot of time over the years telling me how unsuitable I am too. I mean, look at me!'

She gestured disparagingly down at herself. There were pearls at her throat and glittering rings on her fingers, and she was wearing a shirt and a pair of trousers, both made of some pale, silky material and beautifully cut. They had absolutely nothing in common with the shirts and trousers Erin had worn.

'Do I look suitable to you?' she asked Bea.

Bea went back to her casserole. 'Erin says you can ride.'

'Yes, I can ride, but Nick doesn't need a wife who can ride. I don't help out with branding and castrating and those other horrible things they do in the yards. I don't do any of the things Erin thinks makes you a suitable wife, but that doesn't matter to Nick.'

'It matters to Chase,' said Bea before she could help herself.

'He might think so, but he's wrong. All he needs is a wife who loves him. It's too easy to forget that,' Georgie went on soberly. 'That's what Nick and I did, and it nearly cost us our marriage. When I left Calulla Downs last time, I didn't think I would ever come back. I thought I couldn't be the kind of wife Nick wanted, or the kind of mother Chloe needed, and that they'd both be better off without me, but I was wrong.'

A reminiscent smile curved her lovely lips as if remembering how Nick had put her right on just what he wanted. 'It turns out they both like me the way I am!'

'Does that mean you'll be giving up your career?' asked Bea.

'No,' Georgie shook her head. 'Acting is important to me, and I need to be able to do it, but from now on, I'm only going to do one film a year, and Nick and Chloe will come with me. The rest of the time we'll be here, doing what Nick needs to do.'

'I'm glad you've been able to work something out,' said Bea honestly.

'You and Chase could work something out, too.'

She shook her head. 'It's different for us.'

'Is it?' asked Georgie. 'You both just need to decide what you really want, not what Erin thinks you ought to want.'

'We know what we want.' Bea took a deep breath. 'I want to go back to Sydney, and Chase wants Wilbara.'

If she said it often enough and firmly enough, maybe Georgie would accept it.

Maybe *she* would accept it.

'I can't see myself spending my life in the outback,' she made herself say lightly, casually, as if she were talking about a pair of shoes and not about a whole future without Chase. 'Certainly not at a place like Wilbara.'

'Of course you can't live at Wilbara,' Nick said, coming into the kitchen with Chase in time to hear the end of their conversation. 'The place is a ruin. I've been trying to talk Chase out of it,' he told Georgie. 'I've suggested we split Calulla Downs and build him a house of his own.'

Georgie's face lit up. 'Oh, that's a wonderful idea!' she cried, and Nick's hand rested in a brief, revealing caress on his wife's hair.

'I know, but Chase won't hear of it,' he grumbled. 'He's insisting on Wilbara. Can't you talk him out of it, Bea?' he appealed to her, evidently placing as little belief as Georgie in their protestations that theirs was simply a marriage of convenience. 'Make him see sense!'

'It's nothing to do with Bea,' said Chase flatly before she could answer. 'She's going to Sydney.'

'Let me have your address when you get to Sydney, and I'll contact you about the divorce,' said Chase.

The Sydney plane was half an hour late, and they were sitting side by side on the plastic chairs at Mackinnon airport. Bea's hair was styled straight and smooth again, and she was wearing a short skirt, cropped top and her favourite shoes. If she had to go back to the city, she was going back in style, she had decided.

It was just as well it was ending like this, before she had time to do anything really silly like deciding that she was in love with Chase after all. It had been touch and go there for a while, but fortunately yesterday had shown her just how unpleasant and unreasonable and downright difficult he could be!

Bea had spent the night back in the room she had once shared with Emily, telling herself it was all for the best. Chase was in a foul mood because she hadn't raved about Wilbara, but why had he asked her to go with him if he hadn't wanted her opinion? It wasn't even as if he had suggested she might have some stake in the place. He hadn't even *considered* asking her to stay on until the Wet.

No one in their right minds would want to spend the rest of their life stuck in the middle of nowhere, with only Wal, assorted creepy-crawlies, and a man like that.

'I'll write to you as soon as soon as I find somewhere to live,' she told Chase in a brittle voice. 'Shall I send it to Calulla Downs, or are you planning to move to Wilbara straight away?'

'Send it to Wilbara,' said Chase. 'I'll be there.'

'Right.'

Bea tugged off her wedding ring and gave it back to him. 'Here,' she said, flinching inwardly as if she had torn off a piece of her flesh, 'I nearly forgot.'

The skin around Chase's mouth seemed to tighten, but he barely glanced at the ring as he put it in the pocket of his shirt. 'It might be sensible to leave it a little while in case the immigration authorities get suspicious,' he said, his voice empty of all expression, 'but if you meet someone else and want to speed things up, let me know.'

Bea tried to imagine herself meeting another man. She hadn't had much luck so far, what with Phil and now Chase. Maybe it would be third time lucky, she thought gloomily, but it was impossible to picture right now.

Still, Chase might have his own reasons for wanting to be officially single again. 'You too,' she said.

There was another long, bitter silence. Bea stared desperately at the sky, willing the plane to appear, but as soon as it did, she was gripped by panic at the realisation that she was going to have to say goodbye to him.

Suddenly, everything was happening quickly. Too quickly. The plane had landed and there was a bustle of activity on the tarmac as steps were pushed out, passengers disembarked and the trailer loaded with her solitary suitcase trundled out to the cargo hold.

Now the official was opening the door. 'The plane's just

about ready to go,' he called cheerfully, and the two other passengers who had been waiting headed over and joked with him as he tore the stubs off their boarding cards.

Somehow, Bea got to her feet. Chase was standing too, his face closed and bleak. He picked up her bag and gave it to her.

He was going to let her go, Bea realised incredulously. Until now, she hadn't really believed that it would happen. This, then, was it.

She took a shaky breath. 'Well…good luck with Wilbara,' she managed.

'Good luck with your business.' A muscle was beating in Chase's jaw, but otherwise his face might have been carved from stone. 'Thank you for all your hard work,' he added stiffly.

'I should be thanking you for marrying me,' said Bea. 'I wouldn't be able to stay in Australia if it hadn't been for you.'

'I'm glad you got what you wanted,' said Chase bleakly.

Bea didn't even have the heart to pretend that it was true. She hoisted her bag onto her shoulder. 'I…I'd better go,' she said and stepped back before she could throw herself into his arms and beg him to let her stay.

Terrified that she was going to cry, she put on her sunglasses with fumbling fingers and headed blindly towards the door, where the official tore off her boarding card and handed her back the stub.

'Have a good flight,' he beamed.

Bea nodded dumbly, took a step towards the door, and then hesitated. Involuntarily, she looked back at Chase. He was standing there, watching her go, with an expression so stony that her heart cracked.

'Goodbye, Bea,' he said.

Bea tried to smile in return, but it didn't work, and she turned quickly to step through the door before he could see her mouth shaking. The tears trickled down her cheeks from beneath her sunglasses as she walked across the hot tarmac, and this time she didn't look back.

'I'm worried about you,' Emily declared.

She had turned up in Sydney three weeks after Bea, having discovered that her laid-back diving instructor was so laid-back that he had forgotten to mention that he already had a girlfriend back home in Brisbane.

'Another Prince Charming who turns out to be a frog in disguise,' she said cheerfully to Bea, who envied her ability to fall disastrously in love so many times without losing her belief that the right man was waiting for her just around the corner. She was already making eyes at the manager of the bar where she had picked up a job.

'You seem a bit down,' Emily went on. 'I thought you'd be thrilled about being back in Sydney and able to stay in Australia.' She looked at Bea with a puzzled expression. 'You're not missing Chase, are you?'

It was like a dentist drilling on a nerve. Bea flinched inwardly. The truth was that she *was* missing Chase. She was missing him more than she would have believed possible.

She had arrived back in Sydney in high dudgeon, infuriated by his attitude and determined to put the whole episode behind her. Whatever she had felt for him had been mere physical attraction, Bea decided, and even that had vanished when she realised just how stubborn and pigheaded he could be. As soon as she got back to the city she would forget all about him, right?

Wrong.

Bea couldn't forget. She couldn't forget the way he stamped the dust from his boots, the way he hung up his hat, the way he smiled when he pulled her into his arms.

She couldn't forget those quiet evenings on the veranda and the sound of his voice in the darkness. She couldn't forget the sleek strength of his body and how his chest vibrated when he held her to him and laughed. Bea's heart clenched with longing whenever she thought about it.

Six weeks she had been back in Sydney now. Six weeks of missing Chase, six weeks of needing him, aching for his touch, aching just to be near him.

*Six weeks* of realising that she loved him.

She had wanted it to be a physical thing but it was more than that, Bea knew that now. It didn't matter how different they were. Chase was part of her, and without him she felt incomplete. She just didn't know what to do about it.

'You don't belong,' Chase had said. 'I'm holding out for a suitable girl.'

He would never think that she was suitable, not after that day at Wilbara. She had been childish, hysterical, and frivolous, not an appealing combination at the best of times, let alone when she had been busy pouring cold water over his plans and recoiling from a bit of dirt and neglect. No wonder Chase had been glad to see her go.

She could have encouraged him, Bea thought now that it was too late. She could have told him how exciting it would be to rebuild Wilbara and make it a home again. She could have told him straight out that she wanted to do it with him.

But she hadn't. She had screamed and sneered and run away from a spider instead.

That spider had been horrible, Bea tried to be fair to herself. She wasn't sure that she would ever get used to all those creepy-crawlies. It would take courage to live in a place like Wilbara.

But not as much courage as she would need to get through life without Chase.

Bea had made up her mind. She had booked a seat on a plane back to Mackinnon that weekend. She was going to find Chase and tell him that she loved him and beg him to give her another chance. He might say no, but at least she would have tried.

She hadn't told Emily yet. She didn't want her exclaiming and teasing or crowing that she had known all along. She just wanted Chase. She wanted him so badly that sometimes she felt sick and giddy with the longing just to see him again.

One more night of work, and she would be on her way. Without the heart to set up business on her own, Bea had contacted her old company who had welcomed her back with open arms, and she had passed on the contacts Georgie had given her before she left.

'Strictly A-list parties only, darling,' Georgie had promised. 'I'll recommend you.'

One of Georgie's friends was having a party that night in Elizabeth Bay, and Bea was going to supervise the finishing touches to the food.

Wearing a plain black, sleeveless dress, she moved through the throng with her exquisite delicacies, smiling mechanically as she offered the tray to people who hardly noticed that she was there. The chatter was deafening, and longing for the silence of the outback stabbed at her like a knife twisting in her side.

One more day, she reminded herself.

Through the crowds she glimpsed a solitary figure on the edge of the room, looking out into the garden as if hating the party as much as she was. Bea headed that way, desperate suddenly to get out of the crush of bodies and clashing perfumes.

'Would you like—?'

She broke off in stunned disbelief as the man swung round at the sound of her voice. The tray started to slide and would have fallen from her nerveless hands if he hadn't caught it and straightened it for her.

'*Chase*?' Bea stared at him hungrily, unable to believe that it was really him. He was thinner and tauter and out of place in this glittering, glamorous setting, but it was him, it *was*! 'Wh-what are you doing here?' she stammered.

'The hostess is a friend of Georgie's,' he said, his voice sounding strange in his own ears. 'I told her that I was going to be in Sydney and she asked if I wanted to come, so I did.'

'I thought you hated this kind of thing!'

Chase didn't answer. He couldn't take his eyes off Bea. In that little black dress, with her hair smoothed behind her ears she looked alarmingly sophisticated, but there was an air of fragility about her, as if she were tensed against a blow, and he could see shadows beneath her beautiful eyes.

He didn't know how to begin. Four of these horrible parties he had endured before this one, passed around from one of Georgie's friends to another in the hope that someone would have been in contact with Bea. He had dreamt of finding her again, and now here she was, and all the careful speeches he had rehearsed had deserted him.

'You said you would let me know where you were.'

It came out more accusingly than he had intended, and Bea's eyes slid away from his.

'I'm sorry,' she muttered. Now was not the time to tell him that she hadn't wanted him to contact her about a divorce. 'I...I meant to be in touch, but I've been busy.'

'I've been trying to find you,' said Chase. 'I need to talk to you.'

He sounded so serious that Bea's entrails tangled themselves into a tight knot of fear. *Get in contact if you meet someone else*, he had said. *You too*, she had replied, never believing that he would.

Oh, God, was that why he was here? *Had* he found someone else? Had she left it too late?

'What about?' she asked through stiff lips.

Chase opened his mouth to reply when a burst of laughter from a group nearby distracted them both. A girl who had clearly had rather too much to drink was shrieking and giggling as the young men around her attempted to lob canapés down her cleavage.

'We can't talk here,' said Chase, raking his fingers through his hair in frustration. 'Let's get out of here.'

Bea was still clutching her tray. 'I'm supposed to be working,' she said doubtfully.

'You think anyone here is going to notice if you're not here for a few minutes?' said Chase with something of his old style.

He was right. The party was in full swing and there were other waitresses circulating, although nobody seemed to be eating any more. No one would miss her.

Bea followed Chase out through the sliding doors onto a terrace. The garden was beautifully landscaped down a hillside, and a swimming pool gleamed in the moonlight below. Nothing but the best for Georgie's friends.

Setting down her tray on a table, she walked with him down the steps to a curving poolside terrace where they could sit in the shadows under a vine-draped pergola. For several minutes they sat there, not talking, not speaking. In fact, Chase was silent for so long that Bea wondered whether he'd forgotten that he wanted to talk to her.

The silence, at first comforting, began to jangle. Bea hugged her arms together and sought for something to say.

'How's Chloe?' she managed eventually.

'Fine.'

'And Georgie and Nick?'

'They're fine too.'

Another pause.

'How's Georgie getting on with the cooking?' Bea asked.

'We've got a new cook.'

'Oh.' Bea bit her lip, unprepared for the twist of pain at the knowledge that they had replaced her so easily. 'What's she like?'

'She's very good,' said Chase. He seemed relieved that the conversation had got going at last. 'Her name's Morag. She's Scottish, and grew up on a farm, so she feels quite at home in the outback.'

Bea didn't want to know that. She wanted to know whether Morag was pretty.

'Is she nice?' she asked jealously.

'Very nice.'

How nice? Bea wanted to shout. Nice enough for him to want to spend the rest of his life with her? Was Morag the one?

Her heart churned as she sat next to Chase on the bench. After that burst of information about Morag, he seemed to have run out of inspiration, and he was clearly struggling to find the right words to say what he had come for.

This was it, Bea braced herself, but as he opened his mouth, she stumbled into speech before he could say what he wanted.

'How...how are things at Wilbara?' she asked breathlessly. Anything to put off the moment of truth for as long as she could.

He turned slowly to look at her. 'I didn't buy Wilbara,' he told her.

'Didn't buy it?' Bea repeated blankly. 'Why not?'

'I was thinking I might like to spend some time in Sydney,' said Chase. As if aware of how awkward he sounded, he stopped and cleared his throat. 'Maybe get a job down here for a while.'

She stared at him, unable to believe that she had heard him properly. 'You want to come to Sydney?' she said very carefully, and then, when Chase just nodded, '*Why*?'

He glanced away, disconcerted by the incredulity in her face. It didn't make it any easier when you knew that this was the last thing she had been expecting or wanting to hear.

'I thought that if I was here, I might be able to see you sometimes,' he said with some difficulty, wishing that he could remember some of those fine speeches he had prepared to tell her how he felt. 'I thought...I thought it might be easier just being near you.'

'Near *me*?' Bea whispered, terrified that if she moved or spoke too loudly this would turn out to be no more than a dream.

'Yes.'

'I thought you'd come about the divorce,' she said.

'No.' Chase shook his head. 'That is, I did in a way. I wanted to ask you if we could forget the divorce,' he told her. 'I wondered if we could begin again like normal people. I know how much you want to stay in Sydney, Bea, so I thought if I got a job, even if you don't want to live together, we could see each other, couldn't we?'

He was stumbling over his words by then, desperate to persuade her, to hear her say yes. 'If it doesn't work, we could still divorce,' he said. 'If that's what you want.'

Bea just sat there and stared at him, her heart too full to speak, shaking her head at the sheer wonder of it.

Chase misinterpreted her silence. 'I just want you to give me another chance, Bea,' he said urgently. 'I know I don't deserve it. Georgie told me how unpleasant I was that day you left, but you've got to understand how angry I was. Angry with you for hating Wilbara, and angry with me for pretending you would ever think about living there.'

When Bea still said nothing, he leant forward to rest his arms on his knees, not looking at her.

'I was stupid and selfish and too stubborn to admit how much I needed you,' he confessed. 'I tried telling myself that I would get over you, but it didn't work.'

He smiled crookedly, remembering his attempts to forget her. 'When I went back to Wilbara, it was desolate without you and Wal kept asking where you were, and when you'd be coming back, and what I thought you'd want doing to the homestead until I couldn't stand it any longer. I told him we'd decided not to buy the property, and went home to tell Nick and Georgie I was coming to find you.

'It wasn't that easy, though,' he went on, thinking about the last few desperate days. 'You hadn't let me know you

address, so the only thing I could think of was to try all
Georgie's friends to see if any of them had heard from you.
Nobody knew your name, but everyone said to come along
when they were using caterers and maybe one of the waitresses would know you.

'This is the fifth of these parties I've been to in three
days,' said Chase. 'I was nearly ready to give up and try
another way when I turned round just now, and suddenly
there you were.'

He had been watching the pool, but at that he glanced
up into Bea's face. 'There you were,' he repeated simply.

Bea swallowed. 'You said you didn't love me,' she said
slowly.

'I lied,' said Chase, his eyes going back to the water. 'I
didn't want you to feel pressurised. I told myself that it
wouldn't last, and that when you went I would somehow
stop loving you, but I didn't.'

He straightened, and looked directly into her eyes. 'I
missed you,' he said.

Warmth was spilling along Bea's veins like sunshine,
melting the cold knot of misery inside her.

'I said I didn't love you either,' she reminded him quietly.

'I know. I'm not asking you for anything you can't give,'
Chase promised her. 'I just want to be with you.'

A smile trembled on Bea's lips as she reached out and
laid a gentle hand on his shoulder. 'The thing is, Chase, I
lied too,' she said. 'I didn't tell you the truth.'

'The truth?'

'The truth, that I'm in love with you.'

'Bea...' Chase searched her face with eyes that were
suddenly alight with hope. '*Bea*,' he said again, and his
arm came round her to pull her onto his lap. 'Bea, say that
again.'

Her arms wound round his neck. 'I love you.'

And then at last they could kiss, deep, desperate kisses

to banish the memory of the long weeks when they had needed each other and the future had seemed dark and empty.

'I love you...I love you...I love you,' Bea gasped between kisses, pressing her lips to his ear, to his jaw, to his mouth again, boneless and giddy with joy and relief and the dazzling delight of knowing that he loved her too.

'Why didn't you tell me this before?' Chase pretended to grumble, his arms tight around her. 'We've wasted all this time!'

'Why didn't you tell me?' she countered.

'I wasn't sure that you were really over Phil,' he said slowly. 'He hurt you a lot.'

Bea lifted her head at that, and sat back slightly so that she could look into his face. 'Yes, he did,' she agreed, 'but if he hadn't, I would never have found you and realised what love really was. When it happened, I thought my world had ended, but now I know that it hadn't ended at all, it was just beginning. Now I know that you can't be truly happy unless you're with the right person. The right person for Phil is Anna,' she said, accepting at last that this was true, 'and the right person for me is you.'

And she kissed Chase, a warm, sweet kiss to seal her promise.

Some time later, when she was resting her face against his throat and breathing in the familiar scent of his skin, she fingered the buttons on his shirt. 'What about you?' she asked a little anxiously. 'You're over Georgie, aren't you?'

Chase pulled back his head to stare at her blankly. 'Georgie?'

'I was afraid that you might still be a tiny bit in love with her,' Bea confessed. 'Erin kept saying how much you adored her.'

'I've been over Georgie a long time, Bea,' he told her. 'At the time, I thought I loved her, it's true, but it was never quite real. What I felt for Georgie is nothing like what I feel for you,' he went on, lifting Bea's hand to press a warm kiss into her palm. 'It's not something I can put into words, it's just knowing that we belong together, and that without you, nothing would ever feel quite…right. You know that, too, don't you?'

Deeply satisfied, Bea nodded, but couldn't resist teasing as she wound her arms around his neck. 'Even though you really wanted a suitable girl?'

'There's only one suitable girl for me,' said Chase, kissing her again, 'and she's right here where she belongs!'

Bea rested her head back on his shoulder with a blissful sigh and he smoothed the hair from her face tenderly.

'So, wife, can we go back to being married again?'

'We can,' she said happily.

'Let's go and look for a house tomorrow,' he said. 'Wherever you like.'

Bea sat up out of the circle of his arms. 'There's a bit of a problem,' she told him, her face serious.

'What?'

'I don't think you'd like living in Sydney.'

'I would if you were here with me,' Chase insisted.

'That's just it,' said Bea. 'I won't be here. I'm leaving Sydney the day after tomorrow. I've booked my flight and everything.'

Chase stilled in dismay. 'Where are you going?' A terrible thought struck him. 'Not back to England?'

'Well, there's nothing definite yet,' she told him, 'but I *did* hear that there was a property near Mackinnon which badly needs a housekeeper. The homestead needs a lot of work, I gather, but I like the idea of making it into a home, and I was sort of hoping that if I was very nice to the owner, he might make the position permanent. Of course, that was before I heard that he was stupidly thinking of throwing it all in and moving to Sydney of all places!'

It was Chase's turn to stare in disbelief.

'You want to come to Wilbara?' he asked carefully, just to check that he understood.

Bea smiled at him lovingly. 'It's where you're going to be, isn't it?'

'But…you're a city girl. You hate the outback.'

'That's what I said,' she admitted, 'but that wasn't true either. Oh, I have to admit that I'm not that keen on the flies and I really don't like the spiders at all, but I don't hate them nearly as much as I love you.'

A smile started in Chase's eyes and spread over his whole face. 'You love me that much?'

'More than that,' said Bea, and melted back against him for a long, sweet kiss. 'Much more than that,' she mumbled against his lips. 'Much, much more.'

'Bea, are you sure?' said Chase some time later. 'Wilbara's no place for you. It's dirty and uncomfortable and falling to pieces.'

'Then we'll just have to clean it and put it together again.'

'It will be hard work,' he warned.

'I know, but we'll do it together,' she said as she kissed him. 'It will be worth it.'

Chase still wasn't convinced. 'What about all the creepy-crawlies?'

'Wal can deal with them.'

'Seriously, Bea,' said Chase, longing to believe her but determined to make sure she understood just what she was letting herself in for while she still had a chance to change her mind. 'Wilbara hasn't even got basic essentials at the moment, and it's miles from everything a girl like you needs.'

'You mean like shops and bars and cinemas?'

'Yes, that kind of thing.' Seized by fresh doubt, Chase gloomily contemplated how little he could offer Bea. It would be better to live in Sydney than watch her pining for the city.

But Bea was putting her arms around his neck and her lips were warm below his ear. 'I've learnt that a lot of things I used to think were essential aren't that important,' she told him.

It felt so good, so right, to be holding her again that Chase let his last lingering doubts dissolve in the intoxicating promise of the future they would share.

'You'd be surprised at how little I need now,' she murmured, her kisses drifting enticingly along his jaw.

Chase started to smile as his arms tightened around her. 'Just somewhere to plug in your hair-dryer?' he suggested wickedly, and Bea laughed as she kissed him once more.

'And you,' she said.

# Romantic reads to
## *Need, Want*

**International affairs, seduction
and passion guaranteed**
8 brand-new books every month

**Pure romance, pure emotion...**
4 brand-new books every month

**Pulse-raising romance,
– heart-racing medical drama**
6 brand-new books every month

**From Regency England to
Ancient Rome, rich, vivid and
passionate romance...**
3 brand-new books every month

**Scorching hot sexy reads**
4 brand-new books every month

*Mills & Boon® books are available on the **first Friday of every
month** from WHSmith, ASDA, Tesco and all good bookshops.*

## MILLS & BOON®

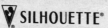

MILLS & BOON®    0107/03b

Live the emotion

# _MedicaL
## romance™

## THE LONDON CONSULTANT'S RESCUE
### by Joanna Neil

Dr Emma Granger enjoys rescuing people all over
London with the air ambulance team. Her boss, Rhys
Benton, is professional, caring and fully in control
– everything a consultant should be. Emma believes
that he could never see her as anything more than
a colleague, but when Emma's life is in danger, Rhys
has the opportunity to show her how he really feels.

## THE DOCTOR'S BABY SURPRISE
### by Gill Sanderson

Gorgeous doctor Toby Sinclair has a reputation as
a carefree playboy. But when his baby son – who he
never knew existed – lands on his doorstep,
Dr Annie Arnold can't refuse Toby's plea for help.
And as Annie watches Toby bonding with his baby,
she wonders if they might just have a future together
after all…

## THE SPANISH DOCTOR'S CONVENIENT
## BRIDE by Meredith Webber

Obstetrician Marty Cox cannot help growing
attached to the baby girl in NICU, but she knows
that the father – when they find him – will want to
take his child away. The attraction between Marty
and Dr Carlos Quintero is instant and, realising how
devoted Marty is to his daughter, Carlos proposes a
marriage of convenience.

# On sale 2nd February 2007

*Available at WHSmith, Tesco, ASDA,*
*and all good bookshops*

*www.millsandboon.co.uk*

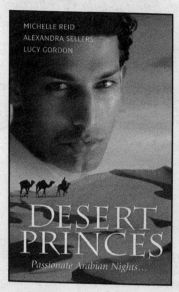

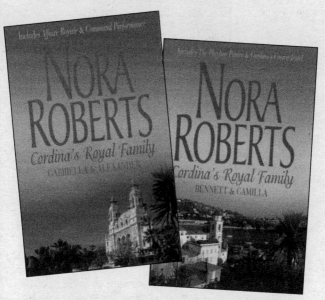